THE INN
AT THE
END OF THE
WORLD

Gene Levin

3563-LEVI

To order additional copies of this book, contact:
Xlibris Corporation
1-888-7-XLIBRIS
www.Xlibris.com
Orders@Xlibris.com

CONTENTS

To Rose

*. . . Your love and understanding
has been the foundation upon which
our life together has been built.*

PROLOGUE

GOD'S AUNT

With the passing of the ages, Lord God the Creator grew increasingly disappointed with humankind, whom He had created in His image. Given to know the difference between good and evil, they continued wicked. Given the ability to reason and renew themselves at will, they continued stiff-necked. And given the power of speech, they continued foul-mouthed beyond the limits of His endurance. It seemed that hardly had man developed two-word sentences than God's ears were assailed with blasphemies. Of all humankind's transgressions, the desecration of creative powers irked the Lord God most.

And there came a time when humankind's repeated blasphemies caused Him to lose His patience. He hurled the pot of celestial fire toward the Earth that the land be seared down to bedrock and the planet be entirely cleansed of abominations. But even as the primordial fire flashed down through the Milky Way, consuming stars, moons and other handiworks, the laughter of a little Chinese girl playing with her cat came to His ear and He recalled His original hope for humankind. He destroyed His missile, pot and all, just in time. The pot, smashed into chunks and bits of rock, He placed in orbit about the Sun between the fourth and fifth planets, where there was room. And with His outstretched finger, God blasted the fire into countless millions of comets and set them to orbiting the

Sun in various trajectories, as occasional reminders to the nations of Earth.

And finally, so that His ears would no longer be subjected to an infantile yammering of blasphemies, curses and maledictions, He created His aunt and proclaimed her destiny: to wander the face of the Earth with a great sack, into which all such transgressions of the mouth would be trapped ere they reached His domain.

Then He took up golf.

That His aunt not be recognized as being from the dwelling-place of the Most Holy, she was to cover her radiance from the face of man. So she was garbed, from wide-brimmed hat to high-button shoes, in the most utter blackness. Black was the veil that concealed her face and neck, black the dress that hung nearly to the ground and black were her coat and shoes. Black gloves covered her hands and the staff that God gave her was black, and such was its power that no creature took notice of her for evil purpose, though she was neither tall nor particularly strong.

At her side hung a sack of undulating, tightly woven metallic thread, designed to attract and hold fast such words and phrases the hearing of which might cause the Lord to forget His mercies and scourge the Earth after all. Indeed, so often did the mouth of that sack widen and gulp into itself curses, blasphemies and maledictions that from within there issued a constant rustle and crackle of sound as though a field'sworth of mice were tumbling about in a box filled with dry straw. The noise rose and fell in intensity, but never fell completely silent, even during the sacred seasons. Such was the state of affairs at the time of our narrative.

The woman in black had walked the face of the Earth for many thousands of years; hardly a patch of the planet had not known her tread at one time or another and she was no stranger to the great modern cities of the world. Indeed, she rather enjoyed ballet, musical shows and was particularly fond of opera, though she had to settle for standing room in the uppermost tier, lest the rustling from her sack disturb her neighbors.

All in all, God's aunt would have preferred a more balanced situation, but this was her raison d'etre and she accepted it, though it was hard on the feet. So one can understand her celebrating the invention of public benches and parks in which to place them.

There are some pleasant enough little patches of green in the Bronx, on both sides of the Grand Concourse. One such mini-park, barely a triangle of grass at the intersection of streets, happened to possess several wood-slatted benches, one happening to face west, and it was to that bench that God's aunt made her way on an October afternoon. She sighed as she eased her feet out of her shoes, wiggled her toes just for the joy of it, then raised her veil slightly that a bit of sunlight might shine on her face, and who can blame her for that? And if she permitted herself doze off? It's not as though she had to manage the sack; it carried on by itself, day and night, deflecting from the Lord's ears humankind's expressions of ingratitude for the gift of intelligent life.

But a nap is not sleep, and a doze is not even a nap, and God's aunt dozed unevenly and without restoration of spirit, for she was vexed. Her feet hurt and the sack had grown especially noisy during this past decade and worst of all, she was tired of finding herself continuously and conspicuously out of style except for Greek and Turkish villages, where she was taken as just another old widow. Also, her Nephew was getting impatient.

A millenium ago, her Nephew had commented that, now that He was no longer assailed by humankind's verbal perfidies, He was newly aware how little wisdom seemed to grow in the garden of human consciousness. Had He not strewn the path of righteousness with wisdom right from the beginning? Was it unreasonable to expect of humankind, after all this time, a begetting? How could it be that, given a multitude like to the stars in the sky, so few sparks of human wisdom reached His ear in these latter days?

Perhaps the precious words, many of them uttered by the meek, were being blown astray by the solar wind or other necessary adjuncts to a functioning system of worlds. That was easily rectified; He gave his aunt a small, silver bellows to carry, that upon encountering wisdom, she might squeeze the bellows and send the precious words directly toward His abode, together with the identity of the speaker and the location of his dwelling-place.

It seemed, however, that God's aunt was always in the wrong place for wisdom, or she arrived too early or too late. At any rate, three centuries had passed since God's aunt had last squeezed the bellows and even in the Bronx, while resting her feet and catching some rays late on an October afternoon, her Nephew's disappointment lay heavily on her.

She woke. Someone was approaching with a step light as a robin's hop. Dropping her veil, she turned her head and tightened her grip on her staff, just in case.

"Oh, my God!" she breathed.

"Shhh!" replied the newcomer as he took a seat beside the woman in black. His dark brown overcoat was several sizes too big and bulged in back, as if the wearer had a physical appurtenance that needed concealing, such as wings. Large, white wings. Though the day was rather mild for October in New York, a silk muffler covered the open space between the coat's lapels, effectively concealing the top of a robe of surpassing whiteness and purity, so long as the newcomer didn't move about too much. A wide-brimmed fedora concealed his brow, but there was no hiding the celestial radiance of an archangel from God's aunt. "It's me— Michael," he said, anxiously.

"Why . . . has something happened?"

"Yes. Have you noticed an increase in . . . the contents of your sack?"

She leaned down and listened to the disagreeable noise as though gauging, then shook her shoulders, uncertain and not anxious to appear an alarmist.

"That may change," the archangel said sadly. "The imposter has gone from the underworld."

"The imposter?" asked the woman in black, peering about to make certain there were no eavesdroppers to a conversation that was unusual, even for the Bronx near the Grand Concourse.

"Wotan," whispered the archangel Michael. "Wotan Allfather, he calls himself. The mote in the Lord's eye.

"I warned the Lord! All of us warned Him not to neglect matters. Golf is not just another hobby, I told Him. It is a passion! But it takes up all His time now.

"So Wotan, unguarded, managed to escape his fate and has made his way to The Inn at the End of the World, where it appears that he has taken over the persona of the Innkeeper, though that is not the end of it. You recall the outcome of his last adventure."

"The Ring of the Nibelungen!" she said. She had seen the Ring cycle once, in Bayreuth. That had been enough. She shivered, recalling the dark legend.

"Twenty hours of lies, thievery, envy, treachery, murder, illicit love, betrayal . . ." growled the archangel.

The woman in black liked many operas; she was particularly fond of Carmen and cried every time she saw Rigoletto. But The Ring . . . was something else. Its dark, powerful music transported one's soul down, down to ambitions forbidden since the dawn of mankind.

"Wotan . . . but have you brought this to my Nephew's attention?" demanded the woman in black. "Will He not take action as He did last time? It's all there in the Ring . . . the breaking down of Valhalla, the destruction of the false gods . . ."

"That was last time," said the archangel, wearily. "I have brought this matter to the Lord's attention, but the timing could hardly be worse. He is wroth at what mankind has made of the gift of life, and still awaits a fruition of wisdom, though with little hope of satisfaction. The higher the hope, the greater the disappointment,' He said. Indeed, his recent interest in golf is a mixed blessing for humankind. Yes, it enabled the imposter to escape his fate in the underworld, but it also provided the Lord with entertainment and diversion, else He would have blasted the Earth to its core in fury at mankind's loathsome behavior over the past century.

"'I will not move against the false god,'" He told me, and those were His words. "If wisdom has been entirely replaced throughout the Earth by lust and vanity and base, unnatural behavior, then so be it. Those who will not serve Me, let them serve Wotan!"

A squirrel emerged from the shelter of a low bush and, with a flourish of its tail, deposited an unopened nut at the archangel's feet. Irked to find his disguise so easily penetrated, Archangel Michael passed his hand over the creature; a blessing. It bounded away and, to the end of its days, was never again chased by dog or cat.

But the archangel glanced about warily; he could not tarry long.

"I have here a curse that somehow missed your sack, some while ago," he whispered. "It may give you some pleasure to know that your Nephew saw fit to grant it. Take it and file it with the others." From a pocket of his coat he drew a bit of parchment and handed it to the woman in black.

She read the legend: "Thirteenth century A.D. From the second wife Shariza of the wealthy Arabian merchant Achmed al-Dira Machmet.

" 'My husband and lord having purchased a pair of youthful virgin concubines with yellow hair, I have this evening after prayer walked out into the desert and with my own hands erected an alter of unhewn rock. The wind is bitter and my hands bleed, yet I pray to the Lord of Lords, to God on High that their bellies dissolve! May their waists shrivel and their bottoms be as that of stripling lads! May their breasts lose their softness and their babes be forced to suck the milk of cows! Let their fingernails grow into the sharp talons of eagles, and their golden hair twist into shapes and stiffen that even the wind cannot move it, nor my lord's hand. Let them bathe in the public water, and their clothing be as gossamer strips, that their ugliness be seen by all.'"

God's aunt stuffed the document into her sack.

"That is all?" she asked.

"No," Michael replied. "The Lord God reminds you of the bellows. He has not tasted the fruit of His labor these three hundred years. If you encounter wisdom, do not tarry; put your hands to those bellows and send Him what He longs to hear.

"Now I've got to leave; my wings ache and someone's coming."

He rose, stepped behind a tree and was gone.

The woman in black sat alone with her thoughts. That little squirrel's devotion had been as close to wisdom as she'd seen in a century. She hadn't had an opportunity to ask Michael, who had the Lord's favor, to transmit her desire for a new winter coat. And now . . . Wotan had taken over the persona of the Innkeeper of The Inn at the End of the World!

A woman came, sat on a nearby bench and opened a small, soft-covered book. God's aunt regarded the woman's appearance and, sad to relate, a pang of common jealousy shot through her. She thought the woman's blonde hair rather long and loose for one who'd not see forty-nine again. Her cheeks were rouged quite nicely, though, and her eyes were shaded in the European manner. Considering the age difference, she was no better looking than God's aunt except that, free to wear what she pleased, she was able to present herself to best advantage. Her simple black coat sported a velvet collar and vertical piping that emphasized her slim figure and was of the latest fashion; her stockings were sheer; on the middle finger of her left hand she wore a simple gold ring with an attractive ruby-colored stone, though it wasn't real ruby at all. God's aunt knew her jewelry.

She glanced at her own unattractive, plain, functional outercoat in dismay; why was she fated to an eternity of dowdiness? She possessed no ring at all and her stockings were plain, durable cotton. Black. It's not that she wanted a coat fashioned from the pelts of minks or beavers or cute little chinchillas; she didn't want furs.

But if she asked her Nephew to permit her to go shopping for purpose of style, He'd shrug His shoulders. He simply didn't understand! Of course, it would go better if she could just bring him a bit of wisdom.

A man came along—"Ah, Adele, a pleasure to run into you like this. What's that you're reading—The Valley of Horses—never read that one." He joined the woman on the bench and continued his monologue, to which the woman responded chiefly by vague smiles. "Do you know I wrote a book once?" he said. "The Boy with No Future."

Evidently she did know about his book, for the conversation lagged for some moments. God's aunt dismissed this one immediately; from his heavy lips she would more likely coax a belch than wisdom. He wore an old brown overcoat that was frayed at the edges, and no hat. His hands were pudgy and his cheeks red, either from the slight chill in the wind or from the strain of keeping his ample belly tight. Most of his remaining hair was grey, but the centuries had taught God's aunt that wisdom was more than a collection of grey hair.

The man bent toward the woman, pointed to the cover picture on her paperback book and whispered something into her ear. She laughed. Not a belly-laugh, but more than a polite, social laugh. His mouth was opening; he was going to repeat whatever he'd said; God's aunt had seen and heard a good deal of human nature over the years and she knew that he was the type to milk a good thing.

But the woman had laughed and she was quite smartly dressed, and presumably sophisticated. Had that old fool actually said something clever? Was there wisdom here? After three centuries, God's aunt was beginning to doubt her judgement. Anyway, she couldn't afford to miss a possible, not if she wanted a new winter coat. Careful to conceal the bellows behind her sack, she pumped it vigorously, not noticing that its nozzle was not aimed properly.

The man spoke:

"Well, what do you think of that, eh, Adele? Clever? As soon as you showed me that book cover with the horses, it popped right into my head! You know, I should write that down and send it to a magazine. If a man's testicles were an inch lower on his body, he could not ride a horse and the course of history would have been different!"

God's aunt stopped pumping.

But Myron Blunger's increment of wisdom flew directly to the Inn at the End of the World, to the ear of the Innkeeper, who was quite pleased to learn the whereabouts of Myron Blunger. The Innkeeper, you see, was in a rage . . .

THE DREAM OF A DEAD MAN

The king of France went up the hill with forty thousand men....

Snore. Snooooore....

The king of France came down the hill and ne'er went up again.

Snooooore... uzgawugzba....

Knock

Nursery rhyme... English... look it up... look it up... look it up... ah, battle of Agincourt. The 25th of October, 1415 A.D. ...glad to... twenty fifth... rent almost due....

Snooooore... uzhawuzha....

Knock

Children's... Reference desk.
How can I help you....
Help you... Help you....

Snooooore... uzawumza

Little Engine that Could?
Third shelf... on the right....

Knock!

The regular, peaceful snoring from within apartment 2C Concourse Plaza came to a snarfling halt. Myron Blunger buried his head more deeply in pillow and projected a weak choliera at the waterhammer from the kitchen plumbing.

KNOCK!

"The door, Sophie," he groaned. But Sophie was in Florida, visiting her sister. Was it Adele? Pretty Adele from the third floor whom he'd spotted reading The Valley of Horses in the park too young to be a widow but she was and she appreciated little kindnesses . . . Adele tapping at his door! Sophie away in Florida. Oh! Oh, my!

BANG!!
A shock wave that echoed in the hallway. A fire, maybe? Blunger, finally awake, fumbled in the dark for his robe, found the armholes and padded heavily to the front door of the apartment. "Who is it already!" His voice sounded harsh, phlegmy. He should have stopped to gargle. Gargle? At two in the morning? Maybe Sophie was right; maybe his brain was acting up. "Who's there?"

"Windbreaker." A commanding voice that Blunger didn't recognize. Ah! Maybe it was the plumber finally come to fix the waterhammer after years of begging and written letters! Blunger opened the door and found himself staring up at a youthful bodybuilder with muscular arms folded arrogantly across a broad chest and long black hair that hung down to the crew neck of a dark green cable-knit sweater.

"You're Myron Blunger?"

Somewhere within Myron Blunger's chest, a bubble of indignation started to percolate. Knocking on doors at two in the morning with insults yet! Sophie insisted it wasn't their fault; the kids today were being born into a rough, hypocritical world and were confused.

Blunger started to open his mouth to tell this young man off. His mouth continued to drop. Sophie was right! Oh, was this one confused! From the waist down, where the sweater ended, he was not an arrogant youth at all, but a horse! Blunger squinted. Yes, a sleek, black horse with broad forequarters and horse's legs at the corners ending in hooves not feet yes, a horse! With a tail. A black tail that was switching impatiently from side to side. Well, whoever heard of a plumber coming at 2 in the morning, anyway? This was a centaur.

Blunger willed a command to slam the door shut, but too late; the creature had clopped inside and with a flick of his right hind hoof, closed the door behind him.

Blunger's right eyelid fluttered; his other muscles were frozen.

"You're Blunger, the writer?" the creature demanded. "Tell me something clever. Something original!"

Blunger wanted very much to be back in bed with the door locked and the king of France marching up his hill. But there was a centaur filling the entranceway of his apartment.

Never again prune compote and milk on top of the eleven o'clock news, Blunger resolved, but his mouth opened and the words tumbled out. "If a man's testicles were an inch lower on his body, he could not ride a horse and history would have been very different. I . . . I never told that to anyone, until today . . . yesterday. In the park. It's . . . the most profound thought I've ever had." Blunger's voice trailed off.

The centaur leaned down and said sarcastically, "And what do you know about horses? Or, for that matter, about testicles?

"You're the author of The Boy with No Future, right? The creator of Joey Willem, modelled—shall we say—after Oliver Twist?"

Joey Willem! Four years earlier, Blunger had succumbed to a creative need (Myron's phrase) or total lunacy (Sophie's description), writing and revising and revising The Boy with No Future; selling it, after the standard dozen rejections, to a publisher. He recalled his exhilaration at the offer by Socio-Real Productions for a possible TV series! Oh, had his brain been supple in those days before the cancellation, before the publisher let the book go out of print.

Blunger backed slowly into his apartment.

Joey Willem, born in a typewriter, had lived through three printings hardcover, one paperback, a TV option and six never-produced screenplays only to be killed off prematurely at the whim of a television sponsor. So maybe Myron had borrowed an idea, a word or two from Dickens but after a hundred fifty years to send out a centaur at 2 AM? What an agent Dickens must have had!

Windbreaker nudged him down the center of the hall runner until they were abreast of the kitchen. "Dress warm," he ordered. "We have a long trip ahead."

Blunger's nervous system, near total shutdown, was revitalized by the bad grammar. "Dress warmly," he declared. "It's an adverb. Also, I don't believe in centaurs so if you don't mind, I'm going back to bed."

Pressing against the wall so as to ease past the centaur's flanks, he locked the front door and started back toward his bedroom with his eyes firmly closed. His outthrust hand encountered an unyielding expanse of hide covered with the kind of hair that horses use. Blunger opened one eye. The creature's front end was in the kitchen busily draping bologna slices from the open refrigerator onto pieces of rye bread.

"Excuse me," Windbreaker said between chomps. "Sorry if I was a bit loud out there in the hallway. Fact is, you startled me. Somehow I thought the creator of Joey Willem would look different."

Blunger thrust out his chin, sucked in his belly and leaned forward. "You gotta look like a movie star that they shouldn't cancel your T.V. series?" he snapped.

Shrugging his shoulders, the centaur, his mouth full of sandwich, mumbled, "More like a . . . man of action. Fast, lean, with not-so-bulgy eyes. You look like a grocer. Anyway, get dressed.

Warm clothes, and hurry!" The bologna sandwich was gone, devoured in four bites.

This was a mistake, Blunger decided. It couldn't be his nightmare that had horse-legs and didn't know from adverbs. "Listen, I'm a retired librarian and I don't believe in centaurs," he repeated. Then, with an anxiety that surprised even himself, he asked, "What about Joey Willem? What's . . . this all about? Joey . . ."

"Joey Willem has run away with the Innkeeper's seven-league boots!" the centaur snapped impatiently. "The Innkeeper is in a rage! You've got to get the boy back to the Inn. You know him better than anyone; it's your job and your responsibility."

Selecting an apple from a bowl of fruit on the kitchen table, he added, "I'd do it myself, if I could. I like Joey. Wherever those boots took him, he must be scared out of his mind. Now, we're in a flaming hurry, SO GET DRESSED FOR TRAVELLING NOW!"

A centaur had come all the way from the Inn to tell him that Joey Willem had run away. From the Inn. What Inn? What boots? What Innkeeper? How to stop this nightmare?

"How can a story character run away?" he said, weakly.

"The same way any kid runs away when he thinks his world's at an end and he has nothing to lose. Now get moving!"

Myron Blunger shook his head. Joey Willem—his Joey Willem—stealing someone's boots? Nonsense. What kind of craziness was this? Not his Joey! Would a child thief go three printings in hardcover? Plus one in paperback? And who knows how far he would have gone on T.V.

Am I insane? Myron Blunger thought. I'm standing in my hallway at two in the morning, defending . . .

Joey. My Joey.

And my Joey's no thief! Street-smart, yes, but not a thief!

As for this creature, Sophie would know how to handle him, he thought ruefully. The same way she handled the landlord, the butcher, the supermarket checkouts who didn't want to take her coupons! This apparition would clop right out with his tail between his legs. But no sooner would she get rid of the pest than Myron would get an earful . . .

I turn my back for a few days to visit my only sister sick in Florida and right away you invite all kinds of crazies into the apartment? Half a horse, yet? You know what it costs to clean high-pile carpet in light blue . . .

And so on. Married thirty-nine years, with two boys raised— a college professor and a pharmacist, no less!—and married to nice girls except for Jason's Princess Shirley. Myron knew all Sophie's lectures by heart. Except the one for getting rid of a centaur. Before Myron could organize an effective ultimatum, he found himself lifted several feet into the air and carried into the bedroom. "Now!" ordered the creature. "You created Joey Willem and you're the only one who can get him back. He's your responsibility, Blunger. And by the way, put on heavy boots."

"Boots?" Blunger asked, distracted from a half-developed ultimatum he was working on. "In October?"

"You'll be cold enough on the Northern Reaches," answered the centaur ominously. "But it's the wolves I was thinking about. They seemed snappish on the way down."

Minutes later, the centaur hustled his booted and overcoated captive through the dimly-lit laundry room of the apartment house, out into the parking lot and into a black van. Even as several sets of hands set about strapping Myron Blunger into a seat, the centaur scrambled in through the rear doors with a great clatter, pulled them shut and commanded, "North!"

"Oy!" the captive moaned. "My brain has snapped altogether. Sophie always said it would end this way; what she would give to see her prediction come true! Ugh!"

This last as a strap was run over his belly and pulled tight. "Stop complaining!" The voice was high-pitched and came from a pasty-white moon-round face framed by a dark hood. "A journey is integral to the thing. You're a writer; you should know that. I'm Yin, by the way."

Blunger's eyes, straining in the darkness, discerned a short, stout figure in black strapping itself into the seat beside him. The van swayed as, behind them in the darkness, Windbreaker settled his considerable mass on the metal floor. Dismayed, Blunger whispered, "A journey . . ."

"A journey," Yin repeated excitedly as the van lurched into the night, picking up speed. "An adventure! A quest! Essential for a good story. If only you'd sent your Joey Willem on a trip of self-discovery, he wouldn't have had to do it on his own. Otherwise, The Boy with No Future was a grand book. I cried at the end. By the way, I'm what you might call a gnome."

"A gnome. A trip of self-discovery . . ." Blunger said, shaking his head. Even as he silently worked on an approach that might effectively cancel this nightmare and restore him to his bed, the van shot onto a highway and accelerated. And continued to accelerate.

"A trip of self-discovery." This in mocking, deep tones from the front seat. An authoritative voice. The driver! This nightmare van was not so magical that it steered itself; it had a driver! A driver meant a driving licence, which implied an exam to be passed and therefore, a degree of normalcy, even if by the faint green glow from the instrument panel, the driver resembled a dwarf/leprachaun/gnome/brownie/whatever! Normal means no kidnapping! But it doesn't mean no practical jokes!

"Well, you fellows are something else," Blunger guffawed in a tone that showed that he knew how to take a joke. "A trip of self-discovery indeed; we must be a mile from the nearest subway station. You fraternity kids do this kind of thing very well, don't you? Very amusing. You can let me off right here; I'll make my way home, eh? And wait'll I see Adele tomorrow in the park; will I have a story for her!" Hope fluttered within Blunger's chest.

"Your subway is far behind," the driver replied in a flat voice, and indeed, Blunger could see no city lights, no house lights, no streetlights. To the left was an endless stretch of barren land painted harsh white by moonlight; on Blunger's right, a forest marched alongside the highway. A dark, forbidding forest exactly like those in Grimm's Fairy tales in which little children lose their way and are found by witches. Blunger shuddered.

"Soon enough there'll be no highway," said the driver. Blunger shivered uncontrollably.

"Then no road at all but an ill-marked path through the forest, which is what one generally gets in trips of self-discovery. By the way, I am Yang, the older and wiser brother of Yin, and I also cried at the end of your book."

"I tried to make it sentimental, but not maudlin," Blunger said, flattered at the attention.

"You don't understand," the driver said solemnly. "I cried because it was a lousy ending to a dumb story."

"A dumb story!" Blunger cried. He could defend his book in his sleep, as Sophie well knew. Indeed, she preferred his snoring to his nocturnal moans about the injustices of the publishing industry. "Is a child of misfortune, poor, without connections, to be denied the opportunity to rise to the top by virtue of effort, thrift and innate goodness?" Blunger demanded. "It's a good, solid story with a protagonist and a major dramatic question."

"Hah!" Yang laughed.

Blunger snapped, "I'll bet you never got beyond the jacket blurb! Where does . . . did Joey live?"

"In the worst part of the Bronx, with his widowed mother," Yang grunted. "He's not physically big—don't you find that humans have a curious obsession with physical size? If turtles wrote fiction, I wonder if they'd favor protagonists with large, colorful shells—and he has trouble with algebra. And he's always the last chosen for team sports. Some protagonist!"

"But he's got pluck! Eh?" Blunger said, proudly. "My Joey has guts! He doesn't give up!"

Inspired, Blunger went on. "During a surprise inspection, his teacher finds a stash of crack in his cubbyhole, where the class bully hid it during gym. He's brought to the principal's office, but he doesn't know anything. After school, the bully beats him up and promises more unless he comes up with the money for the confiscated drugs! To make things worse, while Joey's mom is out working, the bully's gang breaks into their squalid basement apartment and rips off everything they can fence.

"Well, Joey is telling his troubles to his best friend, Armani, who has a secret dog. Secret from the landlord, that is. Using empty crack vials, the boys train it to sniff drugs. They find the bully's hideout, take his cache of drugs to the police and get written up in the newspaper. A decent, rich widower who is not a landlord reads the article and seeks Joey out . . ."

"Stop! Please, my entrails are sensitive."

" . . . takes him under his wing, but keeps it secret from his family because his two grown sons, Reginald and Troilus, are trying to have him committed as senile and incompetent . . ."

"I'm getting nauseous."

"The rich man hires Joey's mother to supervise his staff of servents and run his personal library for double her previous salary, and pays for the boy to go to a private school in Riverdale. When he learns that his own sons are investing in used F-51 jet planes with which to fly cocaine into the country from an island in . . ."

"SILENCE!" the driver shouted. "Listen to me, Blunger. My brother Yin is an idealist, an optimist, a romantic and is frequently disappointed. I am Yang. I expect little and am seldom disappointed. But seldom is not never; my bowels ache from your story. Not that I wish hardship on you, but if I read my entrails correctly, it's just as well you're leaving the Bronx now. Ahead lies a winter of record cold, taxes are rising with rents not far behind and the end of Mankind is near. I am Yang. I speak the truth."

Taxes? Rents? The end of mankind? A kernel, a seedling of hope sputtered in Blunger's chest. He stated, very carefully, "Yin and Yang are Chinese words. I think you're in the wrong nightmare. Also, you should know I was a librarian, a children's librarian; I know something about reading entrails and one thing I remember is you don't read your own."

The driver turned halfway around. Indeed, Yin and Yang were twins, though the driver's face seemed chubbier, more healthy, probably from not being disappointed so much. "I know my own entrails best," Yang said, swivelling his head back as the van veered toward the edge of the highway.

"Listen, Mr. Blunger, and I'll give you the story of life on Earth in one paragraph.

"For a billion years, seventeen trillion trillion trillion plants pumped oxygen into the Earth's atmosphere. Not too much, not too little. Twenty-one percent; just right. For this they got no individual or group credit. Then a host of nameless creatures climbed out of the ooze, learned how to walk and run and fly, following new, uncharted destinies until some of them became dinosaurs, who got to run the place for a hundred fifty million years, after which they turned themselves into fuel-oil, which was very thoughtful of them, eh? Then along came humankind and in a few centuries, you worked your way through the whole lot, plus most of the mineral resources and anything your guts could digest. You sure wove yourselves into the universal fabric, Blunger. Leaving precious little and little precious for your successors."

"Successors?" Blunger managed to whisper.

"Us."

"After . . . humans, come gnomes?" Blunger asked. "My son Irving says the ants will inherit. And he's a physicist, a professor with nine articles published already and when he finds out I've been kidnapped, I wouldn't want to be in your shoes!"

At that, Yang exploded with gasping laughter, his head flopping and rolling around on its stubby neck while his eyes teared. The van careened from side to side; he slowed down until he'd regained control. "There is order in this universe, Blunger," he said, wiping his eyes with the back of his hand. "Dinosaurs, then humans, then us. Ants come at the end, when the Sun is dying and nothing matters any more. So the Innkeeper has assured me."

"Ah, yes; the Innkeeper!" mused Yin. "Once upon a time, he was a jolly fellow who used to help plan each newcomer's accomodations, who hosted wine and cheese parties on important birthdays and wrote overdrafts when his budget didn't balance. But he has changed, and not for the better. At times, he takes the appearance of his old self, but it is not constant. He has an obsession with weapons and power . . .

"Anyway, I'll thank you to keep your thoughts on the Succession to yourself," he said to his twin. "Myron Blunger's going to need confidence and courage, and it's not right to expose him to destiny before he's even gotten started!" The gnome leaned toward Blunger and asked, "Tell me, Blunger, are you at peace with your soul?"

Blunger trembled, managing a nod that was barely detectible in the darkness of the van.

"Good. That's important. Are you stout of heart? Does your mind function okay? Your imagination? That's vital; how's your imagination?"

"A-1!" Blunger said, though in fact his thoughts were elsewhere. His fingers, exploring, had found the release button on his harness and he was concentrating on an escape. If the van would only slow down, perhaps on a sharp curve to the left, he could release himself with his left hand, open the door with his right hand, tuck his head down and roll out onto the ground.

And then what?

Nothing, he realized. They were driving at breakneck speed through dense forest. There was no place to run to even if he weren't afraid of things that prowled woods and forests at night. Blunger sighed.

"Are you afraid to die?" Yin persisted. "For a cause, I mean. Not a stupid death; a glorious abandonment of body in the heat of righteous battle, after which your essence ascends to its rightful place within the universal soul."

"Not yet," Blunger whispered. Blunger knew a trick question when he heard one.

"Good," Yin answered cheerfully. Tapping his brother on the shoulder, he sneered, "You hear that? Passion for life!"

Blunger cried out, "Aha! Prose! That's it! That's your mistake! I'm not Irish! This has all the earmarks of an adventure, and every adventurer is quick of tongue, red-headed and extremely Irish! You could look it up! They get into the most terrible situations and get out by wits or derring-do or other stuff I don't have. We could stop in Mount Vernon and find an Irishman who'd love to go on with you."

"Ho, ho!" cried Yin, slapping his brother on the back. "Didn't I tell you he had the spirit?" To Blunger he said, "Now you're talking! Wits! Derring-do! And most of all, determination in the teeth of adversity! If the kraken pulls you out of the boat, what'll you do about it?"

"Kraken? Boat?" Blunger paled. "I don't . . . know," he stuttered.

"Why, you sink your teeth into the outermost tentacle where the flesh is not yet scaled! Well, it's worth trying, anyway and really, there's nothing else one can do," he said, lamely.

"Try something easier," Yang said. "Suppose a stomachorum starts pulling you into itself, feet-first! What'll you do?"

"Bite it?" Blunger recited weakly.

Yang laughed. Yin groaned, apparently disappointed at Blunger's lack of background and preparation. "Impossible," he said. "In the fraction of a second it takes for your jaw muscles to contract, the acids would dissolve your teeth. You must shout to your comrades, warning them of the danger! If you can't shout, you wave! And if it's got you all the way to the neck and your muscles are already dissolving in the acids, you wiggle your eyebrows!

"Also, don't get down on yourself. Keep a riddle in reserve for when things really get tough. A good story has riddles."

Let me think. After some minutes, he recited,

> "A riddle, a piddle. Your boy's in the middle
> of danger no matter the way of his choosing."

Yin stopped and went into a trance, concentrating on his riddle. With growing alarm, Myron Blunger watched the gnome's face fold in upon itself, puckering up until eyes, nose, mouth and ears had converged nearly to a point.

But then, Yin was a gnome, eh? And Yang was a gnome. And Windbreaker was a centaur. And he'd been conversing with them. Arguing.

The nightmare was winning.

Blunger pulled himself more tightly into his overcoat and shivered. Dead ahead on the horizon was lightning. No more Bronx, no proper goodbye to Sophie and the boys. No hope. Now Blunger's head was shaking wildly from side to side. Desperate to salvage the remnant of his sanity, he said in a small voice, "I still don't believe in centaurs!"

Suddenly his head was gripped as in a vise and Windbreaker's face, inches from his own, was livid. "Must I trample you to confirm my existence? And are your wits so slow that you won't accept dragons until Old Groff turns you into soot and ashes with one snort from his left nostril?"

"Let go! You're crushing my skull! I believe, I believe," Blunger cried.

Windbreaker released his grip on the ex-librarian's head.

Blunger rubbed his temples, groaned and regarded his seat-companion closely as possible in the dim light. Yin's features were restored. Perhaps he had given up on his riddle. "So you're a gnome?" Blunger asked.

"You may call me that," Yin replied.

After a moment's silence, Blunger ventured, "What do gnomes do?"

"We . . . observe," Yin replied cheerfully. "Humans, mostly. You're fascinating, you know! Every one of you is a bonfire, nay, a supernova of the life-force, of passion! You are wonderful to behold! Wonderful! Even your darkest dreams are tapestries of glory!"

A chill ran down Blunger's spine. "Why did you ask about my soul?" he asked.

A bolt of lightning illuminated the heavens and the earth. The driver slowed down and braced himself as a blast of thunder sent the van onto the road's shoulder. A few yards more, and they would have careened into the trees. Only Yang's skill with the wheel and accelerator prevented a rollover. When they were once again hurtling along, Yin said, "In Esfandiary is the universal soul, created by Lord God at the beginning of time and substance.

"Physical birth in Earth Real is accompanied by spiritual birth, as a drop of the universal soul is joined to the new life.

"Be very careful about what you choose to believe in, Blunger. The Inn at the End of the World is separated from Esfandiary by only the thickness of a door, and in Esfandiary, it is not wealth or size or cleverness that matters; one's true beliefs are of the greatest importance."

"Have you been there?" Yang growled.

"No," Yin admitted. "But I've listened to Elf Miki. In Esfandiary there are golden meadows and grand cities backed by high, snow-capped mountains; deep forests and at their edges, charming villages where the roofs are thatched with bundles of straw. There are crystal palaces for the kings, trees that sing in the wind and the Lord's golf course. And the universal soul!"

"And tournaments where a centaur might go up against the greatest knights of the land," Windbreaker added wistfully.

"Neither of you have been there," Yang said. "So be silent. Only romantic fools and humans chatter about unknowns when what's needed is a close eye on the road.

"The words Esfandiary is are without general meaning. According to the Innkeeper, Esfandiary is filled from edge to edge with dinosaurs. One would expect to hear their roars and screams. I have listened closely at the sealed door, and have heard nothing. For all one knows, there could be nothing behind that door except a stone wall, and behind that, the End of Being and eternal cold."

"Pay no attention to him," whispered Yin to Blunger. "One cannot hear what one is not prepared to hear; of this I am certain.

"The attachment of the drop of mortal soul to human babies, whose lives are not yet fixed in Earth Real, is weak. While the infants sleep, their souls, seeking the universal soul, which they miss sorely, return to Esfandiary. They are guarded by elves lest they encounter the dangers of the place. In a few years, this is over and done with, except for occasional fragments of dreams. The souls of some creative ones, artists and writers and musicians also ascend to Esfandiary of nights.

"Elf Miki told me this. Nightly he shepherds the souls of children through that place."

"Elf Miki is kindly and sweet and hopelessly confused," Yang retorted, holding the wheel tightly against a sudden wind-gust from the right side.

"Elf Miki." Myron Blunger was reduced to an echo, his mind adazzle at these words. He saw an opening. "I'm a writer. I don't remember going to this Dreamland, this Esfandiary."

Yang laughed harshly. "You! A writer! Cervantes was a writer; Homer was a writer! Shakespeare! Your Joey Willem doesn't even know who he is! The boy's incomplete."

"So who isn't these days?" Blunger retorted. "Anyway, it's not my fault! The T.V. people made him different and then they . . . they ended the series and my publisher wasn't interested any more."

The van lurched to the right and suddenly was engulfed in a hard-driving snowfall punctuated with blasts of sleet that glazed the windshield as fast as the wipers could clear them. Blunger whimpered as they fishtailed, then stabilized and proceeded cautiously through a blinding whiteness that made Blunger's eyes ache.

I'm dead and that's that, he thought, sadly. I thought it would hurt more. A last fringe benefit from the union. Why couldn't it happen while I was filling out my income tax? Maybe Sophie could sue the government.

Blinking away a tear, and more fearful of silence than anything more that could befall him, Blunger asked of no one in particular, "So tell me about this . . . Inn."

Motioning the driver slightly to the left, which now seemed unimportant to Blunger since he was dead already, the centaur answered, "The Inn . . . well, it's on the border between Earth

Real and Esfandiary, with a door into each place. And a big dining hall."

Yin said, "Pinocchio lives there, and Cinderella and Sherlock Holmes . . ."

"And Black Beauty and Pegasus," the centaur added.

"And Bilbo Baggins and Gandalf," Yang said. "It is a home for all those who have fixed themselves so strongly into human minds that they live on."

"So long as they retain their readership," Yin said quietly. "They come . . . and they go."

"Don't forget the library," Windbreaker said. "There's a grand library with a roaring fire and armchairs, one for the Innkeeper, and one for the Don."

"The Don?" Blunger echoed.

"Don Quixote," Yin said. "He also serves as Maitre d' in the dining hall. In the library there is King Arthur's round table. It is very special."

"For writing?" Blunger ventured.

"No!" All three together. Sharply.

"It is forbidden to write in the library," the centaur said.

"Dangerous," Yang added.

"What one writes in the library of the Inn at the End of the World has a way of coming true," Yin said. "But anyone can read there. There are lanterns and a warm fire, and books by the thousand, in all languages."

"I used to read Latin and Greek!" the centaur said, proudly. "And I may take up Romany. And French, if it's not too hard."

"Why did you stop reading Greek?" Yang asked, ignoring a medium thump on the shoulder by his twin brother.

"Why should I?" Windbreaker snapped. "I'm only interested in getting my curse lifted, and while Greek is probably a great language for turning a curse on, it's not so great for turning it off again." Turning to Blunger, Windbreaker said, "I'll tell you about the Inn. If you were within a dozen feet of its front door and night coming, you'd freeze to death! How about that, eh?"

Blunger decided not to wonder why the centaur had stopped reading Greek. What would this foolish creature say if he knew that he was only a character in a dead man's dream? But there was something wrong with that, wasn't there? Blunger tried to concentrate on exactly when and how he'd passed from life to afterlife, and why he'd not felt pain and how far this creation of an overactive imagination could carry consistent answers and to what eternal destiny he was headed. Hmm . . . questions. Sophie believed in questions. Myron Blunger ventured: "So my Joey ended up at this Inn at the End of the World?"

Windbreaker nodded. "Apparently your novel pulled together enough of a following to give the boy a place. The Innkeeper put him in the juvenile wing and immediately there was trouble between him and Alice, and then with Dorothy."

Alice. Dorothy. Being dead is as consistent as being alive was! Maybe more, even, Blunger thought.

Windbreaker continued, "I had to take your Willem by the arm and have a talk with him. If the Innkeeper had learned of it, he'd have given the lad a thrashing, for sure. Joey misses his mother, you know. And you never gave him a father at all.

"Not that a mother's everything! Mine got me into a lot of trouble. I mean, first she got me; then her husband came home from Troy sort of early and found me there. If it had just been the other way round . . ." he said wistfully. "I wasn't always a centaur, you know. I was born a human, a prince of Greece!" His eyes flashed. "I used to give my teacher the slip and head for the fields, the kitchen, the stables. Of course, that was a long time ago . . ." He sighed.

Blunger closed his eyes, trying to conceal the fact that he was listening carefully. Blunger recognized a possibility when it presented itself. The centaur had a problem. If Blunger could draw upon his background in children's stories and fables, if he could solve that problem, he could trade that for a safe-and-sound, happily-ever-after return to the Bronx! Windbreaker could continue on to the Inn and take care of the boots business, somehow.

"My father, the king, showed up, returned after a ten-year absence with his whole retinue . . . including his wizard," the centaur recited. "I was only six years old. I had a good build even then; could have passed for seven, or a short eight, but not ten. No way ten. Mama didn't have a story ready, dad not being expected for another couple of years.

"I was out riding my pony," Windbreaker said. His eyes were dark and his muscles tense. "The king . . . my father . . ."

"The king threw . . ." Yin prompted patiently.

How old was Windbreaker, anyway? Blunger wondered. And Yin? His mind balked.

" . . . threw me down on the ground and told his magician to make me gone, out of sight and memory. There was . . . there was . . .

"Lightning," Yin prompted.

The centaur flinched, but gamely recited, . . . and I got knocked out and when I woke up, I was a centaur! And banished from the kingdom.

"Having a mother isn't everything. It didn't do me much good. But that's part of Joey's hangup."

Blunger opened his eyes. "Well, you're right; a mother isn't everything!" he snorted indignantly. "Did Dorothy have a mother? Did Alice? I suppose so, but they never mentioned them, did they? Still they made out very nicely and had grand adventures and all that. I gave Joey a thousand hours of my life, just learning how to string sentences together! Is that what Joey Willem wants," he asked, "that I should write another story?"

Windbreaker's answer was whispered, as though the words were forbidden. "No. He wants . . . I think he wants to bring himself to life in Earth Real."

Blunger shivered. To bring himself to life in Earth Real, like Pinocchio. This nightmare is certainly consistent! he thought. Maybe it's a spell. So how to break a spell? Think of something else. Lox on a toasted bagel. The king of France. The dewey decimal system. Concentrate!

Lightning flashed, accompanied by an immediate blast of thunder. The storm was all around them. And the wind was whistling and Myron Blunger was still captive in a black van tearing through the night, captive of two gnomes and a centaur burdened by an ancient curse. He closed his eyes and concentrated on what he knew best.

Ring a round the rosy a pocket full of posies.

Another English nursery rhyme. From the time of the plague.

Lox, four dollars a quarter pound.

Sophie. The boys. Irving is a professor. Jacob owns a combination pharmacy-houseware store.

The twenty-fifth of October. The king of France at the battle of Agincourt. A week till the rent is due.

At that moment, either by design or accident, or simply because the dream was too expensive or, perhaps because the roadway had come to an end, the van swerved wildly, climbed a snowbank, rolled over completely and came to a jolting halt, sending its occupants crashing and thudding in all directions.

Blunger's door popped open! He unlocked his safety belt and tumbled out into a snowbank. By the light of the van's headlights, he found his footing but no sooner had he taken three unsteady steps in as many directions than he was lifted bodily by Windbreaker and placed on the seat of a black troika. Three grey stallions, stamping and snorting impatiently, were in harness. Too astonished to cry out or attempt an escape, Blunger watched as Yin and Yang pulled themselves and each other out of the rear door of the van. Yang, the larger, might come up to Blunger's belt. Both were so heavily cloaked that they could hardly advance themselves through the snow. Were they really gnomes? Did it make a difference, considering that this was all the dream of a dead man?

Supporting each other, the gnomes stumbled and flopped over

the snow to the troika, then climbed and clambered into the driver's seat. Yang took a whip into his hand and with a flourish and one sharp crack, they were off, flying along a narrow trail into the heart of a great woods with Windbreaker cantering alongside. His torso bent nearly horizontal, the centaur was searching out the true path amid a treacherous patchwork of tree-shadows and slivers of brilliant moonlight. While Yang flourished the whip, Yin gripped the three sets of reins, snapping them, spurring the horses to greater speed. So they travelled for a time, with Blunger huddled shivering in the rear seat, his hands pressed against his belly for warmth and his face so buried in the lapels of his overcoat that only the tip of his nose was exposed to the merciless wind. And then Yin turned around and, with a smile of utmost satisfaction, recited:

"A riddle, a piddle. Your boy's in the middle of danger no matter the way of his choosing.
A miser, no wiser, will seek an advisor.
In doubt, higher migher. You'll never be losing."

Before Blunger could ask, "What? What does that mean?" Yang stood up, raised the whip and slashed at a pack of wolves that had just emerged from the forest shadows. They raced alongside, panting, snapping, leaping for Blunger, who had suddenly dropped to the floor of the great sleigh. The centaur appeared at the troika's starboard side. Crying, "Off with you! Get!" he dispersed several wolves with repeated forehand and backhand sweeps of a long-handled knobkerry carried aboard the troika for just that purpose.

Blunger's eyes, narrowed to slits, were fast riming shut but in his despair, he considered that a blessing for surely he was going to die again, torn alive to mouth-sized pieces and eaten in an Artic forest. Suddenly a white wolf, the largest of the pack, leaped into the troika from the port side, safe from the centaur's too-accurate knobkerry. "Kick it out! Kick!" Windbreaker shouted and Blunger's legs came to life, jerking, swinging and pushing spastically with the wolf's jaws tightening their grip on his ankle until Yin, leaning over, punched the animal on its nose. The wolf, yelping, tumbled over the side, leaving the man sprawled on the floor of the rushing sleigh, his boots slashed, his leg bleeding and his heart thumping like the kitchen waterhammer, which he suddenly missed more than anything in the world.

"Bravo!" Windbreaker shouted. "Keep stamping away, there! Good for the circulation!" Blunger commenced a series of furious poundings against the wooden floor that quickly reduced to half-hearted taps as he recalled that he'd deduced himself dead already. "Anyway, they won't dare follow us out of the forest," the centaur added as he swiped at another wolf that had its paws over the edge of the troika.

Blunger, now afraid that he was *not* dead, cried out, "Why not?"

"Oh, they're afraid of the sabertooths on the Northern Reaches," the centaur called over the wind-rush."

Blunger mewed, "Of course. By the w . . . way, I didn't know that wolves snap at empty air."

"They don't usually," Windbreaker called between cupped hands. "Only when they're starving."

Blunger's eyes peeped out from the lapels of his raised collar, scanning from side to side as he tried to anticipate from which direction the next attack would come. His ears, straining for the expected clatter of paws and death-growl, heard only the syncopation of the centaur's hooves in the soft snow, the hiss of the runners, the rush of the wind and the labored, rhythmic panting of the horses. Apparently the wolves hadn't gotten too near the horses, discouraged either by their high kicking, the careful placement and timing of Yang's whip-snaps, or Yin's high-pitched "Hi-yah! Hi-yah!". Terrified that the centaur was about to gallop ahead, leaving him to face the next onslaught alone, Blunger reached out and tugged at the bottom of Windbreaker's sweater. "You know, Mr. Windbreaker, I'm not such a big traveller but small talk does help pass the time. So tell me, wha . . . what's new?"

The centaur laughed. "I like you, Blunger! Somewhere under

that fat, there's style! If you ever take up writing again, maybe you could help me. The Innkeeper says I can shake the curse if I pull off a noble deed. Maybe if you get a chance, you could give me a lead role in a battle scene. A charge, preferably downhill or on level ground. A strong rhythm! Thunder and lightning in the background. You could set it in the Dromedary Mountains, where old Groff is supposed to be hanging out. The barrier's starting to tear open! The sky opens up with an explosive crash. A buzzing violet circle appears in the air. The barrier's torn open just ten yards from where Joey Willem has sought refuge from the storm and now Dragon Groff has emerged from his cave and is scratching at the cave entrance, trying to get at the kid. He's got him in his talon! Lifts him high in the air, right over his open jaws! He's about to devour the boy whole when the Horn of Roland is sounded! There, at the top of the mountain is a centaur with a great bod and an iron spear and a shield. Breaking into a full gallop, the centaur sounds the horn again and readies his spear! The dragon drops the boy and sets his talons in the ground to face this unexpected . . .

"Oh, you can take it from there, Blunger. Just remember to give the centaur some backup; this is Dragon Groff we're talking about."

Blunger nodded. *The horn of Roland. Centaur. Dragon. Spear. The Dromedary Mountains. A barrier. Why not?*

The wolves had been left far behind and no sabertooths had been guarding the passes of the Northern Reaches. Ignoring pails of oats that Yang had laid before them, the horses lay huddled beneath blankets, shivering and staring across an expanse of black, wind-driven water studded with the shards of smashed icebergs. Blunger, his teeth chattering violently, was a bulging knot pressed into the belly of the lee horse. Heedless of the cold, Yin and Yang were preparing a small boat for launching.

"I didn't know . . . north went this far," Blunger muttered after tearing apart his frozen lips. A horse whinneyed. Windbreaker, his hooves dug into the frozen tundra, thrust his shoulder against the boat. And again, calling to Yin and Yang, "To . . . gether . . . NOW!" With a sharp crack, the boat broke away from its bonds of ice and slid an inch.

Blunger persisted. "The creative side of my brain is l-lonely and nervous, not up to c-cold pursuit."

"This is the easy part, Blunger!" Windbreaker called. "Hang tight there! HEAVE . . . NOW!" The boat slid a foot toward the black inland sea.

"The worst is behind us?" Blunger cried.

The centaur threw back his head and laughed. "Behind us? A little snow and a few mangy wolves? Listen . . ."

Blunger listened. In the distance, an iceberg cracked. Then he heard another sound, further out in the blackness. A low-pitched roar as must come from a throat of unimaginable size.

"The kraken," Windbreaker grunted as he and the gnomes heaved in unison and the boat slid halfway into the water. "The trick is (ugh!) to stay close (Heave!) behind the kraken, and let the swell of his wake carry us along. But not too close! Just out of sight."

The boat slid into the water. Yang climbed aboard the troika. The lee horse rose, dumping Blunger into the snow. Slowly, slowly he pushed his frozen body to a kneeling position, then to his feet. "You probably wouldn't believe how nervous this whole thing has made me."

"I! Me! Myself!" Windbreaker snapped. "You'd better start thinking how you're going to get those boots back to the Inn, with or without the boy! Otherwise you're going to have a real problem on your hands, Mr. Blunger the big writer. A real problem! The Innkeeper . . ."

While Windbreaker ranted, Myron Blunger had quietly placed · one numb foot on the giant sled's runner and was reaching up to try to pull himself inside, where he could hide on the floor, or somewhere. That plan was scotched when he found himself being lifted by the centaur and carried toward the boat.

"No! No!" he cried, pointing to the troika. "I . . . I . . . get seasick!" he protested.

"Don't," Windbreaker said. "The journey around the Deep takes too long, and the Innkeeper's in a hurry," Windbreaker said, dropping his passenger into the boat without ceremony. Behind, Yang snapped his fingers; the horses leaped ahead. Backing up onto the beach, the centaur took a running start and soared into the air, barely clearing the boat's coaming before thudding onto the deck. Yin was already hoisting sail as Windbreaker took the tiller.

Waves crashed over the boat's side as though fleeing even colder, darker water below. Windbreaker, legs braced against the gunwales, steered directly toward a phosphorescent swell a distance ahead. To starboard, something large hurtled out of the water, then crashed back, nearly swamping the small craft. Blunger looked longingly back at the icy shore vanishing astern; from the windswept cockle-shell of a boat, it looked steady as a living room.

Grasping the horse-blanket against the shrieking wind, his other hand wrapped around the lantern Windbreaker had given him to tend, Blunger had been silently pleading for a different nightmare, but now gave that up for a new terror. The vessel was coming apart. Driven by the wind to the top of a wave, it would slam down into the following trough and remain there, with water pouring over the side and the floorboards creaking ominously. Soaked through and through and with his teeth chattering violently, Blunger tapped the centaur on a hindleg to bring this to his attention, only to have his face swatted by Windbreaker's tail. Blunger closed his eyes and concentrated on the king of France, reciting it over and over. The little cockle-boat was moving faster now and Blunger became aware of a noise from below, from deep within the water. A pulsating groan, so low in pitch that it was more felt than heard.

The kraken.

They were riding its wake, like surfers.

Blunger passed out and the next thing he heard was Yin crying, "Inn dead ahead!" Myron Blunger squinted from between eyelids that refused to open more than a sliver and even as the gnome pointed to a yellow glimmer of light in the distance, the boat was lifted high above the waves and overturned, its contents spilled out as though for inspection. Blunger hit the water with flailing arms and legs (which retarded his descent into the Deep), a lungful of air he'd been planning to expel in a fruitless scream and his mouth closed. He did not know what manner of creature wound a ropelike tentacle around his abdomen and dragged him down, down. All existence became a terrible thrashing and tossing in that dark sea as his captor was itself attacked. Blunger's last thoughts before passing out was the only part of Yin's riddle he could remember: In doubt, higher migher.

A PROBLEM FOR BLUNGER

Cold. Hard. Sharp in places. Cold! Rocks. Chunks and slivers of ice. Bitter Cold! Hard. Slimy.

Slimy?

Cold and hard wasn't bad enough? Slimy?

Blunger lay on a rock-strewn beach, exactly where Windbreaker had dropped him before diving back into the icy depths to search for Yin. Only the most energetic, the most ambitious of photons could squeeze between the ex-librarian's tightly-compressed eyelids. His efforts to interpret a world gone violet made his head throb. Also his hands and arms were frozen into a block of solid ice and he couldn't feel anything in his legs. Not anything. Preoccupied with these matters, the right side of Blunger's brain, the action-oriented side failed to interpret the clicks and thunks his ears had desperately been sending inward, not for methodical analysis but as a warning to get out of there!

Just outside his narrow field of view, an armored Stomachorum Flexiclaw, alerted by the aroma of warm flesh, had advanced stealthily (considering that she was swollen with eggs from her last mating) and patiently (considering that she had not eaten properly since immediately after her last mating.) And she much preferred warm meat to cold. Having reached her prey, she was cautiously extending her watermelon-sized claws in the defensive posture and probing with her antennae for a chink in its armor. Lo, it had no protective shell at all! Opening her mouth-parts to their limit, she extruded a spongy, bladder-like extensible stomach, with which to soak up the nutritious body-juices before they drained away into the tundra. The morsel's muted cries of welcome were in the exact key as her previous mate's death ecstasy, and her neck-muscles contracted repeatedly, streaming digestive juices over the gift from the sea.

The sudden appearance in his limited field of view of a long, violet antenna provoked Myron Blunger to a degree of anxiety that transcended anything he'd ever experienced, even in the Bronx. Then a spray of liquid fire seared his face, sizzling away the stubble of beard and burning into the skin.

His icebound hands could not push it away, nor could his numb legs take him out of danger. His mouth, clamped shut against the deadly fluid, could not scream aloud. A purple bladder slowly descended over his face, blotting out the violet sky.

Myron Blunger had, for years, secretly steeled himself against the certainty that one day a chunk of corned-beef cholesterol would slip into place in his coronary artery and shut everything down, Thump! thump ... whoooosh ... and Myron Blunger would go out in the same way all of his forefathers had, at the table, licking his lips. Furious that a cruel death by engulfment on a frozen, alien shore was scant seconds away, Blunger tore his lips apart and screamed, "SOPHIE!"

At that moment, Windbreaker burst from the roaring surf, turned and spat a mighty flume of water, green stuff and bleeding tentacle back into the Deep. By the time he'd laid the limp body of Yin beside Blunger, the shore creature was in full retreat, buzzing and clacking alarm to its kind, warning of the new four-footed sea-monster and its trick of setting out warm bait.

The centaur, his legs wobbly from fatigue and bleeding profusely from dozens of wounds inflicted as the price of one of the kraken's myriad tentacles, nevertheless went about resuscitating the gnome, rolling him over a rock and alternately pressing and thumping his back until breathing was restored. Finally, with a blessedly semiconscious but living passenger slung beneath arm, Windbreaker, with the last of his strength, started the long uphill climb to the Inn at the End of the World.

Clangs and tinkles, warmth and the aroma of burning hickory greeted Myron Blunger's returning senses. He blinked, found that his eyes worked properly and his face was no longer encrusted. And his hands worked and his legs had feeling. With a delicious shiver, his body announced that he was alive, alive, and lying on a long wooden table, cocooned in blankets. He opened his eyes wide.

The room was large, lit by firelight and flickering lanterns set in wall-sconces. Its vaulted, age-darkened ceiling was supported by massive columns of iron-bound wood, and the only sound was the crackle of logs in a large stone fireplace. Blunger's librarian's nose discerned the bittersweet odor of slowly decaying, low-rag-content paper and now he saw that there were books everywhere; in shelves that lined the walls from stone floor to ceiling, in rows of stacks, in piles scattered randomly on the stone floor, spilling out of boxes and sacks. Slowly, cautiously, he moved his head to the right. There, stretched out on the hearth, his body covered with gauze and bandages, his flanks twitching and shivering, was Windbreaker. The centaur's eyes were closed; he appeared to be asleep. Yin was nowhere in sight.

"Well, looky who woke up!" exclaimed a gruff but kindly voice accompanied by a fresh round of bongs and tinkles. "Welcome to my Inn, Mr. Blunger. You took exactly twenty one stitches, in case you're one of those who keep track of such things. Now drink up, laddie! There's a job of work awaitin' . . ."

Blunger rolled his head to the left to find a stout old man standing there, his belly pressed into the table. His mane of white hair and thick beard framed a jolly, ruddy face with merry blue eyes, pink cheeks and full, red lips. Beneath the Innkeeper's left arm was cradled a crockery pot, from which a rich, thick vapor spilled out into the room.

"St. Felicia's potion," he chuckled, pouring a ladleful down Blunger's throat—glug, glug—before he could protest.

The therapeutic soup went about restoring the full fire of life to Blunger's insides, blasting away a lifelong buildup of tartar, malevolent viruses, parasitic bacteria and enough cholesterol to cement a hundred-gallon fishtank. Blunger burbled, "Helb!" but the ladle was again between his teeth, the second dosing accompanied by more tinkles and bongs.

Myron Blunger, his internal pathways and byways scoured clean, expelled a prodigious belch and focussed on the Innkeeper who seemed anything but that. His irridescent shirt and vest were festooned with pockets, as were his blue denim work trousers and work apron, and from a wide leather belt hung a forest of loops, thongs and gadget-holders. From all of these protruded the source of the clatter: screwdrivers, wrenches and a claw hammer, measuring cups, spoons and a sheath knife, bandages and thermometers both Celcius and Fahrenheit, dental picks and mirrors, tissue paper, plaster and a trowel, all of which banged and clattered together at the slightest motion. And a book of folk tales, from which protruded a leather placemark. Perched atop his head were two pairs of eyeglasses, with three more dangling by cords around his neck.

Tossing another half-ladleful of the elixir down Blunger's hatch for good measure, the Innkeeper put aside the medicine and, using the ladle as a baton, sang hoarsely:

> "When songs are sung of the heroes of yore, by quaffers old and hoary, let a toast be drunk and the tale told, of a prince of centaurs brave and bold, journeying over the Reaches cold.
> He found his man by the sound of his snore and earned his way to glory!
>
> (Bang, rattle, clatter-bang!)
>
> His thundering hooves scattered the wolves!
> Into the forest he flang 'em!
> To reverse his curse, he bested the beast, diving deep without hardly a peep, sworn to rescue the kraken's prey, he grabbed its tentacle, chomped it away!

Pulled Blunger up to the light of day!
Brought him and Yin to our wonderful Inn!
(Don't leave that out of the story!)"

"How's that, eh? You listening, you horse's ass?" the Innkeeper roared, the force of his voice causing the nearest lantern to flicker wildly. "Blunger here wants to pay his respects and thank you for saving his life!

Windbreaker's head nodded ever so slightly, but his eyes remained closed.

"Give him a thankee," he whispered into Blunger's ear. "He's disappointed that his heroics didn't get his curse lifted. Keep it short; we have work to do."

Thank your kidnapper!

Blunger humped himself to his side so as to face the centaur, and groaned, "I just want to . . . to thank you for a . . . for a very exciting and refreshing vacation trip north, Mr. Windbreaker. You should feel free to drop in for dinner any time you're in the neighborhood." Blunger fell back, grimacing with pain.

The Innkeeper whispered, "Excellent, my boy! Short and to the point. Same as with writing; you don't have to describe every flower in the hothouse; one rose will do if it's the right one. Write what you know."

Blunger closed his eyes. "I gave up writing four years ago."

"Not so fast," the Innkeeper admonished, wagging a forefinger in Blunger's face. A forefinger that seemed incongruously, unnecessarily thick and calloused for a short, kindly old gentleman with blue eyes and pink cheeks. "We have a job to do."

Blunger struggled to his elbow and scanned the library more carefully. His eyes fell upon the wide, triple-bolted oak door at the far end. What was behind it?

Cold, eternal silence. A stone wall.

Golden meadows and the souls of infants, led by elves.

Heaven.

Hungry dinosaurs.

The Grand Concourse and the rest of the Bronx.

Esfandiary!

"I'm retired from jobs!" he said, suppressing an hysteria that was building up just below his Adam's apple. "Your horseman kidnapped the wrong librarian! This is a cataloging job you have; I'm strictly Reference and Children's. The best thing is I take a taxi home and mail you ... very good references ... on the ... dewey decimal ... system."

Blunger's lips continued flapping but no sound came out. Because the Innkeeper was growing taller, broadening across the chest, changing altogether. Accompanied by solid clanks ominously lower in pitch than the earlier clatter, the merry laugh lines dissolved into hard, vertical grooves; the hands clenched and hardened into massive, callused, club-like fists; the white beard darkened and the kindly eyes receded beneath heavy brows and their twinkle vanished. Hardly less astonishing was the metamorphosis of the Innkeeper's loud but harmless array of tools and utensils into a matched set of bludgeons, lengths of heavy chain and a rack of daggers that hung, unsheathed, from a wide, black leather belt.

Blunger chittered, "Sto ... sto ... stop changing, please. Too much change becomes adventure and adventures are for children. English children. You could look it up."

The Innkeeper, who now towered above Myron Blunger, raised muscular, dark-haired arms, clamped a horned, iron helmet onto his now bullet-shaped head. "I took the trouble to adapt a benign, grandfatherly image to ease your awakening and do I get appreciation?" he growled. "'I'd like to go home by taxi, if you please,'" he mimicked. "Well, I've just got a communication direct from the battlefield according to which your Joey Willem somehow made his way across or through the barrier to Upper Muchness and already a griffin is missing from Esfandiary!"

Of this, one word embedded itself in Blunger's mind. "Battlefield! What battlefield?"

The Innkeeper put his finger to his lips and glanced at the dozing centaur. "Did I say battlefield?" he whispered. "I meant valley, of course. The valley of Upper Muchness. A peaceful, serene place which is neither here nor there. Keep that in mind. Read this." From a pocket he took a sheet of paper and thrust it into Blunger's trembling hand. Earlier, in the van, the centaur had wished for a heroic charge; Blunger had dismissed that as prattle. This Innkeeper did not appear to be a prattler. Battlefield!

The paper was apparently the front side of a one-page newspaper; the rear was blank. The nameplate read The Postulate. Beneath that was printed Extra Edition. Beneath that was one brief article. Blunger read it quickly.

> A youth who gives his name as Joey Willem has been found asleep in field 39B by Trenton Interface, the highly esteemed and talented Major Domo of Valleymaster Lucien Broco. Questions regarding his means of transport into the valley, the location of his home and the names of his parents went unanswered. After searching fruitlessly for a lost pet he would not identify or name, he has taken up residence in the mansionhouse of Mr. Lucien Broco. His mass is twenty-nine kilograms (sixty-four pounds). He has a thin face, dark eyes and long black hair and was wearing a horizontally-striped shirt, blue denims and carried a jackknife, which Mr. Interface immediately confiscated.
>
> When found, he was barefoot. His feet were unscratched and had no visible calluses, though he must have endured a considerable journey to reach this most isolated of valleys. Confronted with this oddity, he tried to run from Mr. Interface, who caught and carried him back to the mansionhouse.

Joey Willem! His Joey Willem was real! Fear, pride and astonishment cascaded, collided, coalesced within Blunger's overloaded brain.

"The Postulate comes from Upper Muchness by roundabout,"

the Innkeeper whispered. "It is written by Benison Hawkins, a mathematician who may or may not be crazy. All the same, he has a Theory. Not a theory; a Theory with a capital T. He claims that it explains everything from the ins and outs of gravity to how to set up and run a kingdom. Everything.

"Blunger," said the Innkeeper, staring into his guest's eyes in a manner that Blunger found most disconcerting, "I have a deep and sympathetic interest in human affairs. After all, I have served as Innkeeper to a most diverse collection of guests. And who are these guests? Each and every one is a distillation of an aspect of humankind. And are they a restless and passionate lot!

"I am curious to learn whether this Hawkins fellow has captured in a set of mathematical equations what poets and writers have struggled with for millenia. I want to know whether his Theory explains why nations go to war, and what drives children to learn to walk despite the anguish and frustration of repeated failure. I wish to . . . examine his . . . social map, to see if it might enable someone of Stature and Authority—not a dictator, of course—a benign Manager to bring order to the affairs of the world of humankind. A person who has demonstrated his managerial talents in a related field, such as . . ."

"Running an Inn," Blunger guessed.

"Aye," the Innkeeper smiled broadly. "And while you're about it, it seems that your . . . protege, Joey Willem . . . a splendid lad with a boy's aptitude for pranks . . . well, he seems to have run off with my boots. My favorite boots, without which I cannot hope to safely pass through Esfandiary, where, with those boots, I can travel seven leagues at a step. They do not work in Earth Real, because your kind has adapted a hard, mechanistic view of the universe. At any rate, I would appreciate their return."

Blunger handed back the newspaper and said, "Look, Mr. Innkeeper, I appreciate all this attention, but I have no idea how to get Joey Willem back to the Inn. To tell the truth, Sophie hardly trusts me to go out and mail a letter. You seem to be very well organized. Maybe . . . if you're not too busy, you could . . . it would be much easier . . ."

Fire flashed from the Innkeeper's eyes and his hamlike fist seemed poised to smash Blunger into his constituent parts, but instead it poked about until it encountered a chair, which the Innkeeper swung around and straddled. Taking a deep breath, he said in a low voice,

"You've been very tactful, Blunger. Very tactful and cooperative. You haven't asked why I want the boots at this particular time. You've been a real trooper through some tough going. If you were a lesser man, I'd say that you were afraid to arouse my wrath. That, of course, is not the case. You are most certainly not a lesser man. I will confide in you.

"My main reason for wanting the boots is that I badly need and fully deserve a vacation, with Upper Muchness as the preferred location. Upper Muchness is a valley bounded by beautiful cliffs. Very special cliffs. I wish to sit in that valley day after day, reading wonderful books, including a synopsis of Hawkins's Theory which I will wring . . . I will discuss with him, occasionally looking up to regard and appreciate the interplay of sunlight on the eastern cliff as day descends into night."

But the word that resonated through Blunger's head was Battlefield.

The Innkeeper shook his head and muttered, "But without the seven-league boots, I cannot get there. The route via the Northern Reaches is strewn with dangers. Sabertooth tigers, wolves. And, somewhere on the border of Upper Muchness, a dragon left over from the old days.

"That leaves the route through Esfandiary, and unless I can outrun the dinosaurs . . . you see how it is? So you must get them back, eh? And Willem and the griffin, while you're at it. They wouldn't be happy in Upper Muchness, anyway.

"As for the how of it; why, you're going to write him back to the Inn. With the boots. Be certain of that; I must have those boots!"

At that moment, the St. Felicia's potion, circling around in Blunger's head with nothing left to cure, came upon the tiny nodule of Flamboyant Confidence, buried within a surface convolution and lost since age 3, when Myron Blunger showed his Aunt Bella how he'd learned to balance himself on one foot. Sometimes. The potion dove in.

Myron Blunger sneezed. Once, and again, and a third time, each more powerful than its predecessor. Feeling curiously lightheaded, he cast off the blankets, lifted himself to a sitting position with only a moderately excruciating degree of discomfort, and announced loudly, "Joey Willem's acting out, is he? Well, I'll have him back in two shakes!"

"Now, that's the way of it!" the Innkeeper said heartily, helping Blunger down from the table. "Let's discuss an outline."

Aiming himself toward the front door of the Inn, Blunger cried, "Outline? Nonsense! I'll just trot over to this Upper Muchness valley, collar the little devil and talk to him like a Dutch uncle!" With that, he thrust out his jaw and narrowed his eyes. Just outside the library was a spacious lobby, at the far end of which was the ironbound front door of the Inn. The door led outside, to the road south, to the Bronx, the Concourse, home. He took one unsteady step. Another; his ankle wobbled.

"Blunger!" cried the Innkeeper, taking his guest by the arm. "Where do you think you're going?"

"To the chair beside that coatrack," Blunger declared, pointing to a row of wooden pegs on the wall of the lobby from which a solitary overcoat was draped above a pair of floppy-top, ragged and torn galoshes. "Then out! A straight march to the crossroad, from which I shall follow the signs to Upper Muchness, to my boy Joey and the boots." To himself, he said, South, to a subway! Myron Blunger struck out for the coatrack, supporting himself on the Innkeeper's arm.

"I don't think you'll want to walk out that door just now," the Innkeeper said.

"And why not?" Blunger demanded, determinedly driving his

aching body across the stone floor toward his coat, his galoshas and freedom.

And then a sound came to Blunger's attention. It was a muffled scratching, and it seemed to come from the other side of the door.

"Why not?" the Innkeeper sighed. "First, let me disillusion you regarding the route. There are no crossroads, no signs. Only faint trails in the snow marked by well-chewed mastodon bones and discarded tusks. First you would have to cross the Deep. By canoe, since the sailboat was lost. If you somehow failed to attract the attention of the kraken, which must be in a bit of a snit following the loss of its tentacle, you would then face the long march over the windswept Northern Reaches to the edge of the Forest Beyond, where seven trails converge. Yours is the center one of the three not marked, but you have only to keep the wind to your left and your shadow to the right to eventually arrive at the head of the Valley of Upper Muchness, which is where your lad has ended up."

Reaching the chair, Blunger dropped into it and singlemindedly started to work his left foot into its galosh. "You keep saying . . . you," he panted. "What about Windbreaker? After all, he brought me here."

The Innkeeper shook his head. "Windbreaker took three hundred twenty stitches; he must heal before he goes adventuring."

"What about Yin?" Blunger asked, firmly snapping one galosh and reaching for the other. "He'd be company."

The Innkeeper said nothing until Blunger had pulled on and fastened the other galosh. Then, setting strong, thick fingers in the arterial groove of his guest's wrist, he gripped Blunger's arm in the other tightly, stopping blood flow. Then he said "Yin's recovering from a case of the bends. Twenty . . . thirty . . . And acute hypothermia, oxygen deprivation and hallucinations. Sixty . . . seventy . . . he's under observation."

"Could I see him?" Blunger asked.

"Ninety . . . one hundred . . ." the Innkeeper recited under his breath. Shaking his head, he answered, "Not now. He barely has strength to lift a book. He's a great one for books. Lookin' for a career, he says. And Yang hasn't arrived yet. By the way, I understand that Yin recited some poetry to you on the way up. A riddle or such. Do you recall the words, by chance?"

The last sentence was delivered with a studied casualness that did not deceive our resident of New York for one instant, yet such was the intensity of the Innkeeper's gaze and the strength of the grip on his arm that Blunger, powerless to prevaricate, resorted to a half-truth. "All I remember is: 'In doubt, higher migher'." He waited for the Innkeeper to nod sagaciously, but the Innkeeper seemed as perplexed as Blunger himself. After some moments, he continued his chanting. "One twenty . . . one thirty . . ." Was something wrong? Had he misheard, after all? Suppose Yin had said, "Higher, Mightier!" That made more sense.

"One sixty!" the Innkeeper declared.

"What's that?" asked Blunger. The scratchings had been replaced by a series of chuffing grunts from outside the front door, which seemed to be bending slightly at the center.

"Ah!" the Innkeeper exclaimed. "You noticed. That is a sabertooth tiger out there."

Squeeeeeezzz . . .

Were it not for the St. Felicia's potion in his nodule of Flamboyant Confidence, Blunger would have collapsed to the floor. As it was, he only sagged a few inches.

"A rogue male," the Innkeeper said, releasing Blunger's arm and counting under his breath. "Don't get many of them around here. This one seems to have followed Windbreaker up the path and he's been hanging around ever since. Poor fellow left a trail of blood, you know."

"Two hundred ten over one thirty!" the Innkeeper announced, releasing Blunger's wrist. "A high pulse rate. Some fresh air and exercise would do you good." The quiet was blasted by a great roar of frustration and hunger from outside, and then the iron-bound door bellied inward under the impact of a heavy body.

The Innkeeper pondered the array of bludgeons on his belt,

selected one and slapped it onto his open palm to check its balance. Gripping Blunger by the arm, he pulled him to the door and opened a small peephole.

Keeping his eye at a respectable distance from the aperture, Blunger peered outside and saw death. It had taken the form of a tiger the size of a small horse, with curved yellow daggers protruding from its upper jaw. It had seated itself on its haunches and its steady gaze was fixed upon the peephole, in the manner of a hungry cat expecting dinner.

Handing the bludgeon to his guest, the Innkeeper said, mildly, "Nuisance cat. Well, if you insist on leaving us, I will not hold you back. I will get the cook to make up a pack of travelling grub for you, not forgetting a tot of rum against the cold. Meanwhile, just throw the bolts, open the door and chase it away, will you? A good whack on the snout'll send him flyin'. Then you're off to Upper Muchness!"

As Blunger watched through the peephole, horrified, the sabertooth opened its mouth wide . . . incredibly wide . . .

It roared . . . lunged . . . smashed into the door . . .

Blunger found himself back in the library, huddled deep in the stacks between RO 729.13 and SI 122.880. A hickory log crackled in the fireplace and the gloom of the recess in which he had hidden himself was momentarily relieved by a burst of firelight. Blunger glanced toward the comfortable, peaceful hearth, his internal parts no longer throbbing from an overdose of heroism. The centaur lay on his side, snoring peacefully, soaking up restorative energy from the fire's warmth. An image shot through Blunger's mind of thousands of heavily-bound books waiting to be brought into the light, opened, their stories and secrets revealed. The prospect of bringing order to the library made more sense than starting off on another journey.

The Innkeeper strode into the library, smirking. With a glance at Blunger, he dropped into the armchair.

Blunger emerged from the stacks. What was this bludgeon doing in his hand? he thought as the paralysis caused by his one look at the sabertooth faded. "A wonderful weapon, the bludgeon," his mouth chattered to the Innkeeper all by itself, his brain being semi-paralyzed. "Prefer a blung, myself. Family thing. Blunger. Blung. Heh, heh. Never go outside without a blung, not in the Bronx. You aren't going to open the door, are you?"

The Innkeeper shrugged his shoulders, then led Blunger to the far end of the library, where there was another triple-bolted, iron-bound door. "Perhaps you'd like to try this one. This is the door to Esfandiary."

"To . . ." Blunger whispered.

The Innkeeper nodded. "Based on a pulse rate of 210 per sabertooth, I'd be interested in how high you go face to face with a six-ton Tyrranosaur that hasn't had a hot meal in sixty-five million years. I'll bet you'd hit ten thousand!"

A thought seared itself across Blunger's mind. "Did . . . Joey Willem go through . . .?" Blunger pointed, his lips unwilling to shape the name of the forbidden place.

"Yes, but he had my seven-league boots. My seven-league boots! And the little thief evidently discovered the secret of the door. Even I can't make it open at will."

"Oh."

The Innkeeper turned around, removed his iron helmet, shook himself once, twice, and when he was once more facing Blunger, he had reverted to his previous form. The bludgeons and daggers had metamorphosed into screwdrivers and ladles, rulers and measuring cups and it was a merry-eyed, white-bearded old gaffer who accompanied Myron Blunger back to the hearth.

"That place . . . is really full of dinosaurs?" Blunger asked, pointing fearfully toward the door that led to Esfandiary.

"And worse," the Innkeeper growled. "Dagger-trees and exploding seed-pods, snakes that fall on you from above and tiny flying worms that crawl through your skin whilst you're asleep, and lay their eggs in your warm flesh. They itch like the devil, but not for long; the larvae chew their way out fast enough. The shore critter that almost got you—the stomach-thing Windbreaker mentioned—I reckon it comes from there. Snuck through a weakness in the barrier, probably."

"Oh!" Blunger breathed, watching the door warily. "Who could figure such a thing? And this valley of Upper Muchness . . ."

The Innkeeper nodded grimly. "That's where the boy has to be. It's the only place where the barrier's weak enough so he could sneak through.

"Practically speakin', there's only one way you can get the job done. The way of the writer. You will write him back. In the library."

It is dangerous to write in the library of the Inn. It is forbidden . . . .

The Innkeeper's broad face glowed with pleasure as he continued, his face thrust directly into Blunger's. "In the library of the Inn at the End of the World, a writer puts himself into his storyline, body and soul!

"You will enter the valley of Upper Muchness. You will create a storyline that will bring you face to face with your Joey Willem. You will bring him back to the Inn, to his little friends and his own bed and cubby in the boys' dorm.

"With the boots!"

Then the Innkeeper's eyes glittered hard as diamonds. "And don't think of crossing me; writing in the library of the Inn at the End of the World isn't like making up a grocery list. I'll be right here, watchin' your every move by way of the manuscript with a red pen in my hand. One false step and I'll write you back here to the Inn so fast the air will pop behind you!

"Be careful, Blunger. The Inn is timeless, after a fashion, and some fates are worse than having your neck broke. What I'm saying is, don't mess around! Get those boots back, and the boy if you can."

Then he added, brightly, "But enough business! You're probably hungry. Well, you'll be glad to know I run the best dining-hall in these parts! Anything you want, just tell the Maitre d'; his name is Quixote. Habla Espanol? No? Too bad. Come. And while

you're stokin' your furnace, I'll have the table and chair in the
library set up with paper and pencils. You will address . . . The
Problem of the Missing Griffin. Write what you know, Blunger!
No fancy nonsense! And don't cross me!" he growled. "I want
the boots. They're mine and I need them!"

The Innkeeper guided his guest out of the library, down
corridors, through vaulted chambers and finally to the dining
hall. Blunger stared into an endless, high-ceilinged hall iden-
tifiable as a dining-room by the universal clatter and buzz of
conversation. Innumerable persons of all manner of being and
dress sat around sturdy wooden tables, gorging, eating, dining
elegently, served by buxom Elizabethan wenches, by liveried
servents, by what appeared to be many-armed robots. At one
stein-laden table, students were singing and banging for service; at another, heads were bowed as grace was recited over a
simple loaf of bread.

"The Maitre d' will show you to a table. Remember: The
Problem of the Missing Griffin. Good luck." With that, he was
gone.

Astonished, Myron Blunger eyed the dignified approach
of a tall, thin personage wearing the garb of a Spanish noble-
man of a time long vanished. His bearing was regal, his silver
hair and mustache impeccably groomed, though it was doubt-
ful that his matchstick arms could wield the filigreed sword
that hung by his side. But his eyes shone and his lips were
already rehearsing the phrase that would welcome the new guest
to his domain. After the deepest, most courtly of bows, he took
Blunger by the arm and escorted him to a quiet table by the
wall.

"Aqui es una mesa," he said, with a bow.

Falling into the proferred chair, Blunger repeated, "A kee
ess una meiseh."

The Maitre d' beamed, snapped his finger in the direction
of a Hollandische-dressed waitress, and with a final bow, stalked
off.

"A kee ess una meiseh," Blunger muttered to himself, astonished and bewildered at . . . at everything! It was too much to absorb on an empty stomach. To the waitress, he announced, "I will not write The Problem of the Missing Griffin! Not with me in the story. Too dangerous. A kee ess una meiseh! That's what I shall write."

She nodded prettily and waved her pencil over her order pad.

"A kee ess una meiseh?" she repeated, puzzled.

"It means: A Cow Eats without a Story! I'll start with orange juice, two soft-boiled eggs, some toast . . ."

*   *   *

Windbreaker, his lungs bursting, was enfolded by tentacles pulling him down, down. The kraken had him this time. His arms were pinned to his sides and thrash as he might, he was drowning in the pitch darkness of the Deep. He kicked mightily, but his hooves only stirred up the water. His lungs gave up their last store of air. A fleeting image of his long-gone mother flashed into his mind and then . . . he woke, gasping, and thrust himself up to a standing position, though it cost him dearly in pain.

He was in the library, by the dying fire. He was safe! Safe! It was only another nightmare.

There was Blunger, his head bent over the pad of yellow paper, his right hand steadily working its way from left to right, again and again. A blanket that had covered his knees was half-off and on the floor.

The centaur took a weak, tentative step in Blunger's direction and discovered that he could see beyond Blunger, could see through the writer! Yes, there were bookstacks and a flickering sconce . . . !

Blunger was fading!

And then . . . Blunger . . . was gone!

The pencil lay on the table and the writing continued, and Myron Blunger was nowhere!

Where had he gone to?

It is dangerous to write in the library of the Inn at the End of the World.

A KEE ESS UNA MEISEH

by Myron Blunger author of The Boy With No Future

At the base of the Dromedary Mountains the terrain flattened and the tangle of stunted, barely penetrable brush gave way to a dense forest of precisely the mixture of trees and brambles in which wolves and bears do best. A granite rock marked the northern boundary of the Upper Muchness Valley, and there Myron Blunger paused to extract a sliver of flint from his foot and muse on his options for bringing the Willem boy back to the Inn. During the arduous descent of the near-vertical western face of the Dromedaries (by rope, without light or pitoons), he'd devised several brilliant strategies for retrieving Joey Willem. As for luring the griffin back to wherever it had come from, that presented no problem at all. He would be lying in a field admiring the clouds and playing softly on a guitar while nearby, a tethered cow chewed its cud. Down would swoop the foolish griffin, claws extended for the poor cow's jugular! Out would come the number 5 blung and Pop! The creature would find itself gift-wrapped and waiting for United Parcel pickup!

Now slate grey and pink striations above the eastern cliff announced the eminence of dawn. The ominous western cliff—vertical slabs of midnight-black obsidian, a vast wall of darkness into which night was vanishing—glowered at the interloper who had so boldly penetrated the hidden valley and from its north end, yet!

Stripped to the waist, Myron was applying non-prescription Goldman's Ointment to the many scrapes and rope burns that criss-crossed the bulging muscles of his six-foot-two frame when his keen eyes noticed a rectangular object fastened to a tree some dozen yards to his left. He approached it from downwind, cautiously, yet making lots of noise to announce his presence. His greatest concern was that a predator, thinking it had the upper hand because of its fangs, claws, territorial claims and good night-vision, might attack him. One swing of his number 5 blung would produce a sharp clockwise rotation of its jaw relative to its shoulderbones and it would generally die on the spot, its neck broken. So why litter a virgin forest with carcasses?

The rectangle was a sign, with inch-high letters black on yellow. Approaching, he read in the half-light:

DAWN IS IMMINENT, NOT EMINENT!
PITONS NOT PITOONS
CUT OUT THAT NONSENSE!!
OR I TAKE OVER!—Innkeeper

Undaunted by the absurd message, Myron Blunger threw his broad shoulders back, unstrapped his number 5 blung from its thong and strode away from the arrogant sign. Several yards away, he felt a mental pressure, a cosmic will externally imposed. He paused, turned back. The letters seemed to be wavering, reforming into other words. Ah! Perhaps he had read it wrong; perhaps it contained directions. The wavering ceased and the sign now read:

WRITE WHAT YOU KNOW, EX-LIBRARIAN!
SABERTOOTH STILL HUNGRY.

THE PROBLEM OF THE MISSING GRIFFIN

by Myron Blunger author of The Boy With No Future
absolutely not involved with A Kee Ess una Meiseh

From every direction a problem. Panting, sweating despite the chill wind in his face, Myron Blunger sat where he had dropped, exhausted, at the very base of the Dromedary Mountains. Behind him was the terrifying trail with no streetlights or fences, down which he had scrambled in a blind panic pursued by the night noises of large, starving animals. Whatever in his body wasn't almost broken, was bruised or cut or beating too fast for a retired librarian. Now, to his left and right was a forest full of more starving animals. Myron knew that were starving, else why were they out making terrifying rustling noises in the underbrush instead of being curled up in their dens and caves, sound asleep? One horrible screech had already sent his testicles right up into his abdomen and precious time had been lost coaxing them down.

And ahead was worse! From ahead came moans, hisses and heavy thumps in the darkness and always the cold wind in his face. Myron tightened his muffler and pulled the collar of his overcoat up around his neck. He wished he'd thought to bring a flashlight or at least a tuna sandwich, but who could know everything? How was he to ever locate Joey Willem? And what about the escaped griffin? Exactly what was a griffin? What did it look like? What did it eat? Thrusting his hands into the pockets of his overcoat, he felt a scrap of paper. Pulling it out, he tilted it to capture a thin shaft of moonlight that had somehow evaded capture by cloud or overgrowth.

On it was a sketch of a creature with a lion's body and the head and wings of an eagle. But there was no scale. Was it a very small lion grafted onto a regular, standard zoo eagle? Myron knew better. It was surely a monster eagle grafted onto a standard zoo lion, or what was all the fuss about?

It had wings. Almost certainly it was a swooper, gliding silently as an owl from a treetop . . . from up there where a branch was shaking! Swooping with claws extended to grab him! Or was it so large that ordinary branches wouldn't hold it? Blunger's heart stopped. Of course!

It wasn't a swooper at all! With a lion's body large as a horse, why mess around with trees? For sure, it was a ground nightstalker! A silent nightstalker that hissed and snuffled! Wasn't something snuffling in the brush right behind him . . . its claws extended to take out his eyes and his liver, leaving his carcass for the wolves and bears? A humongous shudder wracked Blunger's frame. He had to find his way out of the forest! A lesser man would have panicked and run, this way, that way until he was hopelessly lost and fair game for the sniffers and trackers.

Myron Blunger was not a lesser man. How many times had den mothers brought their cub scouts into the library to sit in a circle and listen to Mr. Blunger read aloud important passages from The Explorer's Handbook (followed by a dramatic reading of The Monkey's Paw or The Golden Arm)? From the handbook, Blunger now recalled the Explorer's Nightmare: groping blindly through a dark forest in a circle until one went mad. But Myron Blunger recalled the counterstrategy. He set off in the straightest line possible. Being right-brained, he was probably unconsciously veering toward the right. Therefore, at the first ankle-twist, he turned a full ninety degrees to the left and continued. Ah, but certainly he was overcompensating, so at the first stumble, he rotated sixty degrees to the right and so it went—a succession of short march segments interrupted only by ankle-twists and stumblings until he spied, directly ahead, sunlight and a roadway! Not with a curb and a sidewalk, to be sure; a country road made of dirt and pebbles, but a road, and with a signpost! Blunger approached the sign cautiously, from upwind, and read:

BROCO WAY
HELP WANTED: PROFESSIONAL
ADVISOR WITH WRITING SKILLS
ALL OTHERS TURN BACK signed: Benison Hawkins

Blunger's belly rumbled its disappointment. An advisor! What about a restaurant? Nevertheless, he started down the road. How hard could the advisor position be? Compared with being torn apart in the forest by a wolf or a bear, that is. If he could remember just one percent of Sophie's suggestions over the years, he could do it. Then a fragment of Yin's rhyme recalled itself to his mind.

"A riddle, a piddle. Something . . . something . . .
A miser, no wiser, will seek an advisor.
In doubt, higher migher. You'll never be losing."

Yes. That was it.

"A miser, no wiser, will seek an advisor.
In doubt, higher migher. You'll never be losing."

A miser will seek an advisor. But what did the next part mean?
In doubt, higher migher?
Even the Innkeeper hadn't known. It must be very profound, Blunger thought.
Keeping to the center of the narrow forest road and pondering this and other problems, Myron Blunger became aware of something keeping pace with him a stone's throw to the left, hidden by the growth of trees and brush. Something large enough to crack

twigs and fearless enough not to bother with stealth. Something that didn't grunt or snort.

If there's one thing a children's librarian knows, it's animal sounds. Cows moo and do not live in dark forests. Dogs are more likely to dash out onto a road, yapping if they were small, growling if they were on the large side, but dogs do not stalk their prey at a stone's throw, at least not in any book Blunger had ever read. But bears! Why should they grunt, or snort, unless they felt like it? Especially if they're starving. Myron Blunger trembled as his mind followed the logic to its conclusion. Bears eat honey. Honey is nature's substitute for ketchup. And one does not eat ketchup alone!

Myron Blunger's lower organs rebelled. From bladder to gizzard, they voted Enough Already! They wanted out! For starters, he suddenly needed to relieve himself. Backing against an elm for protection against an attack from the rear, he was about to irrigate the ground when a small voice in the back of his mind called to him. Logic! Use logic!

Standing thus and holding, Blunger was reminded of his tenth grade geometry teacher, Mrs. MacArdle. Mrs. MacArdle had been a fiend for logic. But that was so long ago! Now, when logic was life itself, he tried to reconstruct her approach . . .

Logic. You always start with an (a), he thought. (a) for assume. Whatever he assumed, it had better be something powerful; the noises were getting closer!

(a) Assume a sabertooth tiger.

So far, so good. Then came (b). (b) was for bear. Any children's librarian knew that. Then (c). A sabertooth tiger outranks a bear.

A growl from just beyond those dense bushes! Blunger's hands were trembling; there wasn't much time left. (d) Tigers are cats and cats are territorial. (e) . . . (e) . . . he thought desperately. Something large crashed in the dark forest less than a stone's throw away! And his penis was cold and shrivelled and he had no blung! (e) A bear will not invade the territory of a larger animal . . . (f) . . .

Crash! Thud!

It was closing in! The words came like a thunderbolt: (f) was Higher, Myer!

To Yin all western names were the same! Someone else might have called him Jack or Joe; the gnome Yin had simply dubbed him Myer! And what was the first line? A riddle, a piddle! Blunger spun around and piddled up, up as high as he could on the treetrunk, squeezing for all he was worth. In doubt, Higher, Myer! Cats mark their territory, and big cats—sabertooth cats!—mark higher!

Expelling the last of his hope in a grand finale, Myron Blunger turned and ran pell-mell down the road, looking back only as he reached the first bend. Then and there his eyes, after years of fine and reliable service, went berserk.

Myron Blunger was prepared to see a bear, and had just about convinced himself that most bears simply do not bother with humanfolk. They're quite reasonable, really, so long as one doesn't appear to be threatening their cubs or intruding on what they believe to be their territory.

But what Blunger's eyes appeared to detect in the shade of the elm was not a bear at all. It resembled a Pekingese lapdog in all respects except two. It had yellow, forward-set, intense eyes that Blunger associated with wolves, and from its shoulderblades sprouted a pair of long, whiplike, striped tendrils. Curling, un-curling, whipping out at eyeblink speed and retracting slowly, each tendril seemed to have an intelligence of its own, independent of its host. When one came too close to the other, there was a violet electric discharge in the intervening air, accompanied by a sharp BANG!

It did not appear at all interested in a urine-soaked tree. Sitting on its haunches, panting in the manner of canines, it appeared to be solemnly regarding Myron Blunger. Very rapidly, Blunger completed his analysis of this creature. It wasn't attacking because it didn't like to get dirty; one or two more high-voltage electric discharges at long range would paralyze its victim from the inside out, from pure fear. And, despite its diminutive size and wondrous cuteness, it was a wolf. An electric wolf.

Myron Blunger's heart was thumping, pounding as though to escape his rib cage! Closing his eyes against the hypnotic image, he scurried to the side of the road and plunged into the protective cover of the dense woods. He had to hide, to regain his breath, his strength, the confidence shattered by the Innkeeper's interferance and that strange, dangerous creature on the road. But where to hide? Where?

Into the dense undergrowth at the side of the road he plunged. Pressing one hand to his heaving chest, using the other to protect his eyes against thorns and whipping branches, he charged deeper into the woods, crashing and flailing his way through thickets and brambles until he could go no farther.

As he slid to the ground, which was everywhere carpeted with pine needles, lo, before him was a tree nearly as high as a pine, and with a correspondingly thick trunk. Its long, ropy branches radiated outward and down, descending from a bulbous node at the very top of the trunk. Had they carried their full complement of leaves, there would have been excellent concealment within that umbrella-like bower, but, alas, the branches were naked of leaves. Perhaps the chilly October nights had already stripped them of their finery. Perhaps this one was too old to create a full measure of cover; in any case, there was no concealment beneath that tree.

Blunger's ears strained for a telltale rustle that would surely be followed by a growl of the electric wolf sneaking up on him, but he heard only the angry chatter of a distant squirrel. But it wouldn't . sit in the roadway forever! He pushed his way deeper into the woods, further from the road, and soon enough he spied another umbrella tree. From its thin, whiplike branches sprouted leaves galore. Unfortunately, they did not drape all the way to the ground. Perhaps this tree was more succulent than the first and the tips of its tender shoots had been nibbled back by furry rabbits and chubby woodchucks and growing fawns fattening up for winter. Where were these images coming from? Sixty years he'd lived in the Bronx and never had such a thought! Anyway, it was an image for schlemiels and schlimazels; for the chronically unlucky. The fact was that Myron Blunger could see right through this umbrella tree to the dark woods beyond. There was no hiding place beneath this one, either.

But now Blunger knew that he was in trouble. Somewhere ahead he would find a third umbrella tree. Oh, it would appear perfect from the outside, promising shelter and concealment; Blunger knew how these things went. Always in threes.

Too large, too small . . . JUST RIGHT!

Too hot, too cold . . . JUST RIGHT!

But the third choice always led to a trap, and Myron Blunger had no ability with traps. Behind him on the road an electric wolf waited patiently, its abrasive tongue whetting its canines. With an iron band of fear tightening across his chest, Blunger rose and skirted the second tree, heading deeper into the woods until his fear of proceeding further equalled his fear of returning to the roadway. At exactly that point, he spied a third umbrella tree nested beneath tall oaks. As he'd feared, it was perfect. Its branches were still thick with leaves which, draping to the ground, formed a thick curtain, within which he would find concealment. Worse, the ground was neither muddy nor rock-strewn, being thickly carpeted with pine needles.

The perfect umbrella tree. Bnd what awaited him within that curtain of leaves? A bear? An ogre? Trolls?

He could retrace his steps . . . and face the electric wolf out there on the road.

Gathering his courage, with every nerve and muscle tense, Myron Blunger snuck up on the tree, slowly spread the branches apart with his forearms, peered about in the green-and-black mottled semi-darkness, took a step forward, caught his toe beneath an exposed root, plunged headlong into the canopy, landed on his belly and had the wind knocked out of him. "Oof!"

"Eee . . . eee . . . yeeeaou!" someone screeched nearby.

Very nearby. Beneath him!

The someone cried, "Get off of me! Get off before I'm all busted up. Oh ponderous mountain of flesh descendent!" it hollered. "Oh, great nelefant of the woods, please lift your impressive and imposing bulk by the width of an ankle."

Beneath Blunger's belly, something squirmed. Not waiting to catch his breath, Blunger bolted to a kneeling position from which he catapulted forward, slammed his head into the trunk of the tree, dropped to the ground, scrambled around, dazed, to face his destiny and found himself staring wide-eyed at a diminutive humanoid creature that lay in a shallow depression in a bed of pine needles. He had missed seeing it earlier because it was clad in a green garment that blended perfectly with the pine needles and the grey-green motley of shadows in the enclosure. It was rubbing its left ankle and grimacing. Upsidedown on the ground beside it was a brown, leatherbound book. Blunger's eyes widened. This was . . . had to be . . . there was no mistaking . . .

The elf's eyes narrowed. "Myron Blunger!" it piped. "You must be the real Myron Blunger! From the Bronx!" The elf ceased massaging its ankle.

Blunger stammered, "Elf . . . elf . . ."

"I am . . . Elf Miki, nearly minus one ankle, thanks to your profound belief in gravity," the creature replied in a high-pitched voice as it pressed its ankle tenderly. Fortunately, his leg had been caught in the soft press between Blunger's belly and the bed of pine needles that it had made for itself. "Bones . . . bones . . . what a nuisance . . . well, nothing seems broken," muttered the elf with a final massage of its ankle. Then, to the intruder, "There I was saying to myself the last thing I needed was another complication, and boom! you drop in!" Elf Miki stood up slowly and tested his ankle, which held firm. "So there is a Myron Blunger after all. And I thought the boy had made it—I mean, you—up!"

Blunger closed his eyes and started from scratch. "Elf Miki. An elf," he whispered, crawling closer and staring without blinking, his muscles tense in case the elf leaped at him, though it seemed tame enough. It was narrow of face and its brown hair was parted in the middle. No beard, no mustache. It was slender of build and as tall as Blunger's arm was long, and seemed pale of complexion tending toward the blue, so far as one could tell in the mottled half-light.

An elf! How many times had he sat at the center of a reading circle, an adult unbeliever reading Tom Thumb or a tattered, long out of print Book Brownie's Book to a dozen openmouthed, wide-eyed children, hypocritically reassuring his audience of the reality, even the necessity of small folk in a large and often strange and dangerous world?

An elf! "What do you mean, a complication?" he asked.

The elf dropped to the ground, crossed his legs and re-trieved its book from the ground. Mournfully it recited, "You are a complication. Also, I can't find the boots. Or the griffin. The boy's troubled, troubled in his heart. If he had his pet, I'd hoped that might put him into a better frame of mind." The elf shook his own little head sadly. "If I'd known he was going to dash through Esfandiary, I would have met him, escorted him, guarded him. But I didn't and there, alone in Esfandiary where he certainly didn't belong, he encountered something and now his spirit is shadowed."

Blunger feared to actually reach out and touch the little one. He was half afraid that he would find it quite solid and real, and half afraid that his hand would go right through it, that he was conversing with an illusion. Either way, he felt as though his mind was slipping.

"What kind of something happened to Joey ?" Blunger whis-pered. "A dinosaur?"

"Who mentioned dinosaurs?" Elf Miki asked.

"The Innkeeper."

"Aha!" Elf Miki nodded vigorously and, drawing a pencil from a hidden pocket, made a notation on the flyleaf of his book. "That's helpful. Esfandiary is subjective, you know. So the Innkeeper has an obsession with dinosaurs! If Joey entered the Innkeeper's

Esfandiary, that means dinosaurs." Tapping his pencil against the book absentmindedly, he thought aloud, "That would be terrifying enough, but he did have the seven-league boots, and should have been able to outrun any dinosaur."

Blunger said, "This is my Joey Willem you're talking about?"

Elf Miki nodded. "I've read this guidebook from cover to cover, including the appendices, and find nothing about sadness in ten-year old boys. They're supposed to be curious and optimistic and just a bit adventurous. There's a footnote describing `piss and vinegar', though that doesn't make sense to me." He held out the book so that Blunger could read its title: The Book of the Ways of Man.

"My Joey Willem was all that," Blunger offered, declining to hold the book lest he find out that it was solid, real. He felt curiously proud, as the father of a newborn, except that Joey Willem didn't really exist, either.

"You mean, is all that," the elf said.

The word is sent a shock through Myron Blunger and set his head spinning again.

"He certainly didn't enter my Esfandiary!" Elf Miki said. "I take my little charges along the most pleasant pathways. Song-gardens with birds and bunny-rabbits to pet and just enough gravity to know up from down. No scraped knees on my route, even for beginners. Well, why are you here?"

Half apologetically, Blunger answered, "To bring Joey back to the Inn at the End of the World, with the boots."

"Best you turn around and go back," the elf said. "The boy has longings that I cannot fathom, and strong feelings regarding yourself. Joey blames everything on you."

Blames! "Sharper than a serpent's tooth," Blunger said. "Besides, I can't. There's a creature out there on the road . . ."

"A creature?" the elf exclaimed. "Did you happen to notice whether it had fierce eyes, the head of an eagle, the body of a lion?"

Blunger shook his head.

"Perhaps the eyes aren't so fierce; its only a fledgling, you know, and playful," the elf suggested hopefully.

Again Blunger shook his head.

"Well, what kind of creature was it?" Elf Miki demanded.

Blunger described what he thought he'd seen, focussing on the tendrils.

The elf regarded Blunger carefully. "Tendrils?"

Blunger nodded. "Striped."

"A heffalump! I can't do this job alone any more!" the elf wailed, throwing his book on the ground and stamping his unhurt foot. "The barrier is collapsing by the hour! The griffin is out here somewhere, and I can't find the Innkeeper's boots! And Dragon Groff's still missing and now a heffalump's come across the barrier! And I'll get the blame for all this!"

With that, Elf Miki put himself into a power of concentration, closing his eyes and weaving his thin body from side to side and forwards and backwards, moaning and muttering aloud, "What to do first? What comes first?"

"First? What's wrong with my Joey comes first!" Blunger demanded.

The elf stopped his gyrations. "Later," he piped. "When he sleeps, I will enter his mind gently, gently. Maybe I'll learn exactly how he lost the boots and what happened in Esfandiary!

"As for you," he continued, "perhaps you should meet up with the boy. I'll lure the heffalump away from the road. Then I must continue my search! In any case, get out of the woods now and keep to the road. I have to go!"

"Wait a minute!" Blunger cried.

But the elf, clasping his precious book to his chest, had already sprung vertically into the air. His edges blurred . . . and then where he had been was a royal blue, luminescent sphere the size of a basketball suspended in the air not three yards from Myron Blunger. Without buzz or crackle, it rose, slowly at first, then more rapidly until it cleared the top-boughs of the umbrella tree and drifted away as though it weren't quite certain of its direction. Myron Blunger stared until it was out of sight.

Get out of the woods now! Keep to the road.

Recovering his senses, Blunger did that, scrambling through the leaf-curtain and retracing his steps until he was out of the woods and standing in the roadway. There was no sign of the . . . heffalump! A.A. Milne. Pooh. Had Milne made the creature up, or was he one of those privileged to visit the forbidden universe of Esfandiary? Had Milne's soul wandered through a magic universe, escorted by elves, and seen such a creature? Perhaps the same one he, Blunger, had just encountered?

Blunger's heart pounded with joy and astonishment. He, Myron Blunger from the Bronx, had seen a heffalump!

Shoulders thrown back, he strode boldly down the center of the roadway. Yes, he was hungry. Yes, he was thirsty. But the sun was rising over the trees and it was warming up and he'd discoursed with an elf and seen a heffalump! Of course, no one would ever believe him.

Well, too bad for them! He would fulfill his mission, though he now found himself wondering just why those boots were so important to the Innkeeper? The Innkeeper's stories were patent nonsense, of course.

The Innkeeper. Which Innkeeper? The kindly old fellow who'd treated his wounds? Or the stern Viking? Were there more Innkeepers sharing that body?

Pondering the imponderable, Blunger strolled at an easy pace, his hands clasped behind his back. Occasionally he looked back for signs of an electric wolf or a heffalump or whatever sneaking up on him, but he was alone on the narrow dirt road. Soon the trees thinned out as woods were replaced on either side of the road by expanses of cultivated fields that bore the marks of a recent harvest. Strong sunlight warmed Blunger and, as he continued along the road, he removed his coat and slung it smartly over his shoulder, getting it right on the first toss. From the sun-heated soil came a rich, fresh aroma, which Myron Blunger inhaled deeply and savored, as though he were absorbing Mother Earth herself into his bloodstream.

He felt as one with nature and took delight in the swallows darting over the fields and the lack of pigeons, and paused to regard a pair of brown rabbits unhurriedly crossing the road some distance ahead. Natural rabbits, not in a cage. Wonderful.

To his left stretched row upon row of stubble and beyond that, an entire field of tomato vines stripped, alas, of their produce. Whose fields were these, he wondered. To what market was this cornucopia of produce headed? Who had harvested it? And for whom? And were they all sitting down to lunch right about now, and with room for a stranger? So ran his thoughts as Myron Blunger plodded steadily along that country road. He envisaged stalks not broken and dried, but living, green and laden with fruits and vegetables! He heard them crying beneath their ripe burdens, begging to be relieved of a part. The traveller's other nightmare—the mirage—was even more dangerous than the first, and many a lost soul in similar circumstances had dropped to his knees, scooped up double handfuls of loam and filled his belly with dirt only to die a horrible, gut-wrenching death. But Myron Blunger did not succumb.

The dirt road meandered down the center of the valley and it was the nature of this place that instead of the sky coming down to meet the earth, the earth jumped up to meet the sky. Cliffs. There were two of them. The one to his left was banded horizontally with a magnificent array of pastels—lime greens, russets, oranges, violets—that had a different appearance every time Blunger looked. Perhaps it was a trick of the sunlight.

The other cliff was black. Not the flat, non-reflecting black of a nun's habit, but a deep, profound black that threatened to pull into itself Blunger's image as surely as it sucked hungrily at the sun's radiation. If there was anywhere on this Earth a Cliff of Night, that was It. Shuddering, he determinedly kept his eyes and thoughts away from the dark cliff.

Loping, panting, occasionally stopping for a rest in the shade of a tree or bush, he pressed onward while the sun crossed the sky.

Both lope and hope had diminished, one to a stumbling shuffle and the other to a taunting memory, when Myron Blunger spotted a miracle: a man hunkered in a field of ordinary, normal grass beside the road. Not the type of man Blunger would have liked to encounter: an ample human being with whose kind face and double chin were framed by a large napkin and who might be waving a turkey drumstick in the direction of the wanderer. This human being was almost skeletally lean, and the few wisps of grey hair on his broad scalp seemed not to be scratching out much nourishment.

Beside the man, however, was a box. A white, cardboard box; the sort of box that could contain a morsel of food! The man had been involved with the box; now he watched Blunger's approach without expression.

Too parched to croak a proper Hello, Blunger marched stiffly toward the stranger and performed a medium, noncommital nod.

"Are you here about the advisor's position?" the fellow asked sharply.

All others turn back.

Blunger, recalling the sign's final directive and not wishing to be turned away, nodded.

The lean man rose, approached Blunger and hissed, "This valley is owned by the richest man in the world. His workers—members of Henchpersons Local 241—are at this very minute voting on a new contract. What advice have you for him?"

Thirty years earlier, Blunger would have cried, "Advice for that Midas? For exploiting working men and women, robbing them of their very souls? He should be tarred and feathered and run out of the valley!"

Fifteen years earlier, Blunger would have answered, "Advice for him? Advice for them! To the ramparts! Strike!"

But it was now, and Blunger was tired, hungry and thirsty. Thus, the answer did not come from either the right or left hemispheres of Blunger's brain; it bubbled up from his shrunken belly, the exact phrasing tempered by decades spent behind a reference desk in the childrens' section of the Mott Hill library. "He should encourage and support them every step of the way!" Blunger replied. "They should have an alma mater, a fight song and a secret sign. He should provide them with instruments for an orchestra, throw a picnic on the fourth of July, set up a good welfare plan and retirement benefits."

The response to that was a pensive nod. "And what is your authority for that answer?"

"The story of the Wind and the Sun," Blunger croaked, pointedly eyeing the box. "The Wind bragged to the Sun that he was the stronger and suggested a contest—who could separate a traveller from his overcoat. But the harder the Wind blew, the more tightly the traveller pulled the coat around him. The Sun, of course, simply beamed down, warmed the poor fellow up and he gladly took the coat off."

"In other words, smother them with kindness! Very good. Very quick," the stranger said. "Remember to include ancient folktale as attribution. Hey! Watch out!"

But Blunger, succumbing to the urging of the inner man, had dropped to his knees, sniffed at the box and been rewarded by having his olfactory lobes stupified, his nose-hairs seared and all protective fuses blown out. Myron Blunger fell to the ground, stunned.

A rush of footsteps, a wetted handkerchief thrust beneath his nostrils, hands on his chest and a weak attempt at artificial resuscitation. Blunger retched, hiccupped, uncrossed his eyes, blinked in the sunlight.

"In goes—the good air—out goes—the bad." The voice was reedy, thin but precise. "Come on—one good sneeze'll do it!"

Blunger's head oscillated as it slowly tilted back, back, back and then it exploded in a sneeze so powerful, so awesome that the recoil lifted him clean off the ground.

"Fire away!" his rescuer cackled merrily, thumping him on the back. "It works, by thunder! The strongest, most invincible fruitcake in the world! Loretta's masterpiece!"

"That was a fruitcake?" Blunger whispered from the ground after his benefactor had poured some clear, cool water from a flask down his parched throat.

"Not just any fruitcake. That was the Oldest! I was afraid to get downwind of it myself. Stored in an airtight barrel these twenty years against the time when it would be needed most! And that time, sir, is now! Tonight I'll have that varmint glass-eyed and hog-tied, or my name's not Benison Hawkins.

"Which raises the question, what's yours? If you're an advisor, what are you doing sneaking down by the back road?"

Blunger pushed himself into a kneeling position and found himself staring into a pair of unblinking grey eyes. "Eh? Who are you?" Hawkins repeated suspiciously. The grey eyes narrowed.

This was a time for confidence. Hoisting himself ponderously to his feet, he declared, "I am Myron Blunger, an advisor's advisor! And a writer's writer," he added, brushing himself off.

And after all, had he not occasionally, in his other life, contributed suggestions to Sophie regarding menu, furniture arrangements and the like? And does not a librarian correspond with publishers, placing the orders that provided royalties to authors? Wasn't that the kind of writing authors most appreciated?

Myron Blunger took a deep breath of the pure air of that remote valley and found it exhilerating. Indeed, he felt renewed, dynamic, curiously light-headed, as though that fruitcake-induced sneeze had relieved him of a lifelong inner burden.

"An advisor's advisor!" exclaimed Hawkins respectfully, circling Blunger and eyeing him evaluatively. "Well then, I regret your accidental inhalation of the fumes of the Oldest, but in law, air does have the right of way and in any case, I am not actionable or culpable. An advisor and a writer!"

From a trouser pocket, Hawkins withdrew a copy of The Postulate, unfolded it and handed it to Blunger. It consisted of four pages, on the first two of which was printed an article titled Henchmen as Dependents—a new tax writeoff? The third page was devoted to advertisements for financial services and on the last page was a crossword puzzle with the hinTitle Steps in the Amassing of Uncountable Wealth. The remainder of page four was blank.

"The latest edition of The Postulate, which I write, edit and publish for three reasons," Hawkins said. "One: it yields a modest income for my wife Loretta and myself. Two: it provides guidance and inspiration to Lucien Broco, the semiretired but still avaricious multibillionaire who owns this valley. I hope to win Broco's complete confidence by introducing an advice column."

"A whole newspaper for only one reader?" Blunger asked.

Hawkins shook his head. "Two. The other is an innkeeper whose copies are delivered by an indirect route. I do not know his name or interests."

Myron Blunger shuddered.

"The road I came down," he said, "is that not called Broco Way?"

"Just so," Hawkins said. "Lucien Broco owns very nearly the entire valley, from cliff to cliff, from the base of the Dromedary Mountains to the village of Lower Muchness away to the south. When I say owns, I mean that he claims absolute title not only to the ground on which you are standing, but also to the moisture and microbes in it, the rocks and ores beneath it, the grass that covers it, the gravitational field that keeps it in place and the sunlight that shines on it. His landhold encompasses four hundred-thousand acres, a bit more in summer, a bit less in the winter as the land expands and contracts."

Then he turned to the south, grinned crookedly and whispered, "For him, it is not enough."

"He still wants?" Blunger asked.

Hawkins peered in every direction before continuing in a low voice. "Lucien Broco is not merely a millionaire, Mr. Blunger. He is a billionaire. A millionaire must snap his fingers to order a whiskey neat; a billionaire need merely extend his hand and it is there in a crystal goblet."

Blunger accepted the statement.

"Lucien Broco and I exist in a balanced symbiotic relationship, at

which we both strain like flies caught in a spider's web. I need his
financial subsidy while I await tangible evidence that my life's work
has not been in vain. He struggles against time.

"His immense wealth has long since ceased to give him joy.
His doctors are trying to wean him from whiskey neat and many
other imbibements and activities that you and I enjoy according
to our means and tastes," Hawkins continued. "If you are to un-
dertake the post of advisor, you must understand that Mr. Broco is
now focussed and dedicated to the thing most precious, the cur-
rency of life.

"Time. That is why he followed me here, to the valley.

"I am a mathematician, Mr. Blunger. Mr. Broco subsidizes my
journalism only that he may have a window to my mind," Hawkins
said. "My field is the Theory of Partial Inconsistency. Learning of
my work, Broco followed me to Upper Muchness, to this valley,
built himself a suitable dwelling place and waited for the fruit of
my labors, which he intends to usurp to his own ends. During the
past twenty years, our mutual goal has evolved into an interesting
set of obsessions that intertwine on several levels." Blunger, having
worked under a variety of chief librarians in his other life, knew
how to nod agreeably (if not sagaciously), and when to pause and
repeat, "On several levels, you say. Hmm."

"Yes. No journal has accepted my Theory. I have not published. But I will. That is the third and, for my part, chief purpose
of my publishing The Postulate.

"Tell me, Blunger. Can you imagine giving birth to a lion?"

Blunger shook his head solemnly; the very concept was foreign to his background and upbringing, though certain supermarket tabloids seemed to document similar events with a surprising
regularity.

Hawkins continued, his voice dry, steady, hypnotic. "Twenty
years ago, on the last Thursday in October, I interrupted a lecture
on the theory of irrelevant sets of the second kind and walked out
of the classroom at New York University, leaving behind my notes,
my briefcase, hat, coat, tenure and all hopes for a professorship.

Like the explosion of a supernova, a general proof of the Theory of Partial Inconsistency had burst forth in my mind! It demanded only the writing down . . .

" . . . and experimental verification!" Hawkins hissed, shielding his mouth with a dry, veiny hand. "That evening, Loretta and I packed our few possessions into my automobile and wandered up into the north country, seeking a valley with exactly the right geo-mathematical properties. Have you ever heard of Brigadoon?"

Blunger nodded. "A musical show. Very musical."

"A village out of time!" Hawkins snapped. "Oband-Xu? Germelshausen?"

"Gezundheit."

"Fool!" Hawkins shrieked. "These are villages that, according to legend, appear but once a century; then they vanish beyond space and time. Anyway, on the outskirts of a village deep in the Appalachians and half forgotten by the world, I encountered a farrier, an old-timer who had heard of a hidden valley further north. Its eastern boundary was, according to an old Indian legend, the cliff of the sun, and its western boundary, the cliff of the moon. Its north end was sealed by a twin-peaked mountain. The south end . . . the south end, he told me, was queer. Story was, people tried to enter that valley from the south end, and found themselves back outside, no matter what.

"That . . . that was crucial! My Theory was predicated on certain topological quirks I won't bother going into."

Blunger whispered, wide-eyed, "Like Brigadoon."

"Or Oband-Xu, or Germelshausen," Hawkins hissed. "Or a hundred others. Every culture has its legend of a place that only appears . . ."

" . . . once in a century!"

"Not necessarily. The interval between openings depends on many factors, according to my Theory. As does the duration of opening. This valley is, topologically, equivalent to a semi-permeable Klein bottle. It is isolated from the outside world, except . . . But enough! The cliffs were necessary. The mountains and topology were necessary. Together they are sufficient! And in mathematics, sufficient is a royal flush. I drove through the night, took the land-agent from his bed and purchased two acres. Within six hours, the lawyers of Lucien Broco, one or another of whom had been sitting in that mathematics class, taping every lecture and following my every move for years, had bought the remainder of the valley.

"I am no fool, Blunger; the general theory will not be understood in my lifetime; it occupies twelve notebooks in the requisite spidery handwriting. College-lined, no margins. But understanding is one thing; acceptance is quite another. Partial Inconsistency is unique in mathematics in that it is subject to experimental proof of the most dramatic kind! The theory indicates a developing nexus between those twin peaks in the fabric of space-time! When the nexus manifests itself, my theory will be proved beyond all doubt! Oh, yes, beyond all doubt!

"Of course, I will follow the proprieties and publish my results in a special edition of The Postulate. Copies will be sent to the mathematical hierarchy and I will sit back to await the accolades of my so-called peers.

"But now I must return the fruitcake to its barrel before it loses its potency. Come, you must be hungry and thirsty and we have much yet to discuss."

Approaching the box from upwind and snatching it into a plastic bag, Hawkins scanned the horizon in all directions, then started off across the broad field heading southeast, his guest in tow.

After some minutes, it occurred to the mathematician that additional explanation was in order. "Something has been invading my property of nights," Hawkins confided. "Not a fox, not a racoon or a bear. It screams high, then low, and in the morning, some chickens are gone from a coop fenced four feet high. There is no sign of forced entry. Traps are ignored, their bait untouched. I would sit outside with a weapon if I had one, but the night chill is bad for my joints. Nor can Loretta stand guard; the poor thing has suffered from the vapors ever since our daughter, Wilma, reached what she considered her majority and went out into the world to find herself."

He sighed, then whispered, "This fruitcake is not merely another decorative comestible. It is an attack fruitcake."

Blunger wrinkled his nose in unhappy agreement.

"It is my last resort, and for proving its efficacy, I owe you a decent lunch, at least. As for the advisor position, you have done well in direct questioning, but there remains the issue of cleverness. Mr. Broco will have the final say on that. Are you clever? Tell me something clever."

Too weary, too hungry to improvise, Blunger recited: "No matter how much you prance and dance, the last two drops go down your pants."

"True. And spontaneous," Hawkins conceded. "But no citations or cross-references. Anything else?"

Blunger's brain was torpid from hunger. Thus, he recited the only epigram that came to mind, and that only because it was fresh in his mind and he was certainly in doubt. "Higher, Migher," he muttered.

At which Hawkins abruptly halted, his mouth agape, his eyes wide with astonishment. "Higher, Migher! I don't believe it! 'Anything else?' I ask, and you toss off, 'Higher, migher!' as though it were the time of day! In rhyme, yet!

"A thousand pardons, Dr. Blunger! I admit to proposing an interview with Broco purely as a cheap ploy to drive down your salary demands. But to cite Higher Migher right from the shoulder, without hesitation! Your brilliance is galactic!"

Displaying a presence of mind he'd never accomplished when purchasing a major appliance, Blunger kept his mouth shut while he framed and reframed his next, crucial, sentence. Then he asked, as casually as possible, "And how do intelligent folks in this part of the world interpret Higher, Migher?"

Hawkins hissed between gritted teeth, "Not here in Lucien Broco's open field! He claims title even to the trills of the larks and robins. Later we will talk in my home, which you must now consider yours. Loretta went to the village a-marketing; I will prepare lunch. A three-bean omelet, heeble soup, fried prune pate . . . whatever strikes your fancy . . ."

Nothing further was said until, having crossed several more fields, they once more found themselves on Broco Way and not far from a pleasant enough two-story house made of white stucco, with a thatched roof, a red brick chimney and a fenced yard in which a number of hens scratched and clucked in the manner of their kind.

Lunch was prepared and eaten, and Myron Blunger's life-force restored with great draughts of lifeberry juice diluted with spring water. Then Benison Hawkins took his guest into the parlor, pointed him to a comfortable chair by the low fire and took the seat opposite. Closing his eyes reverentially, he sighed, "Higher— H is the eighth letter, of course—and Migher—M is thirteen. Not just another number, Mr. Blunger, eh?" Hawkins placed a long forefinger alongside his thin nose and winked. "And Eight and thirteen are the second two lowest Fibonacci integers whose sum minus their difference yields a perfect square!"

Blunger decided not to divulge his prior interpretation of Higher Migher; this seemed more elegant. With a knowing, appreciative wink, he helped himself to another piece of fresh fruitcake.

Leaning forward, Hawkins whispered, "Not nearly as profound as my Theory, of course, but folks get tenured and even promoted to Full Professor with less. Eh, Blunger?

"Now, regarding your employment as advice columnist," Hawkins said, leaning back. "Your advice is generally sound?"

Blunger nodded comfortably. "In my part of the world, advice comes right along with one's first milk—'Don't gulp!'—and ends only with 'I told you so!' at the final closing of the casket. For example, I am interested in finding . . ."

Hawkins interrupted, "Interest. Yes. It is my experience that the best columnists labor out of interest and prefer scholarship and a cerebral, monastic environment uncluttered by gadgets and gimcracks. Would that describe you?"

"Why not?" Blunger replied easily.

"Excellent. Bed and board, then, with something extra at Christmas." His eyes glittered.

"However," Blunger said forcefully, "I also have a prime interest. I am interested in locating a youth named Joey Willem. And his . . . pet."

Hawkins's eyes flashed. "The boy oscillates between this very dwelling and Broco's ostentatious mansionhouse atop the greensward. But this pet, as you call it . . . does it have a nocturnal lifestyle?"

Blunger shrugged his shoulders.

Hawkins leaned forward. His lips glistened and his nose pinched with excitement. "Is it winged? Does it have claws? Does it swoop down from the sky, screaming until windows crack?"

Blunger's fingers tightened around the armrests of his chair. He narrowed his eyes, determined to match craft with craft. "I'm surprised you should ask such details. As a resident of the Bronx, I try to mind my own business. There's a clause in my life insurance. I take things as they come. Of course, this pet could be in disguise," he hinted.

"Disguise?" Hawkins's voice trembled. "Such as?"

"Such as a kee . . . a cow," Blunger announced with the smallest touch of triumph. "A tame cow, that eats without a story."

The thin smile that Hawkins had pasted onto his lips failed, blown away by Blunger's playfully introduced red Holstein. "Then let us put all cards on the table," said the mathematician. "I have an interest in this creature. My Theory of Partial Inconsistency predicts a local rupture in the reality of space-time . . . somewhere toward the northern end of this valley! Perhaps in the Saddle between the peaks of the Dromedaries. The theory would be proved beyond a shadow of a doubt if a suitably unusual creature from a parallel world were to work its way through into ours. A cow has never, never been used to prove a major theory in mathematics, or even in physics, where they're far less particular. In mathematics a standard cow would not even support a minor theorem or even a postulate."

"But a non-standard cow might?" Blunger suggested. "If, say, it had wings. The head of an eagle . . ."

"Silence!" Hawkins commanded. He scurried from window to window, peering outside each for eavesdroppers, then hurrying back to this chair.

"I plan to set forth this very night to effect the capture of the beast that is raiding my chicken-coop. If it turns out to be a standard cow, it is yours. But if it is other than a standard cow . . . it is mine!"

BROCO

by Myron Blunger

Night's shadows were advancing across the valley and strange and wonderful glitterings were visible against the utter blackness of the western cliff. This was the Kristallfluss, the fluorescence of crystals embedded in the obsidian walls of the western cliff, discharging their daylong accumulation of sunlight. Because of the swiftness of the nightly drop in temperature, the Kristallfluss was more spectacular in the valley of Upper Muchness than anywhere else in the world.

The grand sweep of window of Lucien Broco's library—ninety feet of gently curved glass—had been designed with that kaleidoscopic display in mind. Indeed, the architect of Lucien Broco's retreat had won his commission with the suggestion that each evening, shortly before sunset, Mr. Broco might settle into his upholstered, motorized swivel chair, gesture once and extend his hand. As music appropriate to his mood filled the room, Trenton Interface, his major domo, would measure out a dram of bourbon or Scotch, then stand by while the master of the valley took pleasure in the confluence of harmonies. For variety, Mr. Broco had but to look to the eastern cliff, where bands of stratified minerals shone violet and gold and russet in a pastel salute to the departing sun.

Lucien Broco pressed a lever built into the arm of his swivel chair; his electronic binoculars swung around from standby position to eye level. There had been a time when he could stroll his landhold, carrying the state-of-the-art binoculars and unobtrusively checking up on the field hands and the comings and goings of Benison Hawkins, but now the doctors had limited even his viewing time to forty minutes a day, and that with the binoculars mounted on a cantilevered arm.

Lucien Broco pressed a button; the binoculars began a slow sweep of his landhold. "Why don't I see the henchmen slaving away in the fields? Are they on strike?" he snapped. "Negotiation report!"

The loyal Trenton Interface clasped his hands behind his back and delivered the speech he'd prepared earlier. "As you know, sir, the contract is due to expire on the thirty-first of October, at midnight. The henchpersons' negotiating committee have been meeting around the clock. If I may say so, you've put quite a few issues on the table."

"Did I not have their hovels' insulation doubled, that they might better withstand the cruel blasts of winter?"

"They're most grateful, sir, " the major domo acknowledged. "But there's the matter of the orchestra. Hedley has perfect pitch, and believes that merits a bonus. He's the major holdout, I believe."

"The arrogant swine!" Broco muttered. "To think of all I've done for him, and the other henchpersons. Haven't I spent a small fortune on band instruments to provide them with cultural advantages?"

"Yes, sir," Trenton Interface said. "Four cornets, used but in good condition, a conga drum and . . . something called a battletuba, which I must say is bloody hard on the lips."

Ignoring the complaint, Broco growled, "Perfect pitch, indeed! Inform Hedley that he's nothing but a thankless, greedy swine! Don't put it in writing, though! Damned fools'll move for arbitration." Then the lines on Lucien Broco's face melted into a thin smile. He chuckled. Laughed. Roared until a single tear found its way out of his left eye. "Perfect pitch! Good old . . . Hedley!" he laughed. "The man's got balls! More power to him! Which of my lawyers would have the courage to stand up to the valleymaster of Upper Muchness? A spineless lot of toadies! And that goes for my bankers and managers, too; conniving sycophants, all of them! Hedley . . . Hedley's a man's man! Give him his bonus! Raise Hedley 12 percent. That is, a half percent a month over a two-year contract, not compounded."

"Now, what about the lawn?" he growled. "And the boy!"

The expanse of lawn that fell away from the mansionhouse for a mile on all sides, usually manicured to the standard of a golf fairway, was greatly overgrown.

"No progress, sir," Trenton said. "If you recall, you ordered that the greensward be allowed to grow to a sufficient height that the boy might not . . . er, waste his time kicking that soccer ball about . . ."

"Ah," Broco sighed, extending his left hand without taking his rheumy eyes from the Hawkins house. Instantly his fingers closed on a dram of Kings' Bourbon in a crystal goblet. "The little scamp has outlasted me. I cannot let the grass grow higher. My enemies could be marching on me a thousand strong with cavalry and elephants and I'd never see them! See that it gets a mowing before noon tomorrow.

"News," he grunted, after taking a sip of the golden liquor.

Trenton Interface recited, "The stranger in Hawkins's house is one Myron Blunger. He claims to be an advisor's advisor and a writer's writer. In his initial conversation with Mr. Hawkins, transmitted from a microphone hidden in a bunch of ragweed in field twelve, he referred to something called Higher Migher . . ."

"What?" Broco sprayed half his liquor allowance into the air.

"Higher Migher, sir, though there is no reference to such in any of your encyclopedias."

Lucien Broco's right hand started oscillating nervously. "Migher means wealth in the secret tongue of the Old Merchants' Guild, and Higher Migher is the codeword needed to access MoreWealth, my financial management program. There can't be three people in the world who know that!"

"Hawkins thinks him to be a fellow mathematician," Trenton said.

"Like water, a fool seeks his own level," Broco snapped. "Do
not underestimate this Blunger, Trenton! Hawkins is brilliant but
naive. I have not had an opportunity to read this Blunger's face,
but if my intuition is correct, he may be an economic shark seeking entry to my financial affairs. What more of him do we know?"

Trenton read, "He claims to have outkicked a wolf, outlasted a
kraken and outfoxed a heffalump through sheer bladder-power.
More significantly, perhaps, he has apparently wangled lunch out
of Hawkins."

"A formidable opponent!" the valleymaster grunted. "He will
not fool us so easily, now that we are forewarned. What of the
monster?" Broco demanded.

"There are no sightings yet, sir," replied the major domo.

"Arrgrum!" Broco knocked off the remainder of his drink. "And
the Willem boy? Cheeky little . . . what's keeping him? Why don't
I see him?" Broco snapped. Leaning forward, he toggled the binoculars toward the Hawkins dwelling.

The boy. Trenton Interface, making his rounds of the landhold,
had discovered him asleep on the meadow near the forest. Of trivial
things, such as hunger and thirst, the boy had spoken clearly
enough, but he could not or would not account for his being on
private land without permission or proof of identity. He appeared
to be about ten years old, perhaps eleven, and had the shrewd,
ratty look of a street urchin. Brought to the mansionhouse, washed
and fed, the boy had nearly been sent on his way when a henchman from an outlying farm came flying up the back roadway to
the kitchen door. "Monster, monster!" he'd bleated, pointing north
and cringing into a corner of the pantry. He keened imitatively in
a high pitch, both hands slicing downward, then shrieked as his
fingers extended into claws, closed and roared up, up into the air.
"Chickens!" he'd croaked, holding up two fingers.

"Something from the sky carried off two chickens?" Trenton
interpreted, this intoned with a solemnity appropriate to Trenton's
new title and responsibilities. On his recent promotion from Chief
Henchperson to major domo, Interface had immediately taken to

his room, where, before a mirror, he'd experimented with manners of speech and expression in keeping with his new position. Not blessed with a quick tongue, he had decided that a low-voiced ponderosity of speech would best enhance his new status. Now to find out whether this henchman had really seen a monster, was malingering or was merely testing the new major domo.

"It was probably a male silver-crested eagle and no monster at all, except to chickens," he declared. But the henchman was pouncing around the room, wild-eyed, roaring and hissing in imitation of the creature. "Then again," Trenton continued in tones with undercurrents of suspicion, "it could have been a cloud reflected in the dregs of a sixteen ounce mug of ale . . ."

The henchman was shaking his head and sending both hands in imaginary monster-dives when he spotted none other than the master himself in the doorway. Confounded and abashed, he backed off but halted at the old man's raised eyebrow.

Lucien Broco had not become a multibillionaire by virtue of unbridled greed and hard work alone. He had the knack of reading faces. In his prime, Lucien Broco could measure the emotional state of a broker halfway across the floor of the Exchange, simply by the set of his chin. As a young trader, he had once sold short ten thousand shares of Big Steel, based on the uneven cut of a floor-trader's mustache. Now, for the first time in twenty years, adrenalin surged within his dessicated body as he glanced at faces. Trenton's was, as always, glacially impassive. As for the henchman, that unfortunate was now flopping around the kitchen, making horrible grimaces and growling quietly as he wound up his charade.

But there was a boy at the table. A barefoot boy. A boy with dirty knees and chewed fingernails, long hair and dark, defiant eyes that returned Broco's stare without flinching or apology for being in his kitchen, drinking his milk and eating his sandwiches and cookies. But one instant sufficed for Lucien Broco to take the measure of his spirit, to note the spark in the boy's eyes as they tracked the gyrating henchman. The boy had knowledge of this creature and that fact sealed his fate. Whatever his business in this

private valley, the boy would not take his leave until the creature—be it monster or eagle or something else more rare, more
important—had been brought to light and its relevance to Lucien
Broco's dream, determined and settled.

But the Willem boy proved stubborn and ungrateful. Taken
to the village and outfitted with clothes, shoes and sneakers, pajamas, a toothbrush and a soccer ball, he repaid Broco's generosity
with determined silence. Given the run of the estate, he wasted his
time kicking the soccer ball up and down the greensward until
Lucien ordered that it not be cut until further notice. Perhaps it
the boy had less time to kick his stupid ball, he might become
amenable to a trade; a manicured lawn . . . for information on his
background and on the creature that had accompanied him to the
valley.

But the boy had simply learned to arc the ball high and keep
it suspended in the air longer. Lucien Broco's respect for the lad
doubled; he admired a fighter.

Rainy days were more promising. The boy passed them draped
over a chair or sprawled out on the rich, Persian carpet before the
marble fireplace, working through Lucien Broco's library, book by
book. Trenton Interface surruptitiously kept a record of which books
the boy had read, how much time he'd spent with each and what
questions he'd asked.

The break came when *Treasure Island* vanished from the library and turned up secreted in the pantry with a napkin tucked
into it opposite one of the illustrations. Much of Jim Hawkins's
dialogue was underlined and on the napkin, a single word was
printed. A word that was nowhere to be found in the novel, or in
any dictionary. This was reported to Trenton, who immediately
informed Lucien Broco.

Ordered to the library, Joey Willem found himself standing
before the swivel chair. Mr. Broco was nearly buried within the
folds of a plum-colored woolen blanket, one thin, veiny hand shuddering over the control module and his eyes glittering with anticipation. The window was covered by a great sweep of velvet curtain,

and the gentle hiss of a fire in the fireplace gave the large room a cozy atmosphere. But Broco's countenance was stern; the boy had stalled long enough. "Who are you?" demanded the master of the valley. "Where are your parents, your family?"

There was no running away; Trenton Interface stood by the door, arms folded and his jaw clamped tight. And the major domo was quick and strong. Immensely strong. Joey had not believed anyone capable of kicking a soccer ball ninety yards *up* the greensward, and with his *left* foot!

So this was it. The boy gulped, then said, "My name is Joey Willem. I . . . I came down from the place between the mountain peaks, what you call the Saddle. I . . . have no family." His eyes were bright and he was blinking rapidly, fighting off tears, but stubbornly refusing to cry.

"So I am told," Broco snapped. "But you were not raised by wolves in the forest! Who taught you to read, to tie your shoes? Speaking of which; where are your shoes? When Trenton found you, your feet were bare but clean and with no trace of callouses." Waving the napkin in the boy's face, Broco demanded, "What is Esfandiary? Where is Esfandiary? How did you get into this valley? Why did you mark Jim Hawkins's words in my copy of *Treasure Island*? And what is this monster-pet of yours? Where does it come from?"

For monster there was; something larger and stronger and hungrier than an eagle was carrying off Hawkins's chickens, two at a time, generally late at night when it was darkest and clouds covered the moon. Broco had offered the services of his henchpersons in capturing the beast, but Hawkins refused to allow them on his two acres. Hawkins was playing his own game. But Broco had the boy.

Joey screwed up his face in anguish. He'd absentmindedly doodled the word on his bookmark and now they'd caught him cold!

"I never went to school," he admitted. "Jim Hawkins is my friend, sort of. I don't like shoes; I wear sneakers. Dorothy taught

me to tie them, but made fun because she never seen sneakers.
Alice, too. Little jerk! Dorothy's Aunt Em . . . taught me to read.
I read *Treasure Island* because I . . . think a lot of Jim Hawkins . . .
and I wanted to . . . do like him, so I was studying the things he
said and how he said them. That's all. And there's no monster," he
added stubbornly. "It's . . . just a baby griffin. I call him Roger.
Jolly Roger. From Es . . . Esfandiary."

"From Esfandiary!" Broco echoed reverently, clasping and rubbing his hands together. "Tell me more!" he commanded.

"Esfandiary is . . . someplace else," whispered the boy in a
voice so low that Broco had to lean forward to make out the words,
which were, of course, being recorded for truth-analysis and interpretation. "It's not like this at all. I got the boots from under the
Innkeeper's bed. The door opened for me and I went through and
found myself in a meadow of grass. I wasn't sure how seven-league
boots work, so I took a step, just one step, and I was standing by a
river. That's where I found Jolly Roger. He jumped into my arms.
I took another step, and I found myself before a great castle of
silverstone and a hunting party on horses, with horns and banners, was riding by. They didn't see me.

"Holding Roger around my neck, I took step after step and he
flapped his wings and that's how he learned how to fly! Then I
took a step and found myself in fog at the edge of a big swamp,
with a water pond. There were dinosaurs in the water, big ones
with long necks, and on the dry land behind me, others higher
than trees!" he whispered. "And I couldn't run; couldn't even take
a step! The boots were sunk into the mud and stuck and I couldn't
pull them free until I stepped out of them and yanked hard! And
one of the dinosaurs roared but I couldn't see to get the boots on,
because Roger was flapping his wings in my face and screaming
bloody murder so I couldn't take that one magic step to go somewhere else. I had to run for it between the trees, zigzagging . . .
they were coming toward us, three of them . . . *thump! thump!
thump!* hissing and roaring! I had to carry Roger because he was

only a baby really and he never should have left his nest by the river. And without the boots on I was losing and . . . and . . ."

The boy shivered, blinked rapidly. "And then I saw an opening and went through it and I got here. I was frightened." With that, Joey Willem dropped to the carpet, bowed his head and broke into tears. "And now Roger's gone and I've lost the boots for good," he sobbed. Lucien Broco motioned Trenton, who picked the boy up and sat him in a comfortable chair.

"*Esfandiary!*" Broco whispered, and his eyes derisively scanned the rows of encyclopedias and almanacs and works of the minds of men . . . garbage, to be thrown out in the morning now that he had an inkling of the truth! "A place beyond time! Hawkins is right after all!" Then, to Joey Willem, "This Jim Hawkins!" Broco said unctuously. "Why don't we call him on the phone, invite him to dinner? What's his number?"

Joey wiped his tear-stained face with the palms of his hands, then said, sullenly, "There is no phone."

Lucien Broco *thought* he'd read truth on the lad's face, but Broco's eyes were not what they'd once been. Was the lad playing with him, hoping to remain here in idle luxury?

A muted gong from the wall-clock announced 2:30, time for Broco to take his pills, then a nap. Trenton led the boy to the door, complementing him on his straightforward account and promising that at noon the next day, the greensward would be mowed and he could kick the soccer ball all he wanted. Perhaps he could invite some children from the village of Lower Muchness up for a game . . .

"No," Joey said stubbornly. "I answered Mr. Broco's questions, and didn't get to ask any. I want to know about life. Does it just happen, or do you go out and do it? That's what I want to know," he said. But the boy's eyes were downcast and his step, slow and uncaring. Trenton Interface, though not blessed with the ability to read faces, sensed a great trouble simmering deep in the boy's heart.

"Very well," Trenton said. "Anything to do with Life is automatically profound and surely the valleymaster will respond. At twilight. Question for question. But not now." He shoo'ed the lad out the library door and closed it. It was time for Mr. Broco's nap.

And now the last of the sunlight had crept above the eastern cliff and vanished. Twilight had come to the valley of Upper Muchness. Of Broco's dram of bourbon, one sip remained as he sat in the swivel chair, awaiting Joey Willem's return. Lucien Broco had many more questions and was impatient to trade information with the lad. The meaning of life versus *Esfandiary*, question for question. The boy had gone down to the Hawkins house, ostensibly to pick up the latest copy of that idiotic newspaper the old mathematician put out. More likely, to stuff himself on pancakes. It was reported that the Hawkins woman had barrelsful of pancakes in the attic, as well as fruitcakes.

Broco glanced at a digital wall clock that provided far more information than the old man needed these days. It was ten minutes past sunset. "Time is a thief," he grumbled.

Out of Broco's direct view, Interface shook his head. It was getting more and more difficult to steer his master away from depression. "Time is just nature's way of making sure everything doesn't happen at once," he replied cheerfully.

"Don't be clever with me," Broco said, and then he kept silent, discouraged that this admonition, which should have been roared, or at least, snapped, had come out as an old man's whine.

After a few moments, he said, softly, "Eh, Trenton, stand here beside me and we'll watch the little crystals flash away their souls." But Lucien Broco had not relocated to this isolated valley to watch the *kristallfluss* and both men knew that. He wanted one more shot at life. One more round. And the key to that, if it existed at all, was only a mile away in that house at the bottom of the greensward, in the head of a half-crazy mathematician. Half-crazy.

"Imagine being ten years old again, but with everything we've learned right up front, unforgotten! Wouldn't . . . make the same mistakes, would we? Imagine . . . a second time around, but this time with a map! Eh? What would you give for that chance, Trenton?"

To which Trenton answered honestly though circumspectly, because he knew that wealth does not hear contradictions in any case. "Faust, sir. Tales of Hoffman. Countless stories, most of them bitter and pessimestic, I regret to say."

"Bah!" Broco cleared phlegm from his throat. "Tales written by impoverished, despairing societal rejects. There I have the advantage of worldly experience, Trenton; didn't I create an empire? Jobs for tens of thousands? Wasn't I, through foundations, a patron of the arts and sciences? A friend of the impoverished? And I started with nothing! Nothing!

"Now, what about Hawkins's Theorem?" he continued. "No news from our Beerbakers?"

"*Bourbaki*, sir," Trenton said patiently. "They're still working on his fifth lemma. Stuck on it, they admit."

"Stuck on his fifth lemma!" Broco spat. "Put that in English, man! What page are they on?"

"Page nineteen, sir. Of Volume One."

A slow exhalation, a long silence, then, "Stuck on a lousy lemma! Who is this *Bourbaki*, anyway?"

"It's not one person, sir. They're an anonamous French mathematics society, sir. Membership by invitation only. Hawkins is very anxious for any sort of professional recognition; membership in *Bourbaki* would be a fitting reward for his life's work."

"If his Theory proves out and I get my end of it," Broco said, "see to it that Hawkins is invited into this Bourbaki forthwith. You know how it's done, Trenton. Just type *Bourbaki* into *MoreWealth* and press the *Encircle/Take* button. The program will take it from there."

Trenton knew how it worked. He shuddered. *Encircle/Take* worked through the international bank structure. Within a few months, a net would be closed and the gentle members of that mathematical society would experience personal financial pressures of the first magnitude, with corresponding incentives for cooperation; mortgages in danger of foreclosure . . . or forgiven, loans called . . . or cancelled, investments driven into the ground . . . or suddenly valuable beyond the most optimistic expectations, and likewise with pensions. If Hawkins's Theory proved out, his seat in *Bourbaki* was assured.

"Hawkins," Broco called. "Has he received any professor offers?"

"No, sir. And none would get by our . . . notice, sir. They'd be . . . held up for inspection."

"Indefinitely," Broco said.

"Indefinitely," Interface agreed.

"We don't want some cow college snatching him away," Broco said. Then, with a sigh, "It's taken too long, Trenton. By the time a way is found to this Esfandiary, I'll be a dried-up and forgotten bag of bones. Get me a good book on religion, Trenton old man. Any book, dammit! Any religion! Or all of them together!"

As darkness settled into the valley, Broco called, "Trenton!"

The major domo rushed back from the bookshelves, where he was trying to decide which religion was most optimistic, most likely to prove therapeutic to the old man. Broco had swung the binoculars into position. "The boy's come out of Hawkins's house and something's changed! He usually jumps off the front porch several times, runs the rooster into a frenzy and wastes valuable time rolling in the grass. This time, he's walking slowly up the hill, looking down at the ground. He's going to open up, Trenton! He's decided to show me the way to Esfandiary! Now he's running up the greensward! Ah! Ah! There's something on the road! Behind him. Something crawling up the road but I can't make it out! Can you? What's going on, Trenton?"

Trenton Interface knelt down, peered through the binoculars, switched to infrared and scanned Broco Way. There was the boy, hurrying his way through the high grass. But on the road, some distance behind him . . .

Trenton rose quickly. In his most dignified tone of voice, suitable to the occasion, Trenton Interface announced, "It is a remarkable sight, sir. Of course, infrared has poor resolution. One can be fooled. You'd best see for yourself."

Carefully removing Broco's trembling fingers from the controls, the major domo swung the binoculars into alignment and focus, then stepped back as Lucien Broco peered into the twilight. Against the backdrop of flashing crystals, he saw, centered on the crosshairs, a low shape moving slowly, slowly along the edge of Broco Way. Recast from infrared into hazy white patches, its nature was not certain. There *was* a feline stealth to its crawl, and the way its nose came to a point . . . it *could* be a beak . . . and the palpitations around its flanks *could* be the fluttering of small wings . . .

Cursing the distortions and uncertainties of infrared, Broco muttered fearfully, "Can one be sure? Can they be wings? It's running, gathering speed! Flapping furiously!" Broco sank into his chair, his lips quivering, his heart palpitating wildly. He dared not speak aloud.

Wings on a cat's body! An import from Esfandiary! Perhaps a griffin! A griffin! Hawkins's Theory is correct! I can't believe it! Soon I'll be in Esfandiary! I should really give the old fool a medal or a trophy or something! Perhaps a gold plaque, suitably inscribed. Maybe another for Loretta, in the shape of a fruitcake with rubies in place of prunes and lifeberries! And for me, more precious than gold or rubies . . . another chance at life! And another! Immortality!

Lucien Broco's bones tingled with the immensity of it. But now the Willem boy was more important than ever! *What was the secret of the griffin? Of Esfandiary?* How did one get there? "Go after the boy!" he bellowed to Trenton. "Get him indoors safely at all cost! And roll out the cage! I will meet you downstairs!"

Trenton was already on the way, flying down the great marble stairway and across the foyer, his footsteps echoing throughout the mansion. As he maneuvered a large iron cage on wheels from its shed out onto the driveway, the sky flashed violet and a thundering crash shook the ground. The iron bars glowed briefly and Trenton dropped to the ground, stunned. Lucien Broco threw open the front door of his mansionhouse and raised his right hand. A liveried servent pressed a button set in the marble wall. Powerful searchlights set along the mansion's roof swept the greensward, then leaped out to bathe Broco Way. Guided by infrared sensors, they converged on a remarkable object that stood in the roadway, transfixed by the brilliant illumination.

*   *   *

"What was that?" Blunger asked anxiously. They were seated around the kitchen table; Benison at the head picking at bits and pieces of his dinner, his thoughts elsewhere. Loretta, a large-framed woman who ate with country vigor, sat nearest the stove, sampling as much from the pots as from her plate. Except for golden hoop earrings— her ears were naked—she resembled a Romanian gypsy. Prior to Wilma's departure, Loretta had been the merriest woman in the valley, punctuating conversations, private thoughts and wonderings with extravagent, sweeping gestures of her bangled and much-braceletted arms. Her cheeks were rouged and she was wearing the same maroon dirndl and white blouse that she'd been wearing the day her daughter vanished. The blouse was hand-painted with Wilma's astrological signs, just in case they worked. Her earrings— *all* of her earrings, gold, silver, base metal, carved wood—hung on the porch where they acted as wind chimes, hopefully to draw Wilma home should she come within earshot.

No sooner had Loretta become engaged to Benison Hawkins than she repaired to a university library to study up on it. There she learned that she must reorganize her persona, that future competition would not come so much from other women as from intangibles such as degrees of infinity and lemmas. Above all, this Benison of hers must not be allowed to ignore her. In this regard, Loretta had succeeded; Benison might term her fluttery and deficient in certain graces, but he did not, could not ignore her. As for lemmas, Loretta had figured out long ago how to handle them. Shortly after their arrival in Upper Muchness and just after his completion of volume I of his Theory, she had sent Benison to Lower Muchness for milk for their new baby, Wilma. Hardly had the door closed behind him than she'd run to his study and shifted one—just one!—of the squiggles in the fifth lemma. So much for lemmas.

Now Myron Blunger sat in the best seat in the kitchen, a window seat that afforded a splended view of the Broco mansion in the distance, silhouetted against the violet sky. The violet sky. That was only one of the things that was bothering Myron Blunger about this place. His prior experience with a violet sky, shortly after his encounter with the kraken, had been very negative.

Worse, his soup was chirping like a canary. Earlier, he'd spotted motion within the blessedly opaque, blue-green soup that Loretta had placed before him. Now the sky was violet and the windows were vibrating from thunder and his soup had gone from chirping to turbulant. "What was that?" he repeated.

"Pod soup flavored with heebles fresh from the pond," Loretta said with a broad smile. "It's a noisy soup because of the heebles, but they're good for the brain. Of course, you being a genius as Benison tells me, well, you don't need it. It was Wilma's favorite." She sniffled and her broad face twitched as she fought off tears.

"Your daughter," Blunger offered with a sympathetic nod.

"Our daughter," Loretta said. "Gone out into the world to seek her fortune. Seven years ago."

"Seven's a lucky number," Blunger said.

"You think so?" Loretta sniffed, wiping her face with her apron.

"Absolutely," Blunger said, pushing his bowl into the center of the table. "She'll probably come knocking on the door any minute now with her fortune in a shopping cart. A shame to waste this delicious soup on a genius. Anyway, the noise I just heard was not from the soup. First of all, it was from outside. Second, it was a large noise, like thunder, or a subway train stopping emergency." His face brightened. "You think they maybe just put in a subway up here? The D train . . . I'm just a block from the Concourse . . . I guess not," noting the bewilderment on Loretta Hawkins's face. "It sounded like something else, anyway."

"Like what, Mr. Blunger?" Loretta asked.

Blunger whispered, "It sounded like a second-grade teacher scraping chalk across a blackboard, except not a teacher but a very large cat, and not chalk, but claws and not a blackboard but hard stone!"

Benison took a pencil stub and plunged it directly into his soupbowl, spearing a heeble. He waited patiently while it went through the shades of green, thrust it into his mouth entire, turned to Blunger and stopped chewing long enough to say absentmindedly, "Not just stone. Obsidian. The western cliff is pure obsidian. The eastern cliff doesn't have an ounce of obsidian in it. Peculiar geology, eh?" he chuckled. "Better eat something. We've got a night's work ahead of us."

"A night's work!" Loretta asked, frowning. "You're not going after that thing that's taking the chickens, are you? How do you know it won't carry you off, too? You want to end up being fattened for slaughter in a monster's lair, go right ahead. When the fellow from the Nobel Prize committee comes through that door," she said, shaking a finger at the front door, "looking for the man who published *The Theory of Partial Inconsistency* in *The Pustulate* . . ."

"*The Postulate!*" Benison shrieked.

"Whatever. I'll tell him exactly what happened, that you got carried off by your own theory and are being fattened up in a monster's lair and he's too late."

Growling, "There's no Nobel Prize in mathematics," Hawkins rose and retrieved a heavy knapsack from a corner of the kitchen. "If you're good, you get invited to join *Bourbaki*. Otherwise, you might as well be an accountant. Come on, Myron," he said, "Time to get started."

Loretta rose, clumped resolutely to the back door and stood there, arms akimbo. "I am not moving until you explain to Mr.

Blunger here your Theory and what it really means. He's got a right to know what may be out there!"

The knapsack hit the floor with a thud. Benison glared at Loretta, but she only spread her elbows until they touched the doorframe. Her husband glanced toward the front door, but his wife slipped a key out of her apron pocket and waved it triumphantly.

Benison sighed. "So. Why not? By next week, my Theory will be in all the newspapers anyway." He strode to the window and peered out. The violet had subsided; the black of night was absolute. "In the beginning, Blunger, there was chaos. No universe, no space, no time. Just concentrated chaos. Now, what does chaos mean to you?"

"Insurance claim forms," Blunger replied.

Benison Hawkins turned around, scowled and kicked the knapsack over toward his advice columnist. "Save such cutenesses for your readers. As a lesson, you will carry the knapsack with the fruitcakes.

"For your edification, chaos means that the values of the physical constants, the electron charge, gravity, the speed of light and such, were unsettled. They were oscillating back and forth, each at its own frequency, wildly, erratically. Suddenly—which is a trick in itself because Time didn't exist yet—a necessary and sufficient number of these physical constants simultaneously acquired values characteristic of a consistent, moderately stable universe. Our universe. *Moderately stable*! They had to fit together only to within plus or minus what is known as Planck's constant.

"Presto! Our universe sprang into being and started expanding outward, creating space and time as it went. How are we doing, Blunger?" he asked.

Myron Blunger smacked his lips, rolled his eyes appreciatively, nodded with admiration and finally shook it firmly. "A theory like *that* you don't just *say*, like you say, 'I think it's going to rain,' or 'The Yankees next year, for sure!' A theory like *that* is *presented*, maybe over coffee and danish, put away and taken out for another time. You don't want to wear out a theory like that! To tell you the truth, I never heard a fancy theory like than in the Bronx."

"Umm," Hawkins grunted. "Your concern is appreciated and supports my judgement of your character and quickness of mind.

"To continue, then. The early universe was self-consistent but not very stable. Other universes may have snapped together with other values of the physical constants, also self-consistent. In general, there may be an infinite number of universes, with no points of tangency.

"But along came humankind with its spiritual component, and a new direction for expansion, a direction not in space-time. Suppose that the creative force of the human mind has caused our universe to expand so that it intersects other universes. In volume five of my Theory, I address mechanisms for an increase in stability, possibly at the expense of other universes; volumes six to nine deal with the appropriate conservation principles. What I am saying is that there are locations, such as this valley, where there may be temporary overlap between parallel universes. Perhaps we are in the middle of a nexus, with a maximum likelihood of overlap. And suppose, during this interval, with no preventative barrier, a creature from another world were to cross over . . . perhaps *has* crossed over! . . . into ours. Eh, Blunger? Can you suppose such things?"

Blunger nodded. "It's like the Bronx and Bronxville. Another world, they tell me; I've never been there myself. So you think the creature that's been raiding your chickens is from Bronxville? Or . . . . " Blunger gasped as his full brain absorbed the implications.

"Beyond Bronxville, Blunger. Beyond ordinary space and time."

"Oh." Myron Blunger's right eyelid was trembling. "And your plan is . . ."

"To immobilize the creature by exposing it to the vapors of The Oldest."

"Oy! The poor . . ." Blunger stopped himself. "And then?"

"To bring it before the world as living proof of my Theory. To sit back and soak up recognition and honors. To be offered membership in *Bourbaki*! Perhaps, to decline it," Hawkins chuckled.

"Poor bakee?" Blunger repeated.

"*Bourbaki!*" Hawkins hissed. "A French mathematics society. Membership by invitation only."

"Sahms goomp me," Myron agreed, chewing on a large piece of whackleberry pie Loretta had quietly pressed into his hand. "If things work out, you could apply to get your Theory into the Bill of Rights or the Constitution! Even Einstein never got that far. But while we're supposing . . . suppose the fruitcake doesn't work? And suppose this thing is the size of a subway car, with lots of claws and tentacles? Then what?"

Hawkins walked to the door, took his wife's hand in his own and said gently, "Darling, tonight everything comes together. Like our own, my Theory of Partial Inconsistency is also a marriage. It is a marriage of mathematics, which never lies outright, and paraphilosophy, the science of pure wonder. Have faith, Loretta. If worst comes to worst and I don't return, remember that, to me, you were always more than just the square root of minus one. I love you."

Moved by this unprecedented display of passion, Loretta stepped aside. Hawkins kissed her tenderly, then hoisted the knapsack onto Blunger's shoulders. "As for you," he added, "you'd better eat a heeble or two. Besides feeding the brain, they keep the bowels in order. You may need that before the night's business is over," he added ominously.

Elf Miki was exasperated with the restrictions of humanoid form. It was too stiff, too breakable, though by a succession of miracles, his skeleton was still intact, though he was covered with bruises and scratches. No wonder humans were cranky much of the time.

He'd finally located the fledgling in the forest, crying for its mother, too weak to move. Pushing and pulling, holding its tail away from entanglement with its hind legs, he'd gotten it as far as the roadway, but suddenly there was brilliant light and to avoid being seen by humankind, Miki was forced to keep to the edge of the woods. The half-starved little creature had little strength left

and were it not for Miki's telepathed encouragement, it would
have flopped into the dirt and gone to sleep for the last time.

The account that Miki had telepathically unravelled from the
creature's immature mind showed a human Joey leaping through
Forest Grey in Esfandiary faster than anything on two legs the
griffin had ever seen. Impulsively, playfully, it had leaped from its
nest and scampered after the Joey along the river and out onto the
plains, finally leaping into the Joey's arms only to suddenly find
itself in a swamp filled with meateaters! And then the Joey stopped
running fast as the wind and they were being chased through the
trees until they dove into a grey miasma of fog just ahead of a set of
huge scissoring teeth! Meateaters! Its mother was just starting to
teach the kits about meateaters . . .

Its mother . . . oh, why had it left its nest!

And then the Joey was screaming and the game wasn't fun any
more at all until they fell through a narrow, sizzling halo in the
middle of the air and found themselves here in this new place! The
Joey hadn't wanted to play, but the fledgling had bounded merrily through the woods and onto the great meadow, chasing little
grey things with bushy tails and screaming and chirping and growling back at everything in its own voice! What an exciting place the
Joey had brought it to! Then the Joey had lain down in a meadow
and fallen asleep, and the fledgling had played a trick, stealing its
boots and hiding them in a secret place deep in the forest!

But when it returned, it had found the meadow empty, the
Joey gone! Now it was playing the price of adventure. Lost, hungry, alone and frightened, it wanted its mother very badly.

Instinct had led it to an enclosure of fat, warm-fleshed birds,
but it was not yet weaned and did not know how to eat them.
After carrying them off, it had tried this and tried that, ending up
releasing them in the forest and crying itself to sleep, still hungry.
Night after night, the desperate fledgling returned for more chickens, only to find that they contained no milk no matter how hard
they were squeezed.

Now the Joey was running up the hill, and the fledgling tried to scamper after its friend. "Wee see! Wee see!" it called, but the Joey didn't hear and it wasn't strong enough to press through the high grass of the greensward and now the Joey was almost at its nightshelter.

Stay on the Road! Call for your mother! Miki mind-flashed. *She will come for you!*

Humans didn't believe in griffins, or in elves, for that matter. For some reason, it was important that they not be confused or enlightened. If the fledgling were found by humans, alive or dead, Miki would be blamed and stripped of his responsibilities! Calling upon all his powers of mind, he exhorted the fledgling to crawling toward the high ground, in view of the Saddle. And though exhausted, famished and frightened, its wingtips dragging in the dirt, the little creature crawled up the road, peeping. It wanted to be back in its nest. It wouldn't venture out ever, ever again without permission!

Then there was a violet flash in the sky. The fledgling yelped and redoubled its effort, crying telepathically. Its mama was coming, coming to take it home. It would never run away again. Never.

In the region known as the Saddle, where the barrier between Earth Real and Esfandiary was weakest, thunder rumbled and the air crackled with bolts of lightning, yellow and violet. The rent in the barrier widened . . .

THE GRIFFIN PROBLEM

The knapsack hadn't gotten along with Myron Blunger at all. Pulling his collarbone out of line and causing his spinal discs to press uncomfortably on the bundle of nerves they were sworn to protect at all costs, the knapsack had finally been removed from his back and strapped into an old, clanky child's express-wagon, which the advisor to advisors was now dragging along behind him at the end of a long rope. The rope, which was looped at the tugging end, wasn't getting along too well with Myron, either. Twice it had snagged him, the last time sending him to the ground with a thump that wrenched his right shoulder. "Ugh!" he cried.

Crawling beside the wagon (on the upwind side), Benison Hawkins correctly interpreted the rope's sudden slackness and paused to wonder at his accomplice, hidden by utter blackness and high grass. That Blunger could be overpowered by a knapsack tightly strapped onto his back was difficult of conception; it seemed to violate several topological principles. That he could then trip on a rope slung over his shoulder and trailing out behind violated the third law of the Theory of Knots! Either Blunger was at war with mathematics, or ordinary matter rejected him. Either way, from this point on, Blunger would have to be treated, not as a constant, but as a variable.

Blunger was not an unmixed calamity. Problems breed solutions, and a solution to the Blunger Problem . . . no, the Blunger *Paradox*, could lead to a new theorem or, at the least, a conjecture! Yes, a *conjecture*! It was well-known that a snake held just behind the head was powerless to inflict a bite. Was there an analagous theorem for a rope? Was there a point on a finite rope such that by holding it there, the rope was powerless to trip one up? Definitely worth pursuing.

Furthermore, Hawkins's navigation system would not have worked nearly so well without Myron Blunger. For their foray up the slope of the greensward with not even a sliver of moonlight, the mathematician had discovered that Blunger was blessed with perfect gurgle, the tone of which was proportional to the local slope of the land. Thus, he needed only follow the tone emanating from his advisor's throat, steering him right or left with calibrated tugs of the rope. Of course, one could not have everything; Blunger was apparently unused to outdoor exercise and required frequent injections of confidence.

"I fell," Blunger called back. "I think I lost the rope again."

"Shut up, fool!" Hawkins whispered. "Broco's lawn is festooned with hidden microphones. Keep down. I'm bringing the wagon up." Groping through the high grass, Hawkins followed the rope to his advisor, then pulled until the wagon containing their arsenal clattered up from the rear. Despite the bouncing ride through the high grass, each jolt releasing a burst of acidic vapor from the overripe fruitcakes, the knapsack was intact. The Oldest, travelling separately in a hermetically sealed tin, had started to hiss. Whackleberries from its core had been thrust to the surface. Had the Oldest not been so well insulated, or had Blunger not been so preoccupied, he might have detected the sound of gas compressing in a confined space. But Blunger had noticed something else that demanded his full attention.

"If you have a minute, I have one small question," Blunger said, rubbing his sore right shoulder and worrying.

"Well? What now?" Hawkins hissed, speaking between cupped hands clamped around his advisor's ear.

"First of all, is it always necessary to *prove* a theory?" Blunger croaked. His throat ached from gurgling what he remembered of the twenty-third psalm to the tune of the Ride of the Valkyrie. "Why can't a theory just stay that way? A theory. We could fix it up nice with wide margins, have it printed up, send it to the democrats . . . they could use it for their platform. I mean, it's very dark out here and maybe we should go back and work on its appearance a little. Grammar . . . spelling . . ."

"What's eating you now, Blunger?" Hawkins rasped.

"Don't say that!" Blunger cried, pointing to the western cliff, where the *Kristallfluss* had reached its peak. "Look over there! The eyes of night are twinkling."

"What twinklings are you talking about?" Hawkins asked, his voice sharp with annoyance. "My Theory doesn't provide for twinklings. They are probably eruptions on the Moon reflected in the obsidian cliff."

Then, "Look! In the doorway!" Hawkins hissed. "It's Broco! Get down!"

Light spilling out from Lucien Broco's mansionhouse silhouetted the master of the valley. Lucien Broco raised his right hand. An instant later, a floodlight high on the roof of the mansionhouse burst into full radiance. A circle of illumination appeared on the roadway two hundred yards ahead of Hawkins and Blunger. Precisely centered was a creature quite different from a standard cow. Hawkins rose to his knees, then to his tiptoes, then pulled Blunger up. Trembling, he whispered, "Blunger, you are taller than I am. Cast your strong, certain eyes ahead and define the creature yonder. Start with its head. Is is, for example, the head of a cow? Answer an old man truly, for my soul flutters and my heart veils my rheumy eyes."

Myron Blunger recognized his employer's symptoms as a case of emotions. You had to be careful giving advice for emotions. Blunger's personal cure for a case of emotions was a cup of hot tea and lemon laced with honey. Sophie believed in hot baths. Jacob Minsky, his neighbor before he died, kept his emotions under control with regular enemas, until a bad one did him in. With this mathematician . . . well, who knew? This description had to be handled carefully.

"It could be the head of a small cow," Blunger said cautiously, not wanting to start a heart attack going. Casually he added, " . . .

if a cow were shaped more like an eagle and didn't have wings and a lion's body." That was enough. He did not mention the flurry of green that might have been a trick of the lighting. A flurry of green that might or might not have belonged to a smallish person of a type well known to children's librarians, and had definitely vanished by the time Blunger could properly focus his eyes. The point was, did Hawkins's Theory include elves? Probably not. Blunger knew when not to get involved.

Hawkins, pushing past his deputy, cried aloud, "Enough, Blunger; you have corroborated; the beast is for me to observe, describe and claim." Cupping his hands into a megaphone, he cried, "Let it be known to all parties and their heirs, assignes, trustees and lawyers that on this evening of . . . at . . . o'clock P.M., blanks to be filled in and notarized within twenty-four hours, that I, Benison Hawkins, have deduced from Theory and observed a new species of creature on the public road. It has a feline body and the head of an eagle. Dimensions, weight, talents and disposition to be filled in later, this space left blank for that purpose."

A hundred yards ahead, the creature reared up on its hind legs, extended its stubby wings and produced a terrifying, rasping squawk. There was an answering grunt from the mansion doorway.

"Hold still!" Lucien Broco muttered, wrestling the string and wrappings from a carton stamped FRAGILE—OPTICAL EQUIPMENT. Inside was a fully-automatic, state-of-the-art SMART/CAMERA, a left-handed present from the Henchpersons Union Local 241. Lefthanded, because they knew full well that Broco had no grandchildren and therefore would never have a use for a camera, much less a SMART/CAMERA! Broco chuckled with anticipation as his fingers tore at the wrappings. They would be surprised, mortified, perhaps furious to discover that their present had been the means of the valleymaster's attaining his dream! Broco smiled at the thought of it.

Ah! What was that racket out there? Hawkins! Hawkins was in

the grass, blowing off about his Theory! Let him blow all night; one roll of pictures and a lawyer was all Broco needed to establish ownership and priority of discovery. Should Trenton fail to trap it, or the creature die in the process, the photographs would certify its existence beyond dispute and Lucien Broco would possess a bargaining chip for the way to Esfandiary and life eternal! The boy had kept his secrets long enough!

Cardboard and Styrofoam packing flew in all directions until, exposed at last, was the miracle camera, with built-in computers and tiny motors for loading, focussing and color balance, plus automatic processing into wallet-size prints! Hah!

Keeping low to the ground, Hawkins prodded Blunger forward toward the startled creature, ignoring his advisor's stream of suggestions that they set up a base camp, form a study committee, rent a catapult. At thirty yards range, Hawkins peeled the protective cover from a small fruitcake and pressed it into Blunger's right hand. Blunger's arm went rigid; his eyes fixed on the flashing lights on the cliff. Hawkins pulled his advisor's arm back, then released it. The fruitcake arced high, but wide left, landing directly in the path of Trenton Interface, who was steadily, determinedly pushing the steel cage through the high grass. The major domo went to his knees, gasping, but doggedly pressed on, his eyes tearing.

"Another!" screeched Hawkins, pressing another peeled and primed fruitcake into his advisor's hand. Blunger took a stance, sent his right arm back in the manner of a shot-putter. His forearm muscles had loosened somewhat, perhaps in reaction to the vapors. Closing his eyes, he let fly. The missile travelled twenty feet vertically and three horizontally, falling onto Hawkins's head with a *splat*! Blunger despaired; despite their pungency, the fruitcakes seemed inadequate against the griffin, backed by a thousand-eyed, careening, topheavy obsidian cliff.

Eyes tearing, Blunger reached back into the knapsack and pulled out another fruitcake, tore the cover off with his teeth, and gripped it in his right hand. He did not notice his employer slowly corkscrewing into the ground, gasping for breath. Blunger stepped forward, out of the expanding vapor sphere and it happened that his watery eyes focussed on the obsidian cliff, beyond the floodlit circle and the terrifying creature at its center. The scintillations paused in their random flashings to spell out a message.

> "Were it not for gravity, you would manage to piss in your
> face! Throw like a man!"
>
> Innkeeper

*   *   *

Courage. Throw lefty.
　　Set your feet.
　　Cock your arm.
　　Right foot forward . . .
　　Stride into the throw!

Blunger, obeying this odd and unexpected command, gripped the fruitcake in his *left* hand, stepped forward with his *right* foot and flung it! It worked! The fruitcake soared into the night, arced gracefully, landed and bounced off the edge of the road to roll directly to the fledgling's paws.

　　The lights spelled out:

Now get ready for trouble.

"Hold it! I'm not ready yet . . ." Lucien Broco, his teeth clenched with determination, yanked the camera from its cocoon. Now how did you start the thing, he wondered. Trenton usually took charge of mechanical situations, but he was occupied and this was an automatic camera, eh? Indeed, the body was studded with tiny dots of color, several of which were already lit as though anxious to get to work. A red light on the rear panel was flashing at the greatest rate. Lucien Broco, a respector of squeaky wheels, consulted the directions. Ah. Film. It wanted film. Well, of course! His fingers probed the debris within the carton until they encountered a smooth cylinder, which he popped into place, chuckling to think of the reception his photographs would get within the scientific community! Not to mention his major benefit. Immortality! The rear panel snapped shut with the solid click of a precision fit. The film was automatically wound and a blue indicator light flashed once. Lucien Broco, smiling, centered the creature in the viewfinder crosshairs . . .

"Look this way!" he cried gleefully. He was about to press the shutter release when he noticed an orange light within the viewfinder flashing insistently. "Blast and damn!" Broco clawed through the instruction manual, which was very well laid out, in logical sections. Ah. All the lights were described on a foldout strip, together with their associated buttons. Orange . . . orange . . . ah, the main computer wanted information. How much magnification? Well, of course it had a zoom lens. Broco found and pressed the orange button. Beside the exposure meter, a green light flickered rapidly. Green. Damn, the creature was moving! Green was the desired depth of field! Broco found and pressed the corresponding button . . .

Joey Willem paused in front of the back door of the Broco mansion and peered longingly at the dots of light. The black cliff was beginning its nightly sparkle. Mr. Broco called them *Kristallfluss* and thought they were a natural marvel, something about trapped sunlight. Joey didn't think so.

The fact was, he really hadn't known how to control the boots, and with each step in Esfandiary he'd found himself in a completely different setting. Somewhere there had to be a door, a portal into Earth Real and life! But where? He'd stepped to the right, and to the left, small steps and large. And then he'd taken that one last step to the left and found himself ankle-deep in swamp mud, black and thick and stinking. Jolly Roger clung to his neck, squawk-ing and crying piteously for his mother. Nearby was a pool of liquid dark and oily that reeked of decayed matter; other pools abounded and from them rose large insects with double wings; they swarmed over his face as though seeking the juiciest flesh, then attacked him with stingers, and did not neglect the fledgling's most tender and unprotected parts. Shrieking, Joey slapped the air with both hands, lost his balance and fell backwards onto a root thick around as his body, one of an interlaced network that connected pools and mud, here and there erupting upward into trees from whose trunks oozed a sticky, resinous substance.

Here, in this murky fen, the root system was the parent entity, the trees a secondary growth. Grown to a vast area, the root system had adapted to a steady diet of organic nutrients of which a major component was body fluids squeezed from the prey of carnivores. Its investment in trees brought forth a harvest of flying creatures, which were attracted by sweet-smelling flowers and snared by thick, resin-coated vines suspended from the upper branches.

Unable to step free of the mud's grasp, Joey slipped out of the seven-league boots, slid around on the root, straddled it. Gripping it tightly with his knees, he leaned over as far as he could and grabbed one seven-league boot. Tugging with all his strength, he felt it move. He yanked, twisted, pulled this way and that, his teeth gritted until, reluctantly, the mud yielded and with a final squooshy *squwhoomph*, released the now-slimy mess. Not willing to risk balancing it on the slippery root and needing both hands to retrieve the other, he was forced to grip the first boot in his teeth. As though in revenge, a horde of insects now launched a full-scale attack. Joey could only blink and shake his head.

No sooner had the other boot squished free than the air ex-ploded in a great roar. His heart seemed to stop.

A meateater! Nearby! Jolly Roger was squawking frantically and digging into his neck and the griffin's wings were in his eyes and he couldn't get the boots on! He pulled Roger from his back, tucked it beneath one arm and, with the boots in the other hand,

got to his feet. Then he ran from root to root in a direction he
hoped was away from whatever had made that terrifying bellow.
No thought to direction; he leaped to whichever root was within
reach, large enough to provide a landing space and above the muck.

But something was following him on the left, hissing and clicking its jaws as it closed in. *Thump! Thump! Thump!* Deliberate
steps, closing its claws on one root before trusting its weight to the
next. Joey risked a single glance behind, then ran full tilt, leaping
as he never had! The dinosaur's head was as large as the Innkeeper
and its open mouth was rimmed with dagger teeth and its tongue
was black. Joey could hear the cracking of roots under its weight;
he couldn't look back again. Another roar, and an answer; *there
were two of them now!* He ran, panting, head low against entrap-
ment in the hanging vines. Roger had buried its head beneath his
arm and was bleating softly. Another roar! From the right and
louder, if that were possible!

The boy concentrated only on the next root . . . the next jump
. . . one slip and he'd be caught in the mud and torn apart. Should he
throw Roger into the air, screaming "Fly! Fly!"? He didn't; the fledgling had no chance in that dread place. His chest hurt. For an instant,
he dared rest, leaning against a tree-trunk. Another roar, and Joey
found that he was stuck to the tree! Nearly slipping and falling into a
black pool, he wrenched himself away, tearing his shirt and leaped,
leaped and now scissoring jaws were just behind him. Something
ahead emitted a low-pitched moan and suddenly he found himself in
a fog so dense he couldn't see his hands before him.

Behind him a predator bellowed. Could it track him by scent?
If so, he was a goner; he could no longer run. But neither could he
stay fixed. Just ahead of him, something twinkled red. Another
flash—deep blue, at ground level. Blindly he probed forward toward the blue flash; his foot found a root. He transferred weight.
Another flash—green; he risked another step. Again green, and
again, each taking him to a safe and sturdy root. He was being
guided! Soon he was on solid ground, out of the swamp and running,

running and his pursuers were somewhere behind, enveloped in blinding vapor.

Blinking vapor! Twinkling vapor! And then there was a color before him, a violet portal rimmed with silver and before him, dozens, hundreds of tiny flashes of light.

As he'd stepped through the portal, he knew he'd reached his goal! And when Lucien Broco showed him the *Kristallfluss*, he knew that it had saved him in Esfandiary, whatever its true nature. Perhaps the fluorescent twinklings were individual souls singing the song of life. Perhaps it was a single life-form he'd never heard of or imagined. Perhaps . . . it was the universal soul of humankind.

He entered the kitchen. Why were the kitchen lights off? Where was everyone? He turned them on and stood with his back to the door.

"Hello?" he called.

Joey wandered into the pantry and absently looked for his copy of the book, then remembered that it had been found and taken away. Despondant, without hope, the boy curled up into a corner of the pantry and stared blankly at the cookie jar on the opposite counter. Ordinarily he would have taken a handful, plus two for his pockets. Now he had no appetite.

Time passed. The kitchen remained empty. That was very strange. Usually someone was around, preparing the next meal or cleaning up or baking cakes.

He peeked out of the pantry in time to see the kitchen lights dim, then he heard a loud *thunk* from somewhere in the basement and then the lights brightened. An emergency generator had just started up! Something *was* going on! Joey tore out of the kitchen and shot up to the second floor by the back stairs but the library was empty. Dashing to the window, Joey looked out to find the road and grounds lit bright as day and . . . and there was Jolly Roger on the roadway! His pet was back! But the baby griffin looked terribly weak! So thin and raggedy! Why, he could hardly walk and his wings were drooping! Joey flew down the back stairs four at a time and out through the side door. At the top of the

greensward, he came to an abrupt stop. Trenton Interface was pushing a steel cage on wheels through the high grass. They were going
to put Roger in that cage! He couldn't let that happen! Joey's legs
churned through the high grass.

Lucien Broco placed his forefinger to the shutter release button.
The contact triggered a sensor—exposure imminent! The master
computer scanned the instructions, integrated the focussing and
exposure requirements and automatically set the shutter speed for
optimum contrast. It was a twenty-two step process. At the twenty-
first step, one short of the *Fire* command, the computer initiated
the rapid flashing of a marmalade light within the viewfinder. Now
what did the blasted thing want? Broco had no more time or patience for instructions! The creature was stealthily crawling closer
and closer to Blunger, and Broco didn't want to miss that shot.
"Hold steady, now!" he snapped, and aimed and fired, aimed and
fired. So powerful was the illumination provided by the roof floodlight that the strobe built into the camera didn't even flash.

Click! A great pose, the wings at full extension, the beak agape,
the eyes flashing.

"Hold it!" Broco shouted, exultant, his body surging with life
as it had not in a decade. Damn the doctors and their endless
restrictions and foul medicines! There was old Hawkins, grasping
his throat and slowly sinking into the greensward! Broco wanted a
shot of that. Lucien Broco wanted it all! Click! Click!

The fledgling snapped up the last bit of food. Whatever it was the
two-legged thing had thrown at it, it had saved the griffin's life!
The two-legged thing was its friend. It was large at the middle,
promising an abundance of milk! If the nipple couldn't be found,
the desperate fledgling would just chew its way inside; it *had* to
have milk! After the manner of cats, the griffin sank to its belly and
padded softly through the cool grass. Nictating membranes slid
down over the predator eyes; the floodlight would no longer dazzle
the griffin.

Myron Blunger stepped back, back. The approaching furrow in the high grass matched his retreat step for step, waiting for him to glance away just once so the beast could time its leap! Backwards he shuffled, kicking a path until, trembling with fear, he recalled the cliff-warning—*Get ready for trouble.*—had ended with a period, not an exclamation mark. Without an exclamation mark it was just a sentence, not an exclamation. Maybe, despite its terrifying appearance, the thing crawling toward him was just a small trouble after all. He probed the air behind him with his left hand and encountered nothing. No tree or Hawkins to hide behind, nothing except air, empty air. Unwilling to take his eyes off the furrow, he lifted his leg high and tried to run backwards only to feel his foot gripped tightly. Blunger went down onto the express-wagon, his foot snagged by the loop at the end of the rope. The hard edge of a fruitcake within the knapsack drove into his spine. His terror of being torn apart by the monster's claws, his throat ripped open by its beak, was agumented by the knowledge that he was certainly paralyzed! Together they'd gotten him, the rope and the knapsack! As he struggled for breath, his hand closed over a fruitcake. He threw it in the direction of the oncoming monster. In midflight, the missive came apart. And then the tall grass parted and there it crouched, its beak wide open. It screamed!

To save Roger, Trenton had to be stopped! Joey Willem lifted his head above the concealing grass, then dropped to the ground; Mr. Broco was looking in his direction. And there were violet cracklings and rumbles of thunder from the north and Joey was terrified. Jim Hawkins had been afraid in *Treasure Island* but he'd overcome fear, even when facing Israel Hand, dagger in mouth, on the deck of the *Hispaniola*. Jim Hawkins had managed to get out of every scrape.

But that was then and this was now, and something terrible was about to come down from the north. Something more terrifying than pirates! It had to do with Jolly Roger and it was all Joey's fault for not sending the fledgling back to its nest right away!

It wasn't fair! All he wanted was life! Real life, with a family and maybe a dog to chase over a field and go fishing with. Like Huck Finn, maybe, but he'd only read Huck Finn once and that wasn't enough. He'd read *Treasure Island* three times, including a careful reading in Mr. Broco's pantry. Biting his lip, Joey decided that no matter what, even if everything came to an end right here, he'd try to be as brave as Jim Hawkins and that meant he'd stick by Jolly Roger, the pet he'd found in Esfandiary; no way Mr. Broco was going to put it into an iron cage!

Scooting crablike through the grass, Joey circled the floodlit zone, intending to somehow stop the cage before it reached the roadway. Somehow. He couldn't hope to halt Trenton by leaping on his back or tackling him; Trenton Interface was too strong for that kind of tactic.

Joey's hand encountered something long and twisty at the base of the grass. A snake! Instinctively the boy recoiled, then he stopped. It hadn't slithered away or hissed. He pushed it with his toe. It didn't move. It was not a snake; it was a rope! He tugged it. One end pulled in okay; the other—the end nearest the road-way—didn't give. Joey popped his head up, spotted the cage ahead and off to the left but moving much faster. Trenton had found his rhythm. His head bowed nearly to the ground, Trenton Interface was chanting and grunting as he pushed and heaved the cage through the resisting grass.

Joey tugged the rope as hard as he was able; it didn't come loose. At the point where it vanished into the grass, there was a furrow leading to the roadway. Trenton was steering for that very point. Jolly Roger must have wandered off the road into the high grass! Joey moved swiftly to his left. He would let the front of the cage pass over the rope, then pull it taut and high and let the rear wheels entangle themselves. Trenton would be furious! Mr. Broco, too.

The front wheels passed over the line of the rope. Joey stood up and, pulling as hard as he could, started running to his left. The rope shot up out of the grass but the cage was moving faster than the boy had anticipated and it was the major domo's legs that got entangled. Trenton Interface went down. The loop of rope tightened around Myron Blunger's ankle, yanking him off the oppressing knife-edge of Loretta's fruitcake. His paralysis was cured! He could move!

The griffin advanced through the high grass, savoring the morsel it had snatched out of the air. Hope surged through the creature's body. What a wonderful place, where food rained from the sky! But it wanted, *needed* more! The two-legger had dropped to the ground and had another food and was shaking it from side to side. It wanted to play! Good! The fledgling's nest-mates often played when they were restless. They called the game: *The last morsel.* Usually a head or a wing with scarcely enough meat on it to keep a spider alive. But they leaped at each other, tearing at neck-feathers and clawing at the leathery skin beneath, mock-fighting as though over a dragon's egg, all this in preparation for their post-adolescent life in Esfandiary.

Now the fledgling extended its foretalons, screamed its play-warning and leaped onto the two-legger, delighting in the game! Extending its talons no further than necessary to provide a firm grip, it swivelled its head this way and that, plucking pieces of the good food out of the air as they flew from the two-legger's vibrating hand. Click! snapped its beak.

Click! Click! snapped the shutter of Lucien Broco's *Smart/Camera.* Myron Blunger's hand fumbled within the express wagon, found the Oldest, tore off its protective wrapping. He did not hear the bubbling that came from within.

Click! Click! went Lucien Broco's camera as he scrambled down the greensward toward the doomed Blunger, shooting film as fast as he could press the shutter release.

And then every living thing in the valley froze as the northern sky brightened and a terrible silence rolled the length of the valley. At the center of the Saddle, a roll of thunder ending with a horizon-to-horizon flash of violet-tinged silver lightning marked the tearing of the fabric of space-time. The barrier yielded and something large and fierce leaped into the sky of Earth Real. Myron Blunger's eyes rolled wildly and he passed through the seven stages of man, backwards. His hands clenched and unclenched; his legs, set into sympathetic vibration, kicked against the knapsack repeatedly, sending fruitcakes flying in all directions and on many trajectories. His head oscillated from side to side with fear. Here at the end of time and the world he was about to face judgement, and in his left hand, as a summation of his life's work on Earth, he held, as an offering to the Supreme Judge, the Oldest fruitcake of Loretta Hawkins!

And then the valley from cliff to cliff was filled with a scream and a huge creature was descending from the north with powerful strokes of its enormous wings. The fledgling lifted its head and cried, "*Wee-see! Wee-see!*" and from high above came a wild scream that rendered Myron Blunger momentarily without hearing. Then, with a furious beating of wings, the mother-beast was upon them, her foretalons fully extended, her hind legs retracted under her body, which was far larger than a full-grown lion's. Her hooked beak was full open and tilted to just the right angle for head-ripping! She intercepted in flight a fruitcake heading for her beloved fledgling, devouring it in one gulp. Banking left, she came about and swooped low over the greensward, toward her lost one. Lo, there was something lying on the ground near it; had it made its first kill, all by itself and in this strange place outside of the homeland?

"*Wee-see! Wee-see!*"

The fledgling leaped from Blunger's chest, leaving him with talon-gashes and dizziness and stripes of agonizing pain across his chest. His legs stopped convulsing and went rigid instead. Then the bulk of the monster was atop him, its huge, tawny forelegs planted securely in the ground on both sides of his body rather than in the shaky mound of flesh that was this native two-legged creature. Her eyes were fixed upon Myron Blunger and her enormous beak, as large as an alligator's jaws, slowly opened and closed as though she were making up her mind what to do with her offspring's first trophy. At that instant, the Oldest exploded in Blunger's hand and with the griffin's fierce beak not a yard away. Blunger's eyes started to cross and his nervous system shut down, but his tongue, as though on automatic pilot, tripped through the words as smoothly as though he were again on the floor of the library surrounded by four-year-olds with wide eyes and open mouths.

From deepest memory, slowly and clearly in a pleasant baritone, he recited:

"Now sit anywhere you want and your Uncle Blunger will tell you the story of Little Red Riding Hood. Once upon a time there was a little girl whose grandmother had made for her a beautiful, red . . ."

As Blunger recited, the beak slowly closed and the fire left those hard eagle eyes, replaced by something softer, gentler. " . . . and into Red Riding Hood's basket went a corned-beef hero, lean, with mustard, and a half pound of potato salad and a couple of pickles and a . . . yes, a fruitcake . . ."

Click. Click.

Detecting what sounded like a camera shutter, Blunger's ears suppressed the information as having no survival value. Another sound was deemed important enough to send forward, but found Conscious Brain AWOL and Unconscious Brain very involved with a wolf that had just stuffed a grandmother into a closet! This was a sucking, smacking sound. The fledgling had found its mother's distended udder and was beneath her, its head tilted up, a nipple firmly but gently wrapped in the soft tissue at the base of its beak. It was pulling nourishment, strength, life from its mother . . .

Click. Click.

Minutes passed, measured by the suckling sounds, an occasional gurgling purr from the mother griffin's throat and the sounds of a camera clicking away.

And just as Myron Blunger recounted the dispatch of the wolf by an alert woodcutter, the mother griffin lifted herself, scanned her surroundings and, ignoring him completely, stalked over to the open road, pausing only to cuff her errant fledgling with a foreleg blow of exactly the proper force to make her point. Then she extended her wings . . .

Click! Click!

. . . and leaped into the air, flapping strongly. Up into the night she soared, circled, watched her fledgling try to imitate her. Its strength renewed, it ran down the road on its short legs, flapping its stub wings harder and harder until it gained airspeed, jumped awkwardly into the air, beating furiously to keep up with its mother, who was flying north toward the violet-tinged aura of silver.

They were gone and the irridescence above the Saddle was fast fading, but nothing in the valley of Upper Muchness moved except Lucien Broco's right forefinger. Click. Click. Broco was the first to reach Joey Willem, who had never released his hold on the rope holding Trenton Interface in check.

"Safe!" cried the multibillionaire. "Come, now. We'll disentangle our loyal Interface, then head home for a hot chocolate and a well-earned night's sleep and not a word about the affair until tomorrow!"

"No, sir," Joey said in a quiet voice as he set about unravelling the rope from around Trenton's leg. "I'm not coming back with you!"

Joey's response startled Broco and sent a thrill through Blunger's chest. Character! The boy had character! A father's pride momentarily overrode his chest pains. Hoisting himself to a sitting position, Blunger discretely, gently checked out his lower parts and was rewarded; his testicles had stood their ground! They had not flown up toward refuge! Character! And like father, like son! It was a complete man who removed the rope from his ankle, followed it back to Trenton and helped the dazed Major Domo to his feet. Then, beaming with pride, he turned to Joey Willem. Enough was enough; it was time to take his *son* home. Pausing to kick a fruitcake fragment from the vicinity of Hawkins's nose, he and Interface together dragged the mathematician to the road's edge, where clear country air quickly brought about his revival.

Clapping his hand on the shoulder of his protege-son, Myron Blunger cried out, "I am Myron Blunger, your . . . closest living relative." Oh, that sounded wonderful! And why shouldn't he swell with pride? Hadn't he carried out a difficult assignment honorably, even with distinction? "I've come to take you home," he said kindly, patting the boy. Should he mention the exciting, tumultuous dining room at the Inn, the spacious yet cozy library, the companionship and that remarkable Innkeeper? The boy's face was expressionless, giving Blunger no clue as to how well this was coming across.

"What a time I had locating you, my boy!" he exclaimed. Still no response. This wasn't going well, but he was committed. "I faced wolves, a tiger, a kraken, an electric wolf and now a griffin . . . every one of them starving for manflesh!" As the word passed his lips, Blunger shivered. "We . . . we'll have lots to talk about."

His voice trailed off. Then, taking a deep breath, Blunger said, "But that part's over with now. I . . . I am your *dad*! And we have to go home."

Joey Willem took a step back, releasing himself from the annoying shoulder-thumping. He said, "I don't know who you are, mister, but I ain't going anywhere with you, either."

I don't know who you are! The words hurt more than his

lacerated flesh. Blunger forced a smile. "Very good, Joey. You don't go with strangers, not in these times. I see you still have your street smarts. But with me it's okay. I . . . you're part of me! That's what a father is, eh? So get your boots and we'll go home. To the Inn. To Alice and Dorothy. And Windbreaker," he added with a meaningful wink.

"The boy stays with me!" Broco snapped. "As for you, Mr. Blunger, you've got ten minutes to clear off my property before I have you taken away in that cage! And it's a two-hour trot to the South Gate so you'd better get started!"

Taken aback, Blunger shook his head stubbornly. "Joey and I have a special relationship," he insisted. "We're . . . just like father and son. He *must* come back with me. He's . . . expected!"

Lucien Broco sneered and motioned to Trenton Interface, who was standing dutifully by the cage, taking deep breaths to clear his lungs from the odor that hung over the greensward like gunpowder over a battlefield. In an instant, Blunger's arms were pinned behind his back and he was being frog-marched toward the cage.

"I wouldn't do that, Mr. Broco!" Hawkins called out. "Let him go before he develops grounds for a lawsuit."

At the word *lawsuit*, Broco blanched. There was no need for him to gesture; Trenton released his captive and set about brushing him off, mumbling all the right words.

"Well, why won't you come back with me?" Broco purred to the boy. "I've given you everything a child could want or need, and there's plenty more," he hinted with a wink of his right eye. "A lot more. For starters, I will tell you the secret of life." With a helping hand from Trenton, he squatted so as to look Willem squarely in the eye.

"Land. All things that live, from little blue twitterbirds to the great predators, fight over territory. Territory comes first; all else follows: food, mates, etcetera. Life is a struggle for ascendency and Man is designed to dominate; over nature, over his fellow man, over the momentary urges of his own traitorous flesh! My greatest personal triumph was not to get pulled down into time-wasting relationships, including marriage! Winning, getting, having: that is the secret of life. Now, all I want is the secret of the griffin. And the way to Esfandiary."

From the road's edge, where he sat cross-legged, inhaling deeply, Hawkins cackled. "That, of course, is self-serving nonsense. The purpose of life is to understand nature, not to dominate it. One starts with mathematics. If one is wise, he need go no further. Nature is applied mathematics. I think you'd best come home with me. We will start with the lower algebra, proceed through calculus and the Heine-Borel theorem. Then we will devote ourselves to my Theory. Perhaps, one day, another opportunity will come and we will prove it to the world's satisfaction."

Myron Blunger was dismayed at the shallowness of two intelligent, successful products of the American twentieth-century culture. Hawkins, lacking proof of his precious theory, wanted a slave-disciple to carry on the work and speak kindly of him to posterity. Broco had photographs of the creature, and would offer them in his own time and for a huge price! Blunger knew how rich people worked things . . .

But now he understood his protoge! The boy wanted to know the meaning of life! Well, it was a good thing that he, Myron Blunger, had made it to this point. Meaning . . .

Blunger coughed politely, winced at the pain he was about to inflict on his own protege, his own disciple, his own son; then he spoke.

"Life you want!" he said. "Better come back to the Inn. There is no life for you in this place. You have no home here, no family. Who will take care of you? There is more to life than fighting over land and learning your times tables. Life is family, friends, walks in the park and standing at a window watching the snow come down. And learning right from wrong. Who will teach you right from wrong in this place?" Blunger cast a challenging look at the multibillionaire.

Joey Willem solemnly regarded Broco, Hawkins and his

pseudo-father. Then he said firmly, "I will remain in the valley. I will live in the Hawkins house, with Aunt Loretta."

"What!" Broco exclaimed. "What can she do for you besides fill your stomach with poison?"

"Loretta!" Hawkins gasped. "My Loretta?"

"Why?" Blunger asked as Joey Willem took a step toward the greensward.

"I left the Inn to make a life of my own . . . before it was too late," he said, looking down at his feet in embarrassment. "Everyone has a soul. Except me. The Innkeeper said I was incomplete. I'm going to stay in the valley and try to earn a soul, so I can be like everyone else.

"I'm going to stay with Aunt Loretta because she's lonesome for her daughter and she needs me."

"Hah!" Hawkins shouted gleefully at Lucien Broco. "And in our spare time, child, we'll get started in mathematics."

"Do that," Broco said smoothly. "Meanwhile, I will take my three dozen photographs to *Bourbaki* and claim priority. Of course, I'm a reasonable person, and the photographs are yours . . . if you can arrange safe passage to Esfandiary." Handing the camera to Trenton, he stood triumphant while his major domo activated the develop/print mode.

"Sir . . ."

"Not now, man!" Broco snapped. He was intent on reading Hawkins's face by floodlight, which altered the color balance and concealed flushes and uncertainties.

"Sir, you should know . . ."

Broco turned and cried, "Well, what *is* as important as eternal life? Make it short, or you'll spend the rest of your life sweeping entrails in the slaughterhouse!"

With a sigh, the loyal Trenton whispered in a stately cadence, "The camera was a present from the Henchman's Union, correct?"

"What of it?" Broco snapped.

"And your floodlights atop the mansionhouse. Weren't they

purchased at an Odds and Ends Discount in the village, at considerable savings?

"Get on with it, man!" Broco snarled.

Trenton Interface coughed apologetically. "The camera will photograph only by union light, sir. It has a sensor for that, also. The floodlights do not meet that standard. None of your film was exposed."

the end
enough already

LOOPS

The first sitting for dinner was over; the waiters were busily cleaning up in preparation for the second sitting. So it was done, Blunger said to himself as he sipped a second cup of tea laced with honey and looked with fondness on the last page of his manuscript.

7the end. enough already.

And yet there was an ache in his heart. Joey had turned his back on him! This, after the hundreds upon hundreds of hours he'd spent on the boy!

Well, maybe Joey was better off where he was, Blunger rationalized. As for the boots, a pity they were gone; the Innkeeper would be disappointed. Maybe he could take a tax writeoff. A lost pair of boots, even seven-league boots, wasn't the end of the world, was it? Then again, this was the Inn at the End of the World! That was a good one! Oh, would he have stories to tell Sophie when he got back! Poor Sophie! And Irving, and Jason in his big ranch house in Scarsdale! They must be worrying themselves sick!

Myron Blunger had considered bringing his manuscripts to the Innkeeper's quarters, but why not bring them directly to the Innkeeper's table, which was on a raised platform near the picture window overlooking the Deep and the Northern reaches? The Innkeeper could read them over dinner, which always put one in a more positive frame of mind. Besides, Blunger had twice gotten lost in trying to find his way about the Inn, and would probably get lost looking for the Innkeeper's quarters, which were somewhere near the armory. So it was that Blunger, finishing his tea, edged the pages into alignment and handed his writing to the Maitre d', to be presented to the Innkeeper when he came to the second sitting.

With nothing to pack for the return journey to the Bronx and some time to kill while the Innkeeper read his manuscript, Myron Blunger returned to the library. It had gotten chilly; the fire had gone down again, and there was but one log left in the woodrack. He tossed it into the center of the fire, turned his writing chair toward the warmth, dropped into it with a great sigh of relief and comfort. Red and yellow flame lapped about the log. He closed his eyes. For all its draftiness and the nuisance of the fire needing frequent attention, he'd miss this library. True, it lacked a reference section and the stone floor was always cold, and many books that one would expect to find even in a branch library were absent, yet it had atmosphere. The softly flickering torches, the hiss and crackle of the fire . . .

Indeed, he'd miss the Inn. Who could imagine being restored to health by Dr. John Watson? Or encountering Athos, Porthos and Aramis striding down the center corridor in full uniform, arm in arm, singing a stirring ballad of war and love? Pity he didn't speak French. If only he could have met some of the children! Pinocchio! Jim Hawkins! Tom Sawyer, Alice, Dorothy . . .

But the Maitre d' had been quite fixed on that; the children dwelt in their own wing of the Inn, presided over by Mother Goose, who loved them all, even Huck Finn and the other scamps. With unbounded devotion, she tended and mended and saw that they got their sleep and finished their vegetables and above all, she made certain they remained children. And that meant no contact with the older folk, not even a children's librarian who was shortly to depart. And since most of the grown guests kept to their cliques, or to themselves, and the majority did not speak English, Myron Blunger had not had much opportunity to mix.

As the fire's warmth enveloped him, Blunger felt a pleasant aura suffuse the muscles of his body, which still ached from the climb up the greensward. Well, he'd had quite an adventure, hadn't

he? Odd how he wasn't aware of the transition; one moment he'd
been in Upper Muchness, trying to persuade Joey Willem to return to the Inn. Then, as Lucien Broco argued with his major
domo over the blank film in his *Smart/Camera*, Blunger, feeling a
slight dizziness, felt that he really should sit down and order his
thoughts. Then he was spinning . . . or was the world spinning?
Anyway . . . *poof!*, he'd found himself back in the library, pencil in
hand, writing *the end / enough already* and with a full complement
of aches and cuts, where the griffin had raked him. No wonder he
was fatigued. Fortunately, there was time for a quick nap before
the Innkeeper finished reading.

Softly the log hissed away its meager store of water. Soon Blunger
was snoring, his hands clasped across his belly, dream fragments
whirling through his mind. There was Windbreaker dashing madly
across a plain, and wolves and an elf named Miki beneath an umbrella tree and Lucien Broco's glittering eyes and a huge griffin
soaring and even as his unconscious wove them into a storyline, it
signalled him to wake! Something was happening!

Blunger's eyes blinked open; the fire was still alive; indeed the
log had barely started to burn. Had the Innkeeper finished reading so quickly? Was he come to send him on his way home? Blunger
looked to his left, toward the hallway entrance. No Innkeeper. No
one at all. He glanced to his right, then opened his eyes wide. The
door to Esfandiary was no longer sealed and bolted shut; indeed,
it now sported a translucent glass panel on which was printed:

CHIEF LIBRARIAN

Office Hours—NOW

And the door was ajar.

Slowly, and against his better judgement, Myron Blunger rose.
The translucent panel was backlit by a steady glow of strong, yellow-
ish light, against which the letters stood out, declaring, demanding!

Chief Librarian / Office Hours—NOW. The NOW in capitals. It was a summons!

Blunger trembled. The Innkeeper had said that Esfandiary—the land beyond that door!—was all dinosaurs, but nothing was coming through the open door, not even the grunting or roaring one might expect from thunder lizards. Blunger's instinct was to back out of the library but his right leg took him forward, not backward. And then his left leg also disobeyed, carrying him that much closer to danger. The door opened wider, as though urging him on. He reached the threshold, peered inside but saw only a yellow haze. Was there footing? He looked down. Before him was a floor, an ordinary wooden floor. He took a tentative step in what seemed to be the only direction his body was able to move.

And then he was over the threshold and the yellow haze was gone and Myron Blunger was surrounded by a living, glorious cathedral of light. In every direction and as high as his eyes could discern, vertical streamers of radiance glowed and shimmered. The path on which he stood was covered with a spongy grass that invited ambulation; Blunger knew, *knew* that he could walk on that ground to the end of eternity and beyond without tiring or feeling hunger or thirst. He sniffed tentatively, then deeply, what sweet fragrances eased his soul! To his ears came a sweet bird-trill such as one might hear at twilight in a virgin forest if one were very patient. The glorious sound was repeated. No more did Blunger's body ache, no more was his mind troubled.

He'd made heaven! He'd made heaven after all! Not with an A-plus, maybe, but a passing grade, for sure! For the rest of eternity . . .

"Well, how do you like it?"

Blunger spun around and his heart started pounding. Beside him, standing beside the now-closed door, was a body-head with a single, centered eye, spindly arms and legs and a toothless mouth that spanned the full width of its face. Its nose was small, bi-nostrilled and in place of ears it had gridded microphones labeled *Widest Dynamic Range under No Load.* The apparition was outfitted in orange plaid knickers, a short-sleeved royal blue shirt with a gold crest embroidered over the heart and crimson knee-length stockings. Its feet were shod in brown and white spiked golf shoes and atop the thing was a light gray Tam O'Shanter cap with a gold tassel. Beneath its arm was cradled a number five iron; its hands were full of index cards.

In a rather mechanical voice without overtones, it said, "Well?"

"Who . . . what are you?" Blunger whispered, too astonished to feel threatened. "Where am I, heaven? What happened to the Chief Librarian?"

The apparition turned to the door and crooned, "Wonderful door. Good door. Smart door."

To Blunger, it said, "Didn't door do a wonderful job of matching up your notion of heaven? Majestic, peaceful, eternal, brilliant but not shmaltzy. Approaching Blunger, the apparition whispered, "Door's been concerned about you. Say something nice to Door; it likes to be complimented. Here; Door likes a rubdown." The apparition took a soft rag from a hidden pocket and handed it to Blunger.

Without once taking his eyes off this Something, Blunger managed to give the door a few swipes with the rag, which smelled of lemon furniture polish.

"Well, that's enough of that," the creature said. "Let's get down to business. You're in big trouble." And waving the golf club in a manner that Blunger couldn't follow, the creature dismissed heaven. No shimmering lights, no bird-trills, no celestial orchestra, no soft path . . . they were in an office. A rather cramped, windowless office whose walls were lined with rows of wooden filing drawers of the size that libraries use for their card indices. To Blunger's right was a table loaded high with books, each with a bookmark protruding from its pages. To his surprise, Blunger recognized some of the titles. Indeed, he vaguely recalled having glanced at many of them, over the years. Directly before him was an old rolltop desk.

"There is no Chief Librarian; the Innkeeper has usurped that responsibility," the creature said.

"Then what about the sign on the door?" Blunger managed to croak. At least the door was still there, though it was closed firmly and had no handle.

"Oh! Take a closer look." Blunger peered more closely and, to his surprise, saw that the sign in the panel now read (the lettering reversed):

DO NOT DISTURB

Blunger closed his eyes. This kind of craziness he knew; this was Wonderland *mushagass* and he wanted no part of it.

"And who are you?" he asked, sensing that he would not like the answer to this basic question.

"Your soul," it said morosely.

Blunger opened his eyes. "My soul?" he said.

"Your soul," it repeated. "Every living thing has a soul. I'm yours. Call me Tom," it recited.

Blunger's mouth dropped open. "Why Tom?" he gasped.

"When you were a small boy you secretly wished you'd been named Tom instead of Myron. You would have named your oldest son Tom, but Sophie vetoed that and you settled for Irving. I am your portion of the universal soul, personified on short order for this encounter. Call me Tom."

Blunger's mouth closed. He blinked, stared, clasped his hands to his temples and whispered, "Tom! Not even Sophie knows that! I really have a soul! A soul named Tom! Oh, my God!" Then, with great trepidation, Blunger pointed toward his head and asked, "If you're my soul, why aren't you . . . home?"

"You overdosed on St. Felicia's potion and sneezed me out."

"Wait a minute," Blunger said, "how could my soul look like this? I mean, one eye . . ."

"Many souls are blind."

"But the ears!" Blunger protested.

"They function best with small talk . . . but enough; we have no time for chit-chat now! As I said, you're in trouble, Myron, you know that?"

Blunger shook his head numbly. Then he nodded vigorously.

Tom took the rag from his hand and with short, rapid strokes, proceeded to vigorously rub down the wooden parts of the door. "Doors separate different realities," Tom explained, continuing to stroke the door. The door responded to its rubdown by glowing brightly for a moment, then continuing to sparkle. "Elsewhere," Tom continued, "doors are passive separators, a hallway from a bedroom, a kitchen from a dining chamber, inside from outside. This one also separates what might be from what it feels should be. Door knows what's been going on in the library. The Inn-keeper has exceeded his authority, having you kidnapped, sending you out to Upper Muchness to retrieve those seven-league boots. And worse to come, worse to come. Of course, the Innkeeper is not always the Innkeeper these days; the false god Wotan is trying to take over his body!

"So Door took action."

The false god Wotan! Door took action! The concept galvanized Blunger, who saw that he was surely sliding down a rabbit hole faster and deeper than Alice ever had! Fixing his mind on the Bronx, on the Concourse, he was formulating a good, strong termination of this encounter in his mind—something like, "Tom, it's been a pleasure meeting you. Realizing that you have a massive cataloguing problem and having a few moments to spare, I thought I'd offer my services to the Chief Librarian in an advisory capacity, as I am rather tired from the labor of writing. Now I must prepare to leave; I am overdue at home and Sophie will be worried sick."

But as though it could read his thoughts, Tom said, "We are one, you and I, and there cannot be falseness or misunderstanding between us. In your writings there are errors of fact and errors of judgement which must be set straight lest you fail entirely and cause great harm.

"First, the rescue of Joey Willem in Esfandiary was a heroic act by Elflet Rush. She diffused herself into a living, scintillating fog, blinding the meat-eaters and guiding the boy toward the portal. She is fueled by eagerness and enthusiasm, and you would do well to make use of her in your next set of adventures."

Next Set of Adventures! Elflet Rush! What next set of adventures? A cold shiver ran down Blunger's spine.

"Second, you have set yourself up as an advisor to advisors," Tom said, "but you have little wisdom to offer." Tom folded the rag and placed it on the desk. Then he picked up a pile of index cards from the desk and sorted through them. "For example, it happens that gnomes *do* read their own entrails, though it is just as well you paid no attention to Yang; their predictions are famous for their duplicity.

"Here are some general pieces matched to your life story," he continued. "'Never eat meat in a dairy state.'" Also: "'Beware the gathering of knaves.'" And this: "'Come not between the dragon and his wrath.'" Shakespeare. Here's a contemporary one: "'Marry a girl from Brooklyn; no matter how bad things get, she'll have seen worse.'

"Will you remember those?"

"Absolutely," Blunger said. "I use memory tricks all the time. Brooklyn dragon eats meat at the knave's wedding. She's seen worse."

"Good," Tom continued, then he cupped his hands around his mouth and whispered into Blunger's ear, "Most important; Avoid profundity; keep it light. It is your only hope. Beware the Innkeeper in his wrath and above all," said Blunger's soul, his hands cupped that the words be directed into Blunger's ear, "do not use the phrase, *Deus ex machina.*"

"You mean . . ." His heart thumping wildly, Blunger looked upward as though to see the Diety gazing down, but saw only a standard office ceiling, with cracked plaster and much in need of a dusting. "Oh! Oh my G . . ." He stopped himself.

"By the by," Tom said, "preprints of your manuscripts are attracting attention."

"Preprints?" Blunger said, totally befuddled. "Who's reading my work besides the Innkeeper?"

"You'd be surprised. Now, listen."

From beyond the walls of the office a trumpet sounded. And another. Enter horns, strings, woodwinds, softly at first, then louder. Drums! Deep, bass kettledrums booming softly.

"Verdi," Tom said. "Guiseppe Verdi. God is very fond of his Requium Mass. Keep that in mind for your next adventure. You're not getting back to the Bronx without a miracle," Blunger's soul said somberly. "I'm trying to add God to the distribution list. Remember, no profundity; that's not your bag. Keep it light. Now you'd better return to the library. The Innkeeper's on his way. Mind what I said!"

Blunger heard a click behind him; he turned to find the door open, the fire still hissing, the log he'd just thrown on, half consumed. He had many more questions to ask. How come his soul wasn't where it belonged, somewhere in his head? Where was God? What did God look like? What did He do? Why was there so much pain and trouble . . .

But then he was crossing the threshold, blinking, bewildered, unable to get even one question out before the door closed and bolts slid home. Myron Blunger, his mind whirling, stumbled toward his chair, intending to sort out this latest, most fantastical experience.

The main door to the library opened and the Innkeeper entered. He was dressed in the outfit he used for butchering, old leather trousers, a torn and much-stained flannel shirt and hobnailed workboots. He was holding Blunger's manuscripts in his left hand. His right hand was in the pocket of a blood-stained apron.

*   *   *

The Maitre d' had delayed giving the Innkeeper Blunger's manuscripts until he'd finished his main course, which included a flagon of ale. The Innkeeper had dined alone this evening, which disappointed the maitre d', who was thus deprived of an opportunity to improve the Innkeeper's level of culture. Escorting a guest to the pavilion, as he chose to call the platform on which the Innkeeper's table rested, he would slip the visitor a phrase-card, which carried a choice of opening lines, such as:

"Thank you for inviting me to join you! What a wonderful view! See how the shadows of night creep across the winterscape!"

On the Innkeeper's personal napkin, printed large that it might be easily read from his lap, was a suitable response: "Yes, the eaves of the Forest Beyond are dissolving into the twilight. Soon the last glimmer of sunlight will kiss its reflection in the black mirror of the Deep and the Northern Reaches will vanish into darkness."

The pavillion business, the phrase-cards, the responsa—all were part of the Maitre d's long-term program to imbue the dining-hall with class. A quick reading of Blunger's chapters had caused a pronounced setback in the Maitre d's acculturation program. The Innkeeper's napkin lay balled up some distance away, having been hurled by great force accompanied by a string of epithets that had cleared the nearby tables even before dessert and tea had been served.

At the moment Myron Blunger first threw the log on the fire and settled down in his chair for a restorative nap in the library, the Innkeeper read the final page of his manuscript, pulled a Bowie knife with a nine-inch blade from its scabbard and thrust it through all three chapters of Blunger's writings, pinning them to his table. He had not had to read every word of Blunger's scribblings to determine that the idiot had failed his mission. Neither boots nor boy had been recovered. The Innkeeper looked up, and his countenance was thunder and lightning.

"You! Yes, you, over there!" he roared in the direction of the aptly-named Knaves' Table, halfway across the spacious hall. There sat two men of quite different manner and history. The first to rise was a sturdily-built, grizzled fellow of fifty winters who nimbly thrust a crude crutch beneath his left arm and waited for his companion to join him; one behind the other they wended their way between the maze of tables to the Innkeeper's Pavillion, seating themselves without awaiting the Maitre d's formal introduction.

"No boots! No boy!" growled the Innkeeper. "Blunger's made a fool of me! I'll have him flayed and his hide made into boots! And his guts for laces!"

"Aye, he's makin' a fool o' you, he is!" echoed the Innkeeper's first guest. His eyes were set close to a thick, crooked nose, and a tri-cornered hat sat low on his broad forehead. This was Long John Silver's first visit to the Innkeeper's table and he was determined to make the most of opportunity.

His left eye a-squint and his voice low, the old pirate said, "I know Blunger's kind. He needs an object lesson, such as keelhauling. Let me tie `is hands an' feet an' swing 'im over the gunwale of the *Hispaniola*! Let 'im just *look* down at ten fathom of green, roiling seawater an' he'll have that jackanapes Willem scramblin' back to the Inn *with* the boots an' some good red stripes across his stern! I'll bet me treasure on't!" he said, grinning wickedly. "Oh, I'll set a fast beat so he don't take on too much water!"

The Innkeeper knew well what Silver wanted out of it—the sloop *Hispaniola* and her crew. Mr. Hands. Black Dog. Billy Bones, Blind Pew and just to show there was no hard feelings, old Ben Gunn . . .

Some made the adjustment to the Inn; some didn't. Long John Silver hadn't, even after great pains had been taken to recreate his quarters as close to the *Hispaniola's* master cabin as possible. He missed the sea, he claimed. What he missed, of course, was pirating under the Jolly Roger. Though it was forbidden to write at the library table without permission, more than once had the Innkeeper had caught Long John at the writing table in the library, attempting to write, sketch, conjure up the sloop *Hispaniola*, though whatever knack or talent was needed for this, Silver apparently lacked. No ship or boat had ever been sighted on the Deep.

Finally the Innkeeper had caught the old buccaneer snuck into the library after hours, laboriously tracing from an old print, again trying to summon the *Hispaniola* into existence. Silver had been banned from the library and, for good measure, his old shipmates consigned to the lower level of the Inn, forbidden to consort with their leader.

But now the Innkeeper had summoned him to his table, which could mean anything.

Don Juan de Tenirio, his companion, was a slender, olive-complexioned man in his early forties, attired in the fashion of late fifteenth century Italy, all in black save for a scarlet doublet laced with black needlework of the finest quality. Smooth hands, an arrogant smile on his thin lips and the carriage of a natural horseman and swordsman could have defined any of a hundred heros of the period, but a nervous tic over the right eye and a general air of anxiety marked this notorious womanizer. He had seated himself with his back to the window, affording a sweeping view of the dining hall. His right hand hung inches from the grip of a sheathed sword that hung from his belt. "Well, Don Giovanni?" the Innkeeper said, gruffly. "Blunger has proved himself a fool and a traitor. Long John suggests a keelhawling. What are your thoughts?"

"Please . . . not Don Giovanni," the guest whispered. "Here I am known as Don Juan de Tenirio." He spoke in a low voice, and his eyes constantly and fearfully darted about. Now his right hand clasped the hilt of his sword, though a sign in twelve languages posted at the entranceway proclaimed the dining hall of the Inn off limits to any sort of violence, no matter how great the provocation. "I am familiar with Senor Blunger's attempt to retrieve your property. Indeed, hearing of his abilities at self-transportation, I have had myself added to the distribution list, offering to translate his writings into Spanish and Italian, in case Senor Blunger succeeds in publication. I wish to express a different point of view than Senor Silver."

So Don Juan de Tenirio was Don Giovanni! Long John Silver had not known that. Once a ladies' man, the don seldom ventured from his triple-bolted chamber for fear of encountering the spectre of the Commandant, the father of one of the women he'd seduced, one Donna Anna.

What could this frightened shadow have to contribute to the Innkeeper's dilemma, Silver wondered? More important, what did he want of the Innkeeper, in return for his thoughts? Was this to be a competition? Could they profitably go partners? Silver listened as Don Juan leaned over the table, fixed the Innkeeper with his dark eyes and said, "With all due respect, Myron Blunger may be shrewder than you think.

"It is my belief that Senor Blunger has come to realize, as men do at his stage of life, that the road ahead is shorter than the road behind. Most men content themselves with a new mistress; Blunger, the ex-librarian, seeks immortality! Consider! He wrote a book, *The Boy with No Future*, designing his protagonist, Joey Willem, to carry out a mission! And what was that mission?

"I respectfully submit that Myron Blunger learned of the existence of the Inn, but did not know how to get here. So, he sent Joey Willem up here, a lad of ten with no loyalties except to himself, Blunger. He created a boy with a head stuffed full of adventure and derring-do, for his mission would require courage. In that, perhaps he succeeded. Perhaps not. The final chapter is not yet written."

Don Juan continued in a sibillant, lisping hiss. "I submit that Willem's mission was to act in such a manner than Myron Blunger would be brought here in person! And why? To do precisely what he has endeavored; to remake himself! Look at his first attempt at writing! Is it not a young, virile Myron Blunger who sets out upon his adventure? And was he not acting upon your orders? Oh, he is subtle, this Myron Blunger! He set out at the foot of the Dromedary Mountains, not to retrieve his protege or the stolen boots, but *to establish a base of operation outside your jurisdiction, then to take your position!*"

At that, the Innkeeper roared with laughter, slapping his open hand on the table and calling out for a fresh round of ale. "Replace me! Blunger?" he laughed, his eyes tearing.

Don Juan waited patiently until the uproar had subsided and three flagons of rich, golden-brown ale had been delivered; then he continued, softly. "You thwarted that scheme, in part. Rather than a young, brash swashbuckler, it is our familiar, portly Myron Blunger who has insinuated himself into Hawkins's household with the boy. It appears that he spends the next two chapters accomplishing nothing. But . . . is that so?

"Already he has successfully transported himself to Upper Muchness, by power of belief! Indeed, were it not for the complexity of the thing, he would likely succeed in imagining a subway terminal right here at the front door of the Inn! He will soon enough come to understand the power of writing in the library of the Inn at the End of the World, where one's written words become real *so long as there is sufficient belief.*"

At this, Long John Silver's eyes narrowed. Sufficient belief! This he had not known!

"My thought is this," the don continued, "Myron Blunger doesn't fully accept the reality of Joey Willem, and has no respect for seven league boots.

"But consider . . .

"*The king of France . . . and forty thousand men, marched up the hill, and then marched down again!*"

"And what's that supposed to mean?" the Innkeeper demanded impatiently.

"It's an old song, a children's song about the battle of Agincourt. Apparently he has sung it hundreds of times in his career in the Bronx. I have heard that when he dozes, those are the words he mumbles. Myron Blunger spent his entire adult life as a children's librarian. How do you know he doesn't believe in it with all his heart? Here in the Inn . . . is it not possible that he could close his eyes and *sing* that army into existence? What will you put up against twenty thousand French knights on horse and foot-soldiers with lances?"

The Innkeeper stopped laughing.

"And then there's the question of who taught Myron Blunger to throw lefty."

"Throw lefty!" the Innkeeper snorted. "What do you mean?"

Removing the Bowie knife, the don ruffled through the pages of Blunger's manuscript, and so absorbed was the Innkeeper in the don's train of thought that he did not observe the presence of a mysterious tray which, after gliding through the aisles, had stopped adjacent to the floor of the platform, though there was no waiter behind it, no hands supporting its sides.

On it were three settings of silverware wrapped in linen napkins, a bowl of vegetables and a platter of cottage cheese, a tureen of salad, a pitcher of carrot juice and two small orders of spaghetti and meatballs. As Don Juan searched for the section of Blunger's writings in which Myron Blunger was taught to throw left-handed, the tray commenced a slow, cautious retreat, bobbing and weaving between tables and narrowly escaping collisions with the multitude of waiters and waitresses rushing in all directions.

No centaurs, not even the most athletically gifted and graceful of that species, were allowed the run of the hall, the maitre d' fearing for the crystal-ware and fine china with which some of the tables were set. This meant that Windbreaker was forced to take his meals at a low table at the far end of the room, kneeling on a mattress to prevent callouses. The table was bare, except for a pitcher of water and a basket of raw carrots, which the centaur was rapidly depleting. Yin sat opposite him on a chair bolstered with a thick pillow, making conversation and following his twin's progress from the kitchen toward this most distant table. Balancing the tray bearing their three dinners on his head and two uplifted hands, Yang was invisible. But why had he stopped at the Innkeeper's table? Yin hoped he wasn't spying on a conversation. That wasn't a good idea at all. That wasn't healthy.

Yang had put him in charge of Windbreaker, to make sure the centaur didn't gobble rolls from adjacent tables. Yang had ordered that no roll-basket be placed on the centaur's table; Windbreaker didn't know it yet, but he was about to go on a diet.

Yin, trying to keep a conversation going, inquired whether he'd made any progress on the lifting of his curse.

"Who knowve?" the centaur replied dejectedly, cramming half a carrot into his mouth. Yin regarded the action with dismay; Yang was right, as usual. Windbreaker, who had once been so proud of his physique, had fallen into compulsive eating.

"A curf is eever on or off," the centaur said, chomping loudly on the carrot. "There's no halfway. And who's in charge of them, anyway? Who keeps records? Who makes the final decision to turn it off? No one knows. Not Merlin, not Gandalf. I thought my underwater fight against the kraken would do it, but here I am.

"Where's Yang, anyway?" he grunted, reaching for another carrot.

"By the Innkeeper's platform," Yin replied softly, covering his mouth. "Under a tray. Don't look . . . the Innkeeper's invited Long John Silver and Don Giovanni to his table . . . knaves, both of them. If they spot Yang under that tray we'll have to charge down and rescue him. Don't look!" Come on, Yang! he thought. There was trouble coming up, and Yin felt inadequate.

The Innkeeper was laughing. Was that good or bad? Yin worried. Now he wasn't laughing any more; that seemed ominous. And just as the tray resumed its motion toward their table, the Innkeeper turned about and stared, tracking the tray's mysterious, stately march until it reached the last table in the dining hall.

On the tray were two gnomes' portions of spaghetti and meatballs . . . and Windbreaker's new diet. This was not going to be easy.

Yang arrived, slid the tray onto the table and clambored up onto a chair.

"Where's my dinner?" Windbreaker asked.

"You're looking at it," Yang snapped. "One roll, a half-pound of cottage cheese, a bowl of salad with low-fat dressing and later, if you're still hungry, I'll get you a bowl of clear broth."

Before the centaur could react, the gnome reported to his brother and the centaur, "The Innkeeper's got the Blunger manuscript there in front of him and he's fuming. That filthy old pirate Silver wants to keelhawl Blunger. You know, I'm starting to regret having participated in his abduction. At the time, I thought it was a sort of lark. Eh?"

The centaur, in the midst of taking a bite out of the roll, stopped cold and the blood drained from his face. Dropping the roll, he looked directly at the Innkeeper's table, where Don Juan was speaking to the Innkeeper. They were shuffling through a stack of papers, as though looking for something.

"Keelhaul!" Windbreaker said. "Keelhaul Blunger! He'd never survive it! If the barnacles don't scrape the flesh off his body, his lungs'll bust!" Windbreaker's head was shaking from side to side. This could not be. This would not be. Not to Blunger.

"Relax," Yang said, alert to the centaur's thoughts. "The Innkeeper won't give in to Silver. Not yet. There's the question of who taught Blunger to throw lefty. If Someone with a capital S has taken an interest in the situation, that changes things.

"In the meantime, if we're going to rescue Blunger," Yang said quietly to Windbreaker, "the physical part's going to fall upon you. So you've got to be in shape! You've got to lose the fifty pounds you've put on during convalescence. I'm starting you on exercise. With weights."

Before Windbreaker could protest, Yang went on, "Secondly, stay away from lox, blintzes and kippered herrings. Ever since Blunger introduced appetizers to the chef, the kitchen budget's been stretched mighty thin. I understand the Innkeeper's not happy about that and we don't want to draw attention to ourselves just now."

"No lox. No herring. No blintzes," the centaur recited.

Yang glanced toward the Innkeeper's table. A tureen of stew had been uncovered and already Long John Silver was attacking a generous portion with gusto. The Innkeeper, his brow furrowed, was reading and rereading a page of Blunger's manuscript, his desert of custard pie ignored. Don Juan was picking at a small portion, his eyes constantly scanning the dining hall, his right hand never far from the hilt of his sword.

"We can no longer leave Blunger alone," Yang whispered.

"Right after dinner, you take the first shift," he said to Wind-breaker.

"What I don't understand," Yin said, "is, if the Innkeeper wants the boots back so bad, why doesn't he just go after them himself?"

Yang glanced about the room, covered his mouth with his hand and whispered, "It is forbidden. That's his one restriction. Don't ever mention it to him; he flies into a fury. The chef told me that. Why do you think he sent us to fetch Blunger in the first place?"

Suddenly there was a cry from across the dining hall. Don Juan had jumped to his feet. By the time his chair had crashed to the floor, he had leaped from the platform to the nearest wall and there he crouched, sword in one hand, a poignard in the other.

"*The Commandant!*" he screeched, edging toward the nearest door. "There! There, by the kitchen entrance! He is in white! White!"

As one, hundreds of diners rose and peered in the indicated direction, but saw only a waiter shaking out a white tablecloth. By the time the dining hall had settled down, Don Juan was gone . . . and so was the Innkeeper. And the Bowie knife.

Windbreaker was instantly on his feet and flying toward the nearest exit. Blunger had to be protected!

Yin scurried out, to search for Don Juan. That left only Long John Silver at the Innkeeper's table, and Yang making his cautious way toward the Innkeeper's pavilion, watching the pirate's every move. If Silver appeared to be heading toward the library, or Myron Blunger's modest two-room suite, Yang would have to divert what might be an assassination attempt. But the buccaneer, having finished dinner at leisure, extracted a curved pipe from his coat pocket and slowly, thoughtfully packed it full of tobacco from a leather pouch. Then, leaning back in his chair, he lit up and stared outside into the gathering darkness, in the direction of the Northern Reaches and the Deep.

En route to the library, the Innkeeper stopped in his quarters to discard his casual wear, a comfortable old bearskin shirt and denim trousers, for a set of stained work-clothes topped by a butcher's apron and rubber boots; the garments he generally for messy jobs of butchering. Thus attired, he headed for the library and Myron Blunger. In his left hand, he carried Blunger's manuscripts. His right hand, immersed in the pocket of the apron, was curled about the handle of a nail-studded bludgeon. The Bowie knife hung from his belt.

He entered the library. There was Blunger in his chair, his head bowed down, as though in thought. Was the thieving, conniving underachiever trying to figure out an escape without making good on the boots?

In his mind's eye, the Innkeeper *slammed* his bludgeon down on Blunger's skull with a crash, sending Myron Blunger's brains clear to the Bronx!

But not yet. There remained two problems: the recovery of the boots, and of determining who had taught Blunger to throw lefty!

The Innkeeper, regaining control over his wrath, coughed gently, eliciting his guest's attention, then dropped the manuscripts on the table.

"Well, I've had a chance to look it over," the Innkeeper said, forcing the conciliatory words through a throat constricted by fury. "Not bad for a first draft." His hand tightened on the bludgeon.

"A first draft!" Blunger gasped, bringing himself back to awareness. His passage into Esfandiary flashed out of his mind at the sight of his writings. "What kind of first draft? That's it! I got the griffins back to Esfandiary and closed it up, which took some doing considering I was working without a map, as you might say. The boots are probably lost in the woods. As for Joey, well, you saw what happened! He wouldn't come! That's all there was to it! Not with me, not with Broco, not even with Hawkins. Stubborn little brat!" But the annoyance on Blunger's face was quickly replaced by a broad smile. "But character! Just like my own Irving, when he was that age. I'll send you pictures when I get home.

"Of course, if you hadn't interfered right from the beginning . . .
was it *my* idea to send an unarmed ex-librarian to confront a full-
grown mother griffin separated from her offspring? To outtalk and
outthink a crazy mathematician and an arrogant multibillionaire?
I wanted to send a six-foot-two bodybuilder, a James Bond type.
Joey would have gone to the Moon with *my* Myron Blunger. Of
course he wouldn't come back with yours. Which reminds me . . .
not all of those words are mine!"

Myron Blunger seemed oblivious to the effect his words were
having. He didn't notice the reddening of the Innkeeper's face or
the sudden tightening of the Innkeeper's neck muscles, the tightening that generally preceded the smash on the head that dis-
patched one of the barnyard animals! And he'd forgotten Tom's
cautionary words: '*Beware the Innkeeper's wrath!*'

Just as the Innkeeper was about to terminate the Blunger problem, the door burst open and Windbreaker entered carrying a double
armload of logs for the fireplace. The Innkeeper's right hand relaxed its grip around the handle of the studded bludgeon; the
wrath attack subsided.

The centaur said cheerily, "Fire's gone down a bit, hasn't it?"
though in fact, the log that Blunger had added earlier was burning
furiously.

After tossing another log on the fire, the centaur, though un-
invited, settled himself on the hearth with enough groaning and
sighing to convince the most hardened medical or veterinary specialist that he was still recuperating from his wounds. He blinked
a warning to Blunger with his left eye.

Blunger winked back. Windbreaker settled into a position that
afforded him a view of the Innkeeper's right arm. That unseen
hand held something, and the centaur was determined not to budge
until he knew that Blunger was out of danger.

"Let me ask you a few questions," said the Innkeeper to Blunger,
straining against his inclination to dispose of this problem the
easy way. "Would Lucien Broco really find immortality in
Esfandiary? Have you any idea what Esfandiary is like? What about
Loretta Hawkins and her lost daughter? Is the barrier between

Earth Real and Esfandiary ruptured for good? Did the rupture close by itself? Or did something close it? What controls the strength of the barrier in the first place? What about this Elf Miki you've introduced? What about Dragon Groff?"

And then, in a tone of voice so mellow that even the naive Myron Blunger could not fail to detect overtones of danger, "*And who taught you to throw left-handed?*"

Blunger, shaking with fright and uncertainty, said, "I . . . I did the best I could. I made up only what I needed. Who . . . taught me? You! First you insulted me:

'Were it not for gravity, you would manage to piss in your face! Throw like a man!'

"And then you gave me instructions . . ."

But his interrogator's head was shaking firmly from side to side. "Look at the manuscript. I registered my disgust and signed it. Then there are the stars; that *ends* my . . . contribution. *And then comes the instruction!*

Blunger said, apologetically, "I always thought I was just a lousy right-handed thrower. I didn't know from lefty."

He scratched his head.

The Innkeeper blanched.

Blunger stroked his chin thoughtfully; the Innkeeper trembled.

Blunger shrugged his shoulders. The Innkeeper leaned weakly on the table. A bead of perspiration trickled down the side of his face. "Is anyone in your family a lefty?" he asked, anxiously.

Blunger shook his head.

The Innkeeper gripped the table's edge, took a series of deep breaths and, with considerable effort, regained control of himself. "Okay," he said calmly. "We'll call these Chapters One to Three. Listen carefully now: You're right-handed except for throwing. You never knew this because you never threw anything before. Now get started on Chapter Four, with a mind to closing the loops. And the biggest loop is those boots! I must have them."

And before Myron Blunger could ask what he meant by that, the Innkeeper was gone.

"Close the loops," Blunger said despairingly. "Chapter Four? How will I ever get out of this?"

Windbreaker settled himself beside the armchair and whistled, "Whew! I don't believe it! Frightened out of his mind."

"*He's* frightened?" Blunger squealed, mopping his forehead with a handkerchief.

The centaur nodded solemnly. "The righty-lefty business. If you're on the level and don't know from throwing lefty, that leaves . . ." His eyes rolled left, toward the farthest recess in the library, toward a triple-barred and locked oaken door that led to Esfandiary . . .

"It looks as though Someone Else has taken an interest in the matter of Myron Blunger," the centaur said, quietly. "The Innkeeper's not used to have someone looking over his shoulder. Much less, Someone, if you know Whom I refer to."

For a long while, Myron Blunger sat facing the door to *Esfandiary*. At any moment it would open and harsh judgement would be rendered. A lifetime of blasphemies, hurtful utterances and other transgressions paraded through Blunger's mind. Harsh judgement.

The door remained shut. "So what do I do now?" Blunger pleaded. "What did he mean by closing loops?"

"I used to read more than I do now," the centaur explained (suddenly finding that he *liked* explaining). "Fiction, that is. Not many stories around I can . . . er, identify with. But Yang explained it to me once. The way it works, you start by posing questions, introducing your characters."

The centaur rolled over onto his side, sighing as his wounds responded favorably to the radiated warmth. "With each character you introduce, you open a loop. Each loop must eventually be closed, some earlier, some later. Some clever writers close a loop before opening it, like in mysteries, but that's another story. *Hah*! Get it?"

Blunger winced.

"After all the loops are closed, you write *The End*, and that's all there is to loops."

"That's all there is to loops," Blunger repeated mournfully. "But I don't know anything about Esfandiary and how am I to get Joey back when he won't obey? Or the boots?

And what about Verdi? 'God is fond of Verdi,' Tom said. "You have any ideas?" Blunger asked.

Windbreaker cupped his strong chin in his hand and stared into the fire. After a while, he said, slowly, thoughfully, "Well, there's one thing I know about your protege that you've probably overlooked, and it's plain as the ketchup on your shirt."

"Ketchup?" Blunger asked, looking down his shirtfront. Then, "Oh," spotting the stain. "What do you mean?"

"Food. If you wrote the way you eat, you'd have a whole shelf for yourself in the stacks. But what about Joey? What does he eat? Do you know?"

"Do I know? I created him. He likes fast food."

"Burgers?" Windbreaker suggested.

"Sure, burgers. And pizza. He's crazy about pizza."

The centaur grinned.

"I'm going to get him back with a pizza?" Blunger snorted.

Windbreaker smiled broadly. His eyes were half-closed; it was easier to diet if you took occasional naps. "Not just a pizza," he sighed. "You need a helper. Someone who knows children. An elf."

"Or an elflet?" Blunger said, recalling Tom's first suggestion. "How about an elflet named Rush."

"Is she brave?"

Blunger said, "She saved Joey Willem in Esfandiary, disguised as a cloud of sparkling vapor!"

"An elflet?" Windbreaker muttered, raising his eyebrows.

"An elflet," Blunger said, confidently. "Rush. She's young and quick and just bubbling with enthusiasm."

And pizza. And Guiseppe Verdi.

THE PIZZA VENDETTA

by: A Committee

"I am getting angry, Rush!" But the dense underbrush absorbed Elf Miki's thin voice so completely that a robin ten yards away didn't even interrupt her search for dinner. Standing behind an old stump he'd adapted as his lectern, Miki had *The Book of the Ways of Man* open to page three. They'd started at dawn, and now golden rays slanted into the Teaching Glade from the west and Miki's student had vanished again! "Roaring, hopping, steaming, piping mad!" he shrieked.

This was impossible! In rescuing Joey from the dinosaurs, Rush had demonstrated the maturity and confidence required for the guardianship of a region of Earth Real. And, of course, that would ease Miki's workload. With that in mind, Rush had started her training, under Miki's tutelage.

Rush.

The elflet was well-named. Barely had Miki started a topic than she'd dart off in one direction or another, fluttering along beside a butterfly, chasing a rabbit, or flashing to blue and trading insults with a resident jay. So this was Earth Real! She'd never imagined anything so dynamic, so vital, so full of life! The elflet wanted to know, see, hear, touch everything immediately Now and all at once!

The first day of her apprenticeship was nearly gone, and they had not progressed beyond page three! And now Miki had a *secret mission* to explain and again the elflet had vanished! He slammed the Book shut, expanded to an impressive sixteen inches, clenched his fists and cried, "If you don't get back here this instant I will . . .

3563-LEVI

I will report you and you will spend the rest of eternity herding worms and toads in the Great Swamp of Esfandiary!"

Immediately the elflet materialized at a respectful distance and floated gently to the ground. "I am very sorry, Miki; I will never leave without permission, never, never unless something *very* important happens," she said sweetly, folding her white taffeta dress over her lap and gazing adoringly at her very own mentor with eyes that exactly matched his preferred shade of royal blue.

Frowning, Miki declared, "We should have been well into chapter two by now! Mind-probing! How can you hope to understand humans unless you have some background in their innermost beliefs? How are we ever going to finish the Book of Ways? And how are you ever going to manage this valley if you don't concentrate?" He peered over the stump. The elflet had taken out her little white notebook and was jotting down the three questions in her mysterious, unreadable shorthand, each on its separate page.

"Now stop that!" the exasperated elf cried. "You know very well they're rhetorical questions! Listen carefully, Rush," he pleaded, coming around to the front of the stump in what the Book described as a good technique to create a rapport.

"While you were out exploring or whatever, I received a message from the Inn. We have a new mission, a secret mission. You and I together. It should be very interesting and exciting, but we'll never get it done if you go flitting after every jaybird in the valley. Are we partners?" he asked, anxiously.

"All for one!" Rush screeched, jumping up and clapping her tiny hands. "Secret mission! Partners! How exciting!" Leaping into the air and shielding her eyes with her hands, she asked, "What Inn? Where?"

"The Inn at the End of the World!" Miki exploded.

"Oh, *that* Inn," Rush sighed. "Who sent it?"

"The message isn't signed, but it's on real stationery," Miki said in a conspiritorial whisper. "It must have come from the Innkeeper himself. And, by the way, I wouldn't be surprised if He came over here in person when we least expect him, just to see how you're getting along in your new assignment."

Rush nodded soberly, her notebook open to a blank page, the picture of efficiency except for the sparkle in her eyes. "Good!" she exclaimed. "You can inform him that I already know all about mind-reading and religion. And . . . I have a surprise."

The casualness of the elflet's announcement produced a small knot of anxiety in the elf's innards. "What do you mean?" he asked.

Sensing trouble, he seated himself on a log beside the elflet and whispered into her tiny ear, "I'll tell you our secret mission if you tell me your surprise."

"Okay!" she grinned. "My surprise is . . . I found a religion for Joey Hawkins and he loves it! What's our secret mission?" She twinkled her eyes out of playfulness, but also because she was in love with her silly, stern teacher.

Miki gulped. "Our mission is to bring Joey to the Inn."

"Oh, how exciting!" Rush trilled.

"Exciting?" Miki said. "A secret mission isn't supposed to be exciting. It's supposed to be carried out quietly and efficiently. The orders don't say how to do it, so I'm going to be Peter Pan. Children follow Peter Pan anywhere, anywhen. That's what he does best. We'll take Joey to the Inn, through Esfandiary."

The elflet's eyes widened and for the first time since starting her apprenticeship, she was momentarily speechless. "Peter Pan! Oh, you lucky! Then I'll be . . . Wendy!"

"Wouldn't you rather just be Rush?" Miki asked.

"No!" snapped the elflet. "I'll be Wendy . . . or else I'll tell the Innkeeper and when he finds out how you're going about it, why, he'll just send Peter Pan over to do the job himself!"

Miki frowned, then countered, "Um, that's a thought. Of course, if Peter comes over to take care of it, he'll bring his own Wendy . . ."

"No!" Rush cried. "Orders are orders. You'll do Peter and I'll . . . I'll be myself." That settled, she asked, "Now, what are those?"

pointing up to the darkening sky and changing the subject more quickly than her teacher could possibly follow.

"They are storm clouds," Miki explained patiently, resigned to his successor's hummingbird mind. "Soon water will come down from them and the wind will blow fiercely through the valley, sending all the birds and animals hurrying for shelter."

"How marvellous!" Rush trilled. "Then Joey's religion will come over the mountain and defeat Storm and save the valley from flooding!"

"Joey's religion," Miki repeated warily. What had the elf-girl done now? "Perhaps we should both visit the boy and see what his religion looks like." And in the blink of an eye, they both transformed, Miki to his royal blue sphere, Rush to a pale green tenuousity of uncertain outline. Together they rose into the evening air, two irridescent washes of color soaring over the woods and meadows toward the Hawkins house.

Joey sat on his bed staring out the window. The floor of his room was littered with crumpled papers and he didn't care if Mr. Hawkins got angry or not. He'd *tried* to do the problems; he'd *really tried*, and he'd even written a note to Myron Blunger for help. Now he felt empty and lost. Empty and lost and no one cared. And hungry. He blinked away a tear.

In the instant that his eyes were closed, the elf and elflet slipped into his mind undetected. That's what human blinks were for, Miki had explained to Rush. The trick is to wait out of sight until the exact start of it, then . . .

"WHAT IS THAT?" he telepathed.

"SHH! That is the symbol of his religion," Rush shot back.

Joey's mind was positively afire with a symbol Miki had never encountered! It was a large golden-red circle with dark spots. It was hot, very hot. And the boy wanted it. Needed it! What had the elflet planted in the boy's mind, and with the Innkeeper coming around on an inspection at any time!

"*The Innkeeper must not find the boy in this state of distress!*" he telepathed. "*We must satisfy his religious need quickly and without a direct intervention; that is an absolute limitation.*"

"*What will happen if we fail?*" cried the elflet.

Miki glowed; at last, an opportunity to use *the word!* Miki had found it in the appendix to *The Book* as something called a counterexample. But it was a grand word, and he'd kept it in mind for just such a moment when an elflet might need to be impressed. This called for physical speech, which was much more dramatic than thought-speech. Slipping out of Joey's mind during an eyeblink, they teleported to a promontory of rock atop the eastern cliff. This was Miki's eyrie; it afforded a view of the entire valley.

Clearing his throat, he opened *The Book* to the appendix and recited, "Comprehension of the psychodynamics of human families is *propaedeutic* to understanding the behavior of children." He glanced at Rush to measure the effect of his statement only to find that her attention had been captured by a nuthatch working its way along a tree branch. Had she no interest in her lessons at all?

"I have an idea," Miki said, closing the book. "Why don't you explain Joey's problem as you understand it?"

The elflet's eyes flashed as she stood up, folded her hands behind her back and said, "Joey is trying to become part of the Hawkins family. Mr. and Mrs. Hawkins have gone away to Boston to look for a Wilma. Before Mr. Hawkins left, he gave Joey a problem to solve and he cannot solve it. That is why he was receptive to a religion. A religion is what humans call upon when they are having problems.

"Also, he's homesick for the Inn and he misses his pet griffin and he feels all alone. I think he needs another pet. Maybe a heffalump?"

Miki said, "Heffalumps have no place outside Esfandiary. They're too dangerous. Joey's is a human problem. I will try a human problem-solving strategy. Watch closely." Slowly, deliberately, he shrugged his thin shoulders, scratched his head human-fashion and spat over the edge of the cliff. He waited, but no insights came. Three human stress-gestures, all three worthless in a crisis, as Miki had oft suspected.

"That is an example of the human approach to problem-solving," he explained. "Now, let me concentrate . . ."

Hunkering down, Elf Miki shut his eyes firmly and marshalled his thoughts, projecting . . . seeking an answer to the symbol-problem . . . searching further for help, for insight . . .

And at the limit of his mental range, he found success! There *was* a solution to the Joey problem! What a lesson *this* would be! Miki resolved to write it up and present it to his supervisor, to demonstrate his competence.

"The symbol of Joey's religion has a name!" he exclaimed. "It is called PIZZA! And there is a temple on the other side of the mountain." Miki nodded to his apprentice; together they blinked out of corporeal form and headed north, toward the Snakeway on the other side of the Dromedary Mountains.

Thick, steel-grey clouds rumbled over the Dromedaries as if positioning themselves for battle against the two small figures huddled together against the wind. Elf Miki was anxiously mind-scanning the inhabitants of the few vehicles that ground their individual ways up the steep incline of the highway known as the Snakeway. Beyond the final switchback was the Pizza Pit, a fast-foodery that featured exotic combination pizza-pies. And a hundred yards beyond that, the exit from the Snakeway to Bumbler's Pass. That boulder-littered, deeply-rutted dirt road slithered treacherously down toward the Saddle between the twin peaks of the Dromedaries, then dropped precipitously to the valley floor and the northern entrance to Broco Way.

PIZZA. Neon signs flashed and sputtered. A storm was imminent and Bumbler's Pass would shortly be undriveable. It would take a brave person to bring the PIZZA to Joey. A hero. Windbreaker could do it; Windbreaker could do anything! Miki had heard of his underwater battle with the dread kraken! But Windbreaker was not here and the responsibility was Miki's. He needed a hero. Someone brave ... determined ... a hero ...

Most of the vehicles that passed his vantage point were large trucks. What little the mind-scanning elf could read in their drivers' thoughts and desires was distressingly similar to the belching black exhaust that polluted the air and was gradually choking the clusters of tiger lilies and dragonweed that bordered the Snakeway. Discouraged, Elf Miki was close to sending Rush into the Pizza Pit to beg for a sample of the deity—a direct intervention that would dash all hopes for promotion to a more prestigious post. Then he mind-scanned the occupants of an ancient black Plymouth sedan crawling up the Snakeway in first gear. This was the one! The male carried a grudge so basic to his life, so well-nurtured, that all it needed was reinforcement ...

"How come you slowed down, Augustus?" snapped Louise Vimstetter to her husband. "I don't like this road! Why didn't you take the Thruway like you used to? Once a year we drive upstate to visit my mother! Once a year, and you took this road just to aggravate me!" she whined.

Augustus Vimstetter's massive, work-hardened hands had tightly gripped the steering wheel of the Plymouth ever since entering the series of seven hairpin turns that gave the highway its name. The navigation of each switchback had been welcome, diverting his attention from the increasingly strident lecture of his dearwife Louise.

But halfway through the sixth hairpin turn, he had indeed slowed to a crawl and though his work-hardened eyes continued to pick out the roadway ahead, a new expression had suddenly fixed itself on the leathery skin of his work-hardened face. "Fret not, my lovebird," he said soothingly in a resonant bass. "Someday we will have a T.V. and you will have diversions other than listening to the lady downstairs screech of nights at her husband.

I daresay she has infected your sweet nature with her venomous reproachments upon the poor man.

"I drive the Snakeway tonight for two reasons. One, because I see it as a fitting way to prolong our recent visit. Two, it is free," he said slowly, thoughtfully. "Through no fault of our own, we are poor. Blinking, stinking poor. But soon, we will be rich. Deservedly rich. Filthy, stinking RICH!" he gloated as he took the last switchback and nursed the grumbling old vehicle into the driveway of the Pizza Pit.

It was a miracle! With no time for delicacies, Miki had churned the driver's mind, bringing the ancient grudge from its resting-place deep in the subconscious and mixing it with his Idea. Sure enough, the vehicle slowed, caughed and ground through the last switchback, then wheezed into the PIZZA temple. Two travellers emerged. When, minutes later, the larger one returned to the automobile with a stack of shallow, white boxes tied together, Miki glowed once, then vanished as the first drops of rain splashed onto his forehead.

Having left the Snakeway and crawled, belched and ground down Bumbler's Pass in low gear, the Plymouth suddenly ejected a final poop of soot-black smoke, and died. A string of exotic curses, *maladicciones,* issued from the driver's window. Then, from the defunct vehicle's glove compartment, Augustus Vimstetter took a powerful flashlight and an ancient AAA road map of the surrounding territory. A thick forefinger traced a dotted line down the side of the Dromedaries to the mouth of the Upper Muchness Valley . . . to the seldom-used, northern entrance to Broco Way.

"Can I open my eyes now?" Louise Vimstetter peeped in a tiny, frightened voice.

"Yo hoooo!" roared her husband in a stentorian bass, throwing open his door and stepping out into the rain and darkness. "Rigoletto here! Gilda! Gilda!" Augustus Vimstetter, broad-shouldered and barrel-bellied, paused but could hear no echo. Surely the cliffs extended this far north, or was his memory failing? It had been . . . twenty years . . .

From under the hood of the dying automobile came a final set of pings and one long groan, then it was over for the Plymouth. Reaching into the back seat of the dead car, he withdrew the stack of shallow, white, square pizza-boxes tied with many turns of string.

"You're crazy," his wife announced flatly as she cautiously emerged from the other side of the car. "The storm's getting worse; my knee's killing me. Not just cats and dogs, Augustus; it's gonna rain elephants! While you're pushing pizza slices into your gut, I'll be drowning here in the roadway. Maybe you'll spare two mushroom slices to cover my eyes."

Flashing his torch ahead into blackness, Augustus chuckled and said, "Louise, a long-delayed justice is just three miles down the road. Don't get worked up now."

"Worked up? Me? After that ride down the cliffside chased by thunder, lightning bolts and the devil himself . . . I've never been calmer." With one eyelid tic-ing spastically and the other eye wide open and fixed on her husband, she intoned woodenly, "Four pizzas, large. With anchovies. Mushrooms. Pepperoni and garlic. And . . . and the last one I never heard of . . . a gazpacho pizza! I step into the Pizza Pit ladies' room for one minute and you spend all our money on pizzas! Your greatest pleasure in life is tormenting me, Augustus! First you drive the Snakeway; now, if we ever get there, I suppose you're going to pay the bridge tolls with two slices!

"But I'm calm, Augustus. After all, it's not that we're going to starve to death. I'm sure there are wolves and bears in these woods. I think I just heard one!" she cried, shuddering.

Augustus roared with laughter, then measured off a distance on the map with the knuckle of his thumb. "There is but one predator of consequence in these woods. According to my oldest, most favorite map, three miles ahead, in the Valley of Upper Muchness, dwells a fox named Lucien Broco. The pizzas are an investment, to remind him of olden days . . . and an unpaid debt!

"God wanted me to sing, gave me the tools, but Papa remembered the Depression and said No! Do construction! And Papa was nearer than God, and maybe bigger. So twenty years ago, when I should have been singing *Rigoletto* at the Metropolitan, I was instead working up here at the edge of the world, making a palace for Lucien Broco!

"There were four of us in my crew. We lived on pizza and beer and slapped mosquitoes all night in our tent and bragged what we would do if we had Broco's money. While the muscles in my arms were shaping marble blocks for the grand vestibule of his mansion, my heart was singing *Verdi*!

"And one day, Mr. Lucien Broco stopped and listened! Eh, you hear, Louise? You ever hear the Broco-burger jingle? *A Million a Minute*? And that's just the tip of his fortune! Twenty years ago, Lucien Broco stood beside me, listened to my bass rendition of *Bebiamo* from *Traviata* and wrote the first Brocoburger jingle!"

Louise, dutifully, mechanically, recited her part of the oft-heard litany. "For which he tipped you twenty dollars, which you spent on busfare to New York for another audition. But Maestro Schwindler arrived half-crocked and fell asleep and you never got listened to and you ended up hitching a ride back in a cement truck owned by Lucien Broco."

"They should have heaved Schwindler into the sewer for the rats and baby alligators from Florida!" Augustus thundered. Then as the rain came down harder on his broad forehead, a smile hardened on the swarthy countenance of Augustus Vimstetter.

A branch snapped in the darkness and Louise nervously felt her way around the dead car. "So you'll sing in the shower like always," she said soothingly. "I'll applaud nice and loud and call for encores. Now it's coming down hard, Augie; turn on the flashlight. We'll have to walk back over the pass to the pizza place."

"No!" roared her husband. "As I drove up the Snakeway, it came to me that my star, my destiny was here, in Upper Muchness. This night Lucien Broco will eat pizza and drink beer and laugh and cry and he will again hear me sing Verdi. Then he will sign an agreement to underwrite my premier at the Metropolitan Opera House!"

"Just like that," Louise sneered. "I hope he has a pen."

"Just like that!" Augustus growled. "And if he refuses, and will not take a pen to his hands, I will tear off his finger and he will sign in his own blood!" Clamping his granite jaws tightly, he clutched the boxes beneath his left arm, snapped on the flashlight and started down the road. The faithful Louise limped behind, favoring her rheumatic knee and mumbling darkly.

As he stamped along, Augustus sang the high priest's invocation from Aida in his special key, for which the sixth sub-harmonic exactly matched the resonant frequency of the valley. Soon his powerful bass was joined by a distant echo, and then another, building in power until it seemed that the night-masked cliffs themselves would crack and splinter from the sheer accumulation of resonant energy. Drummed along by thunder and lightning, Augustus Vimstetter made his way south, toward the mansionhouse of Lucien Broco, toward justice.

*   *   *

Myron Blunger shook the cramps out of his writing hand and leaned back in the armchair. His head was buzzing and his back was stiff; time for a break. Windbreaker helped him to his feet and together they headed toward the Great Hall. Blunger would hike along that especially wide corridor for fifteen, twenty minutes, then drop into one of the regularly-spaced sofas to catch his breath while Windbreaker, needing more exercise, would take off at a fast canter, returning winded and glistening with sweat.

No sooner had the library door closed behind Blunger than a cloaked figure emerged from the stacks and approached the writing table swiftly but quietly. Ignoring the sheets of yellow lined paper on which Blunger was currently working, the Innkeeper focussed on the stack labelled Edited.

"Edited? Edited?" he muttered. Was that horse's ass calling himself an editor, now? Glowering suspiciously, he dropped into the armchair, squared the pages by dropping them edgewise on the table several times, and read the title.

THE PIZZA VENDETTA
by: A Committee

By a committee? Why was Blunger suddenly hiding behind a committee? What was he hoping to pull off now? The Innkeeper scanned the pages, nodded appreciatively at Blunger's fine sweep of penmanship, snorted at the plot line, which seemed too complex for the job at hand. And what was this? Mention of the Innkeeper!

THIS BLUNGER FROM THE BRONX DARED INSERT THE INNKEEPER—THE INNKEEPER HIMSELF—INTO HIS PUNY LITTLE STORY, TO BE MOVED AND JERKED AROUND LIKE A CHECKER PIECE!

Enraged, he snatched up the outline, read the first paragraph and his teeth ground. He read the second paragraph and his jaw muscles went into convulsions.

Yes, Blunger intended just that! The Innkeeper was to enter the story, supposedly to carry out a routine inspection, but actually to participate in the kidnapping of the boy! So that if it didn't work out, he couldn't blame Blunger!

Massive hands clenched as if gripping the shaft of a spear with which to spit Blunger from throat to anus! Oh, had Silver been right all along! Keelhauling was too good for the ingrate! But no spear was at hand!

But there was *Wildschweinblutmeister* in the armory, locked in its case. *Wildschweinblutmeister* . . . the great spear of Thor, discarded when the Norse god took up the hammer. And given by Loki (who didn't own it) to . . . to Brunnhilde!

A smile crept over the Innkeeper's grizzled face. Blunger was setting up for a visitor. A visitor he would have. The Innkeeper marched to his quarters, took the key to the armory from its secret place and proceeded into and through the stone-walled repository of weapons until he came to an iron-bound oaken door and there he halted.

Unlocking and throwing open the door, he lit a torch and approached the great spear *Wildschweinblutmeister*, which rested in its open case, awaiting a champion and a cause. He removed the weapon, ran his thumb over the edge of its triple-tempered head, heaved it onto his shoulder. Holding the torch before him, he marched the length of the armory, his footsteps echoing from the damp stone walls and arched ceiling. Past maces and bludgeons, swords and lengths of chain, racks of spears and lances, longbows, crossbows and countless other great and lesser weapons he marched until he arrived at a high door of iron, unbroken by knob, latch or key. Here he hesitated, listened; from within, he heard only a faint crackle, as of a low fire. Removing the spear from his shoulder, he reversed it and smote the door three times.

Boom! Boom! Boom!

The door swung open. Stooping to clear the doorway, he entered a high chamber of dwarf-crafted stone in the center of which was a raised bier surrounded by low orange flames. The Innkeeper hesitated, then took a step into the room. The flames shot up; the fire soared up toward the ceiling.

"Brunnhilde!" he called.

For it was she who lay dormant beyond the magic fire, her life suspended as it had been for half a thousand years while, clad in her shift, she awaited her hero's horn.

"Brunnhilde!"

Beside her were her sword and armor, to all appearances as untouched by time as though they'd been set down just moments ago while their owner took a brief nap.

"Brunnhilde!"

The form shuddered. The fire subsided. The eyes of the giantess slowly opened and life once again pulsed in her body. Lifting herself to a sitting position, she regarded the one who had summoned her. "*Sind Sie mein held?*" she asked, looking the Innkeeper up and down dubiously.

"*Sprechen Sie Englisch, bitte,*" the Innkeeper ordered, infusing her with the language with one pass of his right hand over her brow. "No, I am not your hero. You have been five hundred years on the marble bier, surrounded by the magic fire. You're entitled to a vacation."

"A vacation!" Her bosom heaved as her breathing deepened. Slowly, cautiously, she let herself down to the floor where she stretched her sturdy body to its full height, dwarfing the Innkeeper. "*Ach, eines vaca-tion.* It is good, yes." Slowly she bent her arms, her legs, sensibly easing back her circulation.

"I recommend the Valley of Upper Muchness," the Innkeeper said. "No more than a three day march away. And while you're there, I have a small request. There's a boy . . . a Joey Willem . . ."

How gut . . . good it felt to again carry a spear and stride in the clean air of the northlands with a sword at one's side! After tossing it some fresh meat, Brunnhilde had considered taking along the front-door cat with the big teeth, but it didn't take to the leash and she didn't intend to spend her first vacation in five hundred years looking after a stupid pussycat! Across the tundra she strode, with her armor fresh-burnished and her winged helmet sitting rakishly on her head. Her hair, of course, was a mess, though the girls in the trench—well, here it was indoors and they called it the *powzer* room—anyway, the girls had flattered her to the sky at the thickness and length of her golden braids. Except for some shrimpy blackheads who were beautifully, perfectly jealous. This was a marvellous place where her father, Wotan, had put her. She'd wanted to tarry a while with a mirror, trying out some of the new dresses, but they would have to be made up in her size and the Innkeeper wanted her to start her vacation immediately after lunch.

A marvellous lunch, but such an appetite she'd had! Brunnhilde threw her head back and laughed to think of it. Two waitresses serving, running back and forth to the kitchen with trays of food until they were dizzy! And the stories the Innkeeper told! Yes, he wanted this Willem boy back very much. And his boots! Above all, the magic boots, which a stupid griffin had dropped somewhere in the woods! But magic boots did not have to be searched for; the Innkeeper had assured her that she had only to call to them. They would come of themselves.

Of course, his story about a *pizza* was nonsense, but what did an Innkeeper know about dealing with upstart ten-year-olds? One does not give in to every whim! Pizza, yet, whatever that was! *Donnerkeil!*—a thunderbolt to the rear end was what the boy needed most! But that was the small part of it, and during lunch, the Innkeeper had filled her with the most improbable tales of this Valley of Upper Muchness. Elves and riches, glittering cliffs and somewhere about, even dragons yet! Oh, the girls in the trench— the *powzer* room—had concealed their jealousy! Chattering about *their* vacations. Paris. Rome. The naughty beaches at Cannes. Poor little house-cats . . . well, she would have a few things to tell them when she got back from Upper Muchness! And the Innkeeper had insisted that with all the doings, she must make it her business to get to know Myron Blunger! A charming fellow, not even seventy years old and with a youth's fondness for statuesque blondes. So much the better, she chuckled. Five hundred years . . .

Three days march, nonsense! Maybe three days for the ladies in the *powzer*-room who were afraid to stretch their legs something should fall out . . . a few hours and she'd be at the foot of the Dromedary mountains already. In fact, in the distance she could see dark clouds streaked with lightning. She stepped up her pace, anxious to get to her vacation before the rain soaked her braids . . .

THE DISH BEST SERVED COLD

by: The Same Committee

Lightning flashes and thunderbooms resounded throughout Upper Muchness; to the furies unleashed this night there seemed no end. The rattle of windows in the Hawkins house at number 7 Broco Way was unheard by Benison or Loretta; they were in Boston; Loretta, to do some shopping and search anxiously for her lost daughter Wilma, and Benison, to obtain, preferably at Harvard, a Letter of Testimony in support of his Theory and/or a strong bookcase to hold it.

In his bedroom on the second floor, Joey slept fitfully amid a tangle of blankets and sheets. He had struggled all afternoon with the math problem left by Uncle Benison to *massage his brain*, as the mathematician put it. His tummy was rumbling.

Myron Blunger, the star advice columnist of *The Postulate* was in his unheated room in the attic, wrapped in sweaters and blankets and plowing through a basketful of problems.

> *"Dear Myron: Is there any way film can be coerced, bribed or forced to reveal a latent image of a mythical creature? Mr. Lucien Broco is very upset over the pro-union bias exhibited by a certain roll of film."*
> *T. Interface*

Response-: Dear Constant Reader Interface: There are two answers to your profound question. a) No. Pro-union, left-wing, socially conscious film responds to stark black and white depiction of life's injustices. It is not to be used for trivial purposes such as photographing mythical creatures unless they're certifiably downtrodden. b) No. Right-wing, conservative film sees what it wants to see, in rosy-cheeked color.

> *"Dear Mr. Blungr: I answered all Mr. Hawkinses problems axept this one: If a man and a half take a day and a half to mow a lawn and a half, how long does it take a half a man to mow half a lawn? Also, he wants to know axactly where is the NEXUS to Esfandiary. Its not that I wont answer that. I cant, and not just because I dont really know what NEXUS means. Mr. Broco keeps bugging me, too. I cant, cant, cant! P.S. Thanks for all your teaching about life. Im sorry I cant go back to the inn with you but I cant. Some day if I come down to visit you in the bronx, will you take me out on a drug bust or to watch the Muggers? Will you buy me a 9mm. machine pistol? I hope so. Love and regards, Joey."*

Response-: Dearest Joey my son, Nexus means join and it means we should join forces to look for the boots. But not tomorrow; it's raining now and the woods will be soaking wet. We'll work out the Inn business, somehow.

Regarding algebra problems, whatever we're looking for, we call X. Half a man is X/2. Then . . . you don't mention hills. If the lawn has hills, call them Y. If it doesn't, then label each flat part Z. Now . . . if a man and a half . . . does it say whether the half a man uses half a mower? Do they start at the same time? Don't forget to add an hour for lunch. This is, of course, just an example because there's no such thing as half a lawn, any more than a woman can be half-pregnant. Either she is or she isn't, though the business of wombs for rent makes confusion there also. My guess is the half-man will finish right after lunch of the second day, including raking.

Myron peered out the window into country blackness; no streetlights, no headlights, no sirens, nothing. Just hailstones rat-tatting on the window. About to turn away, Blunger heard a sound that sent an anguished thrill racing through his heart. It was a Bronx sound. A home sound. A police whistle, shrilling in the night, again and again as if to taunt him in his despair. Myron threw open the window and stuck out his head.

A sheet of lightning illuminated the greensward littered with fallen branches and a figure crawling toward the Hawkins house frozen in the act of putting a whistle to its mouth. It was a stringy old man wrapped in a yellow oilskin slicker and clutching a large white object to his chest. It was Lucien Broco himself! Crabbing his way down the slippery lawn in defiance of his doctors, of wind, hail and lightning, his body limned by the wind-pressed slicker, the old man was making for the kitchen door.

"Oh, this is exciting!" screeched Rush from her sheltered perch in a hollow tree opposite the Hawkins house. "But who is this Lucien Broco and what does he have beneath his arm? A present? What happened between him and Augustus Vimstetter? And what about Joey? He's making terrible sounds in his sleep; I think he's hungry. And what . . ."

"Quiet!" Elf Miki pleaded. His eyes were screwed tight in concentration. "The boy cannot be hungry; he had a full dinner. This is the tricky part. The PIZZA reliquaries have made it to the valley, as I'd hoped, and have reached Lucien Broco, who is transporting them to number 7 to share them with Myron Blunger and Joey. But look over there! Vimstetter detected Lucien Broco stealing out the side door of his mansion and down the lawn toward number 7. Vimstetter is even now sloshing down the road with his poor wife in tow and is she angry!

"Vimstetter doesn't trust himself to negotiate the greensward; he's afraid it may be mined. So he's sticking to the road, which twists and turns. Eventually they'll reach the Hawkins house, but long after Lucien has arrived with the pizzas.

"But Broco's whistle is a signal for help! Soldiers, weapons . . .

"Oh, woe, what have I done? We must help Augustus Vimstetter reach number 7 in safety. Joey's anguish is undiminished and now he cries out for the symbols in his sleep!

"What is that!" the elf screeched, looking north. A lightning bolt had struck directly at the center of the Saddle and *had not blinked out*! It was growing . . . turning violet . . . was generating a fearful tornado-roar! A circle of purple fire appeared . . . the very air was afire . . . there was a thunderous crash . . .

"The barrier!" Miki cried, staring helplessly into a roaring vortex within the circle of fire. "Terror of terrors! The barrier is down! I must stay here! Fly, Rush! Fly! Find someone! Get help!"

Hurrying downstairs, Myron paused only to snatch a towel and a dry robe for Lucien Broco. No sooner had he reached the kitchen door than he heard one final, puny squeal from the abused whistle and the gentle, cushioned thud of an immensely wealthy person falling to the ground, exhausted. Unlocking the door, Myron tugged and pulled Broco's frozen, limp figure into the house. What could have caused the old man to abandon the warmth and safety of his mansion on such a night? Dried and changed into the robe, Broco started to shake with an amplitude and frequency more severe than could ever be attributed to physical exposure.

"Sanctuary! Sanctuary!" he whispered, snatching at his rescuer with one bony hand while thrusting the packages into Blunger's arms with the other. Myron realized that it was not rainwater that continued to stream down Broco's age-gullied cheeks. Those were tears, squeezed from glands dormant for countless years. Myron Blunger's heart went out to this neighbor in distress, and he cradled his head in the towel, both to absorb the wetness and to soothe the man's troubled heart.

"Sanctuary," he purred. "Here you are safe." But safe from what? he wondered. As soon as Broco was strong enough to totter, he moved him into the living room, sat him down on the sofa and wrapped the towel around Broco's head. Then, one at a time, he held Broco's packages to the light.

"Mushroom pizza made special to the order of Augustus Vimstetter . . . Best served Hot," he read aloud. Then, "Pepperoni and garlic pizza made special to the order of Augustus Vimstetter . . . Best served Hot. Pizza with anchovy . . . again Vimstetter . . . best served Hot."

The fourth pizza box was heavier and chill to the touch. "Gazpacho Pizza," he read. "Made to the order of Augustus Vimstetter. Best served . . . Cold." Myron solemnly placed it with the others, turned toward the towel and said, "Tell me, man to man, you own buildings? You have a hammer man, a specialist?"

A hammer man! The heart of Lucien Broco, all four chambers of which had ticked in proper sequence whether he was buying or selling, faltered. This was it, then. This Blunger, this so-called advisor, this scribbler of platitudes and homilies for the chronically insecure, was in fact the Angel of Death! As Broco's head tilted forward onto his scrawny chest, his chin hit his breastbone hard enough to re-synchronize his heart muscles. The darkness that had started to film his eyes receded. Life, confidence and strength were restored. He peeped from within the folds of towel, trying, by the light of occasional flashes of lightning, to read Blunger's face. Was it possible that this harmless-looking, bloated wanderer had, in fact, masterminded the invasion of his property by the arch-fiend Vimstetter as a first step in Broco's disembowelment? Could Blunger have sent the boy with his trick griffin to play on Broco's innermost yearnings?

The griffin! Trenton was probably right; the so-called griffin had been nothing but a long-shot offspring from an arranged liaison between an ambitious silver-crested eagle and a dozing lioness. A cheap gimmick. But the appearance of the stonecutter Vimstetter was no gimmick! It had drawn Lucien Broco from the safety of his fortified mansion to this unguarded living room, awaiting a booming knock on the door! As though he had a shortage of enemies in the world . . .

Blunger wanted an inventory of his real estate holdings! That, of course, would be only the start of it. Blunger, whoever he really was or represented, wouldn't stop until the keys to the mansionhouse jangled in his pocket, the access codes to the Cray IV were committed to memory and Lucien Broco was a-shivering in the road, huddled within the folds of a blanket . . .

No! He might be on the threshold of decrepitude, but Lucien Broco could still read faces! And Blunger's face revealed confusion and a primal fear of losing his appetite! No craft! Neither had Augustus Vimstetter designed this operation or Benison Hawkins; both were driven by other forces. But what about Vimstetter's companion? The harpy! *She* was the brains behind the affair! Broco *had to* trust Blunger! *Had to*! Soon enough would come the dread knock on the door . . .

"Man to man. Yes, I own buildings," Broco admitted. "A multibillionaire has social responsibilities, you know, and buying up buildings cheap and converting them to luxury apartments is one of my most important civic functions. These days, it's all done by computer, even evictions. No one uses a hammer any more. That way, if there's a legal problem, we let the software take the fall. Right now, I've got two hard-drive memories doing 60 to 90 days for alleged rent-gouging."

Then, pitiously, "Look, Blunger, I'll make a deal. Delay Vimstetter long enough for my henchmen to get here and you can have your choice of my holdings. Any building in New York. Plus the land," he added when Blunger didn't jump at the offer.

Blunger smiled and shook his head. "Everything you own, owns you. At my age, taking care of a building would be like taking care of an extra *tuchus*. With boils, yet; one for each tenant. You think I want twenty, thirty boils on my *tuchus*, Mr. Broco? It's the waterhammer! The waterhammer has to go. Will you send me your specialist to take care of my waterhammer? Yes, and it's a deal; I'll help you with your Vimstetter problem."

Broco nodded.

Satisfied, Blunger joined him on the sofa and said, "So talk."

Emotionally drained, his eyes closed, Broco talked. "My man Trenton was locking up for the night when he heard three knocks at the front door. Three loud, demanding knocks that reverberated from the marble halls of my vestibule and reached me in my chambers, cutting off an old man's tenuous thread to innocent slumber. I heard Trenton open the door to the chain's limit and accept packages—these packages—that were thrust inside.

"Trenton had the messengers wait in the vestibule and brought me the packages, which he'd assumed I'd ordered. So easily did Vimstetter pass through my gates and defenses! From behind a curtain I chanced a peek. I had to make certain, you know. But there was no doubt. Vimstetter is large and fierce of countenance, with powerful arms and shoulders. With him was a banshee, a harpy, a witch dancing widdershins. She looked likely to do murder with her eyes!

"By ruse, they had gained entrance. Vimstetter knows my dwelling better than I; he helped build it. I had no choice but to flee. Fool that I am; locks and chains are nothing to one who has successfully nursed a disappointment from minor irk to full-grown grudge. I dressed in the dark, snuck out the side door. Trenton would defend me to the death, but while he could handle any two of them, I fear that he is no match for Vimstetter plus harpy plus grudge."

Sheet lightning flashed through the window; Broco shielded his eyes and whimpered, "The last pizza, Myron. Best Served Cold! I did not have to look up the meaning of that. *Revenge . . . is the dish best served cold!*"

Thunder rolled on and on, echoing and crashing the length and breadth of the valley as though a long-awaited judgement were come at last. "Do you understand the nuances, Myron?" he pleaded. "*Best served cold!* denotes a straight revenge. But together with the three warnings: Best served Hot . . ."

"Three! Aha!" Myron Blunger cried, and with furrowed brow and eyes screwed shut, he concentrated on the interpretation. "There is, in the country of my people—the Bronx, just a block from the Concourse—a Mrs. Minsky. If there's one thing she knows, it's dreams and interpretings. Three! Three knocks at the door and three hot pizzas stand for the three beasts that guard the gates of hell and the three ways of getting there. The anchovy is a fish; drowning. Mushrooms . . . poisoning, very painful. And garlic pepperoni . . . fire. Not good, Mr. Broco. A terrible revenge. A complex revenge. A man goes to the trouble of engaging a witch, he means business. What does he want from you?"

Broco shuddered. "Money, no doubt. He is under the impression that I took somewhat from him with but modest compensation. And now he is come back . . . back . . ."

"Took . . . somewhat," Myron prompted.

"A song. A drinking song—*Bebiamo*—from an opera of Verdi, but sung in the sub-bass key of Lowest B, a key not in the standard classification. The human ear responds to music in that key with amplified responses that are no less than commands. *Bebiamo* is a drinking song; one does not drink without eating. A slight modification resulted in . . ."

"The famous, hypnotic Brocoburger commercial!" Blunger gasped.

"Yes," Broco admitted, wringing his skeletal hands. "My only personal masterpiece and the basis for my second fortune. And with Verdi eighty years dead and his works in the public domain, I pay no royalties."

"But why not simply give this Vimstetter a modest settlement?" Myron asked.

Broco recoiled. "It sounds simple, doesn't it? If I were but a millionaire, I could offer the man ten thousand and that would be the end of it. But I am worth billions, Myron. Vimstetter would not settle for less than ten million; no respectable lawyer would permit it! And once the word got out that Broco had gone soft, how many of my old . . . collaborators and their attorneys would be lined up for the like? Broco Way would be filled from horizon to horizon with claimants and their sharks! I would soon be penniless . . . Broco leaned close to Myron and dropped his voice to a whisper. "For myself, I no longer care. I won my race when I passed two billion. My final challenge was to direct the design of my trading program, MoreWealth. That proved successful, and I have no further interest in the whole thing. There is more at stake than money, Advisor. At stake is the most precious thing. Life! Life itself."

"To think that the boy Joey already knows this, and he is so young! I envy him his youth, his opportunities. I must have another chance at it! I will! And to accomplish this greatest of all adventures, I must have resources, and resources cost money!

"The doctors keep me alive with miracles, plastic tubing, mechanical joints and pills . . . fah! They've replaced everything except my spirit, and Vimstetter has come for that. And I fear he will have it, Myron," Broco said, despondently bowing his entowelled head. "The plan for dealing with Vimstetter is in place. My loyal henchpersons, summoned from their hovels in all corners of my landhold, have been provided with devices for music! They consititute a powerful band, powerful! Even now, Trenton is leading them on a northward sweep of the landhold.

"But Vimstetter has one weakness; he cannot resist Verdi! At this instant the upper valley resounds with Verdi. Vimstetter, attracted by the racket, would be lured to the Saddle, singing his head off. Interface switches to a Calypso limbo. Vimstetter goes under the pole, gets bashed with the tuba and falls from the Saddle into the whackleberry brambles below. An accident. Workman's compensation. A slow recovery in a sanitarium in Seattle. Very slow. That was the plan.

"But they will not find Vimstetter! It is my fault; I underestimated his arrogance! Trenton's sweep of the landhold is predicated on Vimstetter's following Henchman's Way, the servants' road! But as I fled across the greensward, I saw him and his medusa start up Broco Way, which is restricted to The Deservedly Wealthy, their sycophants and retinues! He has no *business* taking that road! Alas, the storm holds no terror for a man possessed. Vimstetter is come to destroy me! I whistle to summon the orchestra back before it is too late, before this very door booms thrice under the iron fist of Augustus Vimstetter."

"Such a thing!" Myron commiserated, shaking his head slowly, thoughtfully. "Well, I have a plan also. We will make a counter-move. We will light the oven and place all four pizzas inside, even the gaspacho. When Vimstetter shows up, he will observe our contempt for his warning."

Suddenly the wind ceased, the furious tattoo of hail on the windows diminished and a roll of distant thunder tapered off into the most-feared cry.

"Vendetta!" roared in a stentorian bass that sent a chill down Myron's spine. And again, even more powerful, as Vimstetter's subharmonic found the resonant frequency of the valley. "Vendetta!"

And one more—"*Vendetta!*"—rose in a crescendo above the fury of the storm, rivalling a thunderboom that shook every window in the house and brought Lucien Broco to his knees, whimpering. His head bowed nearly to the ground, Broco turned to his Advisor to Advisors and intoned in a hollow voice, "Is this to be my end? Sucked dry of blood and substance in a cold house not my own?"

Blunger shrugged his shoulders and nodded. "I guess that's it."

Broco stared, unbelieving. "'I guess that's it?' That's what you come up with? An Advisor to Advisors, a writer's writer . . . and that's the best you can do? Is that the meaning of life? At the finish, 'That's it?'"

Blunger pondered, stroked his chin, pursed his lips. A burst of wind rattled the windows. Blunger's eyes darted anxiously from darkness to darkness, then, "Aha!" he said, brightly. And again, "Aha!" followed by, "No, I don't believe it. It's too powerful, even for a Big Shot Landlord!"

"Believe what?" Broco screamed. "What's too powerful?"

Pointing outside, Blunger said, sagaciously, "Mr. Broco, have faith. Like Tevye's and Joseph's and Goldfarb's, mine eyes have been opened."

"Hold it!" Broco snapped. "Who's Goldfarb?"

"My butcher. He used to weigh the meat on paper, all together. No one noticed until I said, You're selling me wax paper, and at $3.80 a pound? You want me to write to the Weighing Department? So his eyes were opened and from that time on, he makes an adjustment.

"But that's not important," Blunger said excitedly. "It's *you* who's important here. You're interested in immortality. You've been a good person your whole life, and God has decided that you deserve another run.

"But how is the Eternal One to accomplish this, so that other folk won't be jealous and cry out He's playing favorites? Aha! The Lord works in mysterious ways. So . . . enter Augustus Vimstetter, who is not only a Dutchman, but is a direct descendent of the original Flying Dutchman and has inherited *the curse.* He is doomed to come to the valley every, let's say, twenty years to try to get what's coming to him. He can't help it. It's a curse, and curses take precedence, even over dying. Of course, the curse is no good unless you're here, also. So, because of his curse, you are doomed to live here forever, and once in twenty years, you'll have to put up with a terrible storm and Vimstetter hollering outside!

"What do you think?" Blunger offered.

From within the folds of towel a single eye blinked.

"Well, it's just an idea," Blunger said. "Maybe we should put the pizzas in the oven before they spoil."

The barrier, so recently weakened, had reopened. Whether it was due to this terrible lightning that was blasting the valley as never before, or to a collective Will from Esfandiary countering, nullifying the fragile thread of human belief . . . or to the anguish of Joey Willem rattling the foundations of reality . . . but this was no time to speculate on causes. Elf Miki was responsible for all life in the valley, and the boy came first! He had to be wakened immediately! For the third time, Elf Miki tried to slip out of this solid trap of a body in order to flit over into the house and the lad's mind. But the atmosphere was too charged with electricity to permit the change! Try as he might, he could not . . . *could not* do it and now he lay in the lee of an old larch-tree, helpless, dazed and weakened by his efforts.

A storm cloud that had drifted south, silently, ominously gathering electric charge, paused directly above the tallest tree in the area, which happened to be a larch whose wind-stripped branches waved proudly to its neighbors, for its trunk sheltered an elf, and how many trees in this neighborhood had ever had *that* honor?

Miki sensed an odd tingling in his hair, a strange sensation throughout his corporeal body, and leaped to his feet an instant before thirty thousand amperes of real current blasted the treetrunk, vaporizing the larch's fluids and creating a thunderous explosion that rent the air, uprooting adjacent saplings and blowing the elf's body a hundred yards through the air into the hedge that borders Broco Way.

A dozen feet above the hard rock of the Saddle, the air crackled, buzzed, sizzled as microorganisms were sucked into a vortex of highly convoluted tensor forces. A vertical halo of deepest violet appeared in space and within it, utter blackness dotted with tiny yellow flashings. Into the center of the halo drifted a pearly-white sphere; it floated, suspended by alien forces, hesitated, then retreated hastily as though something formidable were approaching it from behind.

Through the valley of Upper Muchness, the creatures of Earth Real, sensing the change and impending danger, backed into the deepest parts of their dens and nests, their young behind them. Neck-hairs bristled, ears were pressed flat to the head, teeth bared and claws extended, but there was more whimpering than growling, for an alien thing had come to the valley.

A king griffin, golden crest flared for battle, was the first to come through, leaping earthward catlike, than extending its powerful eagle wings and soaring up with powerful strokes, screaming its lordship of all winds, its contempt for all earthly storms. Then came another, a female, larger but uncrested. Si-

lently she joined her mate. Then it was as if the storm on
Earthside had condensed, concentrated itself into that aperture into the otherworld. With a volcanic roar, a bull minotaur
came to the opening and leaped through, shaking the ground
with its landing. Its sharp-horned bull-head was set on a mas-
sively-muscled, coarse-haired, naked humanoid trunk. Opening its jaws, it roared until the surface crystals embedded in
the obsidian cliff shattered.

Once more it bellowed, then it sniffed the air and its eyes
glowed red. The traitorous wind of Earth, normally blowing from
north to south in all seasons, had freakishly reversed itself and
revealed to the slavering creature the presence in this lush valley of
warm body-juices. The monster broke into a ground-thudding
lope, sniffing, drooling and working its jaw-muscles.

Rush was lost, lost in the dark forest and frightened. *Find
someone!* Miki had commanded. Unable to fly because of the terrible lightning, and not knowing the way in any case, she had
dashed from tree to bush to hollow log only to end up soaking
wet, shivering and sniffling, her back pressed against the damp,
cold wall of a shallow cave that had promised refuge from the
storm. To her left was the narrow entrance, through which rain
and hail slanted in bursts as though Nature were trying to dissolve, drown, do away with the intruding elflet.

Stumbling blindly through the cave entrance, she had not
dared venture far inside, lest an animal follow her in and trap her.
She was lucky to find this shelter, for it was not foul and musty
and filled with ugly spiders like some caves were. On the contrary,
the air was sweet, probably due to the pine needles that covered
the rocky floor. Now she peered to the right, into the darkness,
and saw a cluster of little crimson lights, not close, not far. They
seemed to be regularly spaced and blinking, though in no particular order. Like a family of fireflies all dancing together in the air,
flashing against the darkness slowly, steadily, lending each other
support. There seemed to be ten of them—no, twelve—blinking

steadily, not moving. How many were there? If Rush went a little closer, she could see them better in the dark. She leaned forward. Fireflies, and now they were moving. Together. Swaying from side to side. Together. It was hard to concentrate. The elflet's eyes felt heavy. She'd never stayed humanoid this long . . . humanoid bodies required sleep, didn't they? Maybe she should take a nap while the storm raged . . .

The crimson dots were the eyes of a land-squid, which captured its prey by hypnosis followed by enfoldment, a quick bite at the neck-artery and a complex series of injections and wrappings that preserved the meat for months. The squid was patient and relied heavily on the curiosity of its visitors. For so long as the prey looked directly at it, the squid would entertain it with its luminous eye-blinks. How many eyes were there? Which would blink next? At the proper time, when its guest was off-guard and relaxed, the creature would creep slowly forward, position itself, jump and bite.

Enfolding could take a day for a victim the size of a fox or a bear cub. This one wouldn't take more than a few hours.

Rush's elfen eyes, though half-closed, were adjusting to the darkness and now she discerned the outline of the swollen body in which the flashing lights were set, and the tentacles draped across the floor of the cave. Oh, the cave was home to a creature after all; a creature that had carpeted it with pine needles, which must be fresh by their sweet aroma . . .

One tentacle moved, then another. Slowly, toward her. Now the crimson eyes were blinking in a regular pattern; the creature had started forward! It was large, of uncertain shape with eyes and tentacles and a beak for nipping.

She screamed, a piercing screech that halted the land-squid's advance, but only momentarily. Now *all* the tentacles were moving and she could hear the pulsing of the squid's breathing apparatus. It stopped, swayed slowly, slowly as it gauged its final leap! The longest tentacle was crawling toward the entranceway to bar escape; the elflet jumped over it, darted to the entranceway, leaped outside and was grabbed around her slender waist by something rubbery, sinewy, cold and strong! Her screams were cut off by another tentacle coiling about her throat! She tried to change form, but there was still too much electricity in the air! Her little eyes opened wide with terror and then something flashed before her that was *not* lightning!

It was a tree shaped like a human leg, a lady's leg, and above it, a sheet of linked metal plates that reached up, up and shimmered and glowed and buzzed with electricity. Rush's eyes, wide with terror and wonder, flew upward. The tree *was* a leg, and the sheet was the skirt of a lady, a giant lady whose body soared high above the tree-branches! In her left hand was a torch, in her right, a spear. The grip on Rush's throat relaxed as her captor assessed this intrusion into its world.

"Help! Help!" the elflet cried.

"Who calls?" a voice boomed out over the storm. "Who is down there calling help, help? Answer me!" the voice thundered from high up. "Also, which is the way to Upper Much-ness?" The torch descended in a great arc, but was still high above Rush's head.

"Help!" Rush screamed, for the tentacle about her waist was tightening.

The sheet of chain-mail clanked; the tree-leg tilted, a head appeared, a lady's head descending to the ground together with the torch. "Oho!" boomed a voice, and the great spear *Wildschweinblutmeister* swung once, shearing off two of the squid's tentacles. As the thrashing monster pulled its bulk back into the safety of darkness, Rush tumbled onto the ground and half-stumbled, half-rolled down a rain-soaked hill until she was stopped by a huge sandal-strapped foot and ended up face-down in a mud-puddle.

Brunnhilde, having eased herself down to a hunkered position with back erect, was groping blindly in the mud and would probably have missed or squashed the creature had the elflet not flopped over her foot. Grasping it around the middle, she pulled it free with a *shlurp*, pulled herself erect and hoisted the little noisemaker high, high into the air to see by torchlight what kind of creature was making all that yelping.

"*Donnerwetter!*" she exclaimed. "It is a talking mud-rabbit, then?" For so mud-covered and waterlogged was poor Rush that she could easily have been mistaken for any manner of swamp-thing.

"Not a rabbit at all!" the elflet sputtered, wiping her face with the drenched apron of her taffeta dress. Freeing her eyes, she opened them to find herself encircled by an enormous hand and being stared at by eyes the size of the elflet's entire face. "I'm Rush," she squeaked, "and I was sent by my master and teacher to get help but I got lost and Lucien Broco's henchmen are going to fight with Vimstetter and there's trouble with the barrier and Miki . . ."

Catching her breath, she asked, "Who are you?"

"Brunnhilde," replied the giantess calmly. "You chatter very prettily. I understand nothing, of course, but that does not matter." Peering wondrously at the elflet, she smiled and said, "You are a woman and I am a woman *and* a Valkyrie and we must stand together against the hardness of the world, *nicht wahr*, little one? Of which-speaking, forgive me for picking you up so; I could not bend over to see with the torch. My neck has stiffened; I cannot bend at all. I have been five hundred years asleep on a bed of stone."

"Five hundred years! Bed of stone!" Rush squeaked.

"It was not my idea," the Valkyrie stated without elaboration. "But you look a sight; we must get you cleaned up! Do you know the way to the Valley of Upper Muchness, then?"

The elflet shook her head sorrowfully. "I'm lost, also. Lost and cold and . . ." She started to weep.

"Hush, child!" commanded Brunnhilde. "Listen; I hear battledrums. And where there are battledrums, there is civiliza-tion."

Indeed, between peals of thunder one could discern in the distance a beat of drums, muffled by the dense forest but regular, steady and martial. Brunnhilde's eyes sparkled. "You will ride on my shoulders, little one, holding onto my braids and shielding yourself under the wings of my helmet. Here; dry yourself off and wrap this around before you catch a sniffle." And the Valkyrie produced a large enough pocket handkerchief to serve the elflet as a doubly-folded blanket.

Soon enough they were striding through the forest, the torch held high and the great spear *Wildschweinblutmeister* slung under the Valkyrie's arm. From the throat of the giantess came a song with which the forest soon resounded. It was a riding song, a battle song, Brunnhilde explained, and she sang it again and a third time and Rush, somewhat dried off and her spirits restored, joined in the chorus, "To, ho! Yo, ho!"

The drums grew closer and finally the Valkyrie and her new friend marched out of the forest onto a low hill. Before them were dozens of lights, lanterns and torches, borne by lines of men moving slowly, cautiously along a narrow country road. Some carried wooden clubs, some carried coiled lengths of rope. And all carried musical instruments. There were horns, cornets, a glockenspiel, a whole section of woodwinds, kettledrums mounted on a small cart, a large conga drum and, to Brunnhilde's delight, a grand tuba, which she pointed out to Rush. "But it is a parade, my little one!" she cried in delight. "Imagine, we arrive without reservations or advance notice and despite the terrible weathers, we are greeted with a grand parade! How wonderful is this Upper Muchness Valley! Come, let us descend and join them! Perhaps I will find the *held*—the hero—I am seeking."

But Rush, for the second time that day, was struck dumb. For her elfen eyes discerned, in the darkness beyond, three terrible shapes moving directly toward the unsuspecting band of humans.

From Esfandiary they were! A griffin! Two griffins!

And a bull minotaur!

THE BATTLETUBA

by: the Committee Myron Blunger, chairman

The same wind that carried Joey's spoor to the minotaur transmitted Broco's whistled instructions to Trenton Interface. Wheeling the orchestra about required but one sharp command—"Wheel . . . About!" Then, "Stand by, Hedley."

"Calypso Variations in A minor?" Hedley asked, hopefully. To the fingers of his left hand, he'd affixed lightweight bamboo drumsticks, the better to rap out the intricate counter-rhythm of the Variations. His strong right hand kept up a steady *boom/ta da/ boom* on the bass drum, which preceded him in a cart drawn by two henchbearers. Morris Hedley's steady drumbeat was the key to the orchestra's superb coordination, especially in a raging storm; Trenton was fortunate to have him on his team.

"Not yet," Interface said, thumbing the pages of a waterproof Plan book. "Plan A called for a left sweep across the Saddle. But Plan A is kaput. Interception is projected at number 7 Broco Way, which corresponds to Plan . . . Plan B! A direct convergance on the Hawkins house, *then* the calypso samba with a limbo beat. As you were, Hedley!"

The drummer saluted and continued flexing his left wrist, keeping it limber for the action to come. From the warbly tone and lack of timbre in the final tootle of Broco's whistled message, Hedley surmised that Vimstetter was large, strong and desperate; he must be taken by surprise. Hedley's right-handed drumbeat paced the *Soldier's Chorus* from *Trovatore* as the orchestra doubled back toward the elusive Augustus Vimstetter.

"Monsters, sir," reported Hedley between bangs. "At eleven o'clock and closing."

Hedley had superb night vision; if he saw monsters, then monsters there be. But sometimes even the reliable Hedley neglected vital information. "Monsters in what key, Hedley?" Interface demanded.

"D," Hedley replied instantly as one of the griffins screamed into the teeth of the storm. "King Griffin, male." Yes, Hedley had perfect pitch; you could rely on his D.

Interface raised the tuba to his blistered and swollen lips and blasted out the opening bar to the *Triumphal March* from *Aida*, maintaining it until the entire orchestra had picked it up in D. But no sooner had the ensemble synchronized itself than there was a great bellow in the eleven-fifteen direction and coming fast!

"Minotaur in C-flat, sir!" Hedley reported.

"Minotaur takes precedence," Interface called after a brief consultation with his pocket guide.

"Correction: C-sharp, sir!" Hedley called out. "Rogue bull minotaur enraged from hunger and sexual frustration, begging your pardon, sir."

"Very good, Hedley," Trenton replied admiringly. "By the way, where did you . . . learn these . . . fine distinctions."

"Myron Blunger, sir. Brilliant new advice columnist on *The Postulate*. Subtle. Speaks entirely in parables. Excellent use of subways as metaphor." So well trained was Hedley that he did not miss a step as three huge forms closed in at his right.

"Ah, finally the road comes! Wotan blast these sandals!" Brunnhilde growled, cautiously feeling her way down the hillside with her spear handle. "My feet are killing me. And my neck is stiff as *Wildschweinblutmeister*, I cannot look down. I cannot bend it at all! At the spa I will take a good Swedish massage, I think. Exactly where is the parade, dear? Oh, these breastplates must weigh fifty kilos apiece!"

From the cover of the helmet-wings, Rush piped, "The parade's coming up now! I see two griffins and a minotaur but I don't see

Miki anywhere! Oh, there's going to be a terrible battle! I'd better get down!"

"You stay right there, dumpling," the Valkyrie commanded joyously as she hefted the spear. "If there's fighting, you must be my extra eyes. Two griffins and a minotaur! How wonderful! Much better than the usual filthy boars. What a marvellous vacation place is this Upper Much-ness!" Leaning *Wildschweinblutmeister* against her shoulder, the giantess modestly turned her body away from the approaching line of torches, tugged upward on her breast-plates and tightened their leather straps.

"Maybe you should remove them altogether," Rush suggested.

"But I cannot," Brunnhilde said sorrowfully. "It goes with the stone bed and the magic fire. It is a package curse Wotan has laid on me. Only a kiss from a *held*, a hero, can help. One kiss and they fall off. I tell you, to be a woman is a hard business." Stooping stiff-backed, she reached beneath her mail-skirt and withdrew a package that had hung from her girdle during the entire march from the Inn. As the parade reached them and three huge shapes closed in on the far side of the road, Brunnhilde proudly unwrapped and slung over her shoulders a black battlecloak on which a pair of golden horns were embroidered. Fastening it at the throat with a jewelled clasp and hefting her great spear proudly, she marched into the roadway just as the conga drum drew alongside.

"How do I look, dumpling?" she whispered.

"Great!" Rush exclaimed. "Beautiful!"

"Thank you. Later you will help me with my hair; I may have to cut off the braids. I have it firsthand from some ladies in the powzer room that in Paris they were wearing it shorter just twenty years ago. Now, as for you, it is better you crawl under the collar where it is dry and warm, and just peep out with your eyes. And keep alert for my *held*, dear. *Funfhundert Jahren! Mein Gott, such a curse!*" she muttered.

The Minotaur

{This is too important to be relegated to a small-type footnote. Besides, it is interesting.

The behavior of the minotaur can only be understood in the context of its personal history. Poseidon gave Pasiphae (the wife of Minos of Crete) a white bull as a house-gift. Apparently she took it too seriously and some time later, produced the minotaur. Despised and rejected from birth, this hybrid (a bull's head on an outsized, muscular male human body) was promptly consigned to an enormous but unlit labyrinth beneath the palace. Without the benefit of a sound cultural heritage, of occasional companionship (other than the annual tribute in youths and maidens which constituted its principal diet) or even a modest library, reading lamp and supply of oil, it passed its free time in that pitch blackness by attending to the growth and development of its penis. At the time of its translation to Esfandiary (the minotaur, that is, not just the penis), his organ surpassed in size even those of the largest mastodons that roamed the Lesser Plain, and was comparable with those of the *tyrranosaurs* that populated the Greater Plain in Esfandiary.

Superiority, however, never fails to exact a price. The amount of blood required to inflate this penis, 28 percent of the minotaur's total body supply, so severely depleted the flow to its brain that when properly aroused, it could not *think* at all, not even in the most rudimentary sense of that word. Specifically, it could not alter whatever course of action in which it was currently engaged.

This is mentioned here only so that the creature's subsequent behavior is understood in the light of an upbringing and physiological limitations not of its own making, and (for the benefit of future Ph.D. candidates seeking thesis material) the minotaur is *not* a proper subject for psychological analysis or deconstructionist gobble-de-gook! Thank you.}

The minotaur, lumbering heavily beside the road with the griffins in tow, kept to the shadows and toyed with its options: a particularly chunky henchman busily tootling a woodwind, or one of the drummers who appeared well-fed and succulant. Then, across the road, it spotted a giant female striding along with her head high and boasting a magnificent pair of headwings! All thoughts of food vanished. The half-man, half-bull lowed seductively.

"Tum tum TUM de Tum!" Hidden from human eyes and the weather beneath the collar of Brunnhilde's battlecloak, the delighted elflet clapped in time with the conga drum. Forgotten for the moment were her own discomforts and her failed mission. "Boom Rata Boom! Boom Rata Boom!" she screeched, delirious with the glory of it all. But her keen eyes darted this way and that and still there was no sign of Elf Miki. He *must* have spotted this parade. Perhaps he was at the house, taking care of the boy.

"When I tell you, look to the right, dear child," Brunnhilde whispered excitedly. "Not yet. With the bottom of my eyes I saw a magnificent pair of horns glinting in the torchlight! Is it . . . is it *mein held* at last? Do not stare, dumpling—One does not stare at a *held!*—but look well and tell me . . . is he . . . large? Has he a *heldenbuild?* Do not stare!"

Before Rush could try to follow these directions, which she did not understand in the least, a new sound filled the air. It was the third *Vendetta!* They had arrived at number 7 Broco Way and their quarry was at the door.

"This is it, Louise!" Augustus Vimstetter said. "Between us and justice is only an ordinary wooden door." The worker of stone smiled grimly as he gauged the lock, the hinges, the thickness of the wood panels. He had good hands, and on a summer day with no pressing obligations, would have enjoyed gaining entry by removing the lock, the hinges at his leisure, humming while the trapped Broco pleaded from within. But a grandfather of storms raged about him, and Louise was not adjusting well to this detour in their routine.

There was a tug at his belt. Louise again. She seemed to be shrieking more loudly then usual; something about *behind*, which was foolish as Lucien Broco and justice and retribution so clearly lay *ahead*, and only by the thickness of a lousy wooden door at that! Perhaps she needed music, he decided, and humming the opening bars of *La Donna e Mobile*, Augustus Vimstetter ignored her passionate begging to please look behind them, just for an instant!

The door was a standard wooden front door, no more than a half-inch thick at the panels, perhaps an inch and a quarter through the stiles . . .

Vimstetter inhaled deeply. His fury increased! There was no doubt of it; they were heating up a hickory-fueled oven for his pizzas! *His* pizzas! Oh, it would feel good to choke the arrogance out of that man! And to make it worse, with all the marching and singing, Vimstetter had built up quite an appetite . . .

The best way with this door was to simply run at it and shoulder it open. Vimstetter backed up, lowered his head . . .

Crouched behind the sofa with only his eyes and forehead poked up, Myron Blunger peered with no hope at the terrifying scene beyond the picture window. Lucien Broco's nemesis, head down, was about to ram through the front door. As though that weren't trouble enough, there, beside him in the torrential rain, was what Broco had called a harpy. Broco was wrong; it was a water-sprite. Blunger's Great-aunt Bella had been born and raised in Romania—"Cimpalung!" she would cackle, rocking slowly, her crochet needles clicking at the nine-year-old, fascinated, delightfully terrified Myron. "*Dracula country!*" she would hiss, and then launch into her story about her encounter with the notorious vampire.

Aunt Bella had knowledge of *all* supernatural creatures! She had, by the time she was only *nineteen*, encountered and bested them all! Werewolves, vampires, ghouls, witches . . . and water sprites.

So, thanks to his childhood tutelage, Blunger knew how to watch a water-sprite. The eyes were the giveaway. If this one started to stare at him, Myron Blunger would have to retreat to the kitchen and search for garlic before it got out of hand.

Suddenly, out of the darkness appeared burning torches! Dozens of them marching on the house! And drums! Music! They were saved! It was Lucien Broco's hench-orchestra, marching in step to a highly syncopated rhythm! And in the midst of them, whacking away at a huge conga drum, was a German warrier-lady complete with spear, armor, winged helmet and encrested cloak! Blunger had never observed a German warrier lady at such close range, and a second look resulted in enlightenment and astonishment such as Blunger had never experienced in the Bronx, in the Inn at the End of the World or in a lifetime of reading and telling stories. The reason for the Germans' propensity for battle was that they had *two sets of eyes!* Yes, there beneath the collar of her cloak, was a second set of eyes, smaller than her primary pair set in her face, but quicker, too! They were darting around this way and that way!

No wonder the warrier-lady appeared so radiently confident, so *immune* to the possibility of defeat! This was the secret behind teutonic self-assurance!

But what was that! There, in the shadows, restlessly pacing the edge of the surrealistic scene, were three hulking shapes with predator eyes that glittered in the torchlight. A sheet of lightning illuminated the valley from cliff to cliff. The three shapes . . . griffins . . . not one, but two of them! The third shape . . . the most terrible of all . . . a walking nightmare . . . words buried deep in Blunger's subconscious burst forth to attack his mind . . . '*bust out of the closet and eat you up if you don't go to sleep right now!* Eileen the babysitter when he'd been five and *didn't want to* go to sleep! Myron scurried into the kitchen and did not hear Louise Vimstetter scream into her husband's ear, "Augie! There are things behind us that you should know about!"

But Augustus Vimstetter was past discourse, past reason, past rage; he had slipped into singlemindedness. "When we're rich, we'll go to a marriage counselor!" he bellowed. "Broco! Open up; it's Vimstetter here! Listen!" But his rendition of the Brocoburger jingle was lost amid the strong beat of the conga drum and the Calypso Variations, a samba Trenton had composed in anticipation of this long-awaited moment.

Let's do / the Rigoletto limbo

The duke's got rocks and Aida rolls; native beer tastes best by firelight, Send the fat man under the pole!

Two gaily-costumed henchpersons carrying a brightly-colored limbo pole rushed forward on either side of Vimstetter. Dancing to the strong calypso beat, laughing and singing, they dropped the pole before him and pressed it up beneath his chin, forcing his head back. He passed beneath it, started to rise only to find it again beneath his chin and lower . . . and again, forcing him to arch backwards, spread his muscular legs to the sides for balance . . .

The final pass left Augustus Vimstetter, dumbfounded, bent nearly double, his face lifted to the rain and darkness and a large brass object swiftly descending upon his head.

Louise threw herself over her husband's helpless form in a desperate attempt to save his life, even at the possible cost of her own. With a final, "I told you so!" she tensed for the fatal blow.

Now the minotaur had a clear run to the door. From the periphery, it had gazed upon the giantess with growing adoration and lust. What a figure! The minotaur, however, was clever enough to perceive the need for a proper wooing. The answer to that was the soft, aromatic young flesh of the creature within the dwelling. The bull-man pawed the ground for footing, took a deep breath and charged. Thudding over the ground with head lowered, it smashed through the door as though it were made of spiderwebs, slipped on a scatter rug embroidered with a *Philadelphia A's* logo, skidded on an empty white box and plowed directly into a plaster wall of superb rigidity and stubbornness. His horntips penetrated the house-wiring and soon enough he had three hundred milliamperes at one twenty volts passing from his left horn, through his rudimentary brainpan and exiting through his right horntip. The flow of electrical energy happened to encounter the minotaur's *singularum*, the seat of its id, amplifying the creature's lust by a factor of thirty. Slowly, because it was enjoying itself, it pulled its horns free, shook the excess charge from its brain and tried to orient itself. Its thought processes were starting to slow down but it managed to turn its massive head toward the entrance just as Brunnhilde stooped low to clear the transom. From this angle, her figure was even more exquisite!

Thinking ceased. The minotaur sat on the floor, its huge bull-head swaying slowly from side to side, trying to fit two thoughts into a brain that could barely accomodate one. The minotaur needed a wooing present. The spoor of the delectible youth was strongest by the stairway. The two concepts grappled for primacy and, as blood continued to flow south, merged into one sustainable concept. The minotaur would go up the stairway, impale the youth on its horns and drop the sweet, dripping carcass at the feet of his beloved. Then he would rape her in the fashion she deserved and expected. But so limited was its thinking capacity by then that the mechanics of rising and propelling itself upstairs would take a few moments . . .

As Brunnhilde stooped to enter the dwelling, Rush dashed out from her hiding place beneath the collar of the battlecloak. She had to find Miki! Crawling and scrambling, she clambered up the steep stairway one step at a time, arriving at the top exhausted, sweaty, dishevelled, only to discern no trace of her mentor upstairs or, casting her thoughts further, anywhere in the house! Well, surely he'd be along and he must not find his disciple in such a dirty state! She would have to wash up as humans did, and fortunately there was a room for that, and with the door open.

Brunnhilde straightened up in time to see only the torso and legs of her *held* running up the stairs, his head already out of view. *Mein Gott!* He was already naked! And what a *heldenbuild!* A bit hairier than she'd expected, but good muscles and . . . big! Big was good. But why was he running upstairs? Was he preparing for the tryst? Would he come down right away? Well, she couldn't be seen standing around like a ninny! For her *held*, she wanted to appear feminine. Feminine. Striding into the living room, she spied an old man cowering there, his head wrapped in a towel. Yes, a towel! Excellent! Saying, "Thank you," she took it and started around the room, dusting. Feminine.

"Great place for a party!" she bellowed, in case her *held* was listening, though in fact the fireplace was absurdly small; one couldn't possibly squeeze a spitted ox into that little hole in the wall. "Well, come in, come in!" she called, and the griffins entered, wings carefully folded, perhaps intrigued by this humanlike creature with eagle wings on her head. Before they could start sniffing around and making a mess, the giantess affectionately stroked their neck-feathers and, after whisking a layer of dust from the mantelpiece with the towel, positioned the griffins on opposite sides of the fireplace, legs gracefully folded beneath their lion bodies, their beaks on a level, just so. Very symmetric, and they added style to the modestly-furnished room.

Myron, in the kitchen, had slid the pizzas into the heated oven and was busily rotating them lest they cook unevenly, and pointedly ignoring the general clamor. Sophie was right; don't get involved! Three hot pizzas times eight slices made twenty four slices. The large woman . . . she'd be good for three slices, maybe four. Vimstetter, three. He was just outside the kitchen and making a terrible racket! A Brooklyn boy, no doubt of it! Two slices for Joey. The water sprite . . . hard to say. On the skinny side . . . figure one slice. The griffins in the living room . . . maybe go for the gazpacho . . .

Plan B had called for the rim of the tuba's bell to connect with Vimstetter's skull directly across the Greater Lateral Fissure. If done properly, the force would be transmitted to the *honoris causa* three centimeters below, with sufficient strength to erase Vimstetter's entire package of old grudges plus such items as how to waltz and the laws of heraldry, for which Broco was quite prepared to make adequate restitution. Deflected slightly by his wife's heroics, however, the bell of the instrument had dropped squarely over Augustus Vimstetter's head with great force, forming a press-fit of incredible tightness. A standard tuba would never have held Vimstetter; the built-in escapement would have effected his immediate discharge. But this was a battle-tuba, and there was no escapement. Blinded and panicked, Vimstetter crawled into the house, his wife riding full astride and steering him with rump-slaps to the right or left, whichever seemed more likely to keep them farthest from the griffins, which, uneasy at the closeness of the room, were trying to spread their wings.

Vimstetter, tenaciously roaring the *Vendetta* in a new, even lower key with enormous amplification, paused at the threshold of the kitchen and rose to his full height. The tuba, hitting the ceiling, was pressed onto his head even more firmly; Louise fell off and rolled into a neutral corner as, roaring with fury, Augustus groped blindly around the kitchen until his left hand encountered the hem of a terrycloth robe. A damp terrycloth robe. Slowly, lightly his fingers walked upward until they discerned an object beneath that material. A skin and bones object with the general structure, convolutions and protrusions of a head.

An obscenely wealthy head.

JUSTICE

by: Myron Blunger (Windbreaker being otherwise
engaged)

Augustus Vimstetter's sledgehammer left hand was brought to the aid of its mate and together they clamped, immobilized, captured that object with the general structure, convolutions and protrusions of a head. It attempted to slip away, but the stonecutter's grip held firm. A desperate attack by a set of false teeth, powered by Swedish-steel microsprings, failed miserably; Vimstetter dislodged the teeth with a single fingerflick and they flew out and away.

The object gurgled. Stonemason hands pulled it close and with appropriate care, completed their tactile investigation of its main features.

"The pizzas meant nothing to you?" Vimstetter roared from within the bell of the battletuba.

"Nuvvink!" Broco choked out between his naked gums. "I'm nok allood ea piba! Ony cowage cheece and oa'meal. Go 'way."

"I will go!" Vimstetter snarled and the muscles of his forearms throbbed with an organic need for vindication. "But first I will have *justice!*"

Broco's head bobbed up and down within Vimstetter's grip. "Wuspish. Vewy goob. How mush wuspish? A thouvand dollarv? Dwendon wiw wib it a you. You 'ememberb goob ol' Dwendon from ve ol' dzays, eh?"

"Not wuspish, Mr. Broco! Vimstetter bellowed. "I ... will ... have ... JUSTICE!"

"Huspive. How mush?" Broco bleated.

"Full measure!" Vimstetter roared. "You will subsidize a new production of Rigoletto at the Metropolitan Opera in New York City and I will premier in the title role."

"Ageed," Broco gasped, trying fruitlessly to loosen the iron grip on his head.

"You will provide for my goodwife, Louise. A pair of white dress shoes from Macy's, a fancy gown with lace and beads and other diddles such as may please her. Washable, mind! Something for her head . . . a brooch or a snood or . . . a pin. Yes, a pin. And a box seat smack in the middle with a crate of roses to throw."

"Shoov, gowm, a pin, a cate of rovev . . . to frow," Broco gasped. "Yef and yef," he whispered. "Whipe rovev to frow. I am chokig. Lep me go."

Vimstetter contemptuously dropped the old man but Louise caught him before he could scuttle away in search of his dentures. "Sign here!" she snapped coldly, handing Broco a pen and a piece of brown wrapping paper with the terms written in shorthand.

Broco's eyes glittered with fury but Augustus Vimstetter's hands were too near, too powerful and Trenton Interface was outside, apparently supervising the disbanding of the orchestra. Broco glanced into the living room. His eyes fell upon the griffins. Could he count on them? Were they perhaps related to the Dreyfuss lion? Management symbols . . . stick together and all that . . . but how to communicate his plight without his teeth in place? No, it was hopeless. Hunkered down on either side of the fireplace, their wings folded, they'd fallen into a trance.

Lucien Broco signed the agreement.

To the elflet Rush, the minotaur had been only one of the usual dangers of Esfandiary. Not for herself, of course; in her other form, she had merely to think herself elsewhere and it was so. But for her charges, for the countless souls of Earth-children she'd shepherded in their night-ventures through the dreamworlds of Esfandiary. How many times had she plucked a fluttering little patch of curiosity, nearly transparent in its innocence, from danger?

But now, trapped in this solid body, Rush was frightened. The minotaur was just outside, in the hallway, sniffing along the floor, snorting and grunting like a forest bear. It was sniffing for a scent. Rush had watched bears in the deep forest sniffing thus, nose to the ground, grunting their hunger. If the minotaur found her, it would crush her in its huge mouth like a little grape!

But even worse than that was the fear itself! *This humanoid body was loaded with glands, and they were pumping fear and worry throughout her entire body right down to her toenails!* Why, she could hardly think! Glands! She had never realized how *riddled* with glands human bodies were! Why hadn't Miki mentioned that? His *Book of the Ways of Man*! Hah! It probably didn't mention glands at all! Why, that meant she'd made a discovery! The thrill of it momentarily displaced fear and worry. Just wait until she told Miki *this*! If she weren't eaten up. If she could just think, she could save herself. She could change . . . if not into insubstantial form, then into something else . . . something the minotaur would leave alone . . .

She had managed, by jumping and reaching high as possible, to pull a big bath-towel down to dry her hair. Now she was curled up within it, with only a tiny opening to peek out from. Not strong enough to push the door closed, she lay on the floor, listening. The sniffing and woofing stopped. Her little heart was pounding! Then there was another sound from the hall. From the stairway! Rush prayed, Let it be Miki! But it was loud knocks and bangs. Very loud. Something large and heavy. Not an elf.

From the sniffer/woofer came a new sound, a chuffing purr as though it had scented something new and exciting. Then it was gone and the door across the hallway opened and slammed shut!

Bravely, the elflet crawled to the door and peeked out. It was only Brunnhilde, with her head looking up at the ceiling. Poor lady, her neck must have gotten worse! She had wrapped a towel around the shaft of her spear and was brushing cobwebs out of the corners, humming gustily and whacking in all directions with her improvised dustmop. The minotaur was nowhere in sight!

Suddenly the bathroom door was wide open and the spear-handle was thrust inside and was banging around. Twice it crashed to the tile, just inches from where the elflet had curled up into a tight ball inside her towel, waiting for a crushing blow as her high-pitched shrieks went unheard. "Oho, what is this?" Brunnhilde cried as the spear-handle pressed into something soft on the floor. Snagging it, she lifted *Wildschweinblutmeister* and grasped the bundle. "So! A fresh towel! Better yet!" And casting aside the now-filthy one she'd borrowed from the old man downstairs who hadn't been using it anyway, she wrapped the bath-towel about the shaft of her spear, elflet and all, and turned around.

Her *held* had rushed into one of the rooms. That was good. At the entrance to the helden-room, the Valkyrie took a deep breath, arranged her braids and gave one last heave to the heavy breast-plates, which would come flying off with the first delicious kiss

. . . .

Joey sat up in bed and rubbed his eyes. He was afraid to sleep in the dark, and always kept the door open a crack so light from the hallway could get into the shadows in the corners of his bedroom. But now he heard noises, loud noises!

The door flew open and slammed into the bureau. Something large entered the room. It snorted. Grunted. *Something huge and terrible!* It growled.

Joey's insides collapsed with fear even before a flash of light-ning revealed what had come into his bedroom to take away his life. The Innkeeper had warned him, more than once, "No one goes to Esfandiary! That door cannot be opened!" But he *had* to get away and the seven-league boots didn't work in Earth Real; Joey had secretely tried them out and barely made it back through the library door just ahead of the sabertooth! Now something was in his room, something not of Earth Real. Something that had followed him from Esfandiary.

Tears ran down his cheeks. All hope vanished. There was no running away from this. The thing from Esfandiary was so big, so terrible! There would be pain. He was alone and afraid; he tried to scream but could only whimper, "No, no. Go 'way!" Would it hurt for long? Looming over his bed, dripping thick saliva, its red eyes gleaming, its hairy arms were stretching out for him just the way he'd seen it in nightmares.

All he'd wanted was a life in Earth Real, with a mother and a father and some friends and maybe a dog to play with . . .

A clatter from the open doorway caught the minotaur's eye. Her Loveliness! He'd beaten her to the foodling's room. Now, she had come to him! Most of her. Too tall to clear the transom and too proud to stoop, she had fastened a banner to the shaft of her spear and was playfully poking it into the room, swinging it this way and that, along the edges of the ceiling and into the farthest cor-ners. Swinging it! Into the farthest corners! Oh, the minotaur knew foreplay when it came within inches of his snout and shook a cloud of love-dust right into his nostrils! Then it was that the minotaur discovered the relationship between time and ecstasy.

In the maze beneath Crete, it had lived an unchanging, one-dimensional existence: chasing, mating, eating, sleeping. In Esfandiary, it had been astonished to observe, to experience light and color and open spaces, but to what end? Typecast as a misan-thropic, barbaric loner and dangerous besides, it had not been able to take much advantage of its new social options.

But here!

The glory of the parade! The horns and the drums! And en-countering—and finding himself *accepted* by—Her Loveliness! And now, the most mind-boggling of all life experiences—*anticipation*! Which seemed to indicate the existence of a dimension undreamt-of in the minotaur's not-very-fertile imagination. Time. Space was good for chasing things, but *time* gave Anticipation! In Earth Real, chasing, mating and eating were not static events to be carried out instant by instant and then forgotten. In Earth Real, the order of things was important! This new sensation, *anticipation*, required time! Time itself was delicious! Expectations were delicious.

Enough philosophy. No doubt, the foodling would prove

delicious, also. But . . . to break its neck right here? Or to break it at her feet, so that Her Loveliness would know it for a fresh kill? In Esfandiary that would have been good enough. Here, the minotaur sensed that it was not. Here, Her Loveliness had to know of its feelings in coming to a decision; that was more important than the decision itself. Now there was a delicious pain in its loins and thinking was getting difficult.

Aha! It didn't really matter where the foodling was prepared; the important thing was to make a ceremony out of it! Reaching out for the boy's neck, the minotaur opened its bull-mouth wide and from its throat came a pulsating, throbbing bellow of love.

The bathtowel rapped sharply against the headboard and from within the folds of the bathtowel flew a small furry animal with a speckled brown and white coat which might have almost been taken for a spaniel pup except for the slender orange tendrils, one on either side of its neck. It landed squarely in Joey's lap, growling and spitting, its tendrils waving in the direction of the minotaur. The air around them buzzed and crackled ominously.

Roaring fury and dismay, the minotaur pulled back. Joey, sobbing, reached out to the little creature, but it sidestepped his embrace. The minotaur, snarling, again reached out for the boy but a wave of those tendrils discouraged it. *Crack!* The tendrils nearly touched and between them the air flashed violet and the sharp report was that of a lightning bolt. The bull-man backed off. It had encountered heffalumps in Esfandiary. They had sky-lightning in those whiplike stingers and were best left alone. It backed off into a corner; Her Loveliness would have to forego the wooing present.

With a final, high-pitched growl, the heffalump relaxed its tendrils, lay down in Joey's lap and licked his hand with a thin, pink tongue. Its body was trembling with exhaustion.

His heart fluttering at the narrow escape, the boy slid out of bed on the safe side, cradled his new pet to his chest and sidled out of the room, never for an instant taking his eyes off the terror in the far corner. Bursting through the door, he ran directly into an iron drape! Not a drape, a dress! An iron dress on a huge lady. But huge *to the ceiling*! Wearing an *iron* dress! An electric dog! This was more than Joey could take! Dorothy would have jumped back in surprise (but not so far back that she wasn't perfectly centered on the page!) Alice would have said something real bright, like 'Who are you?' Joey wanted out. He scooted down the stairs, taking the last four in one leap—the first time he'd ever done that!

And then he smelled something hot and spicy, almost like a pizza. Aunt Loretta had made a pizza once, with tomatoes and cheese and stuff. This smelled richer, better, and it reminded him that he was hungry. He took a step toward the kitchen, saw the creatures bracketing the fireplace and froze.

The storm had passed to the south. The griffins, bellies pressed into the warm hearth and forepaws extended, eagle heads facing each other in the classic posture, reminisced in silence. This pair of griffins had been lifemated for so many centuries that their communication required only the slightest of head-nods, the barest twitching of body-muscles. Thus they had stood guard in time past, observing great numbers of these human beings making their triangle-sided monuments under the hot sun when the world was a quiet place. They were content.

One does not appear before one's employer soaking wet, even if it were simply to receive a sacking. Trenton Interface had not stopped Vimstetter. He had failed Mr. Broco. It wasn't that Mr. Broco was harsh; it was simply that he didn't understand failure and had no patience with excuses. Yet it would not do for a major domo to appear before his employer soaking wet and dishevelled, even for that most unpleasant of rituals.

The major domo snuck quietly upstairs only to find no towel in the bathroom. Determinedly oblivious to the distractions all about him—it was not for nothing that his father had taught him the golden rule for getting ahead: First things first!—he slunk into the kitchen keeping his back to the Master of the Valley and headed straight for the paper towel rack by the sink. Removing the entire roll, he proceeded to wrap himself in it from neck to ankles, then hopped solemnly into the living room, dropped onto the carpet and rolled slowly toward the fireplace, letting the paper towels absorb the rainwater that permeated his hair and clothing.

Never had Lucien Broco needed a scapegoat so badly. Pity to lose Trenton; the man had many talents, was intensely loyal and would be impossible to replace. But the Master of the Valley needed a scapegoat and there was no one else about. He rose. Gnashing and sucking his raw, naked gums, he worked his way toward his soon-to-be-ex-major domo. As he sidled past Vimstetter he extended his fingers, his arms, his elbows and his nose, weaving them into the most profound curse body-language could perform, taking arthritis into account. Then he shuffled to the doorway lest Vimstetter suddenly free himself from the tuba and take umbrage at the severity of the *malediccione!*

In the doorway he paused. There was Trenton Interface, wrapped in towel paper between the griffins. A simple firing would not suffice; the man had failed him totally. Storm or no storm, the hench-orchestra would have to be reassembled and Trenton Interface cashiered, drummed solemnly out of the valley.

"Dwendon Interafe!" he started. No good. It had to ring! Without his damned teeth, he couldn't even handle a straightforward firing! Leaning against the wall for support, he tried again, "*Dwenton Inter-wace!*" It would have to do. He raised one arm in a gesture of command. "Your fai-ure do nuwwify Auguspus Wimsdedder as ordered weaves me, as Masder of the Walley, no aldernadiff . . ."

He stopped. The griffins, having watched the approach of the wrapped body in silent astonishment, had risen and were . . . were bowing! It had been four thousand years since they had been hired to guard the Pharoah Rameses II, and had been upset at not being included in the funeral arrangments after a (human) lifetime of service. They had long ago given up, never expecting the reincarnation of their mummy-wrapped Pharoah after all this time.

Glory to the priests! Their beloved Pharoah, revitalized, had returned! Already one of the elders had arrived to do homage, his arm upraised! The griffins rose, flanking Interface as the reborn Pharoah lurched unsteadily to his feet. The elder's arm fell to his side in the most ancient salute. The griffins hissed acknowledgement.

Lucien Broco's jaws dropped. Interface had set the damned monsters on him! They had risen as one, turned to face him and their powerful beaks were open! They hissed. In unison. *In unison*! Talk about playing hardball!

" . . . as Masder of the Walley," he intoned, "I hab no aldernadiff but to doubbu your sarawy for twying . . . as hard as humanwy . . . poffible . . . and, um, I'll have my lawyerv write a new condwack. Pee me av voon av Poppibwe!" Broco's heart was pounding so hard he was sure his chest would be torn apart! His first thought on seeing Interface between the griffins had been despair and defeat. Now he was elated, thunderstruck! The long-sought opportunity was here! But he needed a moment to collect his thoughts! He retreated into the kitchen, and there he spied Blunger and his soul shrivelled.

Absorbed in the tending of the pizzas, rotating them in the oven so they would heat evenly, Myron Blunger was humming rather loudly to himself and was startled when a spring-loaded set of false teeth suddenly flew into the oven and clamped onto the choicest segment of pepperoni. Removing them with some effort, he washed them clean, pondered them at length, closed the oven and placed the intrusive choppers on the table. Then he sat down and in his most scientific manner, opened them wide, closed them and listened carefully to their *clack*. An interesting, hollow *clack*, such as one might expect from a hollow tooth. But hadn't Benison Hawkins recently purchased a new set of choppers? And hadn't he complained of their noisy *clack*? Yes, the *clacks* seemed identical. Probably the teeth were identical. A suspicion was taking place in Blunger's mind and required only a single, confirming experiment. Opening his mouth, Blunger inserted the upper plate and was rewarded by a buzzing, a humming, static and a barely discernible monologue.

> "... *for the tenth time, Loretta dear, I did not steal our return trainfare; I reinvested it. The Letter of Testimony cost more than I had imagined, but it's written in French, eh? Parisian French, which costs more! But we do want Bourbaki to understand it, eh, Loretta?*
>
> *"Anyway, these motels are nothing but roachholes and your purchase of new walking shoes showed a remarkable degree of foresight. They are comfortable, dear? Soon we'll be off this cursed macadam. The roads to Upper Muchness are softer, gentler . . ."*

No doubt inserting the lower plate would have improved the reception, but Blunger had heard enough! Such a business! Removing the upper, Blunger mated it with its partner and, with disdain, slid them over to their owner. "Millionaire, billionaire, *ptooey!*" he spat. "You're a nogoodnik, Mr. Broco. A low-class *finagler!*"

Broco snatched the teeth and jammed them into place, bristling with fury but afraid to upset the new balance of power. Trenton, bless his soul, had apparently come to an understanding with the griffins. What a brilliant move to renew the man's contract! With some persuasion and some greasing of palms, no doubt, his major domo would arrange for the Master of the Valley to accompany the griffins back to Esfandiary!

From somewhere above came the sound of a metallic crash, as might be caused by a barrel of nails being overturned, or a steel-mesh battleskirt cascading to the floor. This was followed by two resounding crashes and a thump that shook the dwelling to its foundations. Lucien Broco ignored the racket. He had to concentrate on his upcoming trip. He couldn't possibly leave without a suitcase! Some letters of credit, a few religious tracts, plus whatever one wore in Esfandiary—a couple of dark suits, his black shoes, some changes of socks . . . Trenton would know what to pack. Trenton always knew. Suddenly Broco was *glad* that he'd doubled his major domo's salary. After all, Vimstetter *had* been neutralized and the harpy wasn't causing trouble. She was leaning over the table, quietly underlining certain key elements of the agreement. At any moment, Trenton would appear at the doorway to inform him that all arrangements had been made and he, Lucien, could leave for Esfandiary! Meanwhile, there was nothing to do but to keep this advisor fellow pacified. While not dangerous himself, Blunger had a talent for attracting complications!

"A finagler!" Blunger repeated. "You finagled your dentist into yanking Hawkins's teeth and replacing them with radio-teeth, just so you could keep track of whatever he was saying."

Broco put his forefinger to his lips and nodded apologetically. "I am a finagler," he admitted.

Blunger drove it in further. "And a nogoodnik!"

"And a nogoodnik," Broco agreed, glancing toward the doorway into the living room. Were the griffins stirring? What was keeping Trenton?

There was movement from the doorway. It was Trenton! He seemed oddly disoriented. Well, it had been quite an evening, eh? Broco smiled reassuringly. The major domo didn't respond; he seemed to awaiting orders. "Get some beer," Broco called out. "A case of beer!" tracing out in the air the outline of a large suitcase, with a handle and pointing in the direction of the mansionhouse.

From above there was a series of crashes and thuds, shouts and muffled grunts and whoofs and a final howl that rose in intensity until one of the lamps flashed out with a *Pop!* This was followed by the sound of flowing liquid and then a strong voice in high G shouting, "*Hooray for the donder und blitzen!*" This was followed by silence.

The cuckoo clock above the sink peeped once. Myron announced, "The pizzas are ready!" Skirting Vimstetter's sprawled bulk—the poor fellow, having snagged the edge of the battletuba's bell on the table leg, was endeavoring to use leverage to work it off—Blunger made his way to the oven just as a wide-eyed Joey crept into the kitchen, clutching a small puggish thing to his chest. "There was a monster in my room," he announced.

Myron Blunger chuckled. "A monster! *Tsk, tsk*. I have a theory about monsters. Monsters come to young fellows who don't finish their vegetables, or who don't brush their teeth carefully. You wouldn't believe it, but in the Bronx, not washing behind the ears also brings monsters. Now, what kind of pizza do you like? I have a special piece I saved just for you, with mushrooms. And what about your little dog, there?"

"It's not a dog. It's a heffalump. His name is Rush. He talks in my head, sort of. He saved me from the monster. Mushrooms are *uchey*. Could you take them off? Please?" he added. Myron Blunger slid the pizzas out of the hot oven. They were warmed to perfection. Donning oven mitts, he picked up the mushroom pizza, carried it to the sink and tilted it to let the excess oil drip away.

Through the open doorway it flashed, grazing Blunger's left shoulder, tearing into the exact center of the pizza and pinning it to the cuckoo clock above the sink. The oaken shaft of *Wildschweinblutmeister* was not vibrating in the slightest; it had been a perfect throw. Blunger, his hands exactly fourteen inches apart and pizzaless, went rigid; before him, the pizza was dripping oil. The spearhead was dripping crimson. Slowly he turned and faced the open doorway that led to the living room. The Valkyrie stood at the far end, frowning as she appraised her aim. Probably the same Valkyrie he'd noticed outside in the rain, earlier.

He watched as the giantess stooped through the doorway and continued into the kitchen, crawling on her hands and knees. Her face was flushed, her hair unbraided and she was without helmet. Her armor was askew and the steel-mesh kirtle was rent in several places. Rising to her feet, she peered slowly around and her grim countenance dissolved into a sheepish grin. On the third try, she managed to seat herself. Then she exhaled; her breath fogged the air.

Brunnhilde was drunk. Eyes-crossing, down-falling, tongue-twisting drunk. Solemnly she formed a fist with her right hand, studied it for a moment, then discarded it for a left-hand fist. This apparently met with her approval, for she used it to pound her breastplates one, two, three times. They clanged solidly. Too solidly.

"Still here, you see!" she announced. "He was *not* a *held*! HE WAS NOTHING BUT . . . AN *ANIMAL*!" she roared, smashing her hand onto the table. Then she sniffled and cried, "So, what can a girl do?" she shrugged her shoulders. "Oops! But my neck is *aaalll* better!" she trilled with a false gaity that did not fool Blunger. "And now, who is my friend here wearing the horn?"

Augustus Vimstetter could only emit a weary sob, but Louise, tucking the signed agreement away in her bosom, answered, "He's Augustus Vimstetter," she said. "He's my husband. He sings and lays stone."

The Valdyrie's eyebrows lifted. "So. You are a lucky girl then. And this is no ordinary horn he is blowing! It is a *battletuba*! But he is blowing it from the wrong end," she cried. Planting her foot on Vimstetter's shoulder, she took the bell of the instrument in both hands and heaved mightily. With a resounding *thwap!*, the tuba flew off, leaving Augustus curled up on the floor, his hands cupped over his ears, moaning in agony.

Putting the battletuba to her lips, Brunnhilde inhaled deeply, then sounded the horn. The resulting blast blew out the kitchen windows and stopped the cuckoo clock forever. "That . . . ", she announced, "is for *mein held*!" And she tossed the tuba into the living room.

The glorious sound, followed by the appearance of the instrument itself, meant only one thing to the griffins. The Pharoah was ready. As one they rose, squeezed through the open doorway, spread their wings and screamed to the world and the winds, *The Pharoah comes! Prepare for the return of the Pharoah!*

But the way had to be prepared! The Pharoah would desire meat and drink! Music!

The griffins stretched their flight muscles, beat their wings, then leaped as one into the night sky and circled once, dipping their wings to the elder who had rushed after them and now stood in the roadway, singing the praises of the Pharoah and wishing them goodspeed! But they could not remain to attend his farewell speech, though it was spoken loudly enough.

The Valkyrie, in the exact state of self-pity where inebriation is most helpful, leaned toward the small child with the pet and said, "My name is Brunnhilde. What is yours?"

"Joey. And this is Rush."

"Good. I will not ask your age, which is the business of you and your pet, if you don't ask mine, which is . . . is . . ." Wiping away a tear, she cried out, "Why is there no beer at this table!" and reaching up, yanked her spear from the impaled clock and dropped the pizza in the center of the table. "Ach, this is good! Joey, this is *Wildschweinblutmeister*. *Wildschweinblutmeister*, meet Joey. And I . . . I am Brunnhilde!" she giggled.

"Pleased to meet you," the boy said. "What does *Wild* . . . *Wildschwein* whatever mean?"

"What does it mean?" Brunnhilde snorted. "Why, it is a name! It means what it says. *Wildschweinblutmeister*. Master of the blood of the wild pig. That is its name *now*! It will change, I hope, to something better. And soon," with a meaningful glance at Blunger which rattled his confidence.

"What will it change to?" the boy persisted, taking a bite out of his slice and offering some to Rush.

"*Drachblutmeister!*" she said, savoring the first syllable.

Blunger paled. Why had she looked directly at *him* while reciting that ominous name?

"Master of the blood of the *dragon!*" she intoned.

"Is that red stuff on the spear . . . dragon blood?" Joey whispered, transfixed.

The Valkyrie laughed. "No, little one. That is something else yet."

Deciding that the strategic moment had arrived, Myron

Blunger took the remaining pizzas from the oven, then bowed and introduced himself. "I am Myron Blunger. Please take a slice," passing half of the recently-transfixed pizza toward the lady.

"Why, just so!" the giantess laughed, helping herself to a slice, tearing off and dropping half of it into her open mouth. "I must soak up the excellent *compote* I have been sampling earlier."

Waiting until the giantess was busily chewing and could not interrupt, Blunger made his statement brief and to the point. "I am pleased to welcome you to this, our farewell party. Joey and I have been guests at this house too long already and now it is time for us to be returning to the Inn. To the Inn at the End of the World," he said with a meaningful wink to indicate that he was aware, that he *knew*. "He has missed . . . er, too much school already. In fact, as soon as the food is gone, we will be closing and locking up the house. If you're going in the direction of the Inn, you might want to accompany us. In the meantime, take another slice, by all means."

Brunnhilde did so, then replied, "But I think not!" Raising her spear, she thrust it directly toward Blunger's chest, playfully stopping it only when it was inches away. "After *funfhundert jahren* on a bed of stone, I am on a vacation. I want everything I was promised! Everything, *verstehen*? Elves. Perhaps to find mein *held*. And definitely a *drach*!"

"A *drach*?" Blunger whispered.

"A dragon!" Brunnhilde shouted, exasperated. "Pay attention! I would prefer not to name my beautiful spear, so nicely balanced and sharp in the head, *Blungerblutmeister*! So, where are the dragons?"

Blunger tried to fold himself a slice of pizza but dropped it. This wasn't going as he'd hoped. "By the way," he said by way of diversion, "where's your friend? The big fellow with the bull-head?"

Brunnhilde burst out laughing. "But I do not know! I think he fell in altogether!"

"Fell in!" Blunger gasped, glancing at her torn kirtle.

"Into one of the barrels, of course!" Brunnhilde roared. "He could be running around outside with his head in a barrel still!" Then, more softly, "But he tried. He sang. I think. But he had no patience."

Blunger turned pale. Next to his room in the attic was a storage space containing barrels of Loretta's preserved lifeberry compote, some of which were nearly twenty years old and highly fermented.

"You were up . . . in the barrels?" he said.

Shrugging her shoulders, Brunnhilde cried, "Oh, we wanted to be alone, you know. But I only opened one little barrel myself."

"You drank a barrel of fermented lifeberry juice?"

"One? No, I think. *Zwei.* Two. Two barrels," she giggled. "My friend opened the other with his horns. He had *such* trouble reading the labels. 'Luff-bezzy' was as close as he could make it out!" the Valkyrie roared. Then her head was swinging from side to side and she was crying bitterly, "Oh, *mein held, mein held!* But that one had no patience. *Animal!* In the end, I had to dump him into the barrel and help myself. Yes, I think he left already, wearing the barrel for a crown.

"So, let him go. Now where is this dragon? And some elves, please. One, at the least!"

At that, the heffalump jumped from Joey's lap onto the table, spun around once and vanished in a swirl of green fog. Rush reappeared, in diminutive humanoid form with her taffeta dress all cleaned and pressed, for the electricity had gone from the air! "I am an elf," she announced. "And I've had a lovely time being a heffalump and saving Joey and I'd stay for the dancing but my teacher is missing; I have to go find him. Thanks for everything." And with a charming curtsey, she spun around once more and was gone in a swirl of green mist.

The Valkyrie led a round of applause. "So! An elf!" she cried joyously. "Very good. But I do not leave until my spear has tasted the blood of the dragon!" And she put a protective arm around the shoulder of Joey, who, astonished and dismayed at the sudden loss of his pet, was starting to weep.

The Valkyrie lifted the sniffling boy onto her lap, leaned over the table and whispered softly enough to only rattle the kitchen window slightly, "A dragon. For me, and for the boy, who has lost his pet. And not a little shrimp-*drach*! Dragon Groff!" As she rose to her full height, the front door was flung open and Trenton Interface appeared, bent under a half-keg of beer.

"I couldn't find the case, Mr. Broco," he said, staggering inside and laying the half-keg on the table. But Mr. Broco was some distance away, still running down the road he'd built and named for himself, waving his arms toward the now-vanished fluorescent halo in the Saddle through which the griffins had vanished.

"Oops!" Brunnhilde cried delightedly. "But here is some more vacation, with singing and then a hot bath and a rubdown and then I will go to sleep somewhere near the fire. Tomorrow night is Halloween, the very best time to find the dragon." And, beaming, she lifted the half-keg to her lips and opened the tap.

"Dragon Groff." Myron Blunger carefully folded a mushroom pizza and munched it thoughtfully.

Not just any dragon. Dragon Groff.

Oy!

OY!

From the notebook of John H. Watson, M.D.

While echo-tapping around his head to determine the cause of the Innkeeper's present severe headache, I have made a dreadful finding! I dare not tell Holmes; he'll just make one of his caustic remarks regarding my medical competence.

The Innkeeper's brain is no longer divided into hemispheres! The halves have fused!

Somewhere within the confines of his skull, our kindly old Innkeeper exists, entirely suppressed in favor of another entity entirely, one whose unique monolobular (?) structure apparently affords him freedom from conflicts of right vs. wrong. This entity is always of one mind on any issue and wastes no energy on indecision. Sadly, he seems to believe himself to possess latent godlike powers and seems bent on establishing himself. All this from echo-tapping his skull with tuning forks while asking judicious questions. Can Holmes fail to be impressed? Especially if I succeed in curing the malady and restoring the old Innkeeper to his rightful place in his brain!

But first . . . research must be carried out! A theory is needed. Here it is.

My theory is that bilateral brains are designed to withstand conflicting views and indecisions that oscillate between hemispheres at low frequencies. A properly balanced bilateral brain is probably capable of sustaining a remarkable degree of hypocrisy without breaking down. Indeed, I submit that the properly balanced bilateral brain is capable of endorsing totally incompatible beliefs, simply because the two loosely-connected hemispheres pulse against each other until their energy of agitation dissipates. According to my new insight, some inconsistencies might vibrate thus for a good part of a lifetime, the organ appearing all the while in reasonable working order.

The Innkeeper's brain, with no mechanism for energy loss, is susceptible to massive oscillations of agitation in the radial mode. These may be triggered by catastrophes, such as prolonged opposition on any issue, by the noise level in the dining hall exceeding a certain threshold or, as in this instance, by a seemingly minor incident. A single word.

The word, 'Oy!'

[Note-obtain blank monograph paper from Holmes and write this up.]

From forehead to throat, from ear to ear, the Innkeeper's head felt like a volcano. Bright light was intolerable; the kerosene lantern glowed a dim yellow. Compresses covered the patient's face and throat, and the floor was littered with towels wringing wet from persperation. Having just refreshed the patient's throat compress, Dr. Watson was placing hemispherical shells the size of ping-pong balls into a pot of boiling water heated by an alcohol burner.

In the half-light Dr. Watson squinted at the water, anxious to get the procedure started.

"Watson! Watson!" the patient meant to call, but what started out as a roar in the Innkeeper's mind was squeezed to "Wah . . . Wah . . ." by the time it emerged from his raw throat.

Dr. Watson handed his patient a glass of sweetened grape juice spiked with lime (against the scurvy, as a precaution). "Drink slowly," he said.

The Innkeeper squinted at the practitioner with fever-bright eyes. "I want Myron Blunger gone from the Inn," he wheezed, doubly furious over his inability to thunder. "Gone! His carcass thrown to the sabertooth and his sojourn obliterated from the records and neither his arrival nor his departure an allowed subject for epic poems, limericks or even scrawls in the restrooms! His name is to be blotted out!"

With each rise and fall of the Innkeeper's chest, Dr. Watson could hear, even without a stethoscope, the wheezings and gurglings of bad blood, circulating deep inside. His order that the Innkeeper remain silent, conserve his energies, were in vain; now his patient was off on another tirade.

"Don Giovanni was right; he's set . . . to destroy me!" The Innkeeper gasped. "You hear? *The Pizza Vendetta! The Dish Best Served Cold! The Battle Tuba!* and now, *Justice!* And still the boots aren't back, nor the boy and now I've got Brunnhilde out there looking for her damned *held!*

"And the kitchen budget is *donnerwetter* out of whack! I myself watched Myron Blunger eat John Henry under the table, and him a pencil-pusher and Big John still laying a half-mile of track a day just to keep in shape!

"Every time he sorties out to collar the brat and get the boots, he ends up with a full belly, lame excuses and a new request for the chef! Lifeberry compote, now! Herring in cream sauce at three dollars a jar wasn't enough! And you saw how Chapter Ten ends? With an *Oy!* If Blunger were here right now, I'd . . ."

Using a forceps, Dr. Watson removed one hemisphere from the boiling water, tested its temperature against his wrist and placed it on the Innkeeper's chest.

" . . . take him by both ends, shrink him around the equator and stretch him from pole to . . . Arrgh!" the Innkeeper screamed. "Take it off! It burns!"

"Would you prefer the leeches, then?" Watson asked quietly, placing a second, then a third heated cup near the first and ignoring the resultant roars of pain that came out as strangled squeals. It was a rhetorical question; the Innkeeper was deathly afraid of the squooshy little bloodsuckers. "Have patience; as they cool off, cups draw the bad blood to the surface. Just hold still, now. Three more . . . and try to keep calm or you'll burst a pipe!" the good doctor advised sternly. "I'm also going to dose you with St. Felicia's potion; that and the cups should turn things around, but only if you rest quietly and give them a chance.

"In case you're interested . . . there's another cup set; that wasn't so bad, was it? . . . I have a theory about Blunger's use of Oy! Not my own theory, really; I've been reading Freud. It is not impossible that immediately upon being born, the first word Myron Blunger heard was Oy! or something much like it. That is part of the ordinary birth trauma, and is usually buried beneath many layers of ego. I suspect that Myron Blunger's ego has worn thin, eroded, perhaps from living in the Bronx.

"Another cup . . . there! And one more . . . the bad blood's already coming up; you're skin's turning dark red. You're not to leave this room until your symptoms subside. I prescribe warm compresses, lots of fruit juice and a committee to handle the affairs of the Inn until you're up and about."

The doctor found his arm encircled by the Innkeeper's powerful grip. "A committee," the Innkeeper whispered, grinning wickedly. "The very thing! A special committee to address and solve the Blunger problem. So be it! Form a committee, Watson! Chair it! Get sensible types. Public domain old-timers. No self-centered whiz-bangs with their endless squabbling over paperback sales and television rights. Meet in the library. Get Paul Bunyon. He's slow, but steady. Not his damned ox, though! No oxes in my library! No D'Artagnon or Carmen; not steady. Jiminy Cricket, if you can find him. Sensible. And a knave or two, for balance. Every committee has a knave or two. The boy's fixed on *Treasure Island*. Get Silver. Yes, get Long John Silver.

"And the Don. That's two. Better to hand-pick your own knaves than to have to keep your back to the wall."

A kick of exasperation was barely strong enough to set a chamberpot rattling on the night table. With a sudden gleam in his eye, the Innkeeper pointed to it. "And I want a new chamberpot, " he ordered. "And not a plain one! Go to the art studio. Tell whoever's there I want it painted. On the inside. A portrait. Of Myron Blunger. Yes, Blunger. Smiling! Eating! Hah! Yes, smiling and eating! His name will be blotted out, but I, *I*, will think of him twice a day!"

With that, the Innkeeper fell back onto his pillow, coughing and wheezing. "Twice a day," the Innkeeper added, smiling.

Watson frowned. Sometimes the Innkeeper seemed heartless. Painting poor Blunger into a chamberpot? After all the chap had been through? And with a weak ego? Dr. Watson was about to remonstrate with his patient when he remembered Freud. He hadn't finished the book, but suspected that one shouldn't act impulsively when chamberpots were involved.

Extracting a newspaper from his black bag, Watson selected the economic forecasts and used them to wrap the Innkeeper's chamberpot, which would be needed for sizing. A ladleful of St. Felicia's potion, removal of the now-cooled cups, a final touch to the forehead and Watson stole out, quietly closing the door behind him. With no time for silly errands, the doctor was pleased to spot Windbreaker down the hallway, apparently practising his cantering. Calling the centaur over, Watson gave him the chamberpot and the errand. "The fever's gone to his eyes, you know," he said by way of explanation. "He can't read as much as he'd like and would appreciate Blunger's likeness at hand, so to speak. It doesn't have to be *too* close a likeness, if you know what I mean." Saddened at how readily the half-truths had rolled off his tongue, the doctor went off to start rounding up a suitable committee.

There was no getting around it; the Blunger problem was serious. Like most guests of the Inn, Dr. Watson had been following Myron Blunger's manuscripts as they appeared on the writing table in the library. Everybody knew what the boy Joey was after. Life. What's it all about? How do you do it? It was fortunate that Watson had taken up reading Freud just at the right time.

The Blunger problem was the problem of life. Which left Dr. Watson wondering how to set up and chair a Committee on Life? There were so many approaches to it! So many perspectives! One shouldn't overlook the furred creatures, should one? Speaking of which, there was Pooh by a window, totally absorbed in the route of a raindrop that might or might not succeed in trickling its slow way to the bottom of the pane. No, Pooh just didn't have sufficient intellectual staying-power for a Committee on Life. Watson hoped the honey-bear didn't find out about the committee, or wonder why he hand't been selected for it. On the other hand, Pooh was always happy. Always cheerful. Maybe they should send Pooh to bring the Willem boy back; maybe Pooh knew the secret of life as well as anyone.

Watson made up a list as best he could, then gave it to Peter Rabbit. "Meeting in the library at teatime," he said. "I'm chair. If anyone asks, the name of the committee is . . . The Innkeeper's Temporary Council of Administration. That covers it, I believe. ITCA. Might not be too deadly, at that. Now hop along. Teatime, promptly, or they're off the committee!"

Chairs were still scraping across the library floor as Dr. Watson called the first meeting of ITCA to order. All of Blunger's manuscripts were laid out before him on the writing table, as well as a fresh pad of paper and small rectangular scraps, in case a ballot were called for. He started the agenda with a medical report.

"As most of you are aware, our beloved Innkeeper broke out in . . . ahem . . . symptoms while he was reading Chapter Ten of Mr. Myron Blunger's latest . . . ahem . . . effort. He is resting comfortably and has requested that this committee be created for the express purpose of addressing the Blunger problem, which he wants resolved as expiditiously as possible. I am empowered to tell you that immediately following the solving of the Blunger problem, the Innkeeper will host a gala costume party with a twelve-piece swing band, a Roaring-twenties open bar with mock- gangsters and molls, a joust between Ivanhoe and our own Windbreaker, Morris dancing and magic firework hats designed by Merlin!"

The applause lasted some time, and subsided only when Paul Bunyon raised one enormous hand.

Watson cleared his throat and continued. "Now . . . I believe that you have all read Myron Blunger's manuscripts. Let us . . . ah, Mr. Bunyon. Have you any ideas on the Blunger problem?"

The lumberjack, seated Indian-fashion on the floor, nevertheless towered over the others. Pulling a single, scrawled sheet of paper from the pocket of his checkered shirt, he read aloud, his voice booming. "I want to make a kitchen report."

Watson shook his head rapidly. "Mr. Bunyon, the Blunger problem is our first priority. If you . . ."

"A kitchen report," Blunger's voice rumbled doggedly and his forefinger, as thick as any other lumberman's wrist, traced the statement he'd printed in large block letters just for this meeting. "Staples are in good supply. Down to a hundred dozen eggs but a delivery is expected before long."

"I object!" It was the Little Red Hen. Flapping, with much clatter and squawking, to a perch atop the stacks, she cried, "Eggs are not on the agenda! I don't use eggs in my baking and resent their mention! Personally! The agenda is Blunger and his problem. Also, the treekiller uses the phrase . . . before long. This is improper and smacks of timeliness, which is a danger to all of us here at the Inn! No eggs! No time! Stick to Blunger!"

The room echoed with cries of, "Hear, hear!" and "Well said!" and "Plunger? Who's Plunger?"

"A kitchen report *is* a Blunger report!" Bunyon boomed. "I admit, my whole life all I ever knew was flapjacks. Thanks to Blunger, we hope to soon have blintzes on the menu, which are flapjacks rolled around a cheese stuffing. Also with stuffing is something called a *gefilta* fish, which is either whitefish stuffed with pike, or pike stuffed with whitefish, depending on whichever swims faster.

"Blunger is clever, but expensive. *The Pizza Vendetta* created a new demand, and I report that our kitchen staff is turning out pizzas as fast as they can pull them out of the ovens. But unless we get a larger budget, there will not be lifeberry compote on the menu. Satisfied, he leaned over to Don Juan, and whispered, "I make it clear, you think?"

The don nodded abstractly. His mind was elsewhere.

Dr. Watson accepted the report and jotted down some figures. "Farmer John? Any ideas on the Blunger problem?"

Farmer John was a prototype, an old timer whose shrewd eyes peered out from beneath overhangs of brow and whose lank frame unfolded like a carpenter's rule as he rose. Arcing a stream of tobacco juice into the fire, he hooked a strong, spatulate thumb into his overalls and, in a flat voice, said, "Yup." Then he refolded himself into his chair.

Thoughtfully, Dr. Watson bounced the eraser of his pencil on the table several times, then asked, "Could you elaborate on that, please?"

"Yup." Again, Farmer John unfolded, rose, rehooked his thumbs and said, "Sour cream and cheese for the *blint-zers*, I got. Ten barr'l worth. No lifeberries. They like altitude and mountain shade; leastwise, that's how I read it. And no herring. Ya cain't farm herrings. Leastwise, I cain't. End of report."

"Thank you, Farmer John. Mr. Silver?"

Planting his wooden crutch firmly on the floor, a grizzled seafaring man with his head bound in a red kerchief hoisted himself out of a chair by the wall in one fluid motion. "Ay, Doctor Watson, sir!" he said with a broad smile as his sharp, protuberant eyes scanned the room. "Long John, my friends calls me. You'll excuse an old lame seaman for anchoring away from the fleet, but it's frightful awkward in close quarters with my stump flappin' and my crutch pokin' helpless as a harpooned sea-turtle.

"This lad Joey . . . why, he reminds me of my old friend Jim Hawkins! Why, Jim Hawkins and me got along famous for the most part, even at the end of our adventure. Now, I don't doubt but that this Myron Blunger and the rest of his gang done their best to get a hold on Joey, but it's a known fact that around age ten, eleven, twelve there's nobody a boy'd rather adventure with but a seafarin' man." Then, in a lower voice and one eye half-closed, "And expecially if that man's sailed from Madagascar to the

Spanish Main under more colors than a bloody rainbow, and has had a passin' 'quaintance with the Jolly Roger!

"Ay, Cap'n Watson," he growled, advancing with thumps of this crutch that echoed ominously from the stonework, "I remember when I was a ten-year-old tyke in Londontown like it was yestidday. It weren't chicken-eggs or tree-cuttin that I read about with a candle borreyed from church and snuck under the cover of my bed in the attic, and the night-wind howlin' and tryin' to cut its way right through the scantyboards that wuz the roof! I didn't pay that no mind, mates," and supporting himself on the edge of the writing desk, he swung the crutch around the room, "I wuz scramblin' over the side of a three-master onto the deck of a fat Spanish galleon fresh from the gold-mines of Mexico, with a bloody saber in me mouth and glory on every page! Ay, it's readin' sets the mind afire! Why, if it wuzn't for readin', I'd never of found me occipation in life!"

Swinging around, Long John Silver thrust the crutch hard into Watson's chest and whispered, "I'd lay a thousand pieces of eight against a rusty anchor that I could talk our lad back to the Inn faster'n old Flint'd lay out a slow deckhand!"

Withdrawing the crutch, Silver turned about and faced the committee. "I been guestin' here at the Inn long enough. The Innkeeper's up against it and someone's got to volunteer. I know me dooty. It'll be hard and dangerous, just the travelling of it, but that's been me line of work, eh? Might as well send old John than risk someone ain't suited for the job. What do you say, mates?"

Long John didn't bother mentioning his interest in Lucien Broco.

"Thank you for the offer, Mr. Silver," Dr. Watson said drily. "Mr. . . . er, Don Juan?"

Dr. Watson had counted himself fortunate to get the don on his committee. After all, Willem's interest appeared to be Life, and who would know more about life than the most famous lover of all time?

Don Juan sprang to his feet, bowed deeply to the assembly

and said, in Castillian-accented English, "Senor chairman Dr. Watson, honorable ladies and gentlemen, dwarves, gnomes and others," dipping his head toward Peter Rabbit, the Little Red Hen and representatives of several other species of creature. "There are those who believe that if a dog could sing and play the guitar, it would still be a dog. Others believe that if a dog could sing and play the guitar, it would not be a dog. But can it be stated that a creature that sings, plays the guitar and chases rabbits *must* be a dog? I mention this only to demonstrate that I have philosophy and know something of life.

"Regarding the boy Joey. He is doing well. He has befriended a griffin, has ingratiated himself with the only women available, the ever-charming and formidable Brunnhilde and Loretta Hawkins, whose young, adventurous daughter, Wilma, though she has yet to make an appearance, has already aroused within my breast the fires of love. Regarding the secret of life, one need only tell the boy that before puberty, life is running and playing with a dog at one's side. After puberty, life takes on new meaning. It is, of course, very difficult to be a woman. A man has a moral obligation to provide consolation against the internal storms of passion that accompany womanhood. That is nature. That is life.

"My colleague, Mr. Silver, has offered to go to the valley of Upper Muchness to bring the boy back. As a man of honor, I likewise offer my humble services to the solutions of Myron Blunger's problem.

"Quien va!" he snapped and in an instant, Don Juan had whipped a sword with a filigreed blade from its scabbard and thrust it before him in the direction of the dark entranceway to the library. "Who goes there?" By the time he'd repeated his challenge in English, he had wrapped his silk scarf about his left forearm and assumed a classic dueling posture. "The Commandant?" he whispered, his eyes wide with terror.

Not until half a dozen of the committee had searched the entranceway and the stacks did Don Juan reluctantly slide the sword back into its scabbard. It was the Don Juan case that had driven Dr.

Watson to his readings of Freud. The facts were simple. The don had killed the Commandant in a duel over the old gentleman's daughter. Not unique in history. But Mozart had gotten hold of this particular killing and put it into an opera. A brilliant, frequently-produced opera. Even now, somewhere in Earth Real, a Don Juan was plunging his sword into a Commandant. Even now, somewhere in Earth Real, a marble statue of a Commandant was descending from a marble horse and escorting Don Juan to hell. And here at the Inn, the spirit of Don Juan was ever watchful against the arrival of the wraith of the stern, vengeful Commandant. And so it would until the curtain fell on the final performance of *Don Giovanni*.

Unless the don could find his way to Earth Real and obtain a court injunction. His lawyer, Portia, was ready for trial, with surefire medical evidence that would clear the don of all culpability. A successful lawsuit would put a stop to the Commandant. Yes, the only chance the don had of eliminating the old buzzard was in a court of law, where he had one major advantage. Portia had Shakespeare behind her, and NO ONE but NO ONE outranked Shakespeare when it came to straight and fancy talking. Also, she was sensational in bed.

After the meeting, in a private conversation with The Old Woman Who Lived in a Shoe, Dr. Watson suggested a meeting between her and the don. "It will be mutually beneficial, Madam," he explained. "The Senor is a good man, vivacious, courteous and patient, but," with a sad shake of his head, "he has absolutely no idea of the consequences of . . . certain actions, whereas you are . . . the embodiment . . . defined by those very consequences if you'll pardon my saying so. It's astonishing, really. And, frankly, you seem a bit peaked. I think you could use . . . a bit of sparking, if you catch my drift . . ."

He was unable to find the don, however, to firm up the assignation. Afraid to return to his quarters, Don Juan had slipped into the stacks, where he would be safe from the Commandant. Falling into a light slumber, he was awakened by a strange occurrence.

The pain was excruciating. One step at a time, Myron Blunger had made his way down the corridor toward the library. Gaining entrance, he stopped to lean against the wall, moaning the anguish of the thrice-afflicted. The room was half in darkness, most of the kerosene lanterns having gone out. Blunger lined up a direct route to his easy chair, which someone had turned to face the fire. Eight short steps should get him there, but he dreaded the thought of sitting down.

"Well, it's about time!" someone piped up. From around the back of the easy chair peeked the gnome Yin. "The meeting ended a long time ago! They've gone to write up the minutes and prepare a report for the Innkeeper. Where have you been?"

"Administering to my hemorrhoids," Blunger sighed. "What meeting?"

"The meeting of a committee to solve the Blunger problem," Yin replied. He dropped down from the chair and turned it back to the writing table, on which Blunger's manuscripts were stacked exactly as Dr. Watson had left them.

"My problem!" Blunger exclaimed. "This place is truly astonishing! How did they learn about my problem? It just happened! I'm near the end of chapter ten, I shift my *tuchus* in the chair and *Zupph*! Hemmorhoids! Not one! Not two! A whole flock of them, and they all turned on at once! I even finished the piece with an *Oy!*" Then, "You looked at the stories? Four of them, and still no progress! The last is called *Justice*! So what did you think? Honestly."

"What I think isn't so important," the gnome replied evasively. On the other hand, Blunger had said, *honestly*. "You should know that your ending to *Justice* has caused some comment around the Inn."

By this time, Blunger had reached the chair and slowly let himself down with a humongous groan. He drew from his pocket his notes, flipped through the pages, and nodded. "As long as you're interested . . . the pain was so bad I just wanted to send everyone home! But they wouldn't obey! You believe that? Only the griffins; they left quietly."

"That's the characters taking over," Yin suggested, recalling the phrase from a writing course he'd started. Dr. Watson had taught it right here in the library, but had never gotten past Lesson One: Never, never put yourself into a story with your protagonist! If things don't work out . . .

Everyone at the Inn knew the situation, of course. Dr. Watson had failed to sufficiently flesh out Irene Adler in *A Scandal in Bohemia*; clever and beautiful did not suffice to build up a sufficient readership to get one to the Inn. Which left Holmes rooming with Dr. Watson for the rest of eternity, and smoldering . . .

Blunger started to repeat, "But what do *you* think of the writing?" but he didn't because in the darkest corner of the library, so poorly lit that the shelves were used only for annotated High School editions of *Beowulf*, there appeared a blue light. A sliver. Powder blue, as from a summer sky, but so intense Blunger could not look directly at it. It came from the edge of the door that led to Esfandiary.

The memory of his previous summons into Esfandiary flashed through Blunger's mind: the glory and beauty of heaven, the encounter with Tom, the advice he'd received and tried to implement, to little avail. But one item eclipsed all others, even the glorious possibility of a discourse with God. The color of the light then had been yellow; this was blue. Powder blue. This was not the same Esfandiary to which he'd been admitted earlier.

Nor was the Door waiting for him to walk in under his own power. The light flooded the library and Blunger found himself pulled out of the armchair, found himself prone on the floor without memory of falling, and became aware of a universal force pulling on him. Not a single force acting on arm or leg alone, but, like gravity, pulling on every part of him, inside as well as out! Pulling him toward that terrifying, unearthly brilliance. Pulling harder, more insistently, summoning him to . . . to what? His hands, encountered a sturdy bookshelf, clung to it desperately. Two hands.

He stopped sliding. And then Blunger's eyes truly widened, for the doorway that led to Esfandiary started *coming toward him*!

Floor, walls, bookshelves melted before it as the doorway approached and reached him and now his chin was over the threshold. Direct exposure to that unbearable radiance would destroy his vision, his brain, his soul! Folding his forearms across his eyes, he managed to croak, "Help!" as the door slid beneath him. "He . . . eelp!" His feet left the stone floor of the library of the Inn at the End of the World and now Blunger sensed that the intensity of light was diminishing. Not all at once, but at a rate exactly matched to Blunger's inbred notions of awesome power, of a universal control tempered to the limitations of humans.

Behind him the door closed with the precise and irreversible *thunk*! of a bank vault.

So Myron Blunger was summoned to Esfandiary for the second time.

GUIDANCE

Dragged over the portal and the door slammed shut! No warm, yellow glow this time; no heaven; no celestial radiance; no music. Blunger found himself in total darkness. What had Tom said? For his last summons, Door had matched Esfandiary to Blunger's expectations. Well, that was last time, and this was this time, and this Esfandiary exceeded Blunger's worst nightmares.

In Esfandiary, one's true beliefs are of greatest importance.

Yin had said that, in the van on the way up. Whose true belief had put Blunger in total darkness? *Was this the Innkeeper's vision of Esfandiary?*

If so, the dinosaurs would be coming along any minute, necks stretched forward and down, jaws wide open. He scuttled back on hands and knees until his rear butted up hard against the door. His eyes reported not a trace of the intense radiance with which he'd been pulled into the dread Esfandiary. Not a sliver of illumination from within the library sneaking around the edge of that aggressive door, not even a single pinpoint of starlight! Myron Blunger curled up into a tight ball and prayed for a quick dispatch with as little pain as possible.

His ears, however, did have a message. A *whoosh*! in the distance. Most likely a *pterodactyl* homing in on him. Of course, a *pterodactyl* was not a standard dinosaur at all, being more of a flying mouth mounted on bat-wings and filled with razor-sharp teeth!

Beneath him was what felt like grass, and further down, earth. He took his hand away; in Esfandiary even the grass was probably aggressive. Well, why not, after being trampled by dinosaurs all day? Myron Blunger knew about dinosaurs from storytelling where it seemed that nowadays every other children's book was about dinosaurs.

It hadn't always been that way. Once, the children's books were merry stories about cute animals gone adventuring, about dogs named Spot and Rover, about shiny red cars that Daddy bought for cash from chubby little salesmen, and little chug-chug locomotives with courage. Now the children's books were different.

CRAWL EARLY, CRAWL HIGH—The Road to Harvard Starts in the Cradle! . . . Mommy's and Daddy's Divorce may NOT be your fault . . . Stupid boys and Menstrual Cramps—Growing Up With Jennifer.

And hundreds of books on dinosaurs. Pop-ups with mottled green, scaly superlizards that literally jumped out at you. Blunger took a deep breath. Ahh! Why, the air of Esfandiary was sweet, heavy, pungent like the orchid house at the Bronx Botanical Gardens!

WHOOSH! Closer? Louder? He cringed. And then a flat, impersonal voice called out: "Guidance! Guidance for Myron Blunger! Scene one; take one." And there was light, a uniform blue-grey illumination in a cloudless, infinite vault. Myron Blunger blinked, peered around warily to find that he was on the side of a grassy hill at the edge of a wide plain. There were other low hills nearby, several copses of birch trees and what appeared to be patches of pure white sand further away. Somewhere beyond, the land became a haze of blue that blended with the sky; there was no horizon. The door to the Inn was directly behind him, built into a hillside, but again it had no handle. As for the source of the *whoosh*, why, it wasn't a pterodactyl at all. It was a flying mountain in the distance.

SWOOSH . . . VROOOM! It roared by from left to right, soaring up into the atmosphere, dwindling until it vanished. After some moments, it reappeared out of the haze *to his left*, zooming across, grazing the plain, then *whooshing* up, up along the same trajectory until it again passed out of sight.

THE INN AT THE END OF THE WORLD

"A flying mountain," Blunger said aloud. "A flying mountain. A flying mountain." Three times he said it, then pushed himself to his feet and shook his head. A flying mountain his brain couldn't digest. Not now. Not ever.

More important, there was no place to hide on that unbroken plain, in case a dinosaur happened to come along. He knocked, pushed, kicked the door but it remained closed.

"Hold on, hold on; I'm coming."

Blunger heard footsteps. He peeked to the right, to the left, then slowly turned, tensed for disaster. A moment earlier, he'd been the only creature from horizon to horizon. Now someone was hurrying across the grass toward him, huffing and pumping its way up the hill. Blunger's heart started pounding. The Something was vaguely humanoid. It was Tom!

In a mellow voice without overtones, it said, "Sorry . . . I'm late. Short notice."

"Tom!" Blunger cried.

"There's no time for chit-chat!" Tom gasped in his monotone. "Sit down and take off your shoes!"

As Blunger did so, he heard the *whoosh* once more and saw the flying mountain. Pointing toward it, he got as far as, "Flying mountain," when his soul cut him off.

"Lord God," Tom said, still catching his breath. "Nowadays golf is His real passion. Those are just practice swings. Soon He'll do some driving; *that's* worth seeing!"

For a long moment, Myron Blunger sat, eyes fixed on the now-vanishing mountain. "God," he said weakly.

"That's why you took your shoes off," Tom whispered.

"God plays golf," Myron Blunger said.

"Most of it," Tom said. "He leaves out the profanity. Pity you don't play the game; He's always on the lookout for a good round and many of the better golfers are . . . somewhere else if you know what I mean. Profanity. And failure to keep to Just Measures, which includes counting." Pulling a sheaf of papers from some hidden pocket, Tom said, "While we're waiting, I have a copy of your manuscript here. You're swimming in very deep water, Myron. It was decided that you need more guidance than can be written on a cliff-side."

"It was decided," Blunger said. "By God? God is reading my . . . my writing?"

"In this case, reading is too strong a word," Tom said. "But He did ask that I communicate some advice before you cause real trouble."

"God wrote those instructions on the Cliff of Night?" Blunger asked, his entire nervous system throbbing and pulsing. "About throwing lefty?"

Tom shook his head.

"Elflet Rush, then?"

"No."

A moment's thought, then . . . "It was you! You saved my life!"

"With help from the Universal Soul," Tom admitted. "Oh, watch this!" he said.

Blunger turned his head in time to see a billowing, surging cloud appear in the middle distance and settle gently to the ground. A puff of wind dissipated the cloud, leaving a white sphere perched upon a sturdy red pedestal. A white, dimpled sphere. The sphere had to be a mile in diameter, judging by its dwarving of an Allosaurus that had dashed out from beneath the cloud, running frantically as though it had had experience with what was to come and wanted no part of it.

An *Allosaurus*.

Running frantically.

In Blunger's general direction.

Tom didn't seem surprised. Blunger, understanding for the first time the purpose, the *blessedness* of the coma state, feigned calm.

The mountain came down from on high to rest momentarily against the sphere. Blunger then realized that what he'd thought a mountain had structure, that its leading surface was flattened and gouged with regularly-spaced horizontal canyons. Protruding from its top was a slender silver column that reached up, up, tapered by perspective until it vanished from human sight.

The flying mountain was the Lord's clubhead. The club head swung back slowly, arced up into the celestial pearliness.

Tom was pointing at something over Blunger's shoulder; he turned to look. It was the moon. The full moon; it hadn't been there before. *WHOOSH*! Vroom! CRACK! Blunger turned back in time to observe the club go through its swing, into the follow-through, arc up, out of sight, and the ball tearing its way into space at unimaginable speed. Miraculously, it didn't vanish. As though he'd been given telescopic vision, Blunger found that he could track its trajectory out, out and saw that it was headed for the surface of the Moon. Blunger's view continued to telescope, tracking the drive until the sphere impacted just outside the largest of the moon's craters.

Cupping his hands, Tom shouted, "Great shot! An Eagle for sure!" adding, to Myron Blunger, "That's nearly a quarter-million mile, par four hole! Don't play the game myself, but I understand He has to allow for the solar wind, the Sun's gravity, comets and asteroids . . . it's a head game."

"Good Lord!" Blunger said, hastily amending it to, "I mean, good shot, Lord!"

And a response rumbled down from an unmeasurable height, rolling over the plain. "Thanks, Myron."

Myron Blunger awoke with a cold compress pressed against his forehead. "You passed out," Tom said in a quavering voice. "The Lord God asked me to apologize for startling you thus; so often He's spoken to humans—heart to heart—without any response at all, that He just forgot."

Some time passed before Myron Blunger's chest ceased heaving and speech returned to him. "God spoke to me," he whispered. "God spoke to me, God spoke to me. To me, God spoke! You know, my name in Hebrew is Moses. He also spoke to . . . the other Moses! You think there's a connection?"

Esfandiary exploded in a dazzle of light, the blast of a thousand volcanos. Every molecule in Blunger's body spun around and jumped around and kicked off an electron.

Myron Blunger regained consciousness to find himself stretched out on the grass, inhaling a strong odor very much like ammonia. Above him hovered a Being swathed in a golden radiance of such brilliance that Blunger was forced to avert his eyes. Beside him lay Tom, greatly diminished in size and apparently unconscious. Another Being knelt beside the soul, whispering restorative prayers into its ears. As Blunger watched, Tom seemed to grow, fill out, wiggle his extremities, blink. Both Beings left Blunger's field of view and when he sat up and tried to find them, they were not there.

Tom sat up, blinked, oscillated uncertainly, then said to Blunger, "You were perfect!"

"Perfect," Blunger repeated dazedly. "What happened?"

"You compared yourself to 'the other Moses,' as you call him. And the Lord God laughed! Laughed! It's a first! I was summoned, and returned. He won't laugh again. He told me to tell you and I quote: 'For the sake of his ancestor Morris the Decent, who lived in difficult times, I will no more trouble Myron Blunger with My laughter. And, I will leave him with a benefit, that he recall this meeting and hearken to my guidance.'

"How do you feel now?" Tom asked.

In fact, Myron Blunger felt as though every part of his body, from the largest muscle to the tiniest nerve ending, had received a Swedish massage, a needle shower, a powdering and a dose of tonic. Blunger sprang to his feet, overwhelmed and strangely exhilerated.

"Much better, thank you. Much better. But frankly, I'm upset," Blunger said. "All humans are supposed to start off the same, equal! Now I just put myself in the same *sentence* with the other Moses, and God splits His sides! Was the other Moses ten feet tall? Did he have two heads? Am I chopped liver? What happened to the equal?"

Tom eyed Myron Blunger critically, then sighed. "You need

guidance. We'll start with faith. First, take my golf club."

Blunger complied, wrapping both hands awkwardly around the handle of the five iron.

"Good. Now, there's a ball; stand up and give it a good whack."

In the distance, someone called, "Action! Take two!" Blunger stood up and there, at his feet, was a regulation golf ball where there had been *absolutely, positively* nothing a moment earlier. But Myron, freshly recombined, reborn as it were and feeling his spirits, welcomed a chance to prove himself. For sure he knew more about golf than the other Moses, who was undoubtedly short, hot-tempered and impatient with games. How far could such a person hit a golf ball?

Blunger imitated what he recalled of the Lord's backswing, then brought the club slashing down at the ball, missing by only a foot or so. His second attempt, with a shorter backswing, was more productive; to his delight, the club hit squarely with a sharp *CRACK!* and the ball soared over and behind the next hill, where it bounced off something and went even farther!

The something the ball had bounced off raised its head above the hilltop. Slowly, slowly it swung around the horizon, seeking out its challenger. It was a reptilian head the approximate size of a Bronx apartment refrigerator and brownish green in color. Blunger, horrified at what he'd summoned forth, watched the Allosaurus's head rise above the crest of the hill, followed by a thick neck and trunk. Blunger noted the yellow, vertically slitted eyes and a mouth full of dagger teeth. A black tongue. When the head was pointed directly at Myron Blunger, it ceased its swivelling. Two steps, surprisingly rapid for a creature of such size, and a flick of its tail brought the Allosaur to the top of the hill, its taloned forearms poised for combat, its tongue flicking from side to side as its jaws opened and closed slowly, thoughtfully. Endless rows of pointy teeth. No molars. Allosaurs were meat-eaters, Blunger knew. Not quite as large as their more famous cousins, Tyrranosaurus Rex, but with much the same attitude and longer, stronger forearms.

Frightened rigid, Blunger stared without hope. Now the creature's tail was swinging slowly with the sway of its body. It lifted one foot and planted its claws in the soft ground, securing its weight without committing itself. Would it plod slowly or come in a series of quick dashes, grinning and advancing ten or twenty feet at a stride? Or would it make one rush, snorting and bellowing to paralyze its prey?

"It's a test of faith," Tom said, perched calmly on the ground. "Take your golf club and hold it up before you, like Moses's staff. It only works if you think very, very positive. Faith and Belief are important here."

Blunger lifted the club. The beast snorted. Blunger shook the club. The beast hissed. Blunger dropped the club.

The Allosaur ceased swaying, ceased lashing its tail. Lowering its head, it started forward at deliberate speed, prepared to cut off a lateral dash. Its slit eyes remained fixed on Myron Blunger.

"Stop it!" Blunger screeched to Tom.

"I can't!" his soul said calmly. "All I can do at this point is vanish, which would leave you alone. You have to save yourself with an act of faith! It has to come from within you! That's the whole point of humankind! Of all creatures, you are one with the Creator. Close your eyes and concentrate! Be strong! It's still a hundred yards away."

Blunger closed his eyes and recited lines from the twenty-third psalm, which he was getting to know quite well.

From a great height came the still, small voice that had spoken to the other Moses from a burning bush. "Cup your hands!"

No thunder. No lightning. No M-1 tank, no cannon, no John Wayne angel diving down on the monster with rockets and tracers spitting out from beneath his wings. *Cup your hands!* God had given the other Moses a staff that could turn into a snake, that could smite water from rocks, part the sea into dry land . . . .

What did he have? A golf club! It wasn't fair!

God hated him. *Hated him!* Dropping to his knees, Blunger wept.

"*CUP YOUR HANDS!*"

Blunger did so. And within his cupped hands, something fluttered weakly.

From on high: "*Now open your hands!*"

Out flew . . . a butterfly with blue and gold wings.

A butterfly. Oh, was God angry with him! This could only come from telling blasphemous jokes. Blunger swore he'd never, never tell one again! Yet the monster advanced, closing to within fifty . . . thirty . . . now twenty yards and now he could hear its hissing breath. All this for likening himself to Moses!

A butterfly!

Upwards it fluttered in the clear air of Esfandiary, upward as if to try to lure the beast away. The Allosaur was not interested in butterflies. Ten yards away was a quaking, warm-blooded meal without claws or spikes. Five yards. It paused, opened its jaws wide and tilted its head, judging the angle for the quick kill.

The sky parted and a narrow beam of purple and silver radiation from the heart of the Sun flashed down, caught the butterfly and was diffracted by its wings into the eyes of the Allosaur, a high-intensity golden-yellow shaft into one eye, a piercing blue shaft into the other. Dazzled, blinded, the Allosaur bellowed its pain and dismay, turned and lumbered away.

Blunger's knees gave way and, from the ground, he clasped his hands and prayed his thanks, briefly and with no wasted words or false promises.

"You're welcome," came the gentle reply from high above. "For your information, the *other* Moses would have met the lizard half-way down the hill, smote him with whatever he had at hand—staff, golf club or his fist—and then beckoned to his six hundred thousand followers to resume their march.

"You, on the other hand, have so far been unable to entice one ten-year old orphan back to an Inn, where food and drink and companionship are plentiful and the library contains good measure of wisdom among the nonsense and perversion. That is the difference between you and . . . the other Moses, plus measures of faith, belief and determination beyond your imagination.

"I can do no more for you. Address your soul, Myron Blunger. Answers spring from within the soul. Hearken to it."

The sky darkened. Myron Blunger took a deep breath and addressed his soul. "First of all," he said, "I'm sorry. You know what for. You're my soul. You know everything about me from day one. I don't have to spell it all out.

"But now I have problems, real problems. Every time I work out a plan to get Joey and the boots back to the Inn, a dreadful creature appears from nowhere and I have to deal with that. And the characters don't follow my directions!

"And Windbreaker's appointed himself my partner and all he wants to do is write in glorious charges (preferably downhill) with the horn of Roland blaring away. And I've got an oversexed Valkyrie to worry about. And Sophie must be beside herself with worry that I haven't written. And what about Joey? The boy wants life and I have no answer for him. Help me, please."

For answer, Blunger's soul intoned, in its usual monotone, "Hope is the fuel of life. Also, I am instructed to remind you that you will be left with a benefit that you not entirely forget this happening. Perhaps others can give council. Let us see. Fear not; I will be nearby."

The light went out. A male voice some distance away called, "Guidance for Myron Blunger! Scene Two; take one!"

And they turned on the Sun and there was light and Myron Blunger found that he was standing alone by a dirt road on a warm day in summer. A golden meadow stretched away in all directions and birds darted overhead. He could hear rustlings in the high grass and crickets chirping. And another sound. Rhythmic, nearby and coming closer! He turned. Ambling toward him on the road with an easy, rocking motion was a long-snouted, shell-back marsupial, a cross between an elephant, an armadillo and a possum, and mostly elephant from the size of it! It was carrying four young in individual pouches, slung two by two under its belly. They were singing,

> "*Hey, hey; what a day;*
> *Momma takin' us out to play . . .*

"Silence!" the mother thing trumpeted to her young, and they obeyed as she came to a halt not ten feet from where Myron Blunger knelt, transfixed. "Call me Ishmael," she said, studying Blunger with large, brown eyes.

"Ishmael," he screeched, obediently. Then his mouth betrayed him. "You can't be Ishmael. Ishmael is a sailor, a whaler, an Indian man!" He clapped both hands over his hyperactive mouth, but too late.

"Aha!" snorted the creature, tapping each of her young to pay attention. "Lesson one. Never let me hear you say *I can't*! You can be anything you want to be: a sailor, a whaler, even an Ishmael if you're willing to work at it! Doors are made to be opened! Tell that to Joey Willem! And, by the way, I say he got himself off to a good start by running away from the Inn. All he needs now is a boost in confidence and a bit of learning. He's too old to be playing with griffins and rolling around on the greensward and running errands for that old miser Broco; send him to school!"

"Is everyone in the universe reading my manuscript?" Myron blurted out, astonished.

"There's a copy making the rounds," the mother-creature said. "My final suggestion is to . . . Stop that, now!" This to her rear starboard offspring, who was starting to squirm about in his pouch and whacking the forward port offspring, who had started to make faces at Blunger.

"My final suggestion is . . . you were saying,"
Blunger called out anxiously as the creature started to amble off.

"I don't remember," the creature called back. "Too much on my mind these days. Four more at home gestating in their sacs, and six going through adolescence . . ."

But the creature's young were starting to quarrel among themselves, hooting and spitting and flicking each other's fan-like ears with their snouts. The mother creature resumed her stroll down the country road. "Sorry, got to move on," she called over her shoulder. "Goodbye, and good luck. And from this time on I shall use the name . . . Ishmael!"

Myron Blunger called after her, "Hold it a minute! Hold on, there! Who are you?" But between the hootings and hollerings of her offspring, whom she was methodically, systematically whacking in turn with whichever leg was momentarily off-ground, and an apparent desire to make up for lost time, she did not respond. Afraid to move, Blunger called after the creature, "You read the manuscripts? What did you think of them? Were . . . they . . . any . . . good?" But she was out of earshot altogether. And then the light dimmed and went out and Myron Blunger was again in absolute darkness.

Moments passed and then Blunger heard, "Guidance for Blunger! Scene Three; take one!" And there was light. Not a uniform illumination, or even a landscape to illuminate. Only a circle of light cast by a streetlamp of antique design and construction, with a cast-iron, fluted post and an acorn-shaped lamp housing. Somewhere in the darkness, violins and flutes were playing and a slim, youthful woman, dark haired and of wondrous beauty entered the circle of light. She wore a diaphenous, crimson ballet gown and toe slippers, and atop her head was a silver tiara. Stepping gracefully into the circle of light, she proceeded to dance slowly, sensually, and passion and the promise of fulfillment were in every movement of her lithe arms and legs. She positioned herself against the lamppost, smiled and the parting of her lips exhumed a miriad of Blunger's adolescent and not-so-adolescent sexual dreams and longings, promising an eternity of fulfillments that set his brainpan afire. The music diminished; she spoke, and each word was a nightingale released to fly to the ears of a bloodied but unvanquished hero.

"Stay with me. Let time plod for those bound to weary Earth.

Stay forever in the magic land and be mine, and I . . . yours for all eternity.

Walk with me in sun-dappled paths beside gentle streams and we will talk and dream and laugh and love . . . .

Dwell with me. Rest thy weary head upon my breast . . ."

"Cut! Cut!" from the darkness. The scene vanished as the lamp was turned off. "Wrong script! This is Myron Blunger . . . from the Bronx! Take two!"

Again there was the circle of light about the lamppost, but the person who entered onto stage center was . . . was the image of his long-deceased neighbor, Jacob Minsky!

"Myron?" Minsky called, peering about into the darkness. "You out there?"

"Jake!" Myron called, his voice as raspy as when he'd been alive. "This way!" Myron would have run down the slope onto the stage to embrace his old friend and learn, from one who was now beyond it all and therefore smarter than the doctors what to do for hemorrhoids, but was stopped by Tom's hand on his wrist.

"Myron!" Minsky croaked. "You hear me good?"

"I hear you!" Myron answered.

"Wonderful! Listen then. They're letting me prophecy with upraised fingers and a convincing voice," he recited, pointing upward with all four fingers of his left hand.

From the darkness, someone hissed, "The line is: 'They're letting me prophecy!' One finger, a forefinger, please, and the convincing voice are stage directions! Keep going!"

Minsky waved the director off, advanced to the front of the stage and whispered loudly: "Beware of Don Juan de Tenirio; he's *meshuggah* and a murderer and his philosophy stinks! Here's some philosophy in case you should need it, and it's grade A stuff, not Tenirio's horseshit.

"Each of us casts two shadows. One in space and one in time. The shadow in space is a thing of the moment. The shadow in time is the story of our life. Extending into the past, it is recorded in memory. Extending into the future, it is hope. Hope is the fuel of life, and is the whole point to human existence."

"God told me the same thing," Blunger said. "The last part, anyway."

"I know. The word gets around," Minsky replied earnestly. "One thing you learn up here—God knows what He's talking about."

With that, the light suddenly went off and again Blunger found himself in darkness, with Tom's hand still around his wrist.

"Enough guidance?" Tom asked.

"No!" Myron said. He thought desperately. With all this guidance he was getting, they—*they!*—knew there was trouble ahead. Big trouble. *Hope* wasn't enough; he need *major guidance!* "The king of France! And forty thousand men!" he said.

"The king of France!" Tom exclaimed. "And . . . and forty . . . thousand men!"

"Forty thousand." Speak up! Remember the squeeky wheel . . . That's what Sophie said. But sometimes she said, *Half a loaf is better than none.* Should he settle for twenty thousand?

Tom released his wrist and went off, muttering. Time passed. There was a drumming in the distance. A fife chimed in. Then there was a drum roll in the distance and a voice called: "Scene four, take one."

And again there was light and Myron Blunger was standing on a low hill, looking out over a great plain as it might have been painted by one of the Impressionists with objects represented by spots of paint. From horizon to horizon, he saw regularly-spaced blobs of dark yellow—haystacks?—and small dabs of red and blue arranged in clusters and moving in fixed arrays.

"What's this?" Blunger asked.

"The king of France," Tom answered testily, as though he'd been put to some trouble, "and twenty thousand men." Blunger squinted. It didn't help.

"Sing your song," Tom suggested.

Cupping his hands around his mouth, Blunger shouted,

The king of France and forty thousand men marched up the hill and then marched down again!

The scene came into clear focus. Blunger gasped. What he'd taken for haystacks were the tents and wagons of a great army! The dabs of red and blue were divisions of soldiers marching in rank and file, wearing red and blue tunics and white breeches and black boots and Blunger could hear their tramp, tramp even at that distance. And there were horses by the hundreds being groomed and Blunger saw the captains and the majors and the colonels and one who, from the wondrous plume that emerged from his helmet, had to be a general. And in conversation with him was one seated upon a white horse, wearing an ermine cloak and a golden crown that shone brilliantly in the sun. Before each group of tents was a thin pole, atop which streamed a pennant, and Blunger had no doubt that he was looking upon the army of the king of France.

As soon as they heard his song, the soldiers would wheel about and raise their arms and salute him with a grand hail that would roll over the land! And no matter what danger or evil he faced in time to come, he would be able to count on the King of France . . .

Any moment now, they would hear his cry and declare their . . . and declare . . .

By now the sound should have reached them! He shouted the song again, but the army continued its drills and marches; the drums rolled and horses neighed . . .

And then the lights went out and he was in darkness.

Then came a cry: "Out! Out, all of you! Clear the set!" A rush of footsteps, muffled shouts, a distant crash as of a great host, an army moving out. From an infinite distance came Tom's voice, "Give the boy hope. Hope is the fuel of life."

A wind lifted Myron Blunger and pressed him back to the door, which opened at a touch and accepted his passage back to the library of the Inn at the End of the World. Myron Blunger found himself sitting on the floor, shivering, sobbing yet ecstatic. The radiance from the doorway diminished as the door slowly, dramatically closed. Before it clicked firmly shut, however, Myron

Blunger thought he heard, or sensed, or perhaps imagined one final sentence from the other side.

"When you next come before Me, Myron Blunger, son of Hirsh the Unenlightened, see that you are twenty pounds lighter."

The exit and return of Myron Blunger was witnessed from the library stacks by Don Juan de Tenorio, who had remained after the meeting of Dr. Watson's committee and now found himself rewarded by a solution to his problem with the Commandant.

TREACHERY

*In which Don Juan and Long John Silver work out plans of
escape according to their various competencies and desires.*

23,912: I regret having seduced Donna Anna; I sincerely regret
having dueled with her father the Commandant (though I did
warn him to keep out of it); I urgently and continuously regret
having run him through. signed: Don Giovanni (Don Juan de
Tenirio)

23,913: Barefoot and hatless by my grandmother's grave, I beg
pardon for having seduced Donna Anna and for dueling with her
father the Commandant (though I did warn him not to draw sword
against me); on my knees at the edge of the living universe, where
life begins and ends, I urgently and continuously weep for having
run him through. signed: Don Giovanni (Don Juan de Tenirio)

23,914: I'm sorry I screwed Donna Anna; I'm sorry I ever pulled a
sword on her father the Commandant (but he started it!); I'm
sorry, sorry, sorry I ran him through. signed: Don Giovanni (Don
Juan de Tenirio)

23,915: I regret that I chose Donna Anna as a receiver of swollen
goods

The point of his pencil stub snapped off and flew somewhere among
the books. Concealed in the stacks of the library, Don Juan threw
the inch-long, unsharpenable stub against the wall and broke down,

weeping silently. His stock of personal stationery long exhausted and paper being in short supply, he'd been carrying out Dr. Watson's prescription by scribbling his apologies on the flyleaves of library books, of which there seemed an inexaustible supply.

Now he'd have to get another pencil. Where? In The Inn at the End of the World, pencils and writing paper were at a premium, as many of the guests were busily rewriting their personal histories.

The Innkeeper was dangerously close to a wrath attack, according to Dr. Watson; no more borrowing pencils from him. And Watson needed his supply of writing materials for prescriptions and a monograph he was working on.

How was the don to carry out Dr. Watson's prescription, calculated according to Freud?

No less than fifty thousand handwritten, signed apologies—no two alike!—to be presented to the Commandant in a spirit of contriteness along with his sword and the most profuse, abject, self-denigrating verbal statement he could compose.

Fifty thousand! No two alike! And suppose he managed to complete the fifty thousand apologies, only to have them dismissed and rejected by the Commandant? No, Don Juan de Tenirio's only hope lay in escape from the Inn.

His lawyer, Portia, in the course of one of their many meetings, had discovered new evidence which favored him mightily. Indeed, Dr. Watson, after a thorough physical examination, had written a deposition that would exonerate Don Juan once and for all from the charge of willful and premeditated seduction! If only he could escape to Earth Real, to a court of law, he might beat the Commandant yet!

But how to escape to Earth Real? Over the Northern Reaches, as the Valkyrie had? Impossible. She was a Northlander, with blood so thin it had not ceased to flow even during a five-hundred year forced hibernation. The red cells of Southern blood were thick-walled, highly elastic and supercharged with nutrients; they could endure hours of passion without breakdown. The price paid—there is no free ride in this universe—was high viscosity at low temperatures; the subarctic conditions of the Northern Reaches would freeze him solid from the inside out within minutes, leaving him a salt-lick for the sabertooths.

Nor could he hope to escape through Esfandiary, as Willem had. Not without seven-league boots.

On the cold, stone floor he squatted, exhausted, dejected, his sword at hand but with little strength to defend himself should his nemesis appear. What would happen if the Commandant were to suddenly appear with drawn sword, and Don Juan's muscles couldn't respond for a lack of adrenalin? So it was that Don Juan fell into a shallow sleep, trembling and twitching.

He did not stir when Yin entered the library, nor did Blunger's hemmorhoid-induced moaning lift him from his fitful doze. He was jolted awake by a sudden infusion of brilliant light into the room and the clamor of someone screeching. His hand found the hilt of his sword, his pulse quickened, he looked around wildly to find that the room was filled with powder blue light so intense he was forced to squint! This was it, then! Oh, the Commandant knew how to exact a revenge!

And for what? For unselfishly helping the Commandant's daughter discover her innermost fires? They must have it out, here and now, and if he were catapulted down to the lowest circles of hell, so be it!

Sheathing his sword, he drew a poignard from his boot and scuttled to a position where the narrowness of the stacks would preclude sword-play, but a single thrust of a dagger might dispatch his enemy for good and ever. Peering through the narrow space between the tops of books and the next layer of shelves, he was astonished to observe that the door to Esfandiary was open, that it was from there that the terrible radiance blazed. The dreaded Commandant was nowhere in sight, and—Dios Mio!—Myron Blunger was vanishing into that fearful place, feet first!

The don watched Blunger disappear into the glare and then the door closed with a solid thud! Oddly enough, the gnome Yin stood motionless, his mouth open, gesturing with one hand as though, for him, time had stopped. Don Juan forced himself to remain silent, watchful.

Though they both hear everything, the stone is more learned than the tree, for the tree sighs in the wind; the stone reveals nothing.

This Don Juan had learned as a child from his mother. Thoughts of his late *Maman* led, as they always did, to remembrances of his cousin Carlotta. Carlotta, with yellow roses braided into her long, black hair and lips the color of port wine. When he was no longer a child, Carlotta had taken over his education.

He was still recalling and relishing those memories when suddenly the door flew open and Blunger tumbled back into the library, landing in a heap and followed by his shoes! During that entire time, the gnome had stood rigid as a courtyard statue, his eyes fixed on the spot from which Blunger had been taken, one hand still gesturing the thin air and his mouth half open. After the door closed, Yin's arm moved and he completed his thoughts. "Anyway, here's my opinion of chapter ten.

"First of all, a real hero has a dynamic interaction with his environment. Your Joey is okay so far, but Myron Blunger, your alter ego, is a washout as a protagonist. He doesn't handle terror well. He should really be in a cookbook, if you know what I mean. And now you've got Brunnhilde to contend with. If I were you, I'd . . . what's the matter, Myron? Are you all right? You *did* ask my opinion . . ."

But Myron Blunger was on hands and knees, staring blankly, abstractly at something beyond the library walls. His face was pale and an artery in Blunger's neck was pulsing wildly. The expression on his face was grim and determined.

With Yin's help, Myron Blunger lifted himself to a sitting position on the floor. His eyes still fixed on the door to Esfandiary, Blunger cried, "He saved me with a butterfly." Tears coursed down his cheeks. "'Hope is the fuel of life!' God told me that. Do you hear? I spoke with God!" After a moment, he added, wistfully, "A butterfly, with blue and gold wings."

Yin said slowly, thoughtfully, "In Esfandiary you were saved by a butterfly. Saved from what?" Suddenly it dawned upon Yin that he had reached a branch point in his existence! He could remain a gnome, somewhat below dwarves and way below elves in status. Dwarves had no music or magic, but were superb craftsmen; gold-and silversmiths. Elves were only cobblers, but had magic powers and sang well. Gnomes were considered to be 'dark elves', guardians of the underground, but with none of the respect accorded to craftsmen.

But *he, Yin, could be a scholar*! He could ask questions, write down the answers, fill notebooks! He could do real, academic scholarship! He could be an academic scholar, Yin thought excitedly, a professor with a tasselled cap and a gown with velvet stripes, and deep pockets full of notebooks and references! All this, in one flash of thought.

"Saved from what?" he repeated, affecting a scholarly tone of voice, though it was somewhat warbly.

"A dinosaur!" Blunger exclaimed. "It was a test."

Yin approached Blunger and stared anxiously into his eyes. To his astonishment, he found that he could see deeply into Blunger's innermost self, into his very spirit! And at Blunger's core, he found another Blunger! *Another Blunger*! Yin's temples pounded with excitement! Yes, scholarship was his career!

Buried within the familiar self-image of the rotund, retired, amiable children's librarian, Yin discerned a youthful Myron Blunger, a passionate imaginer and dreamer, a ten-year-old Myron Blunger suffused with the life force! What was the relationship between this pre-adolescent, zoo-visiting, infinitely curious Blunger-in-the-making and the adult they'd kidnapped? How had Life in the Bronx, marriage and fatherhood and running a children's library shaped, chiselled, formed the one into the other?

Yin concentrated as hard as he could, and at the limit of his resolution, learned why Blunger had *not* become an engineer or a doctor, or achieved the position of chief librarian. The spirit of the young Blunger had, early on, been nailed flat by a field of X's and Y's, the heads and tails of a host of algebraic equations that had appeared in the fifth grade, had been rein-forced straight through junior high, high school and college, and never expunged *or solved!* And gnawing at Blunger's core was a snakelike coil of slowly twisting, multiply linked, irre-ducible fractions *with no lowest common denominator!*

Nor was the contemporary, retired Blunger free of the heebee-jeebees! The adult spirit showed emotional bruises that had appar-ently been inflicted by something called a waterhammer!

A waterhammer! Barbaric humans! If Windbreaker knew of this, might he not abandon his quest to rejoin this race?

But he had discovered his talent in life, and Yin stepped back to consider his next course of action.

Scholars publish.

It was true, wasn't it, else why all these books? And a publica-tion might or might not be the equivalent of a nine minute head start in life, but it couldn't hurt! If Yang was aware of this gnomish power, he'd never mentioned it. Had Yin finally surpassed his twin?

And what about Blunger? What was happening to him? Was he undergoing a metamorphosis? Did he need watching?

And what to say to a human in the throes of metamorphosis? What to do? Yin suggested he put on his shoes.

Blunger, surprised to find them removed, did so, then stood up slowly as he tried to understand his experience. Turning to the gnome, he said, tentatively, "Maybe only one dinosaur means not so bad at all. Maybe I didn't fail . . .

"They *did* put on a show for me and I got lots of good advice from God and Jacob Minsky. And God gave me a golf lesson. And something named Ishmael has been following my writing . . ." Blunger exclaimed, rubbing his hands with satisfaction.

"Your writing," Yin interrupted, anxious to distract Blunger from the evolutionary or revolutionary process taking place within his mind. "Let's go back to your writing. *Justice* isn't so bad. It's just that . . . well, Oy is not a suitable chapter ending. Also, there are loops still unclosed. Dragon Groff, for example. And Brunnhilde. We have to prepare a new outline. I'll help you."

But Blunger had stopped listening. He had taken several steps forward, backward, had knelt down, straightened, stretched, wiggled his rear in several directions, and then gone off mad, running, leaping around the room.

"No more hemorrhoids! No more hemorrhoids!" Blunger cried joyously. "God promised a *benefit*, and He kept His word! No . . . more . . . hemorrhoids!" Stooping, he embraced the gnome and did a little jig in place, laughing. "Maybe I didn't fail His test after all! Maybe God gave me a C plus, or a B even! And for your information, Mr. Yin, B is a better-than-passing grade!

"God said, 'Hope is the fuel of Life!' And you know something; God's right! Joey's out there trying to make his own life, without a mother, without a father for guidance and encouragement. And what am I doing for him? Instead of helping him find his way, I'm shilling for the Innkeeper to bring him back! Well, no more of that!" Blunger announced, squaring his shoulders and loosening his writing hand with a fancy shake of the wrist.

"I'm going to make him a home! A home in Upper Muchness, with warmth and a good school and any future he wants! Close the loops, the Innkeeper said? Okay, I'll close the loops! I'll start with Dragon Groff!" And to demonstrate his renewed confidence, he snapped his finger three times.

"Dragon Groff is not to be dismissed with a snap of fingers, even if you had ten on each hand!" Yin whispered fearfully, determined to humor and stand by Blunger to the end. "It is said that Dragon Groff was master of the valley when the ancestors of humans were first dropping out of the trees! It is said that he sharpens his talons against a diamond whetstone the size of a bear's head! There are ancient memories passed from generation to generation of the wild creatures . . ."

But Myron Blunger, full of *Guidance*, dismissed the gnome's plea for caution with another finger-snap. "You don't understand! I have guidance from God! Of course, I was flustered a little; there's a lot I could have told Him if I didn't have all that pressure! About women, for example. Their arms are too short; Sophie can't reach high shelves. And Social Security . . . why shouldn't I qualify for maximum? You know why? Because you have to be a Rockefeller or a landlord! And speaking of landlords . . ."

Blunger took a deep breath and dismissed all that with a wave of his hand. "But God is on my side! Now I realize why I was summoned to Esfandiary!

"Hope is the fuel of life! With hope you create your future!"

Pointing a forefinger at his head, he exclaimed dramatically, "When I first sat down to write about Joey Willem, I was really writing about *me*, aged ten! When the rest of the class was learning how to add fractions, I was looking out the window, flying a P-51 or capturing tigers for the circus, or punching Lenny Barther, the class bully, down onto the floor with a right and a left and a Joe Lewis knockout punch right in the *kishkes*! Mrs. Andrews said I had a *hyperactive imagination* and reported I should get dosed with salts and cod-liver-oil!" She didn't know that while she was hocking fractions, I was living three lives in my head all at once! Just wait! Wait until I tell Sophie I spoke with God!

Clapping his hands to his head, he cried, "Sophie! Poor Sophie! What am I going to do? When I started to write *The Boy With No Future*, she was my best supporter, in a way." His head was spinning, and he had a job to do.

Sitting himself down *comfortably* at his writing table, Blunger wrote at the top of a clean sheet of paper:

THE DON AND THE CAPTAIN

by Myron Blunger, with GUIDANCE!

As he jotted notes on his outline for *Hope and the Dragon*, he proceeded to tell Yin everything that had happened since the door to Esfandiary opened for him.

And hidden among the stacks, Don Juan listened. And a means of escape from the Inn and his nemesis hatched within his mind entire: the means, the timing, the arrangements to be made!

The plot was bold, linear and foolproof! There were parts for the horn of Roland and the MasterWeapon Excalibur. There were parts for Windbreaker and Long John Silver. And there was even a part for Myron Blunger. A difficult, unpleasant part with no curtain call.

There was no part for the Commandante! Let the dread figure prowl the Inn, search its hallways and ramparts, haunt the lower levels; the don would be a guest of honor at Lucien Broco's mansionhouse in Upper Muchness, responsible only to his bodily needs, free to enjoy life's givings and takings!

But half the job is the preparation; any housepainter knew that. From the stack behind him, he withdrew an old, leatherbound volume written on heavy paper and carefully tore out a blank flyleaf. It had no crest or watermark, but it would do, it would do. A loveletter to a woman might be scratched on rock with base chalk from the ground, yet it will send her heart pounding . . .

The don waited patiently, silent and hidden, until Blunger and the gnome had left the library together to take dinner and discuss plot outlines for *Hope and the Dragon*. Alone at last, the don slipped to Blunger's writing table, took up a pen, dipped it in ink and in a fine hand, wrote:

My dearest, darling Wilma,

> "Thank God I waited for you! I have just now learned of your brave journey out of the Valley of Upper Muchness seven years ago, in search of your personal life-road, and your story has struck a resonance within my heart. My own quest for love and fulfillment has, unfortunately, only led me to false and shallow dalliances, hard women and would-be lovers blinded by my modest store of worldly goods, inherited from my loving, deceased parents and three wealthy, childless uncles. Believing that truelove had eluded me forever, I have gone each night to my bed alone, cursing the caskets of baubles, the closets filled with seasonal vanity and my landhold, for I had no wife to walk by my side, nor heir to teach the ways of estate management. My life-path was indeed strewn with thorns discarded by happier men as they embraced the petals of their beloved roses, etcetera.
> But hearing of your beauty, character and stamina, I have faith in you as in the sunrise, that we are kindred spirits, darling Wilma. Our destinies are intertwined. Writing this is difficult, for my eager fingers caress the instrument that should be you, my dearest. It is my hope, my dream that even now as I pen this too-brief note in the comfort of my extra-wide downy bed, beneath a canopy of white satin, you are at last making your way home, to your beautiful, gracious mother Loretta, to your clever father, Benison . . . and—dare I hope?—to your truly intended,"

Don Juan

That would do the job.

But the don's heart was light, his hand supple and the book

had *another* flyleaf! And Wilma's whereabouts, after all, were unknown, even to her mother! And a bird in the hand . . . there *was*
a bird in the hand, wasn't there? Another lady demanding attention . . .

He tore out the second flyleaf from the book and, dipping the
pen into the inkwell once more, composed a second letter:

Dearest Brunnhilde,

"Thank Wotan I waited for you! I have just now learned of
your five hundred year ordeal on the bed of stone, surrounded by fire, and your recent search for a *held*, a hero
worthy of your passion for life! Know that your story has
struck a resonance within my heart. My own quest for love
and fulfillment has, unfortunately, only led me to false and
shallow dalliances, hard women and would-be lovers blinded
by my modest store of worldly goods, inherited from my
loving, deceased parents and three childless *heldentenors* on
my father's side. Believing that truelove had eluded me forever, I have passed my days in *heldenactivitaten*, fighting
and slaying and riding my horse into a lather . . . and going
each night to my bed alone, cursing my collection of rusting
armor, my unscratched shield, my untried broadsword. The
harvest bounty of my landhold awakens bitterness in my
heart, for I have no wife to walk by my side beneath the
grape arbors, nor heir to teach the ways of estate management. My life-path has indeed been strewn with thorns
discarded by happier men as they embraced the petals of
their beloved roses, etcetera.
But hearing of your beauty and character and immense
physical strength, I have faith in you as in the sunrise, that
we are kindred spirits, darling Brunnhilde. Our destinies are
intertwined. Writing this is difficult, for my eager fingers
caress the instrument that should be you, my dearest. It is
my hope, my dream that even now as I pen this too-brief

note in the comfort of my extra-wide downy bed, beneath
a canopy of white satin, you are preparing to bid adieu to
those glorious but confining breastplates, and welcome your
held. It is time *Wildschweinblutmeister* was retired to a closet.
Give my regards to your father, Wotan the god.
*y*our truly intended,"

Don Juan

Folding both letters, he addressed them:

To Wilma Hawkins, originally of Upper Muchness, present
address unknown, and,
To Brunnhilde the Valkyrie, daughter of Wotan the god, c/
o #7 Broco Way, Upper Muchness.

Exiting the library, Don Juan dropped his letters on the sideboard
in the *outgoing* mail basket, then proceeded directly to Dr. Watson's
rooms for a brief chat. Learning of the Innkeeper's new chamberpot,
he laughed quite merrily, for this development suited his plan as
though made to order! Before departing, he planted into Dr. John
Watson's consciousness one word, one single word of prescription
upon which his scheme revolved. The word was *neutralize*, and it
was critical that Watson keep that word in the forefront of his
memory when next he examined the Innkeeper.

Satisfied in all respects, Don Juan made his exit, then strode
quickly to the quarters of Long John Silver, keeping his back to a
wall and his sword drawn against a surprise attack by the Commandant.

Immediately upon entering Silver's quarters, Don Juan had misgivings. Could he put trust into such a one as could willingly live
in this loathsome cell? Don Juan's own suite was decorated in plush
velvet, with musical instruments in the corners. His canopied bed
was large and could be quickly adjusted from soft to extra firm by
means of a clever air pump operable from atop the bed itself. His

sheets and covers were of satin and the walls of his bedroom were functionally decorated with gilded mirrors and sensual paintings.

Long John Silver's rooms, modelled after a ship's cabin, were dark and sparsely furnished, with heavy beams running across the low ceiling and dozens of maps mounted on the walls. Those maps, marked cryptically with ink that had faded to light brown, were Silver's most precious possessions. A heavy oak table—the only other pieces of furniture in that chamber were two straight-backed chairs and a narrow bed set hard against the wall—was edge-lipped and gimballed against the roll of oceans remembered. The room was lighted by the steady glow of a thick, yellow candle set on a coin large as a child's fist and made of solid gold.

A porthole looked out upon a barren, snow-covered downslope, and beyond that, the greyness of the Deep. Set into a wall just below the porthole was a short length of discolored wooden dowel, a parrot's perch from the claw-marks and general messiness, though no parrot was in sight.

Beneath the bed was a small, iron-bound sea chest, on the side of which was carved the name *Hispaniola*. In that chest, along with a modest treasure in gold doubloons, was a pistol. Silver himself had let that fact slip out early in their acquaintance, and the don had not forgotten. Had he known of the pistol, the Innkeeper would have confiscated it upon Silver's admittance to the Inn.

"I can take no more torment from the Commandant," Don Juan sighed, throwing himself into a chair, "or from *Don Juan in Hell*, which mercifully is losing its popularity. It's all very well having a strong opera like *Don Giovanni* supporting you, but the other one . . . it's very title is debilitating to the spirit."

The pirate grunted, then returned to stropping a razor edge on his dirk. Indeed, he'd been pondering his own problems and regrets when the don had knocked on his door, and the don's agitation merely underscored his own.

Don Juan leaned forward across the narrow table. "I plan to escape," he announced. "I'm doomed, anyway. And so are you. And everyone else at the Inn. We're all thinning out. That's the way of it; a while at the Inn, a decline in belief and *whoosh!* Out, like a candle. But it doesn't have to be that way, eh, senor Silver? Joey Willem found another way, didn't he?"

Indeed, the pirate's mind had been wandering down much the same line of thought. Where were Flint, Mr. Arrow, Blind Pew or even old Black Dog to share his rum and talk about the old days, here at the end of it all? Below deck, that's where! Rotting away in a bloody dungeon. Aye, the don didn't have to press on so about shrivelling away to nothing.

"The whippersnapper had a pennysworth of pepper in his guts, didn't he, though!" Silver said, pensively. "I mean, the lad done it! Aye for 'im, over there in the valley, fast making hisself 'is own man! And us? We're as others have drawn us! Plain or fancy, to their liking, not ours! Like speared fish, we flop and wiggle to order!"

"But maybe you're right, mate; maybe there's another way for it! In Earth Real, where you make your own life! We could run a tavern together; aboard the *Hispaniola* I was knowed as *Barbeque,* ye know. Ship's cook, and not half-bad at that.

"You could teach dancing to the daughters of the rich, or . . . or even try out for a sailor if you've the spine for it! The boy found the way; he's free and doing just fine *for hisself.*" These last words were hissed. "But how to get there without the boots?" He sighted along the blade of the dirk, whose blade he held in an odd three-finger grip. Then, with a snap of wrist too fast for the eye to follow, he let fly; the dagger entered the doorpost with a satisfying, solid *thud.*

So, the pirate was not above trying to impress him; that was good, Don Juan thought. "It can be done," he said. "And without the seven-league boots."

"How? By crossing the Northern Reaches, as the Valkyrie did?" Silver demanded, his swarthy face creased in doubt and distrust. "I'm as brave as any man above deck or below, but I'm not eight feet tall. There are sabertooths out there, and other creeturs even more fearsome."

"Nor is my sword the equal of Brunnhilde's lance!" Don Juan agreed. "Yet there is a way."

Silver's broad face shook in puzzlement. "Are you proposing we hike through Esfandiary, assuming we can get by the door and find our way without getting et up?"

The don smiled. "I intend to fly through the air astride the fastest of all creatures. Pegasus."

Silver spat. "Arrggh! Yer daft, now! The Innkeeper would draw and quarter anyone beside hisself daring to ride the winged horse!"

"Not it if were put to him properly," Don Juan said, leaning back in his chair and stretching his legs out confidently. "Incentive is the key to it all. And at the bottom, supporting everything, is the fact that the Innkeeper's impatience with Blunger is growing into a gnawing, all-consuming fury!"

"Ah?" Silver grunted.

"Yes," said the don, patiently. "There is a level of society, my dear Silver, where a deficiency of *machismo* or even a breech of etiquette calls for the sending of a white feather. The result is a ceremonial duel, which ends when the injured party has received a superficial cut.

"And there is a level of society in which a breech of etiquette results in the sending of a dead fish. The offender lives for the duration of one *Hail Mary*, unless he happens to know how to breath underwater."

The don lowered his voice and leaned over the table. "And finally there is a social order in which a breech of etiquette—an abuse of hospitality, perhaps—results in the sending of a chamberpot! The message of the chamberpot is more terrible than the sending of a white feather or a fish, to one who knows how to read messages. It foretells destruction from within, slow and terrible. The Innkeeper in his wrath ordered such a Pot made. And it been sent to and received by Myron Blunger, freely and of his own will.

"One does not know in what manner the Innkeeper intends to

dispose of Myron Blunger, but it will be neither quick nor merciful. Oh, no, senor," Don Juan shook his head, smiling coldly.

"Perhaps the Innkeeper intends to force Blunger to write himself out of existence through excessive dining, with our visitor from the Bronx so bloating himself that his arm will no longer reach around his belly to the writing table.

"Perhaps Blunger will die poetically, at his writing table, still trying to uncover the infinity of meanings of *Higher Migher*. I say poetically, because he will have written his own epitaph. *Oy*. The final word of *Justice*. Beneath his gruff exterior, the Innkeeper has a taste for poetic justice.

"And there is more," Don Juan hissed, leaning over the table toward the buccaneer. "The Lord God has indeed taken up golf. I had heard rumors for some time . . . they are true! He has turned His back on humankind. He, who could have transported Myron Blunger back to his beloved Bronx in an eyeblink, dismissed the poor buffoon with an ineffectual slogan. *Hope is the fuel of life*.

"And in conversation with our beloved Dr. Watson I have learned that a new spirit inhabits the Innkeeper's body. The spirit of Wotan! Do you think it trivial that the Innkeeper sent Brunnhilde to Upper Muchness at this time? *Brunnhilde the Valkyrie is his daughter*! Now that the Lord God has turned his back on humankind, and likely on all that He created, the way is clear for Wotan to set himself up, first in Upper Muchness, then everywhere.

"Think, *hombre*! Everywhere! The seas could be yours! For myself, my needs are simple."

The don cocked his ear to the door; was that the squeak of a loose floorboard outside? Was the Commandant waiting, waiting . . . .

"But first I must escape! While I get Pegasus aloft, I must have a guard against my nemesis." This latter word hissed so that the candle fluttered. "As centaurs go, Windbreaker is not half bad. He is obsessed with obtaining the horn of Roland," said Don Juan, "that he might fulfill his destiny. Let him have the horn, if it gives him courage. But for the task of guarding my ascent, I prefer that he wield Excalibur.

"That's fine as it goes, but even Pegasus can't carry two of us out of here, to Earth Real," Silver said in a low voice. "Eh? Where does that leave me?"

The don smiled. "You forget. Myron Blunger is not writing on a kitchen table, or at a desk or sprawled across a double bed; he is writing in the library of the Inn at the End of the World, where belief is a high power! And Blunger seems to have a great power of belief. You sat there yourself on more than one occasion, endeavoring to recreate the schooner *Hispaniola*. Suppose you tried again, *with* Blunger beside you, your dirk at his throat instead of wasting its point in the doorpost!" Don Juan hissed. "Suppose you had your crew at hand, instead of rotting in the lower level of the Inn like rats! All of you together, concentrating on the *Hispaniola*, her shape, her fittings, her sails . . .

"Indeed, why not take Blunger along on the *Hispaniola's* maiden voyage?" the don suggested. "Desperate and out of wind, he's still a threat to all of us so long as he's at that writing table. Cornered, he could write the destruction of the Inn, with all its inhabitants! Taking him along with you would be a final act of loyalty to our friends."

"What makes you say Blunger is out of wind?" asked Long John Silver.

Don Juan adjusted his position to let the candle light his face from below, which emphasized the strong vertical lines of his face. "While composing some letters in the library just now, I scanned his writing. He has outlined a tale titled *Hope and the Dragon*.

"The dragon is Dragon Groff," said Don Juan.

"Then he's a bloody fool," Silver grunted.

"No matter," the don exclaimed. "The writing of *Hope and the Dragon* will not take him long; we must act quickly to prepare our escape. First, we must enlist Windbreaker. By stationing him at the paddock, he will be kept far from the library and any possibility of rescuing Blunger, who will be your captive."

"And what am I doing in the library with the *Hispaniola?* Am I to sail her between the stacks?" the pirate growled angrily.

"Nay," laughed Don Juan. "Myron Blunger has twice visited Esfandiary, and there is an old saying: *Third time pays for all.* You and your crew and Myron Blunger will troop through that door, which Blunger will open, one way or the other. You will find yourselves at the edge of a great ocean, with the sloop *Hispaniola* armed, provisioned, at anchor and a longboat ashore and ready. You will sail away in the direction of Upper Muchness. You will . . ."

"Avast, mate!" Silver growled. "You will please explain to me how all these *you wills* are to be done up proper."

"That's the beauty of the thing," the don exclaimed, rising and retrieving the pirate's dirk from the doorpost. "In the library of this Inn, at that table, you have only to believe. Believe with utmost fervor, believe as you believe in your next breath, your next heartbeat . . . and it is so! And all of you, Blind Pew and Black Dog and the rest . . . and Blunger, who has been given to hope by God Himself . . . all of you together will *create* your ocean to order! And the *Hispaniola.*

"You wish to sail to Upper Muchness, with a following wind? So it shall be. If you will it, you'll make landfall on the north side of the Dromedaries, upwind of the valley, with no more than a three hour march over the Saddle and along Broco Way to the door of the mansionhouse. Of course, there is no need to take Blunger all that way; he could be dropped overboard, permitted to swim the last few miles. To take his mind off his other problems. Also, he could use the exercise."

"And what do you want from me?" the pirate asked, too old a hand not to know that each word of the Don's carried a price.

"Your pistol," said the don matter-of-factly. "I seem to recall that you have a cannonbarrel flintlock in your possession, perhaps having forgotten to declare it upon arriving at the Inn. With some preparation, the Innkeeper will gladly trade the horn and the sword, and an airing of his favorite horse, for a pistol. A pistol of quality sufficient to neutralize Blunger. Not to destroy him utterly, for you will have need of his specialty, but to neutralize him sufficiently that he participate in the creation of the *Hispaniola* with the proper fervor and dedication, as a means of escape from the Inn."

Long John Silver met the don's knowing smile with silence and the merest of nods, signifying interest, but not commitment. As Don Juan proceeded to outline his scheme, the pirate sat, narrow-eyed, hardly listening, considering, weighing.

To write the Hispaniola into being . . . to hear gulls once more, and the snap of canvas, to feel the wind and see the bow wake . . . Blunger writes . . . belief is a high power!

Silver recalled his first voyage as a 'prentice seaman at the age of twelve. Sent aloft with a dozen others in a full Cape storm, he'd found himself straddling a rain-slicked yardarm, clinging desperately to a line with one hand while the other, stiff with cold, pulled on heavy canvas mains'ls that snapped and cracked and tried again and again to slap him down into the angry grey water. Above, the masthead glowed and crackled with St. Elmo's fire . . .

And then there was the *Treasure Island* affair. A chestful of treasure, guns and rum and the company of men. Ah, win or lose, that had been *sweet*! Aye, better to end up swinging on the dock, or tasting the business edge of a cutlass than to sit here, rotting away. How he longed to heave his sea-chest to his shoulder (an' Cap'n Flint aboard the other), and make his way to water's edge. There'd be a dory waiting, and Mr. Hands and the others at the oars, and a few hundred yards offshore, the *Hispaniola*.

. . . *where belief is a high power* . . .

In the end, Silver insisted that they share a pull of Jamaican Dark to seal the pact. A toast to Myron Blunger, and then the pirate exhumed his pistol and its accessories from the bottom of the sea chest. The weapon had been well-wrapped against moisture; the powder was dry. The Innkeeper would find no fault with it. They would work the trade in the morning, directly after Dr. Watson had finished with his patient, when the Innkeeper's temper was at highest tide.

"I have also thought of a suitable code-phrase for this operation,"

Don Juan said, laying the dirk on the table and rising. "What think you of *Deus ex machina*?"

"Dees . . . ex . . . mackina," the pirate repeated. He nodded.

So it was settled. Don Juan slipped out of Silver's quarters. Gaining his room, the don locked and bolted the door behind him. He laid out his best clothing, that he make a good impression in Upper Muchness and, for the last time, prepared for sleep at The Inn at the End of the World. His last act before turning down the kerosene lamp was to scrawl on the wall above his bed, boldly, in red ink:

13,915: I regret nothing.

Long John Silver opened his sea-chest, replaced the pistol until it would be called for on the morrow, and withdrew a brass spyglass wrapped in black velvet. Tucking his crutch beneath his arm, he thumped his way out into the corridor and toward a stone stairway that led upward to the roof. With his crutch tucked beneath his arm and keeping a firm hold on the railing, he nimbly hopped up the stairs until he came out onto the roof and a widow's walk that faced out upon the Deep.

When loneliness was hard upon the ex-pirate by day or night, he came to this place in secret, sometimes alone, sometimes with Cap'n Flint aboard his shoulder. Here he would pace in private, reminiscing to his parrot and lamenting that he was all alone at the end, all alone and stuck with a strange lot of landlubbers and no prospects of ever again going adventuring for treasure. Then he would plant himself by the railing, spyglass extended, scanning the Deep.

The Deep was a considerable body of water, with many coves and inlets and what appeared to be a riverhead off near the horizon, visible only with the spyglass fully extended. More than once, Silver had dreamt of spotting a patch of white moving close to the wind or running before it, the dark line of a ship's hull low on the water or, at night, a dark shape sailing by starlight. His heart ached for the roll of a deck, the smell of salt water, the creak of lines and tackle and the mournful cry of gulls!

Settling himself by a parapet, he sighed as he again pondered the don's phrase: *He is writing in the library of the Inn at the End of the World, where belief is a high power!*

He concentrated on his memories of the *Hispaniola* with eyes shut tight and his hands pressing into the railing so hard that beads of sweat appeared, veins stood out on his temples and his muscles trembled with the work of it. He opened his eyes, fixed his spyglass and scanned the Deep.

He saw only black water with a streak of moonbeam down the center. Well, this wasn't the library, was it? And he needed some sleep; tomorrow would be demanding of strength and determination. He collapsed his spyglass, planted his crutch beneath his arm, crossed the walk over to the stairway and was about to descend into the Inn when he heard the clatter of hooves against stone.

The sound came from the direction of the trail that led down to the Deep, and carried clearly in the still night air. He strode quickly to the parapet and listened, wondering what urgent errand warranted riding so near the Deep after dark. There were dangerous shore-creatures that dwelt among the boulders at water's edge, and one must not forget the kraken. While the kraken was known to be a sea-creature whose fate was to dwell beneath the waters and gnaw at the roots of the tree of life, it was said that at the end of days it would rise onto the land . . .

He waited impatiently while a cloud passed before the moon, then raised his spyglass and was rewarded by the sight of Windbreaker cantering downtrail, a lantern in one hand, a lance in the other. Something was slung across his back. A body? The centaur reached water's edge, spun around and headed back up toward the Inn. Silver lowered his spyglass and shook his head in wonder. Don Juan had selected as his rear-guard one so stupid as to dash up and down the shore-trail at night, armed only with a lance?

Well, that was not Silver's concern. He scuttled to the stairway and down to his quarters.

Had he waited some while, Long John Silver would have spotted something remarkable. He would have seen an object large and black heave its fore-parts out of the shallows onto the silver grey of the tundra. It possessed no eyes, but from its head-section, two trunklike tubes swept the trail that led to the Inn. It sucked air into itself, exhaled quietly, then sniffed again and knew that somewhere nearby, somewhere on this dry land was the half-horse, half-man, who had bitten off one of its lesser tentacles.

Slowly it retreated into the water, slipping its carapaced head and powerful tentacles beneath the dark surface so smoothly, so quietly that hardly a ripple remained to show that it had been there at all. Its sensor-trunks, as though reluctant to cease smelling the spoor of the half-horse, splashed as they re-entered the Deep. The half-horse, half-man had been here; it would come again. It would not leave.

The final grains of sand funnelled through the neck of the egg-timer. Three minutes. Yang inverted it, shut his eyes and cupped both hands behind his ears, straining to hear the sound of hoof-beats down the length of corridor. Nothing. The fine, pink sand in the egg-timer accumulated in the bottom section of the egg-timer. What was keeping Windbreaker?

The centaur was carrying two hundred pounds of flour sacks strapped to his back. One of them had sprung a leak, and patches of white flour marked Windbreaker's first two runs of the evening; they formed a trail down the center of the main corridor that ended at the double-doors that led into the kitchen. From there, Yang knew, they led through the service entrance to the outside, to the trail that led down, down to the shore of the Deep. So out of shape was the centaur that on his first two runs, he hadn't even reached the shoreline before he turned around and scratched and clawed his way up the steep hill to the Inn. Three miles, total.

He should have been back already . . .

Half the sand gone—three minutes plus one and a half minutes—and Yang heard not even a distant clatter of hoofbeats. Perhaps the centaur was still too far away to be heard. Too slow, too slow! They'd set a mark of under five minutes, and Windbreaker hadn't even come close on his earlier trials. Could something have happened? Yang had wanted him to run figure eights in the paddock, with was within the outer walls of the Inn. Windbreaker would have none of that. "Figure eights?" he'd snapped. "I'll go out of my mind! I'll carry a lantern and a lance, in case the sabertooth is prowling around."

The concept of a nocturnal confrontation with a sabertooth tiger sent shivers through every muscle and nerve in the gnome's body, but Yang was afraid to discourage Windbreaker. In the end, his only hope of gaining his life's goal was through bravery, and one doesn't learn bravery from textbooks, doing calisthenics or running figure eights in a protected paddock. And there was the possibility of things out there even more dangerous than sabertooths, though Yang could hardly imagine what they might be. As the very last grain of sand trickled into the lower section of the egg-timer, Yang heard hoofbeats in the distance. Irregular, unsynchronized! What had happened out there?

Six minutes! Again he inverted the timer. The clattering increased in intensity and finally the centaur appeared at the far end of the corridor. Clearly he was winded and struggling, but still he galloped, galloped, his arms swinging and his chest heaving as his wide-open mouth sucked in volumes of air.

The lantern had gone out and the lance dangled at his side as he pulled alongside the gnome, changed gait to a canter, then to a trot, then to a walk. His entire body was drenched with sweat, perspiration poured down his neck into the collar of his heavy-knit sweater, and yet, he was shivering. "The path is too uneven," he said, glumly.

"Also, as I came up to the door, I thought I heard something splash. Something big. Why can't we work out during the day-time?"

"We've been through that," Yang said guardedly. "I want to keep your progress secret. The Innkeeper blames Myron Blunger for his problems. Myron Blunger is an ideal scapegoat. Sooner or later, something will go seriously wrong. When the mob forms, with pitchforks and torches, you will be Blunger's only hope of escape. I think we owe him that much. But you're not ready yet."

No, the centaur wasn't ready yet, Yang thought. Blunger weighed about the same as the four sacks of flour, and despite the centaur's confidence, there was no way Windbreaker, with Blunger aboard, could outrun a hunger-crazed sabertooth. But he had to help the centaur maintain his confidence. "We're through for now," Yang said, reassuringly. "You're running okay . . . steady gait, good endurance. Before you know it, you'll be running down to the edge of the Deep and back in less than five minutes. Take a shower and get a good night's sleep; I'll see you tomorrow at early breakfast."

CHOLENT AND THE INNKEEPER

The morning of Myron Blunger's final day at the Inn was different from all other mornings. Generally, by dawn, the aroma of fresh loaves, rolls, muffins and sweetcakes permeated the corridors and hallways of The Inn at the End of the World. On this morning, a new and rich scent emanated from the kitchen. It originated in dozens upon dozens of heavy iron pots filled with chunks of meat, potatoes, carrots, herbs and spices. They had simmered and bubbled all night in the baking ovens under a low heat, and would be at their peak of flavor by dinnertime.

The aroma drifted down to the lower level where Long John Silver's cohorts and a host of other scoundrels and knaves were wasting away in a communal cell. Yes, even in that dismal dungeon, the succulent aroma of simmering *cholents* displaced the foul, dank, mildew-laden air and lifted the spirits of the imprisoned buccaneers, on the morning of Myron Blunger's last day at the Inn.

Hurrying to the Innkeeper's quarters before breakfast, Dr. Watson took no notice of that rich scent. He was greatly disturbed and most uncharacteristically, his shirt-tails were hanging out, his belt-end was loose and flapping and his stethoscope trailed from his black bag. Awakened before dawn by an evil dream in which Holmes had replaced him as a roommate by Irene Adler, he'd been unable to return to sleep. Turning to Freud for insight on what this meant, he'd happened upon a passage he'd never read before. Alarmed, he'd dressed hurriedly, dashed out of his quarters, a replica of the old 221b Baker Street digs, and ran headlong to examine his patient afresh.

At an intersection of passages, he came upon the gnome Yin who, too excited with his new life as a scholar to sleep late, was wandering about, notebook in hand, looking for another opportunity to carry out research. It came to Watson's mind that, for what lay ahead, it might do to have an assistant.

"Remain out of sight until he's completely under, and be prepared to take notes," Dr. Watson whispered as they approached the door to the Innkeeper's chambers. Yin obeyed, bending low and scooting inside unseen as Dr. Watson opened the door of the darkened room.

"Well, let's take a look at the patient," Watson said cheerily, concealing his fears. "First of all, we need sunlight." With that, he threw open the curtains to admit strong early-morning rays. With a hoarse shout of pain, the Innkeeper shielded his light-sensitive eyes with his left arm.

The Innkeeper's bedchamber had undergone a marked change since Dr. Watson's last visit. Now the oak wall was lined with daggers and hammers, each fitted to its own sheath or loop of iron. A score of banners, battle-tattered and faded, formed an arch over the bed. At the center of that arch was a great shield suspended from eight ropes and below that shield was a plaque crafted in a dark wood and on that plaque was written in letters of gold: *This be the shield of Achilles that was fashioned by Hephaestus.* All these things had been retrieved from the armory. Why? And why now?

Seating himself at the edge of the bed, Dr. Watson opened his black medical kit and carried out his examination in silence. His patient's blood pressure was alarmingly high, his pulse had too much thump, even for a Viking, and a close examination of the pupils of the Innkeeper's eyes led to a new and somber diagnosis.

"Your blood's thick with wrath," Dr. Watson explained as he wrote the R_x on his pad. "The slightest anxiety, such as worrying about the kitchen budget, could trigger curdling. That explains the failure of the cupping and the powerful St. Felicia's potion. Too much inflammation.

"Work on reducing the wrath," Dr. Watson ordered. "Get your mind off Blunger! Neutralize thoughts of Blunger!" *Neutralize* had been the word suggested by Don Juan the previous day. Good word. Should use it more often, he thought. He tore off the prescription and put it in the Innkeeper's right hand.

The Innkeeper's eyes, unfocussed and bright with fever, half-blinded by the strong light in the room, discerned from Watson's penmanship a series of ink-swirls, dots and crosses that seemed to spell out the instruction *Neuter Blunger*. Slowly his pressure dropped, his pulse normalized and the anguished expression on his face dissolved into a calm and profound smile.

For Myron Blunger was to be neutered.

Doctor's orders.

The profound smile dissolved into anxiety as the Innkeeper watched Dr. Watson lay out an array of gauze pads, metal pans and forceps on the night table. It degenerated into a frown as the doctor went into his pre-surgery litany of mutterings, "Tape . . . tape . . . alcohol . . . cotton . . . ah, here we are . . . our little friends . . ."

"Now, how's our patient's right arm?" he asked with old-fashioned professional joviality, unscrewing the cap of a wide-mouthed jar. But his back was to the Innkeeper.

The Innkeeper raised himself on one elbow and squinting, tried to peek around the doctor's body. "You know why my pressure's up?" he said hoarsely. "I gave you the leadership of the most diverse, broadbased and powerful committee ever assembled at the Inn! And what did you do with it? Did you solve the Willem problem? No! Did you retrieve my boots? No! Did you order Myron Blunger to stop introducing expensive delicacies to the chefs? No! You created fourteen pages of minutes in doctor's writing that no one can read! *That's* why my pressure's up and my fever has . . . risen . . . what are those?" as Watson turned around. "What are you doing?

"No! I won't have them again! I . . .

"Aaarrgh!"

So it was that the Innkeeper was given over to the leeches for a second round of bloodletting. Only by keeping his eyes averted could the Innkeeper tolerate their presence on his right forearm, which, apparently because of its superior musculature, the blood-suckers found more congenial than the other. The Innkeeper de-manded, at the least, that they be covered with a towel, but of course that was out of the question; this particular breed of leeches preferred to work in the open . . .

From his waistcoat pocket, Dr. Watson took a gold watch on a chain. He seated himself at the edge of the bed so that sunlight reflected from the watch. Slowly, slowly he twisted the chain, send-ing a spot of golden light dancing around the room and occasion-ally into the Innkeeper's eyes.

"What you need more than anything," he intoned in a sooth-ing, low voice, "is to take take your mind off the bloodletting, off Blunger, off the Willem boy and off your boots, off the kitchen budget. Think of music. Music. Music. Mu . . . sic. Gay Italian music." Watson nodded to Yin, who, squatting beside the bed, had his notebook out and pencil ready.

"*O Sole Mio.*"

The Innkeeper shook his head, but not vigorously; he was going under.

Yin jotted down the response.

"Something more . . . meaty, perhaps?" Watson suggested. "Verdi's *Requium Mass.*"

The Innkeeper ground his teeth and growled, but his features were relaxed. He was completely under now.

Yin jotted this response in the notebook, wondering why the doctor had suddenly turned pale.

"*A German Requiem.*"

Watson nodded to the gnome. Now for the big one. Taking his patient's wrist in hand, he whispered, "How about some Wagner? *Das Rheingold! Die Valkyrie!*" He hummed a few stirring bars of Valkyrie flight-music.

The Innkeeper's abdominal muscles twitched violently, his pulse rate surged and his eyes glittered. The Innkeeper could not hide the sudden burst of emotion from one who had worked with Sherlock Holmes and knew his methods.

So, thought the good doctor, releasing the Innkeeper's wrist. "Who are you?" he whispered, aiming the golden reflection directly into the Innkeeper's eyes and beckoning the gnome to join him now that the patient was hypnotized.

From the Innkeeper's throat came a growl. That would be the dominant patient, Watson knew. He brought the golden light closer and repeated the question. "Who are you?"

"Wagner," the Innkeeper whispered. "Richard Wagner." Watson motioned to Yin: *get this down*!

Richard Wagner was but the first layer of deception. Leaning over the Innkeeper, he shone the reflected light directly into the Innkeeper's right eye and demanded, "Who are you?"

The reply came from deep within the Innkeeper's body and was low, raw, fundamental. *"Ich bin Wotan."*

John Watson, M.D. had experienced grave danger in his army career, and had shared many a terrifying adventure with his roommate Holmes[1], but nothing in his past had prepared him for the shock of learning that the body of the Innkeeper harbored the spirit of the ancient Nordic god Wotan. Watson scribbled his thoughts on a prescription blank.

Freud: In a wrath attack, the dominant personality ejects the other. Alas for the Innkeeper we have known and loved; the dominant personality in this case believes himself to be a god.

I need more theory.

---

[1] Including the adventure of the Giant Rat of Sumatra, for which the world is very nearly ready.

Try this: Without recourse to bilateral oscillations as a mechanism to dissipate battle-energy, the monolobular brain can only pump radially in and out. Too much out and either the skull cracks from pressure or the subdominant personality (the loser) is extruded from the ears and nose, along with pus and brain-substance. Try hypnotism to explore and exorcise the hidden patient.]

Remember: Music has charms to soothe a savage breast. See under breast: moon, teacup, planet, cigar.

Watson was too shaken to continue; passing the golden watch to Yin, he watched as the gnome twirled it, peering deeply into the Innkeeper's grey eyes. And Yin saw into the soul of the usurper, into the soul of the false god Wotan!

I, Wotan Alfdaur, was a god and the father of gods! Wotan Allfather, they called me.

Then Asgard, my home, was destroyed and I was sent down, along with the others, even Freya. Even my poor wife, Freya.

Where is my son Thor? And Frey, brother of Freya? And Loki, Heimdall and Bragi?

Sent down, all of us. For a word. A title. That title that the Lord hath reserved for Himself.

Now I am an Innkeeper! But not forever will I be thus!

Yin concentrated, searched the unfathomable depth of soul of one who had called himself a god. He saw how Wotan had escaped his fate of perpetual torment in the underworld, by trickery. Clever Loki! The false god of lies and treachery had taught Wotan how to trick Door into opening.

And there, penned into a corner of the mind by the dominant power of Wotan was the frightened, shrunken soul of the original Innkeeper, Blondevik Ungdworker! Yin strained to catch the final thoughts of the mind-usurper.

. . . bring the others over to Earth Real. Freya, Thor, Heimdall, Loki . . .

Ull, Bragi, Ull, Balder . . . . We will rebuild Asgard, but in a warm climate with a good sea-view and mountains in the background.

The giant wolves Geri and Freki, as guards . . . A few creature comforts. reasonable banking arrangements . . . frequent parties with music . . . occasional recognition of my accomplishments . . . once in a while, a parade in my honor . . . .

The Innkeeper blinked; the hypnotic state was dissolving. His eyes focussed on the doctor, who was still shaking.

"You need diversion," Watson said. "Shall I get the three witches from Macbeth?" whispered the doctor, feeling very much out of his depth.

"No!" the Innkeeper growled. "Last night they crept into my dream and prophesied over their damned stewpot."

"Ah!" Dr. Watson said, standing up and looking outside into the harsh sunshine rather than at his patient, giving his professional manner a chance to reassert itself. Dealing with a personality under attack was far trickier than he'd anticipated, especially when the interloper believed himself a god. Wotan, no less. "And what did they prophesy?"

"Remove the leeches and I'll tell you," the Innkeeper groaned.

"The leeches stay," Dr. Watson said firmly. There was no immediate danger; Wotan had apparently submerged for the time being; this was Ungdworker talking now. But an Ungdworker with a bit of Wotan in him. A considerable bit. The doctor could not appear weak, indicisive. "What did they prophesy?" he demanded. "This could be contributing to your fever. Tell me; I'll look it up in Freud right away."

"They hailed the next Innkeeper!" Pushing himself to a sitting position and pulling at Dr. Watson's jacket with his left hand, the Innkeeper hissed, "My successor!

"I could not see him aright, of course, nor would they spill his name. That's how it goes with those hags; you can't get a straight prophecy out of them! But I saw a form, a bloated, misshapen form appear out of the shadows, approach the stewpot. It bent over ... sniffed at the vapor ... reached into their wretched pot with a puffed and grasping hand ...

"I have seen that shape before, and that hand gripping a ladle, sampling of soups and sauces, omelets and pies still a-baking ... you can shove Neptune's trident up my arse if it wasn't the hand of Myron Blunger! They have prophesied Blunger to be the next Innkeeper! *This will not be!*" The Innkeeper nearly choked as waves of rage constricted his throat.

With his left hand, he clutched at Dr. Watson's waistcoat. "Not that I expect to be Innkeeper forever," he snarled in a low voice. "I have my plans. And when I am good and ready, I will appoint the next Innkeeper! I've been thinking of the Don taking over."

"Don Juan?" asked Dr. Watson, pausing as he laid his instruments back in his black bag. Frowning, he regarded his patient's face for signs of teasing or mischief; there were none.

"And why not?" demanded the Innkeeper.

Dr. Watson pointed to the R_x and snapped his black bag shut. "Follow my prescription," he said tersely. "Don't think about Blunger or the kitchen budget. And I would suggest you find another replacement for yourself than Don Juan."

"Why?" the Innkeeper demanded impatiently.

Packing the rest of his instruments into his black bag, Watson closed it and snapped it shut. "He is unstable. It is not his fault. Medical ethics prevent my discussing it in more detail."

The case flashed through Dr. Watson's mind. In the course of preparing her case-at-law, Portia had discovered that Don Juan had been graced with balls the size of Valencia oranges. A complete examination by Dr. Watson, at Portia's insistance, had revealed that the don's sexual hyperactivity was driven by an overactive prostate that periodically charged itself up to five- to seven times standard pressure! To hold a man culpable for seeking relief from such anguish ... why, it was a wonder Don Juan hadn't exploded long ago!

Indeed, this had become the backbone of Portia's case at law. The introduction of Dr. Watson's signed medical report in any court in the world would result in dismissal of the claims of all those pleasure-seeking females who had selfishly taken advantage of the don's weakness, which was not of his making and over which he had no control. Besides, he was betrothed to her, as soon as his problem with the Commandant was settled! All this Portia had discussed with Dr. Watson, in strictest confidence.

"Whom would you like to have sent over, then?" Dr. Watson asked. "Hurry, I have other calls to make."

"Don Juan," the Innkeeper replied. "And Long John Silver," he added.

Well, the company of knaves was better than lying here in bed, seething with anger and bringing his blood to a full curdle, Dr. Watson rationalized. He opened the door; Yin scuttled out, unnoticed.

The Innkeeper sank back onto his pillow, weak and despondant. Myron Blunger *deserved* neutering. But how? The first round of leechings had drained the manhood from the patient's right forearm. And now the worms were at him again, sucking away his remaining strength. Shortly after the Innkeeper had fallen ill, the don had paid a visit during which, through plot diagramming, he'd analyzed *The Problem of the Missing Griffin*, nee *A Kee Ess Una Meiseh*. The conclusion was inescapable; Myron Blunger was endeavoring to replace the Innkeeper!

The Innkeeper had immediately sent for a mace from the armory with which to break Blunger's skull, only to find his leech-weakened right arm couldn't swing it. He'd sent for a sword, only to have it clatter to the floor after half a slash. He had not the strength to wind a crossbow properly, nor the experience to place a throwing-knife where he wanted it at ten paces.

He wanted it at the point of the V of Myron Blunger's crotch. '*If a man's testicles were an inch lower on his body, he could not ride a horse and the course of history would have been very different* . . . ' That phrase! That stupid, unprofound phrase! The very thought of Blunger sent it booming through the Innkeeper's mind like a temple gong. But the phrase would dissipate with the absence of its originator . . .

The problem remained, how to do it? The Innkeeper's personal armory was replete with maces, halberds, lances, swords, crossbows, daggers, bludgeons . . . all requiring strength, all useless now that the leeches were at his right arm. Leeches! Ugh! The sight of them made the Innkeeper nauseous and dizzy.

Of course, the pulling of a trigger required virtually no power and his right arm had not lost its steadiness, but guns were forbidden at the Inn. Not one blunderbuss, matchlock, derringer, pistol, rifle or machine gun was permitted on the premises, by order of the Innkeeper. Now he was regretful, not of the law he had set down for the preservation of order, but of his lack of foresight—idiocy!—in adhering to it himself!

Breakfast was served, without rolls. To his surprise, the Innkeeper found that he had an appetite. Only after he'd finished every morsel of food, eating with his left hand, did it occur to him that his hunger had been stimulated by the loss of blood taken by the leeches which remained dangling from his right forearm by their raspy mouthparts. Enraged, he hollered for a kitchen minion, then shied the entire tray into that unfortunate's midsection as soon as the door was opened.

His mood improved at the direct hit, he dozed until awakened by a knock at the door.

"Come in!" the Innkeeper called hoarsely.

Long John Silver and Don Juan entered, the don orienting his chair so that he could feed Silver his cues unseen by the Innkeeper.

Silver straddled a chair at the foot of the bed holding a package crudely wrapped with string. His eyes glittered brightly, for everything was falling into place and his parrot, Cap'n Flint, had decided to come along, as though it sensed adventure coming and would not be left behind. Green and red, with a narrow head perpetually cocked to the left and a black tongue that flicked slowly between its half-open jaws, it squatted on the pirate's right shoulder, squawking "*Pieces of eight!*" at intervals.

Don Juan scratched his nose once. The signal. Silver leaned toward the Innkeeper, smacked his lips and reeled off his lines, "Pleased to hear that your appetite's improved, sir. Have you tried that new dish Blunger has introduced? A rare treat. Expensive, I hears, but worth it. *Cholent*, he calls it. Did you know he puts two pints of premium beer into each pot?"

"Quiet, man!" the Innkeeper wheezed.

"Beans, chuck steak and pastrami in a rich sauce," the pirate continued, "and brisket and carrots, with seasoning and a few potatoes and onions thrown in. First-cut brisket, so I hear," he added, slapping his knee and smacking his lips.

"Quiet, I say!" the Innkeeper croaked.

"But it's the simmer what makes it different. It sits overnight in a bakery oven at low heat, bubbling in its juices . . ."

"Shut up!" the Innkeeper bellowed, though it cost him dearly to squeeze that through his inflamed throat. "I know all about *cholent!*" he whispered. "I couldn't get a roll with breakfast this morning; all the ovens were full of *cholent! Cholent* is Blunger's latest weapon in this warfare he's waged on me! Exotic pizzas! Chopped herring! Smoked salmon on toasted bagels with cream cheese! Blueberry blintzes with sour cream! Delicacy after delicacy until my kitchen budget has been totally destroyed!

"Now it's *cholent!* When I get out of sick bay, I have sworn to throw a grand party, and the main course will be *cholent a la Blunger!* One part *cholent*, two parts Blunger, cooked in wine for two days and dished out of a giant earthenware pot decorated with Blunger's portrait." The Innkeeper's right hand clenched and unclenched, veins protruded from his temples; the whites of his eyes were flecked with red as the wrath pulsed and streamed throughout his body.

Approaching the bed, Don Juan said in a silky voice, "I truly regret the anguish caused by my plot diagramming of Blunger's first batch of manuscripts. I only meant to amuse you. Come, let me try again. I've brought the pieces for *The Pizza Vendetta*; let us examine the plot." Don Juan smiled as he cast upon a section of bedcover a handful of brightly colored cardboard triangles, squares and coiled oaktag.

"First, the triangles . . . one for each character . . ."

He connected a number of triangles of various sizes in a roughly linear pattern, some with edges in contact, some touching only at vertices. One, large and red, remained isolated. "This represents yourself," he announced.

"The squares are plot segments," the don said, reminding the Innkeeper how plot diagramming worked, and soon a dozen squares had been placed below the triangles in a connecting gridwork. "And coils, for musical themes and special effects." Don Juan bent himself over the array and skilfully, carefully, clipped a dozen coils in bright, primary colors, so that each piece connected with at least two others, the connected colors matching perfectly and forming a continuous arrangement with a well-defined backbone from which hung fragments of various lengths, not unlike the arrangement of a parsed sentence.

Save one. The large red triangle stood alone, exposed on all sides.

The don picked up the lone red triangle and played with it, muttering as though surprised, as though he hadn't rehearsed his line of patter quite thoroughly that very morning. "Ah," the don exclaimed sadly. "The Innkeeper remains. Apparently you were to be lost in the storyline of Blunger's little tale, done away with, eliminated! Just as in our first little demonstration. I am sorry . . ."

As the Innkeeper's face reddened with fury, the don quietly gathered his pieces and thrust them into a pocket, his eyes downcast.

"Eliminated!" the Innkeeper thundered. Not only was Myron Blunger after the Innkeeper's job; he was determined to erase the Innkeeper's very existence!

"I'm afraid so," the don replied. "I regret having brought this activity to your sickbed. I will replace it with something more suitable to recovery. A *Parcheesi* set, perhaps.

"Of course, that doesn't address the immediate problem," he mused as though to himself. "Suppose Blunger were to attract a rabble, to descend upon you in this room, helpless, unable to wield sword or mace . . ."

A drop of blood trickled down the Innkeeper's cheek; it had started from the corner of his right eye. His blood was dangerously near curdling. "Defend myself against . . . a rabble," he whispered, horrified. "If only I had a pistol . . ."

"If . . . you had . . . a pistol," the pirate exclaimed, raising his eyes in wonder. "Who would have figured . . . ?"

The Innkeeper regarded Silver's face, then stared hopefully at the package on the pirate's lap.

"By a remarkable coincidence," Don Juan said, "Mr. Silver has brought you a pistol. Think of it as a get-well present." The don was pleased. The sequence of events that had occurred to him in the library had come to pass! The planning would have been easier if he'd just cast in his lot with Long John Silver, travelling to Upper Muchness on the *Hispaniola*, but one did not know how long that would take, or whether the schooner could actually be materialized.

And there was the time factor; he was in a great hurry and Pegasus would be in Upper Muchness long before Silver's *Hispaniola* made landfall north of the Dromedaries. Portia being fully occupied with the preparation of his brief and unavailable for sex, the pain in the don's groin had become unbearable, beyond the capability of any ordinary lady to alleviate. His only hope lay in the giant Valkyrie, Brunnhilde.

The Innkeeper's eyes narrowed. "Talk plain," he demanded, sensing a string attached to this get-well present.

The don did so. "In return for this pistol," he said, "we ask only three small favors. For me, the use of Pegasus. I must leave the Inn. The stablemaster will permit no one but you to ride him, and since you took ill, the horse has been off his feed for lack of exercise."

"And I'd like one more go at the writing table in the library," Long John Silver said.

The Innkeeper nodded shrewdly and his lips curled in a smile. "You're leaving, too?" he whispered. "Both of you?"

There was no use in dissembling; it was time to turn all cards face up. "Correct," said the don.

"Aye," said Long John. "We're thinnin' out here. For me, I'll take my chances in Upper Muchness."

"You still think you can bring her back? The *Hispaniola?*" the Innkeeper said, doubtfully.

The pirate nodded. "Not by myself," he admitted. "I'll need the likes of Mr. Hands and Blind Pew and the lot . . . assumin' they'll be willin' to give up reg'lar meals and the comfort of warm berths to go off with me on shares."

Reg'lar meals . . . the comfort of warm berths . . . How it pained the buccaneer to utter those words! Before sunrise that morning, Silver had bribed his way into the lower level of the Inn where his old mates were being held for various acts of misbehavior. It was common knowledge that hardly had Mr. Hands arrived at the Inn than he found out the location of the children's wing and tried to get barehanded revenge on Jim Hawkins for shooting him into oblivion, especially with the tale not nearly over. Later, Miss Muffet had brought charges against Mr. Arrow for shameful behavior on a picnic and who knows what Pew would have done to Rapunzel up on the ramparts had Nancy Drew not happened by, and that in broad daylight . . . .

But the sight of his old shipmates in their cold, damp communal cell near broke Silver's heart. Hands, once a soldier of fortune feared from New England to the Spanish Main, now shuffled like an old man; his head was bent and his hands shook and he was fading, fading. And who was that by himself in the corner, all hunched up and shrivelled-like? Was that Black Dog, who had once been the terror of the king's soldiers? Aye, more than one had hurled himself overboard to the sharks rather than die on Black Dog's bloody cutlass. Silver fancied that he could almost see through to the buccaneer's bones, so close was he to being gone.

And Blind Pew and Mr. Arrow and the others—they were living ghosts, wraiths, nearly forgotten by readers. But they weren't out yet! And they still had their power of belief, though they had precious few other powers now.

Aye, would they help *believe* the *Hispaniola* back to existence? Would they sign on once more, with Long John Silver as captain and a go at Tortuga, where Kidd's second largest treasure lay untouched? That's what Silver had growled through the small, barred window of their cell in the lower level of the Inn that very morning as he handed them bowls of cold porridge. Would they?

The response was a weak, pitiful scattering of "ayes" that barely made it through the small, barred window. Them that had pulled true and strong at the capstan, raising anchor for the voyage to Treasure Island, that had sung of pirating, rum and treasure so long ago, were now ghost-men. Soon they'd be gone entirely.

And what about Long John? they'd asked. How come he looked so solid, so ready? Well, he'd gotten more play in *Treasure Island* than the others, he'd explained apologetically. He'd been formed sharper, more durable-like, but his time at the Inn was coming to an end, also.

Would they join him?

Aye! They did believe in the *Hispaniola*, they swore, and such was their collective power of their faith that if he could get them up on deck, they'd drop to their knees and *believe* the schooner into existence, with the Jolly Roger already flyin' astern . . . .

Well, double rations of rum and a heavy dose of Blunger's *cholent-stew* might get them going again, Silver thought with a cynical smile as he regarded the Innkeeper.

"And you? Are you also going to Upper Muchness?" the Innkeeper demanded of the don.

Don Juan nodded.

"Have you fear of heights?"

The don tossed his head.

"And you know horses, eh?"

The thinnest of ultra-confident, Castillian smiles played briefly across Don Juan's face.

"Very well. I'll write a note to the stablemaster, authorizing the exercise. See that you don't take Pegasus too high up, mind, and not too fast until he's used to your handling. When you're delivered, see that he's fed and rested." With his left hand, he awkwardly scribbled a note and signed it. Spying the package on Silver's lap, The Innkeeper asked, "Is that it?"

The pirate nodded. "A cannon barrel flintlock pistol . . .

{Author's note: The Cannon Barrel Flintlock Pistol (ca. 1750-60) has a .586 bore, weighs over a pound and change and is just under a foot in length. It is recognized chiefly by the lip at its muzzle, its oval, vented pan of average depth and the superior grin on the gargoyle that resides on its butt cap. The frizzen, snaphaunce and Dog-lock are exactly what one might expect in a. weapon of this vintage, except that the scearenose projects horizontally through an aperture in the lockplate, rather than vice versa. A unique pan/frizzen design provides for protection of powder against the elements, except for oxygen, which prevails. It is a hand-cannon of fearsome capability, favored by pirates and landlords.}

in perfect condition. With powder and balls. I've no use for the thing; it's just a memento of the good old days. Many's the time . . ."

"Spare me your wind," the Innkeeper growled. "Done and done, before Blunger shows up at the door with his rabble and me, unarmed. On one condition. If you raise your ship, take Myron Blunger aboard, alive or dead. Remember that he was my guest, and is to be treated at all times like one of the family. If dead, place his body near the mess hall, that he may check each morsel on its way to the table. If alive . . . he is a gourmet and likes his food fresh. When he calls for kippered herring, tie him by the ankles and lower him overboard that he may catch the fish himself with his bare hands, and some seaweed besides.

"He likes to write. When the sun burns hot overhead and there's scarce enough shadow for a deckrat to cool his whiskers and a man will kill for first feel of the breeze . . . send Blunger belowdeck to write undisturbed.

"And when the night is blackest and the vessel is pitching and rolling fearful, and seasoned hands who ain't heavin' their guts have took to their bunks, elevate him to a position of respect. Send him aloft to the crow's nest to stand watch against the attacks of whalefish and God's lightning."

The Innkeeper raised himself from his pillow and his teeth were chattering from the fever, but he said slowly and clearly and now the words came with a strong Nordic accent, "Above all, see that his feet never touch land from now until the end of days!"

That said, the Innkeeper reached out for the pistol, but the pirate did not release it. "Good and good, all around," said Silver. "Mr. Blunger'll be welcome aboard the *Hispaniola*. Just one more favor we ask, as gentlemen. We'd like the loan of the horn of Roland."

"The horn of Roland?" the Innkeeper growled. "Why?"

Silver said, "For Windbreaker."

Don Juan elaborated, reciting his set piece earnestly and fervently as though charming a lady, but not at such length. "His body has healed up nicely but he is depressed at not having earned a reprieve of his curse. He desires the horn of Roland above all, and we thought it would be nice to let him . . . have it for a while. Is it not good for the general morale? Also, is it not good public relations?"

Long John Silver nodded in agreement. It seemed best for the centaur, whose loyalties and interests with respect to Blunger were unclear, to be diverted far from the library and possible interference with Blunger's abduction.

Yes, and yes, mused the Innkeeper. He didn't have the strength to fly Pegasus to Upper Muchness himself. Not now. Not while Myron Blunger was destroying him from the inside. But as soon as he had his strength back, he would exert his will, putting Lucien Broco's henchmen to a scouring of the valley from cliff to cliff, searching for the lost seven-league boots. And once he had those boots . . .

All that was surely worth a horn. The Innkeeper acceded graciously to the pirate's request. "After all, it isn't the only MasterHorn in my collection," he grunted. "Give it to him. You'll find the horn of Roland in Brunnhilde's chamber. To open the door, you need a MasterWeapon. *Wildschweinblutmeister* is not available— Brunnhilde is still on vacation—but any MasterWeapon will do."

From beneath his pillow, the Innkeeper retrieved a ring of keys, selecting a small key with intricate wards and serrations and handing it to the don with his left hand. "This one will open the display case of *Excalibur*," the Innkeeper explained. "Rap on Brunnhilde's door three times with the butt; the door will open. The horn is on a high shelf.

"And these will open the lower level," the Innkeeper said, indicating the three iron keys on the ring. He tossed the ring to Long John, who handed over the package.

Silver's eyes fixed on the three keys. Soon, soon he'd be in the library surrounded by his mates, remembering with every manjack of them concentrating, believing the *Hispaniola* into existence!

"Now, what have we here?" the Innkeeper grunted as he awkwardly explored the contents of the package with his left hand. "The pistol . . . powder, balls, a good flint . . . Ahh." The Innkeeper managed to load the weapon. Bracing it against his bedpan, he pointed it at the doorway, adjusting the aim at the point of the V of Blunger's crotch, to the best of his memory and estimation.

The flintlock, heavy with shot, wavered. This was no good; the Innkeeper's left hand had not the steadiness for the job. Without looking at the leeches, he transferred the pistol to his right hand, his gun hand. Though weakened, it was more reliable than his left. It would be a blind shot so that his eyes would not happen upon the leeches and nausea foil his aim. He fixed the position and angle of the pistol in his mind, and to himself thought grimly, I'll have Blunger bring his next and final literary creation to me himself. As soon as he opens the door, he can whistle Goodbye to his balls, for they will be but a memory! Then let him ride horses to his heart's content, or take to the sea, under the tutalage of Captain Long John Silver!

The Innkeeper slipped the gun under his pillow and patted down the telltale bulge.

Don Juan and Long John Silver (with Cap'n Flint once more aboard his shoulder) made their exit, walking quickly in silence until they came to the entrance to the armory. There they stopped and, ascertaining that no eavesdroppers were about, divided up the Innkeeper's keys.

Don Juan turned toward the armory. Excalibur, then the horn of Roland had to be obtained and handed over to Windbreaker. Then to the stables. Even before his visit to the Innkeeper—which would have been accomplished somehow even if he hadn't been summoned— he'd bribed the stableboy to spike Pegasus's mid-morning meal with wheat germ and wild honey, that he have strength for the flight. But it would take several hours for the wonder-horse to convert that en- riched food into sufficient energy to fly all the way to Upper Muchness . . . no brousing in the clouds, eh? Then freedom from his nemesis, the Commandant! But first, the horn and the sword to Windbreaker!

In the don's pocket was the brief written for him by Portia, whom he truly regretted not being able to take along, but truth to tell, all those hours spent studying the law had taken its toll in the lady's endurance. And his problems required a lady with stamina!

As for the rest of it, his needs were simple. His sword, a bar of perfumed soap, a hair tonic many ladies had found irresistably aromatic, some silk handkerchiefs, his mustache scissors and a poignard, in case of trouble at short range.

Back in his quarters, Long John Silver removed his maps from the walls and laid them out neatly in his sea-chest, which he then strapped. He whistled once; his parrot took his post aboard Silver's shoulder and the pirate was off to fetch his crew, his cutlass swinging at his side, his dirk strapped to his back but within easy reach, and the cell keys jingling in his pocket.

*   *   *

Windbreaker was delirious with joy. He'd been applying Dr. Watson's prescription salve to his wounds when Don Juan, entering his unlocked quarters, presented him with the two objects most dear to his dreams: Excalibur, and the horn of Roland! And all he wanted in return was that Windbreaker guard the paddock while the don took Pegasus for a flight!

"But I'm not ready . . . not showered . . ." Windbreaker said.

"Prepare yourself," intoned the don. "And you have my permission to take any weapons or defensive gear from the armory you may deem useful. Eat lightly and be at the entrance to the paddock directly after the first sitting of lunch. That is when I shall appear; know that the Commandant will not lightly permit my mounting of the flying horse, Pegasus."

With those few words, Don Juan had departed, leaving Windbreaker hurriedly preparing his morning ablutions; it would be a sin to touch the sword of King Arthur or the battle horn of the great knight Roland with unclean hands!

He needed a complete grooming, a combing down, and a particular set of leather body-armor that he'd long admired in the armory! Assuring the don he'd be right along to defend him at the appointed hour, he started to brush his body vigorously with a stiff, long-handled brush.

Rat-a-tat . . . Rat-a-tat . . . .

Blunger groaned in his sleep. Rat-a-tat . . . Rat-a-tat . . .

"Sophie . . . " *Uhzawuzha* . . . he snored. "Someone at . . . door . . ."

Rat-a-tat . . . Rat-a-tat . . .

The waterhammer! He'd been spirited home! A miracle! He blinked, opened his eyes. Sunlight poured in through the window. His heart pounding with excitement, Myron Blunger rolled out of bed and stood up on a sun-warmed patch of shag rug. Shag rug. Not carpet. His heart sank. He was not home. He saw no familiar apartment house across the street, making a shadow across Arthur Avenue, no row of tightly parked cars, no Pilnuk's deli, no Korean grocery on the corner.

He was still in the small two-room suite he'd occupied since arriving at the Inn. His uncurtained windows overlooked a barren, snow-covered plain that swept all the way to the horizon. If Blunger did not exactly welcome the mournful sound of the wind, he appreciated it, for during those brief intervals when the wind died down, all he heard from beyond his window was silence. Cold, bone-cracking silence.

There was no fire in the small fireplace and his teeth chattered from cold and his feet didn't want to stand in one place, even on the rug. So why not go back to bed?

Rat-a-tat . . . . Rat-a-tat . . .

A noise from the corridor; the living nightmare continued. The writing of *Hope and the Dragon* had proved difficult, even with *Guidance*, but it was finished. *Too Little* remained troublesome. After setting down three possible outlines, he'd found that he didn't recognize sentences he'd written just minutes earlier. Suggesting that the characters had taken over with a vengeance, Yin had prescribed a good night's sleep; surely the storyline would move better in the morning. But it wasn't just the characters who were out of control; the whole storyline was running wild.

And with the fire low and the library cooling off for the night, Myron had finally given up and taken to his room. He'd tossed uncomfortably the whole night while his mind was tortured with brilliant turns of plot which dissipated as he struggled for wakefulness and a pencil. Snippets of clever dialogue and repartee flared up like Fourth-of-July sparklers, only to elude memory when, half-awake, he tried to recall, to reconstruct them. And now there was sunlight in the room and there was something making a Rat-tat-tat out in the corridor . . .

Wrapping his blanket, a big cozy Afghan he'd found in his closet, about him, he emerged from his room; some distance away there sat Yang against a wall, closely watching a three minute egg-timer.

"Excuse me," Blunger said hoarsely as he trudged over, not quite awake, "but I heard a Rat-a-tat in the hallway . . ."

The gnome, not taking his eyes from the egg-timer, pointed to the far end of the corridor. And there it was again—Rat-a-tat . . . Rat-a-tat—and here came the centaur galloping, galloping at full speed down the center of the corridor. The centaur's nether coat was freshly combed and sleek and his hooves, newly shod, clicked loudly on the stone floor of the corridor . . . Rat-a-tat . . . Rat-a-tat . . .

Windbreaker's mouth was wide open and his chest heaved as his double set of lungs processed huge volumes of air. In his right hand was a sword with a golden crosspiece and blade so brilliant it hurt the eyes to look at it. In his left hand was a horn, a simple one-loop horn with dents and scratches. Windbreaker hadn't ever mentioned an interest in music! Blunger raised his estimation of the centaur, who was now bearing down on him, hair flying in all directions! Blunger, taken aback by the sheer power and *grandness* of the charge, hugged the wall as the centaur swept by with a laugh and vanished at the other end of the corridor.

Why the sudden fit of galloping? What was the gnome timing? Why all this racket so early in the day?

Yang called out, "Two sandfalls less the third part of one. Six minutes less a third of three minutes . . . five minutes!"

"Algebra?" Blunger asked, wincing.

"We're timing figure eights around the paddock. Hey, how about a quick run down to the Deep?" the centaur asked brightly. "Just you and me. No sacks of flour."

Blunger shook his head.

Windbreaker returned, still panting, eyes gleaming. *"Excalibur!* And the horn of Roland!" he exclaimed proudly. "Don Juan lent me them! Just for guarding him against the Commandant! Be right back; I have to pick up some body armor and a decent set of lances."

And the centaur disappeared down the corridor at full gallop.

Disgruntled at being awakened so early for such foolishness, Blunger returned to his bed but it was midmorning and sleep was now impossible. He washed, dressed, paused for the briefest breakfast and then hurried to the library, where he found a note from the Innkeeper inviting him to carry his current manuscript to the Innkeeper's chambers himself; a celebration was in order! And the beautiful ceramic pot the Innkeeper had sent earlier was freshly filled with peanuts, potato chips and pretzels!

How thoughtful! Of course, he wouldn't touch them; he was on a strict diet! But it was nice that the Innkeeper had sent them.

Blunger felt a surge of confidence. It was the start of a new day and God had given him a benefit, and the Innkeeper was a hundred percent on his side! And he was sure he'd lost three pounds already! Maybe five! He'd been too weak with Joey; that had been the problem all along. And why? Because he'd been reluctant to force discipline on a child.

And as though a floodgate in his mind had been opened, ideas now started to flow without cease. His hand was a bird flying freely across the page over and over, lightening, fading from view, independent of him! Myron Blunger made the transition into his attic room in the Hawkins home in Upper Muchness and *Too Little* came into being. Blunger's last thought before vanishing into the storyline was that his relations with the Innkeeper were improved and a celebration would be in order!

Yin tiptoed into the library, anxious to research Wotan but afraid of interrupting a writing session, especially with Blunger's habit of vanishing into the storyline. One didn't know the consequences of interrupting a transition. Peeking around a corner, he saw that Myron Blunger was bent over his table, all concentration and starting to fade at the edges! The gnome stopped in mid-step, tempered his breathing, afraid that the slightest noise might cause a disaster.

Soon Blunger was no longer at the table, yet the writing continued, the words appearing on the yellow pad, line after line! Yin crept close, quietly placed another log on the fire and headed for the stacks. Watching Blunger's writings appear as if by magic was fascinating, but he had to learn whatever he could about Wotan, and fast! There was more than abstract scholarship at stake here. Seating himself cross-legged in the stacks, the gnome dug in, filling pages in his notebook as quickly as *Too Little* came into being on the nearby table.

Time passed. A charred log crackled in the fireplace, broke in half, sending a shower of sparks several feet into the air. A vague outline shimmered in the air beside the writing table, then pale colors appeared as Myron Blunger coalesced, darkening and filling in until finally he had returned entirely. He was breathing heavily, his eyes half-closed, his fingers firmly grasping the moving pencil. It took him several minutes to reorient himself. He sneezed once and grinned self-consciously upon spying Yin curled up in the stacks, surrounded by books. Yin was sound asleep.

The little fellow had probably sat there the whole time, Blunger thought, watching over him and making sure the fire didn't go entirely out. Touched at the gnome's friendship, Blunger rose quietly, edged the manuscripts into two neat piles and with a farewell wave at the sleeping gnome, left the library.

Making his way down the central corridor, Blunger headed for the Innkeeper's quarters with a grand feeling of accomplishment in his heart and *Hope and the Dragon*, and *Too Little* beneath his arm. This was his most ambitious writing yet; only one chapter remained, and the Innkeeper wouldn't—*couldn't*—renege on their understanding.

The pistol was within easy reach of the Innkeeper's right hand, its positioning fixed in memory that he not have to endure the sight of the leeches. If he had made a mistake in bring Myron Blunger to the Inn, and in trusting him not to abuse his library privileges, Blunger had made a worse mistake in trying to do away with Wotan Alfdaur, the father of the gods, risen from Hades to take his place in the world!

LIVING MARBLE

"This is . . . not going . . . to work," Yang squeaked unhappily as Windbreaker trotted down the East corridor. The gnome, against his will and better judgement, was in a saddle at an unimaginable distance from the safe, solid ground. His hands had a deathgrip on the pommel. Directly ahead were the high double doors that led outside to the stable area and the paddock and a terrible, one-sided battle which the centaur could not win. "Slow down. I'm getting . . . seasick," he moaned. "And I'm sweating; I think I have a fever." Against the arctic chill that lay on the Northern Reaches from mid-September to May, he'd wrapped himself in two turtle-neck sweaters, a warm jacket and a muffler, topped off by a color-ful wool tam. Gloves were out, as he'd need his hands free to flip pages in a tactics book he'd taken from the library. The book, and another from his own collection, were in a jacket pocket.

Yang had envisaged for himself the role of a strategist, helping to outline a battle plan, providing some last minute cautions, load-ing lances into their sheaths, spitting on their points for good luck and, during the conflict, shouting advice *from a safe distance.*

While Windbreaker was off selecting body armor from the armory, it had occurred to the gnome that the centaur, though on the threshold of battle, knew nothing about his opponent, the Commandant. A quick dash to the library had yielded a synopsis of a hundred operas, including *Don Giovanni.* What Yang had learned in a quick read was not encouraging. "Living marble," he'd said glumly, sitting on a low bench while the centaur enjoyed a pre-battle rubdown from one of the stablehands. "Did you hear? You're going up against a statue returned to life! Even Excalibur

will not cut through living marble! The Don snookered you! Sword
. . . horn . . . you'll not live to enjoy them! He sold you a black
camel at midnight!"

But Windbreaker, stretched out on a wide, matted exercise
table continued to smile, the horn of Roland gripped in one hand,
Excalibur in the other! It was a delicious moment.

Yang snapped the book shut; the fool wasn't even listening!
He turned to the other reference he'd taken from the library. Windbreaker, of course, hadn't thought to research tactics any more
than he'd looked up information on his opponent. Yang, searching the card files under the subject heading *Fighting tactics for
centaurs*, had found nothing; under the broader heading *tactics*,
he'd come across *Modern Field Tactics*, by Parnell and Gross, second edition. The contents made no sense to the gnome, but Windbreaker had mentioned field tactics and this was as close as Yang
had found. The book analyzed tactics and strategies, with diagrams for both offense and defense, and was well illustrated with
diagrams and color photographs. Apparently it was weighted heavily
toward football, though it also covered soccer, lacrosse and basketball, of which the gnome understood nothing, though he did notice that, for some odd reason that was probably characteristic of
human interactions, offensive tactics were called *plays*. In a quick
glance down the index, Yang had found nothing about lance tactics, swordplay at close quarters or hand-to-hand combat between
men and centaurs.

"Forward pass . . ." he muttered. "Full court press . . ." He
shook his head; the terms meant nothing to him.

Watching Yang thumb through the book on tactics, Windbreaker came up with his best idea yet. Yang would serve as an
onboard coach, calling charges and feints even as the centaur hurtled
downfield toward the enemy. Two heads were better than one, and
Yang would be Windbreaker's secret weapon against the Commandant.

Girded for battle, Windbreaker was no longer the ageless, adolescent bodybuilder. From forelegs to hind, his lower body was

encased in a battle sheath of thick leather, from which protruded the handles of a half-dozen lances and a longbow flanked by two quivers full of arrows. For close combat, Windbreaker had Excalibur. His lucky cable-stitched sweater was covered by a silvery vest of close-linked mail borrowed from the armory. This was the warrier Don Juan had contracted to protect him from his nemesis.

Indeed, the centaur appeared formidable, but against *living armor!* Yang slid the sixth lance into its sheath and complemented Windbreaker on his appearance, pleading all the while that this was not a good time to go up against the Commandant! Why not have his portrait painted, return the horn and the sword to Don Juan and forget the whole thing? Even as he made this plea, he found himself hoisted farther from the ground than he'd ever been in his life.

"What can you do against *living marble?*" he pleaded as they started out. "Man and horse!" he exclaimed. No battle plan, no lance or sword could defeat living marble. The horn of Roland would strike no fear in the heart of one who had been through death and renewed uncuttable, unspearable, unhewable. The don had suckered him . . . .

But Windbreaker advanced down the corridor toward his appointment with disaster, heedless of the futility. "Can't you slow down, at least?" the gnome repeated plaintively, holding onto the pommel for dear life, certain to fall on his head at any moment.

"No!" the centaur snapped. "I have three speeds—trot, canter, full gallop—and one for show, a sort of circus-parade-march that bores me to death. I never learned to walk, horse-wise. I'm not a pony, you know. Press your legs against my sides and let me concentrate. This has to look good."

"I . . . I can't," the gnome wailed. "They don't reach." And they didn't, sticking out to either side uselessly. "Will you promise . . . I won't fall?" Yang asked as they approached the double doors. "Maybe I should stand at a distance and direct you with signs?" He peeked down at the ground; it was too far to jump. But not too far to fall.

"When elephants fight, it is the grass that gets trampled," the centaur said. He had no intention of releasing his onboard coach from what the centaur regarded as a moral obligation to see him through this.

He unbolted the doors, threw them wide open and strode out into brilliant sunlight and subzero air that sent waves of chills into his double pair of lungs and down the length of his spine. He permitted himself one shiver, then thrust out his chest, determined to look the part. This was Windbreaker's chance to carry out a deed, to pick up some points toward curse-reversal. Careful to close the doors behind him, he slowed his gait to what he termed his circus-parade-march, and advanced into the open ground, his double hearts pounding in synchronization, the horn of Roland in hand, Excalibur at ready.

He was at the edge of a great field. To his right, several hundred yards away, was the exercise paddock, surrounded by a white picket fence high as a stallion's shoulder, and lined with bales of hay. The gate was open. Some hundred yards from the gate were Pegasus and the don. The flying horse—huge, creamy-white— was snorting vapor, pawing the ground, his great wings flexing. Used to the stablemaster's touch, it was apparently unwilling to be saddled by Don Juan. Rearing, the horse neighed loudly and pedalled his front hooves, sending the don back several paces.

Windbreaker trotted toward the paddock to try to help the don. As he did so, he saw, from the corner of his eye, movement in a line of trees that marked the edge of the Forest Beyond, a quarter-mile away to his left. Windbreaker halted, turned slowly so as not to spill his passenger-coach.

From the treeline emerged a horse and rider and both were white as alabaster from the crown of the rider's bearded head to the hooves of his steed, a stallion larger than Windbreaker by every measure. No vapor issued from the horse's nose, nor from its rider's, despite the cold air. Beyond need of helmet or armor or fear of death, the rider sat erect, his sword not drawn. As though one with its master's mind, the steed advanced quickly out of the trees toward the paddock gate. The don didn't see his nemesis and, having again thrown the saddle over Pegasus's broad back, was trying to fasten the cinch.

The white horse, now galloping, was fast closing on the paddock gate.

Windbreaker burst from standstill into a full gallop. "What now?" he cried to his coach. "Hurl lances? Shoot arrows at long range? Close in for hand to hand?" The Commandant had a lead and the ground thundered under the hooves of the stallion. Yang released one handgrip from the pommel, took out the tactics book and opened it to a page at random. Windbreaker raised the horn of Roland to his lips, sounded it once, then called back as he sped toward the paddock gate, "Call a play!"

"Forward Pass!" the gnome screeched, reading what his eye happened to catch.

Taking a lance in hand, the centaur cocked his right arm and, as his right hind hoof dug into the hard ground, let fly. The lance whizzed over the Commandant's head in a shallow trajectory and dug its head into the turf beyond. The Commandant didn't even slow down; his stony eyes were fixed on the don, who, alerted by the hornblast, redoubled his efforts. Pegasus, perhaps intrigued by the approach of strangers, held still long enough to permit the cinch to be fastened under his belly.

"Next play!" shouted Windbreaker, blowing his horn again.

Don Juan yanked the cinch fast, slipped a foot in the left stirrup and leaped onto the horse's back, clutching a handful of mane as he thrust his right leg over. Without bridle, reins or spurs, he bent low and slapped Pegasus sharply in the ribs.

Now the Commandant's steed was but a hundred yards from the gate. "Screen play!" Yang shouted. The centaur veered off to the right, no longer trying to beat the Commandant to the gate. Ahead was the white fence, lined with bales of hay, that lined the paddock. Yang shut his eyes and tucked his head down, prepared for the crash. Windbreaker, for all his dreams of glory and transformation, had gone berserk.

The don kicked and slapped and shouted Pegasus into a slow gallop, and his body was pressed to the horse's back, his head tucked between the great bulge of muscles that powered Pegasus's wings, which were outstretched, but not flapping with power. "Vaya!" cried the don, steering the horse into the wind with adroit heel-pressure into its side.

The Commandant's stallion surged through the open gate. Some twenty yards to the right, Windbreaker timed his strides, took a deep breath and leaped over the fence. The sudden upward acceleration sent Yang into the air, free and clear, clutching only his precious tactics-book. Windbreaker soared over the fence and started groundward without his coach, who tumbled through the air until he landed on his padded belly on a stack of hay-bales, screeching "Living Marble" until the wind was knocked out of him. Windbreaker landed some ten yards behind the Commandant, who had now drawn his sword and held it out before him. Pegasus, some fifty yards ahead, had begun to flap his wings in earnest, though the great horse was nowhere near takeoff speed.

Living marble! The centaur drew a lance, grasped it at the center, spun it in a horizontal plane and threw the whirling shaft, aiming for the legs of the Commandant's steed, hoping to cause it to stumble. The lance was shattered into three pieces; the white stallion didn't even break stride.

Screen play! Windbreaker veered left and urged himself to greater speed, closing in, interposing himself between the Commandant and Pegasus. Then he was beside the Commandant, matching his powerful horse stride for stride and shielding Pegasus as best he could. Whether the flying horse had been goaded to flight speed by the don's incessant slaps and kicks, or whether he just enjoyed the glory of the race, the great animal had now achieved full gallop and his wings were beating furiously.

Living marble! Windbreaker drew another lance and brought its shaft down against the Commandant's sword. The lance was slashed cleanly in two, nor was the Commandant's attention diverted from his prey. Directly ahead, great white wings beat the air furiously as the wonder horse fought for lift. The Commandant roared; his steed thundered over the ground, coldly, effortlessly pressing Windbreaker to the right, opening a direct lane for a final charge. The centaur pulled Excalibur from its scabbard and brought it down on the Commandant's outstretched sword with all his strength.

Neither weapon broke but the Commandant was forced to glance at this interfering half-man, and in that moment, Pegasus lunged and rose gracefully into the air, out of range of the Commandant's upraised sword.

The Commandant slowed to a trot, as did Windbreaker; side by side they went ahead as Pegasus rose higher, higher. Curiously, the Commandant seemed relatively unperturbed that his long-sought prey had escaped. Indeed, his white lips were compressed in a thin smile.

The flying horse beat through the air with great sweeps of its wings, and the Commandant, who had now halted his steed, pointed his sword skyward and laughed a long and bitter laugh.

"Bon Voyage, runt coward!" he called in a stentorian bass. "May it pleasure you to know that so long as you kept to the Inn, you were protected by absolute law, safe from retribution, except for that inflicted by the guilty conscience of a knave despoiler of innocent women. In Earth Real, there are no such constraints. *Arrivaderci, senor don!*"

Whether he heard that farewell or not, Don Juan directed Pegasus to the right, arcing over the trees of the Forest Beyond, then continuing in a straight line toward the valley of Upper Muchness. Windbreaker broke off and bounded back to where his battle-coach lay, dazed and confused. "Blunger," Yang whispered as he was pulled up and replaced in the saddle. "It's all Blunger's fault." His eyes rolled upward and he passed out.

The Commandant, who had accompanied him, said gravely, "We will meet again." Then, as the centaur headed back to the Inn at his slow circus-parade-march, the white horse turned aside and quickly disappeared into the woods, following the direction Pegasus had taken.

*   *   *

Had God not put him on a diet, Myron Blunger would have stopped in the dining hall for a light lunch. Cottage cheese, dry toast, an apple . . . nothing rich. But he had to lose twenty pounds and you don't fool around with God!

Ever since the Innkeeper had taken to sickbed, Blunger had wanted to pay him a visit, or at least to send him a get-well note or flowers. But Dr. Watson had dissuaded him, suggesting that it would be best for all if he finished up his project and got out of the Inn as quickly as possible, preferably by the back door after the sabertooth had been lured away with a bushel of table scraps. The doctor seemed to believe that the Innkeeper held some kind of grudge against Blunger.

On this matter, Blunger knew that Dr. Watson was wrong. And he had proof! Had not the Innkeeper sent a pleasant note, asking that Myron bring his latest work in person, and the sooner the better? And what about the gift of that beautiful ceramic pot with his picture painted on the bottom, grinning! Not a very flattering likeness, but it must be difficult doing portrait work on the inside of a wide-mouthed earthenware pot with flared edges. It was a thoughtful present whose contents—pretzels, potato chips and other snacks—would have been greatly appreciated by the old, pre-diet Myron Blunger, especially when designing transitions, a part of the writing craft that Blunger found particularly difficult and appetite-stimulating.

The note from the Innkeeper had hinted at a surprise. A farewell celebration . . . or a prepublication book party! When *The Boy with No Future* had come out in print, the publisher had thrown Myron a wonderful book party in Pilnuk's Deli, with platters of

sandwiches—corned beef and turkey and pastrami, potato salad
and real sour pickles right from the barrel . . .

In the distance, a horn blared. That must be the centaur,
practicing. Could the party be starting already? He should bring
something . . . but what? There was no place to pick up a bottle
of wine or a cake. But he couldn't drop in on the Innkeeper
without a get-well gift. Something suitable for a celebration.
Of course! A *cholent*! He'd bring a *cholent*! What better get-well
present? Blunger's spirits lifted, his mouth watering in anticipation. Not that he'd eat any, of course. The ovens were filled
with cast-iron simmer-pots, all bubbling away . . .

Smiling, Myron Blunger headed for the kitchen. As always, he
found a whirlwind of confusion and tumult as the first lunch sitting was getting underway. No one noted or cared that he took
two oven mitts and lifted a steaming *cholent* from its nest in the
oven nearest the door . . .

Yin's slumber on the library floor was not due to the soft, hypnotic
hiss of the fire or physical fatigue; the gnomic brain has a buffer
region, which periodically puts the organism on standby while it
pumps accumulated data into the main-section for sorting and
incorporation into existing files. When the buffer region is depleted, a buildup of brain-enzymes causes an increase in curiosity,
hence the gnomic passion for understanding.

Saturated with data gathered during his latest round of research, Yin's fore-brain had simply called a time out while it relieved the pressure. As he dozed in the library stacks, his main-
brain accepted and slotted the new data and generated an hypothesis.

Research needs an hypothesis; if it survives three working days,
one is entitled to call it a theory.

The hypothesis, based on the knowledge gained from Yin's
Blunger studies, was this: in humans, socialization, including per-
sonality, character and outlook on life, was shaped in the womb.
Abstract thinking, such as aptitude for mathematics, was shaped

during puberty and depended on factors beyond one's control, such as seating charts in home room in the seventh grade.

Thus: Myron Blunger's lifelong interest in food probably had its origin in an umbilical cord of surpassing diameter. His sedentary lifestyle, which reflected a dislike of acceleration, was due to the near-certainty that during pregnancy his mother had not jumped about much.

Yin woke, found this hypothesis installed in his main-brain and, in an ecstasy of creativity, scribbled the word *Wombics* in his notepad. A whole new science of cause and effect! The effects of womb-size on future accomplishment. Wall texture and pre-natal entertainment! Can there be too much of a good thing?

Wombics, it would be called. And he, Yin, had created it!

But it was the mathematics angle that excited him the most. Earlier, in his first close examination of Blunger's inner self, he had seen only the effects; now he understood the cause. He began writing down the mathematics part as fast as he could before the insight fled.

Apparently the young Blunger had shown up at P.S. 19 at age thirteen and a half fresh from a summer of reading, movies, daydreaming, bicycle repair and model airplane building. Pumped to the brim with sound advice and armed with a fresh notebook, two sharp Mongol pencils and a ball-point pen guaranteed not to skip, the young Myron Blunger had taken his seat in home room at 8:40 on the first day of the eighth grade. This *would* be a good year! He *would* really learn algebra and word problems and the geography of South America, and clear up his confusion on dividing fractions. He *would* live up to his potential and make his parents proud! That was at 8:40 A.M.

At 8:42, Myron Blunger's world turned upside down. A girl—not a girl, a *woman* slid into the seat next to his and tossed her strawberry-blonde ponytail once. She turned and smiled and said her name was Elise and she had just moved up from Atlanta, Georgia. Her ponytail flicked enchantingly with

each motion of her slim body, and her blouse—white with
blue border-stitching—was wondrously filled out.
And therein lay the root of Blunger's difficulties with mathematics. Mathematics was taught in home room. Mathematics
never had a chance. Myron Blunger graduated into the ninth grade
only because English, geography and history were taught in other
rooms and there was no co-ed gym.

Was it a general design weakness of the human brain not to
isolate the emotional fire-zone from the rational? Was concept-
placement guided by a master blueprint, or did learning simply
dive into brain-cell zones chosen at random? Had Myron Blunger
developed intellectually according to a chance arrangement of learning in his organic brain? Or had he been shaped for life by an
enlarged womb, an oversized umbilical cord and a mother who
didn't ski, play tennis or indulge in competitive shopping?

Did God, when not playing golf, play dice with human genes?

Most definitely an area for future scholarship, Yin thought
with satisfaction. Why, one could devote a lifetime to the study of
just one human brain in action. *Wombics.* A pity that Blunger was
so anxious to return to the Bronx . . .

What a start to his career as a scholar! Yin thought, excitedly. Of
course, it would be wise to keep this discovery secret until he'd published—oh, would Yang be astonished! But respectful! Oho . . . respectful!

But now he needed a sample of scholarship, just for the
format . . .

Opening *The Book of the Ways of Man*, Yin studied the layout
of the thing. There were footnotes, appendices, references, a bibli-
ography, a table of contents, an index . . . a lot of detail went into
scholarship. Most of it drudge-work, from the looks of it, and
right now he was too excited for drudge-work! Yet he had to put
something down on paper, to prove priority of discovery! He could
write an outline . . . but even that would take too long! Perhaps an
introduction would do . . .

The Tragedy of Blunger. Good working title.

While Yin lay on the floor of the library, emulating scholarship, and Myron Blunger entered the kitchen of the Inn at the End of the World to select a suitable present for the celebratory party in the Innkeeper's quarters, Yang was lying on a bed in Dr. Watson's small but tidy infirmary, to which Windbreaker had carried him. It was but a slight concussion, Watson concluded after a thorough examination, and soon enough the gnome would cease ranting about living marble and such nonsense.

Dr. Watson wanted to observe him for twenty-four hours. Yes, twenty-four hours, and to hell with the Inn being Timeless and all that rot! It might be that the gnome needed a good leeching. The Innkeeper should be just about through with the little beasts.

A CURSE IN THE DARK

Myron Blunger peered into the oven, trying to decide which of the *cholents* had reached fullness of taste and character. The celebration in the Innkeeper's rooms would probably be the culmination of his sojourn at the Inn and he wanted to bring nothing less than a world-class gift. Suppose the Innkeeper asked him to recite from his latest work? Should he read from *Hope and the Dragon*? Or *Too Small*?

Setting his precious manuscripts on a table, he slipped his hands into heavy oven-mitts, reached inside the oven and gripped the handles of a *cholent* whose bubbling was nothing less than joyful. The pot and its dome-shaped lid were made of heavy cast iron. He worked it out, then closed the heavy door with a jaunty swing of his behind.

Blunger set the steaming pot on a trivet, removed the lid and, with a wooden ladle, punched through the thin crust. He sniffed lightly, then stirred, inhaled deeply, closed his eyes and held his breath; the aroma of the simmering stew was a foretaste of paradise. In the old days, he would have scooped out a sample, blown on it, risked burning his tongue against a little taste. But God had put him on a diet to lose twenty pounds! Of course, one shouldn't lose too much at one time . . . a pound a month seemed wise . . . easier to go on a diet at home . . . and suppose the *cholent* needed salt . . .

No! With a blast of will power, Myron Blunger dropped the ladle, replaced the iron lid on the pot and tucked his manuscripts inside his shirt, freeing both hands for the burden of the *cholent*.

Gripping the pot-handles, he lifted his present. On to the Innkeeper's rooms!

Who'd be at the celebration? he wondered. Windbreaker, no doubt. And Yang. And Yin, if he wasn't too busy with his research. Dr. Watson, probably. Wouldn't it be fantastic if Sherlock Holmes showed up, and was willing to chat a bit! Robin Hood! Snow White! Uncle Remus! Ivanhoe! Scarlett O'Hara! *Sheherazade*! His pulse throbbed with excitement! What stories he'd have to tell once he got back to the Bronx!

But how to carry the steaming pot through the dining hall without accident? The room was crowded with the first lunch sitting and waiters bustling and hurrying in all directions. Even though the cover was a tight fit, he'd never make it through without spilling hot *cholent* on someone. The service entrance, he was advised by an apprentice cook, led only to a series of store rooms, each with a massive, oaken, double-bolted door to the outside. Spotting another door to the left of the refuse drums, Blunger, proudly carrying the *cholent* before him, marched toward the rear of the kitchen, crying loudly over the din and clatter, "Hot stuff! Watch out . . . hot stuff!"

Above the door was a sign that read:

To Refuse Pit and MtW, Small Folks Wing, Lobby
DON'T FORGET TO RETURN THE KEY!

Hah! Blunger chuckled; the hook was empty. Oh, did Sophie let him have it when he forgot to return the house-key to its hook by the toaster! For all its size, this place was rather homey.

From the lobby, Blunger would easily find the Innkeeper's quarters. He set his burden down for a moment and shook the ache from his arm muscles. My, the *cholent* was heavy! The pot, having started off chest-high, was now warming his belly. Just before he reached the Innkeeper's rooms, he'd rest a moment. He very much wanted to march inside with his *cholent* held high, as befitting a gift of value.

The door was double-bolted, and fitted with a snap-lock. He noticed a hand-lettered sign to the right of the door:

The Butcher, the Baker, the Candlestick maker, were pleasant and charming signori, but they ventured out back on garbage patrol, each of them with a drumfull to roll; none ever returned from the refuse hole, *'cause none of them took a good story!*

Take One!

Beside the words *Take One!* was a long spike that protruded from the wall, from which hung one scrap of paper, on which was written in red ink:

STORY STACK—REFILL AT ONCE!
DID YOU RETURN THE KEY?

Had Myron Blunger's thoughts not been so fixed on the savory *cholent* or the celebration at the Innkeeper's quarters or the tales he'd have for Sophie and his sons Irving and Jacob and their wives, and especially for his grandchildren, he might have paused to wonder at the possible significance of the doggerel, what type of stories the spike usually held, and why all the fuss over the key? At the very least, he might have wondered why this door was double-bolted, with a snap-lock. That he completely overlooked the cryptic MtW is understandable, considering his state of excitement.

He threw the bolts, then simultaneously twisted the snap-lock, pushed the door open against a spring, lifted his present and backed into the rear passageway. Behind him the door closed with a solid thump. Regret flooded through him instantly.

The corridor was cold and damp, and there was mildew on its stone walls. The only illumination was a dim greyness that came from above, where a residue of daylight managed to penetrate snow-encrusted, narrow windows set high in the left wall, which Blunger correctly guessed to be the outside wall of the Inn. Between windows, the corridor was dark as a subway tunnel. Blunger heard an eerie, deep sound echo in the passageway. A sound not unlike the croak of a frog. A frog the size of a horse. And not exactly a croak; more a belch.

Then it came to Myron Blunger that this passageway, like everything else in the Inn, was modelled after fiction! Suddenly the most dreadful thought whirled through Blunger's mind. Was this passageway inspired by the terrible wine-cellar of Montressor's palace in *The Cask of Amontillado*? What if he encountered a freshly walled-up section, and heard muffled screams from within? What would he do? What would he do? It was one thing to read Poe's story under your blankets with a flashlight at the age of fourteen; it was quite another to find oneself locked into such a passageway.

Blunger tried the door, but the snaplock held. He pounded, but heard no footsteps. Blunger made a promise to God that if he lived and got back to the Bronx, he wouldn't breath a word to anyone! Not even Sophie! If she asked where he'd been . . . he'd . . . he'd say he didn't remember!

The door did not suddenly fly open, nor did anyone appear.

A thought came unbidden to Blunger that the *other* Moses would have marched forward, right down to the bowels of the Earth if necessary, waving his staff. The reminder of Blunger's shortcomings dejected him.

From somewhere ahead in the darkness came another croak-belch.

"Hello?" he called ahead, timidly. "Is anyone there?" He heard no response. Shivering, Blunger suspected that if he turned his head farther to the left, he would see, at eye level, a huge spider-web with its hairy, venomous-looking owner motionless at the center. Slowly, cautiously, he did that, and was rewarded by the sight of *two* such arachnids, each at the center of its rectangular floor-to-ceiling web, each with a row of glittering, red eyes, legs that could span a dinner plate and a hairy abdomen large as a mouse! Something descended onto his head and gripped the flesh of his scalp with tiny but sharp pincers. "Argh! Argh!" he screamed, dropping to the floor, gripping the *cholent* pot to his chest, mindless of the heat. Blunger screeched, waved, kicked out in all directions and thrashed his mitt-covered hands frantically in the near-darkness as a monstrous spider scrambled down over his right ear, leaped to his shoulder, scuttled down his arm and vanished, presumably having descended via a thread, though Blunger didn't care, for he continued to thrash and yell until he lay, exhausted and panting, against the door. Blunger hammered and kicked at the locked door again and again, but it didn't open. No one had seen him enter. And such was the clatter of pots and pans out in the kitchen that he'd *never* be heard.

The keyhole was right there before him. With no key, he put his lips to it and called, "Help! Help!" though it probably came out more like "Hoop! Hoop!" on the other side. It didn't matter; no one answered.

There in the half-light he squatted while his pulse slowed and his thoughts reordered themselves into a rational, life-preserving way.

Hope. The fuel of life. God had said that hope was the fuel of life, but had God ever been set upon by spiders? In fact, had God ever subjected Himself to affliction and danger? No, Blunger decided, for if He had, He'd be more tolerant of human shortcomings. God had permitted disappointment with humankind to fester to calamitous proportions, and golf did not provide suitable refreshment; it was too much of a head game.

Now *that* was philosophy! Wouldn't it be wonderful to be sitting in his kitchen back in the Bronx, trading philosophy with Jacob Minsky? Or sitting in that armchair in the library of the Inn before a gently hissing fire, with a sound dinner under one's belt and grand philosophy running through his head. But Myron Blunger was stuck in a dark corridor, thrown upon his own resources, with no weapon but a hot *cholent*.

First things first. That was the theme of his bar mitzvah speech and by a quirk of memory, he'd never forgotten it. Blunger rose and stepped into the darkness ahead, the hot *cholent* held before him like an amulet. His arms were starting to ache and the pot now hung at knee leve.

First things first. Get past the refuse pit, then MtW, whatever that was, then the small folks wing, then the lobby, the Innkeeper's rooms and a grand celebration! Cautiously he proceeded, keeping to the center of the passageway, away from those spiders. Regrets competed for his attention. He shouldn't have retired. Having retired, he should have taken up karate, or crossword puzzles or parsing sentences or advanced grammar. Anything except writing a children's book! He should have accompanied Sophie to Florida. He should not have answered Windbreaker's knocks in the first place. Most of all, he should have yelled his head off while Windbreaker was frog-marching him outside and into that black van.

The passageway was widening and the ceiling seemed further away. His shoulders ached from carrying the heavy pot but he didn't dare pause to rest. He heard noises. Squeaky, scratchy noises. Grunts? Woofs? *Growls?* Should he turn back and wait by the door until someone opened it? Or had the noise come from behind? Had something foul and hungry come out of a hidden recess to trail him, sniffing and growling and licking its chops?

He couldn't tell because of the echoes.

Blunger strained to penetrate the gloom, but couldn't see more than ten feet in either direction. Slowly, prepared to throw the heavy pot at anything that moved, he advanced one cautious step at a time, his back to the right-hand wall. A strong reek of decay assailed his nostrils. Here there were no windows at all. Darkness closed in on him like a shroud. His eyes ached from peering. He could only move by feeling his way along the wall! Now there were loud squeakings ahead. And near. The refuse pit was probably filled with rats! A sharp stink hit him from the left; the pit must be at hand! Pressed against the right wall, he hesitated, ready to throw the *cholent*, pot and all, at anything that started to climb his leg.

And then, from the heart of darkness that surrounded him, came a dreadful, high-pitched, sibillant hiss.

*"May his food taste like bile and the soles of his feet bleed as he
makes the rounds to collect his rents."*

Blunger's heart skipped a beat!

The eerie voice continued its chant: *"May his ancestors' graves open
and their grisly, shrouded tenents converge upon the hall where his daughter is about to be wed."*

Blunger's scalp tightened and his knees trembled as the remainder
of the curse—*his curse on his absentee landlord and all of Knight
Management, the syndicate his nameless landlord hid behind*—was
spoken in the darkness. The words he'd composed at three in the
morning of the previous January 19, the night the waterhammer
woke him from the well-earned slumber of a retiree . . . those words
echoed within his mind even as they resounded from the dank,
encrusted walls of this dread passageway in the Inn at the End of
the World!

*"May sweetwine turn to vinegar in his mouth, and every time
he passes wind may the gases ignite in a blue flame and torch his
hemmorhoids! And may his hearing treble in sensitivity so that
he can hear the steady tread of cockroaches in the walls of his
tenements, the flushing at all hours of night of every commode on
which he collects rent! And most of all, may the noise of my
kitchen waterhammer resound within his skull without cease!"*

And then from the utter blackness directly ahead there issued a
low-frequency crackling vibration that continued steadily, ending
in an explosive belch and carrying to Blunger's overloaded nostrils
a fragrance composed, apparently, of equal parts of sulfur, sewer
gas and garlic. It *was* a belch! And it was followed by a profound,
basso grunt, and then by a voracious sniff and the sudden appearance of a pair of large, green, unblinking eyes at waist level.

"Monster!" Blunger shouted, retreating until his back pressed against the wall. He kicked out with one leg in all directions while he managed to balance himself and his burden.

"Monster!" he shouted, not realizing that the reason there was a solid wall behind him instead of a passageway down which he could retreat was simply because at the sight of those green eyes, he had turned to put his *cholent* pot between him and certain death.

The creature spoke, uttering words that Blunger didn't understand, and lo! there was light, a deep blue St. Elmo's fire that crackled at the tip of a staff held in the creature's hand. "Monster, am I!" it growled in a deep bass. "Don't you know a warlock when you see one? The only reason I don't send you screeching into the bottomless pit is because for you, Myron Blunger, that would be the easy way out! Also—sniff, sniff—something smells good and I deserve a hot meal!"

The self-proclaimed warlock was a stumpy thing with an enormous, bearded head which seemed to erupt from its trunk without the need of an intermediate neck. It licked its thick lips and its eyes glittered as they focussed on the pot of *cholent*.

It was garbed in a midnight-blue robe inscribed with half-moons, formulas and scribblings in unfamiliar symbols. The robe was gathered at the waist by a living belt of closely intertwined, eyeless, size 12 snakes. Blunger watched the belt slowly advance around the warlock's middle in a counterclockwise direction, permitting the snakes in front to forage briefly in their master's beard for bits and crumbs of food, while the remainder waited their respective turns.

Now Blunger's eyes had grown dark-adapted enough so that he saw, behind the warlock, a high-arched tunnel that branched out perpendicular to the main passageway and angled down for some distance until it vanished, undoubtedly into the refuse pit, which might well be bottomless; Blunger was willing to take the creature's word for that.

But the warlock wasn't alone! Seated on a high stool at the

tunnel entrance was a woman dressed entirely in black, even to the veil that covered her face. She wore a long, black coat similar to Sophie's, and beside her was a stick stout enough to qualify as a staff for casting spells. For a moment, Blunger thought he'd seen her somewhere before, perhaps in the Bronx before all this happened. But he dismissed that as impossible, even for the Bronx.

Blunger focussed on the only aspect of this apparition that offered any hope at all. The woman's coat. That coat was at least ten years out of style. Blunger's heart rose; maybe she wasn't a witch; maybe she was a *balabustah*! Who else, besides Sophie, knew how to make a winter coat last so many seasons?

Then Blunger noticed beside her three wicker baskets, each carrying a crudely printed label: Grade A Curses—profound, elaborate, permanent; Grade B Curses—heartfelt but retractable; Grade C curses—spur-of-the-moment, unintentional. So much for the *balabustah* theory.

Beside her was a large sack, from which ensued an odd rustling noise. In her hands were several slips of paper. One of them, Blunger realized with a heart tired from sinking, looked disastrously familiar. Written on the blank side of a Waldbaum's flier, he could tell even in the midnight blue illumination that the writing was his own. The woman in black was holding his original curse on Knight Management and on his hidden, nameless landlord, written on his kitchen table during a night made sleepless by the sudden commencement of the waterhammer.

"Plagiarized!" hissed the woman in black.

"What do you mean, plagiarized!" Blunger cried.

For answer, she reached into her sack and removed another sheet of paper, unfolded it and read in that same dreadful hiss:

"May his liver turn to water, and the bones of him crack in the cold of his heart.

"May dog fennel grow upon his ancestors' graves, and the grandsons of his children be born without eyes.

"May whiskey turn to clabber in his mouth, and every time he

sneezes may he blister the soles of his feet. And the smoke of his pipe—
may it make his eyes water, and the drops fall on the grass that his cows
eat and poison the butter than he spreads on his bread."

"The Transformation of Martin Burney," she said. "O. Henry.
You took the meter, the structure . . ."

"It was three in the morning," Blunger pleaded. "I couldn't
sleep for the waterhammer! Sophie sleeps through garbage collection, car crashes, fire engines! I had to put my anger down somewhere! I phoned Knight Management at three in the morning and
talked to a machine! My landlord? For years he was a nameless
shadow, but I'd bet my pension it's Lucien Broco.

"I had to get the anger out, or I'd explode! O. Henry helped a
little!"

Blunger gave up. What kind of help can one expect from a
witch?

Focussing on the stump-man, Blunger clutched his pot to his
belly and said, steadily, "I'm unfamiliar with warlocks. My specialty, before I retired, was children's books, which mostly use
witches." Nodding politely to the lady in black as in taking one's
leave, he took a step to his right, toward the Small Folks Wing and
the lobby and the celebration.

"Witches!" the warlock snapped. "They get all the P.R. You
think a witch could survive pit-duty for one hour, freezing her
buns off down here, beating off rats, vampire bats and blood-spi-
ders, and all the while, grading and matching up incoming curses
with stories? Which reminds me; have you a story, a funny story to
cancel that dreadful curse you wrote?"

None came to mind. First things first; he took another step to
the right.

"I have no story," he admitted. "If I hear one, I will certainly
send it along," he said politely, as one does when about to add:
"It's been a pleasure, but I have to get along, now, Mr. Warlock."

"Call me Meyer. Meyer the Warlock."

MtW stood for Meyer the Warlock! Meyer! Blunger, his leg muscles

alerted for flight at an instant's notice, hesitated. "Have you anything to do with *In doubt, higher migher?*"

The creature's response was to scuttle to the tunnel's edge
and, grumbling, *ascend the sheer wall*, apparently by finding mi-
croscopic purchases. Reaching his destination, a high ledge quite
near the ceiling, the warlock swung around, seated himself and
clapped onto his head a conical hat inscribed in the same manner
as his robe.

"Higher Meyer!" the warlock snapped down at Myron Blunger.
"You satisfied? As I was saying; life is all connections! The Wicked
Witch of the West happened to connect up with a dumb, pre-
adolescent idiot girl who didn't know enough to get in out of a
cyclone! For this she gets a cushy room in the tower for as long as
the Wizard of Oz is in print! And the Wizard! You should see how
he's made out, the phony!"

Higher Meyer! Why couldn't Yin have explained this in the first
place? Blunger was embarrassed at his string of misinterpretations
of the cryptic message.

Blunger firmed his grip on his *cholent*, took a deep breath and
ran, achieving exactly three steps in the direction of the Small
Folks Wing only to find his way blocked by the warlock, his glowing staff held before him!

The warlock snatched his pot and set it on the ground, heedless of its heat. Removing the lid, the warlock inhaled deeply of
the rich aroma. "Just in time," he said, glancing at the woman in
black, who had now risen. She took a step toward Blunger, who
remained paralyzed. "I'm Myron Blunger," he whispered.

"I know," she said. "I know everything."

"You know? You believe?" he exclaimed, relieved beyond words
that instead of ridiculing him or turning him into a frog, she had
spoken plain English. "I tell you the truth; I believe only ten percent of what I've seen with my own eyes! But it's good you believe;
that saves time." Pointing surruptitiously toward the dwarf who
was rapturously inhaling the *cholent* vapors, he whispered, "Careful what you say; he thinks he's a warlock."

"He *is* a warlock," she replied in a pleasant enough contralto, presumably her voice when she wasn't reciting curses. "Meyer the Warlock. Be careful what *you* say. I'm God's aunt and I'm exhausted and my feet hurt and . . . my, that smells good. What is it?"

"*Cholent*," Blunger replied, his momentary hope dashed into full despair. *God's aunt.* Another *meshuggah.* Was this place full of them? What was coming next, trolls and ogres? He looked wistfully in the direction of the Small Folks Wing and the lobby.

"A *cholent*! Wonderful," she exclaimed. "I'm famished! Three for luncheon!" she said, raising her staff.

This was too much for Blunger. "Wait . . . that's my *cholent* . . ."

"Three for luncheon!" she cried, and she flourished her staff three times. "And don't forget plates, napkins, utensils and a liter of house wine, chilled!" There appeared a whirlwind of screaming darkness, within which one heard scrapings, thumps, the clatter of silverware and the clink of crystal goblets. Quickly enough it subsided, leaving behind a card table covered with a red-and-white checked cloth, place settings for three, including wine goblets, an open bottle nestled in an ice-filled cooler, condiments, matching napkins and a bud vase in which was a single rose, plus three folding chairs. Meyer picked up the pot and plunked it down in the center of the table. Blunger could only stare dumbly.

"It's a present for the Innkeeper," Blunger whispered, half-hoping that no one would hear the protest dictated by his sense of justice.

Jumping up into one of the chairs, Meyer the Warlock spooned still-bubbling *cholent* into his plate and growled, "Too heavy. Too much *cholent.* The way you were carrying it, the pot was almost to the floor."

God's aunt hefted the pot, stared at Blunger and nodded. "We'd better lighten it by two pounds," she said, helping herself to a generous portion.

Thrusting his fork toward Blunger's belly, the warlock said, "So there's no misunderstanding, God's aunt and I are not eating this cholent out of greediness or base motive; we are doing it to save your life. Pass the ketchup."

Save my life! Ketchup on cholent! "Okay, okay," Blunger said. He watched dispiretedly as the warlock shovelled a good portion of the stew into his maw without saying grace or so much as by-your-leave.

The woman in black helped herself to a sizeable portion also, but paused to say grace before taking even one bite, which she conveyed to her mouth without lifting her veil. *God's aunt.* Blunger took nothing, finding, for once, that he had no appetite.

"What's in the sack?" Blunger asked.

"Curses. Maledictions. Blasphemies," answered the woman in black. "It's my job to scavange them before they reach my Nephew's ears and cause Him even more distress. Meyer collects jokes, poems, songs. We match these bits of merriment and good cheer against the *agita*, which they neutralize. A story, especially a funny story, extinguishes one of these maledictions. Well? Anything come in since my last visit?" she asked the warlock.

Between mouthfuls, he growled, "Frog joke."

The woman in black spread Blunger's landlord curse on the table, pressed it flat, then nodded.

"There was this beautiful, ripe princess, see?" the warlock recited. "And she went for a walk in the forest and sat down and up jumped a froggie right into her lap. Heh, heh."

Through her veil, God's aunt threw him a look of warning and the warlock, clearing his throat, continued, "'I'm really a handsome prince,' said the froggie, 'changed into a froggie forever and a day unless I spend a night on the pillow of a true princess.'

"With that, the princess, who was very kind and beautiful, with big . . ."

"Just tell the joke!" God's aunt snapped.

"Anyway," the warlock recited, "she snuck him home and that night put the froggie on her pillow and the next morning when she woke up, sure enough, there was a handsome prince in bed beside her.

"Would you believe that to this day, her mother don't believe that story?" the warlock chuckled.

To Blunger's astonishment, the writing vanished from his Landlord curse. God's aunt crumpled the flier with its 6x6 tomatoes at 99 cents per pound and sent it down the tunnel. The paper half-flew, half-rolled directly to the edge of the pit and was gone.

The warlock, having cleaned his plate, drained his wine-goblet at one continuous swallow, leaned back and delivered himself of a stentorian burp. "That was a rare treat, sonny," he sighed.

"Because that *cholent* was really excellent, I will prophecy! Stand back!" With that, he stood up, closed his eyes, leaped about in a seemingly aimless fashion, then fell to the floor and spun around three times. "Aha!" he announced. "Here it comes! To open the door to Esfandiary, you have only to cry, 'Fore!' F. O. R. E. Not Four F.O.U.R.; that won't work. You see, Door knows that God is always looking for a golf partner."

"Fore," Blunger said, sadly eyeing the greatly reduced *cholent* in the pot.

"That's it," said the warlock, hauling himself to his feet.

God's aunt rose, waved Blunger away from the table together with the pot containing the remaining *cholent*. She tapped the table three times with her staff. A whirlwind enfolded the table and chairs, and with a clatter and a rattle and a clunk and a thunk, carried them down the tunnel, and vanished into darkness.

"Be on your way, and good fortune be with you," said God's aunt to Blunger, and he lost no time, but ran as fast as he could along the passageway toward the Innkeeper's quarters, hoping they hadn't started without him.

"Well?" said the warlock, after Blunger's departure. "Does he have a chance to get out of this?"

The veil oscillated slowly from side to side. "No. As we speak, Don Juan circles Upper Muchness on a flying horse, probably looking for a virgin to land upon. Even now pirates are in the library, conjuring up their ship. As their readerships decline, others will flee the Inn, fearful of fading into oblivion without souls. And there is the problem of Dragon Groff and the ineffectiveness of the barrier between Esfandiary and Earth Real, in that odd valley of Upper Muchness.

"I have spoken to my Nephew; He will not intercede, despite Myron Blunger's having given Him his greatest laugh since He invented the duckbill platypus. Blunger has no idea of the magnitude of the Original Dream, and therefore cannot fathom the perhaps inevitable disappointment."

For some while there was silence, then God's aunt spoke: "The *cholent* was excellent, wasn't it. Perhaps . . . perhaps I shall try again. Not in Esfandiary, though. There is no help for Blunger in Esfandiary. I even approached the King of France; he wouldn't see me, because of my *patois*, as his aide termed it. "No, I will gamble on the human heart. The lightspeed system is in order?"

The warlock grunted.

"You have been sending copies of Blunger's early chapters to his wife in Florida, in care of her sister Gertrude?"

The warlock nodded and yawned; hot meals made him tired.

"Good. Have you copies of these latest chapters, *Hope and the Dragon*, and *Too Little*?"

The warlock nodded sleepily, pointing toward a rock shelf in his living quarters, a spartan alcove several steps into the tunnel. God's aunt saw a slim package wrapped in brown paper and tied with string. She wondered whether the warlock, who had much time on his hands, had gotten around to opening this material for a quick peek, as he had with the first and second batch of writings.

"Good. I will take them myself." With that, the woman in black took up her staff and sack, retrieved the package and strode down the tunnel past the bottomless pit until she vanished in a different direction altogether.

Windbreaker had carried Yang into Watson's small dispensary for first aid. The gnome's eyes were unfocussed and his words were a babble of nonsense. Dr. Watson's theory was that the fall from Windbreaker's back into the hard-frozen hay bale had jarred Yang's forebrain, throwing certain disparate thoughts into sudden juxta-position. As a precaution, the doctor had strapped the mumbling, hallucinating gnome onto his bed. Watson sat beside, and used the time to write down his notes on the Innkeeper.

"In summary, the Innkeeper believes himself to be Wotan," he muttered as he finished his thoughts. Beside him there was a stirring on his bed.

"Wotan," Yang whispered.

"No," Watson said, determined to correct the gnome's confusion before it set in. "You're Yang, and you're in my care at The Inn at the End of the World. I'm Dr. John Watson, companion to Mr. Sherlock Holmes, with two stories in my own right."

The gnome turned his head and now his eyes were focussed quite nicely. Yang said, "What about Wotan?"

Watson was reluctant to divulge a professional confidence, but was equally anxious to see Yang through this concussion-caused amnesia. "The Innkeeper believes himself to be Wotan. How many fingers am I holding up?"

"Twelve, you fool!" Yang snapped, struggling to rise.

"Not yet!" Watson cautioned. "If you stand up, you'll get a splitting headache."

"Windbreaker . . ." Yang dropped back as his head throbbed and the room began to spin in both directions at once.

" . . . went back outside to practice his horn," Dr. Watson continued, taking the gnome's pulse. "He's a bit disappointed that he didn't do better against the Commandant."

As though cued, a horn sounded in the distance. Yang closed his eyes. His head hurt and he couldn't think properly. *Wotan!* Did this fool doctor realize who Wotan was? The effort of thinking was too great; Yang fell into a shallow doze.

Dr. Watson loosened the restraining straps; it was time to take the leeches from the Innkeeper and he didn't want Yang to waken and panic at finding himself immobilized.

"Make way! Hot stuff!" Blunger called, wending his way through the lobby. "Make way! Watch it!" Though the pot was certainly lighter than when it had started out and no longer threatened to scrape the floor, he was unable to carry it directly before him, as a proper present; it hung below his belly. A hundred yards from the Innkeeper's door, he knew he wasn't going to make it without a rest. Endeavoring to set the pot down on a narrow side-table, he missed entirely, lunged forward and fell to the stone floor, the pot clanging loudly. That the pot didn't break was because of its heavy iron construction.

Blunger lifted the pot onto the table and sank into an adjacent chair to catch his breath and relax his arm muscles. Had he not been mindful of God's order regarding diet, he would have broken down and taken some *cholent*, for strength.

The loud clang that accompanied Blunger's dropping of the pot alerted the Innkeeper, whose corporeal self was now driven ninety percent by the spirit of Wotan. He glanced at Dr. Watson, who had extracted some blood from one of the leeches and was examining it under a microscope for signs of curdling. The Innkeeper's mouth tightened in a crazed grin; his eyes widened with anticipation.

Blunger was coming. Blunger was announcing his approach by banging on a pot. How fitting. With his left hand, the Innkeeper drew the loaded pistol from beneath his pillow, where he'd hidden it from Watson's view, and positioned it exactly at the point of the V shortly to be occupied in space by Blunger's crotch. Then, lest he catch sight of one of the bloody leeches, he turned his head away, transferred the weapon to his right hand, tightened his right forefinger against the trigger and listened intently, waiting for the door to open.

In the distance a horn sounded, starting soft and of a single pitch, as though feeling its way, then growing louder and richer in overtones until it sounded like an army of horns. Then it stopped abruptly . . . .

Blunger flexed his shoulders, picked up the *cholent*-pot and resumed his awkward march, staggering and shuffling down the middle of the corridor, determinedly holding his back straight, trying to hold the proof of his good intentions belt-high. After all, he couldn't march into the Innkeeper's chambers like a *shlepper* with a pot dragging on the ground!

A horn was blowing. Already the musicians were tuning up for the celebration!

The Innkeeper heard the *clang* of iron being set down on stone just outside his door. Labored breathing. A knock.

"Who's there?" he growled and the forefinger of his right hand tightened on the trigger.

"Myron Blunger."

A pause to savor the moment, then, "Enter."

A click, a creak of hinge as the door opened. From the corner of his eye, the Innkeeper saw Blunger's smiling face. He waited until his guest had taken one step into the room, then closed his eyes and squeezed the trigger firmly.

BANG! boom . . . boom!

A loud, echoing *clang*, a scream of excruciating pain mingled with cries of rage triumphant, screeches, yelps, howls and the sound of running feet and still the discharge resounded, echoed throughout the hallways and corridors of the Inn.

Windbreaker had carelessly left the door open, and the sound of the explosion, echoing down the hallways and corridors, carried out to the paddock so magnified and unending that one might have thought a major battle was taking place. Windbreaker instinctively reared up on his hind legs. Then someone came charging out of the Inn shouting, "Run! Run for your life! His blood's curdled!" Then more guests poured out of the doorway, screaming women clutching at their skirts that they might run faster, children crying with terror, men shouting in many tongues, "Get out! Run!"

"What's happened?" Windbreaker called.

A whiskered man wearing a chef's hat yelled, "The Innkeeper's shot Blunger! His blood curdled! He's gone mad! Run for your life!"

Dropping the horn of Roland into a saddlebag, the centaur focussed on the rescue of Myron Blunger from whatever had befallen him. To try to enter the Inn against the outpouring tide of humanity was out of the question. The only way to get inside was around the perimeter of the Inn, then in through the door into the library. The area patrolled by the sabertooth.

The wall around the paddock was high enough to keep the sabertooths out. Was it too high for a centaur to leap? Was the ground outside level, or was there a ditch? He didn't remember. Why hadn't he prepared more thoroughly? Yang had been right all along; taking advantage of his recuperation, he'd gotten lazy and stupid and now Myron Blunger had been shot and where was he? Out in the paddock, practicing blowing a horn! It was his own fault!

Picking his way through the gathering crowd of bewildered, shivering guests, Windbreaker gained open ground and broke into a full gallop. Thirty yards from the wall, he gauged the footwork for that leap that would take him outside the boundary of the Inn. Nearing it at top speed, he timed his leap, shot up into the air, tucked his legs beneath his body, cleared the wall by inches and landed not twenty feet from the sabertooth.

It had dug itself a shallow groove in the hard snow, and there it lay, panting, alert to the tumult on the other side of the wall but concentrating on something beyond the centaur's field of view. The tiger's grey stripes on white fur blended in with the landscape, so that Windbreaker, sailing over the wall, didn't spot the tiger until it had leaped up and was bounding toward him, snarling.

In a long run, the centaur knew that he could outlast the sabertooth. But there would be no long run; it was nearly upon him, snarling and bounding at top speed! Planting his forelegs into the tundra, Windbreaker whirled about, timed the huge cat's motion, then kicked back with all his power. The tiger weighed hardly less than the centaur, and though it caught the hooves in midair and directly in the head, its momentum sent Windbreaker crashing to the ground. Knowing that the tiger would regain its footing faster than the centaur possibly could, Windbreaker swivelled about on the snow and kicked, kicked, trying to keep it at distance while his hands sought weapons. *Excalibur* was beneath his bulk, trapped. Arrows. He snatched a handful and threw them at the tiger's head.

The cat ducked, ignored the minor stings of the few arrows that found flesh, swiped at the centaur's flailing legs; by the time it decided to jump over them, Windbreaker had managed to pull a lance from its sheath and try for footing. He was still off-balance, kneeling as the cat screamed, jumped, came down with its forelegs extended and its knife-claws raking the air as they would slash his exposed neck and face. The centaur lowered his head and managed to set the butt of the lance in ground; the lance-point met the sabertooth in mid-flight, penetrating its white chest. The hurtling beast impaled itself until the lance-head erupted between the powerful muscles of its back. Yet its foreclaws slashed Windbreaker's face as its momentum carried it crashing into the red snow.

The dying beast screamed and its yellow eyes were fixed on something beyond the centaur. Windbreaker, lurching to his feet and wiping the blood from his face, opened his eyes and was stunned.

The kraken had left the Deep. The sightless monster, huge beyond reckoning and festooned with tentacles and snorkels for sniffing, had somehow worked its way up the trail and was at the boundary wall of the Inn. This . . . this was the thing Windbreaker

had fought *mano a mano* in the Deep! The centaur had pictured it
as a super-octopus; it was not. Its body was segmented, the myriad
of tentacles knotted just behind the head-segment, to which two
grey snorkel-tubes were attached.

The kraken knew the scent of the half-horse that had bitten its
tentacle. Reversing its snorkels, it vented a noxious, dark gas that
blinded Windbreaker. Living whips slashed at him; the centaur
gained its feet and leaped blindly, came to earth and leaped again,
only to land on a tube of flesh. He pulled *Excalibur* from its scabbard, swung it to the left, to the right, fought to get to the open
ground, but he was blind, trapped in a living forest of writhing
tentacles. Coughing, winded from his exertions, he slashed and
hacked, but the kraken, driven by a fury that transcended its primi-
tive instincts, lashed at the half-horse regardless of the loss of body
fluids, of flesh, and now it had all four legs of the half-horse wrapped
and immobile. Its powerful fore-tentacles swung over to encircle
the thing's body, to crack it in half . . .

BANG! boom . . . boom!

An explosion! Yang slipped from Dr. Watson's restraining cuffs
and lurched, still dizzy from the concussion, into the hallway. He
smelled gunpowder and saw a puff of dark smoke down the corridor, in the direction of the Innkeeper's quarters. Something crashed
to the floor with a resonant *clang* and there was Blunger backing
out of the room, doubled over, bellowing with pain, horror and
shock! He was clutching his abdomen, mindless of the mess streaming over his hands, his trousers, splashing into a rapidly growing
puddle on the floor. His head shook wildly from side to side in
denial but there was no denial.

The Innkeeper appeared in the doorway, a huge pistol in hand.
From his mouth came wild, maniacal shrieks that went on and on.

Dr. Watson was on the floor of the corridor, his hands and
shirt streaked with blood. "Get away! Get out of the Inn!" he cried
at Blunger. Even after decades of exposure to violence, the loud-
ness of the explosion had so startled him that the bloodsucker he'd

been studying was quite squashed. "The Innkeeper's blood has curdled; he's in an uncontrollable rage and I'll not answer for his actions should he encounter you."

"Argh! Argh!" Blunger screamed, clawing at his burning midsection. "Hot! Hot!"

Yang wanted to hurry to Blunger's side but his head was splitting and it was all he could do to crawl like an infant. He could see Blunger in the distance. The man's trousers were stained red and brown, and on the floor was a large pot, still ringing like a bell struck at its center of percussion with a hammer . . . or a lead ball from a cannonbarrel flintlock.

Had Blunger not been transporting the iron pot at exactly the proper height, his private parts would have been disintegrated into their component molecules by the shot. And had his manuscripts not been tucked deeply into his trousers, it is likely that the heat of the spilled *cholent* would have seared and scorched those sensitive and unprotected appendages beyond recognition or use. As it was, he was suffering more from shock than from damage, though a hot and alien fluid *was* dripping down his trouser-leg.

Blunger, terrified, ran wildly, blindly. Yang, some fifty yards down the hallway, saw a hand reach out and take hold of Blunger's elbow. *Long John Silver!* Yang tried to stand, holding onto the wall for support, but fell in a heap as pain shot through his skull. He watched the pirate pull Blunger toward the library, and an instant later, saw the Innkeeper himself appear in the doorway, barefoot, the right sleeve of his pajamas rolled up to accomodate the tenacious leeches, the flintlock in his right hand, his countenance fiercer than Yang had ever seen it. With a horrifying yell, the Innkeeper started after Blunger, lurching, pushing aside whoever got in his way, reaching into his pajama pocket for a fresh charge and powder even as he followed his nemesis, who no longer had a pot to hide behind.

Had the Innkeeper not paused to reload his weapon, he might have overtaken Silver and his captive. But the Innkeeper—wholly Wotan now—was single-minded. Blunger, alive, was a threat to his plans. Blunger, dead and martyred, could be even more of a danger. But Blunger emasculated, Blunger a laughing-stock with an empty, flapping scrotum—Blunger no longer interested in the effect of testicular engineering on the history of humankind—could be sent back to the Bronx on horseback, or walking, or by his precious subway; it would not matter.

BOOM!

The lead ball would have disembowelled Myron Blunger, upon whose rear the library door had not quite closed, had the weapon been aimed properly. But the Innkeeper, using his right hand, had been distracted by the hanging leeches and his arm moved. The shot, however, found a window and, beyond, the sensitive tip of the tentacle that was wrapped about Windbreaker's upper chest. The kraken recoiled, permitting the centaur to fasten a two-handed grip on the living rope that bound his legs.

Windbreaker slashed a tendril that had probed its way to the flesh of his arm, but not before an electric shock coursed through his body. His arm muscles were convulsing, yet he slashed, thrusted, scrambled for balance.

And as he thrust *Excalibur* into the base of a great knot of tentacle, he reached into his saddlebag with his left hand, withdrew the horn of Roland and put it to his lips.

Fatigued, still entangled in the beast's tentacles, Windbreaker gathered air into his double sets of lungs and blew. Startled and confused at this unprecedented sound, the sightless kraken paused in confusion, only for the few moments needed to sniff air and ground, to determine that no new enemy had appeared.

But those moments sufficed. The sword of King Arthur again flashed in great arcs, desperately slashing the leathern ropes of muscle. Blowing the horn again and again, the centaur scrambled out of the imprisoning maze of tentacles. Out of the darkness he leaped, soaring over writhing coils until he reached clear ground and charged for the library door, hooves pounding rhythmically.

He felt a pain in his chest . . . wasn't getting enough oxygen . . . couldn't gallop much further . . .

He reached the door that led into the library and pounded on it with the butt of *Excalibur*. There was no sound from within. He glanced to his right. *The monster was no longer pulling itself along like a worm; it was humping along the ground caterpillar-fashion, sucking in great volumes of air through trunk-like tubes that extended from its head!* Windbreaker pounded on the door, which he knew was triple-bolted on the inside. It would take time to undo those bolts!

Footsteps. Weighty footsteps. "*Hurry up!*" Windbreaker sounded a discordant *blatt* but that only seemed to speed the kraken up!

At the other end of the library, the Innkeeper was pounding on the door with both hands, threatening total devastation if the door weren't opened immediately. The repeated impact, together with the torpidity of the Innkeeper's blood stunned Dr. Watson's leeches. They started dropping away from their host's forearm.

"Blunger!" bellowed the Innkeeper, smashing the butt of the flintlock on the thick oak door. "Send out Blunger!"

Deep in the stacks, where he'd been carrying out research since breakfast, Yin gave up. The noise level had become unbearable. First it was the pirates, trooping in with their "yo-ho-hos" and a great chest, which they'd dropped onto the floor without a by-your-leave. Then an explosion outside, and much shouting, though the gnome was determined not to let that kind of nonsense interfere with his research career. Even the arrival of Myron Blunger with that ugly pirate hadn't broken Yin's concentration.

But now they were pounding on both doors and the pirates, plus Blunger with a dirk against his Adam's apple held by the ugly one, were seated around the table concentrating. Yin rose quietly and headed for the outside door; the pounding seemed more urgent, and he didn't like the tone of voice coming from the Innkeeper.

The pirates were concentrating with a power that astonished

Blunger. Indeed, so vivid was their reconstruction of the Hispaniola
that it was projected into Blunger's mind! Having no sympathy
for their project, Myron Blunger had tried to concentrate on the
antithesis of a three-masted schooner riding high in a placid la-
goon. Blunger had imagined in as much detail as possible a storm
bearing down from the north, icebergs in a sea roiled by undersea
volcanos, lightning attacking the masts and . . . and a horde of
giant cockroaches climbing out of the sea, over the gunwales . . .

It was a standoff, the twelve pirates' assembling of the
Hispaniola alternating with the collapse of one part or another,
until Long John Silver had put the dirk to Blunger's throat and
demanded that he get the door open, one way or another. And he
had done so.

"Fore," he'd whispered, hoping it wouldn't be noticed. But
the door had swung open and there, just as they'd imagined it,
was the start of a sandy beach, and beyond that, open water that
stretched to the horizon. A gentle surf rocked two longboats which
rested at water's edge. Not far offshore and pulling gently at anchor was a slightly fuzzy three-masted boat with sails furled. At
the stern a white skull and crossbones flew against a black background. But the schooner was gaining in clarity and detail; soon it
would be real. Also, Blunger couldn't keep this up much longer;
he was getting a headache and Silver's dirk was pressing too tightly
into his throat and someone was pounding on the door. On both
doors.

The dirk dropped away from Blunger's adam's apple as the
head pirate poured his determination into the completion of the
schooner. Blunger peeked from between narrowed eyelids. The
reconstruction of the *Hispaniola* was only minutes away.

This would be a good time to depart, but how? The Innkeeper
was at the inside, lobby door, and it seemed clear that this wasn't
a matter of liking or not liking *cholent*.

Someone was pounding on the outside door; it followed that
the sabertooth must have gone elsewhere. That was his best bet for
a fast exit. Blunger rose and tiptoed in that direction only to find

Yin already there and trying to throw the bolts, without much success.

In the hallway, the Innkeeper, having given up on threats, was carefully loading a double charge of powder into the flintlock.

"OPEN THE DOOR!" Windbreaker roared. An eye was at the peephole. "Oh, my!" someone said dazedly. The peephole closed. It was Blunger!

"OPEN THE DOOR!" the centaur thundered. A bolt was thrown.

A forest of tentacles was snaking *past him*, closing off escape, and the tubular snorkels were at his feet. Windbreaker kicked at the closest one.

"OPEN THE BLOODY DAMNED DOOR!"

As soon as the semi-circle was complete, the kraken would close in.

Another bolt was thrown. One remained . . .

From inside the library, there was an explosion . . .

"Blunger?"

What had happened? The centaur lashed out at the door with his forefeet, swung *Excalibur* wildly, ineffectually! The encirclement was complete; the centaur was trapped unless that door opened *now*!

While Blunger struggled with the final bolt on the outer door, the Innkeeper aimed at the lock mechanism of the inner door of the library, shielded his eyes and fired. The heavy brass lock of the inner door was gone. The door swung open and a thick cloud of dense, acrid gunsmoke billowed into the library. The Innkeeper, his eyes closed, felt his way inside, curdled blood dribbling from his nose, spraying from his ears, oozing from the pores in his forehead and from beneath his fingernails.

Stooping, Blunger jammed his shoulder beneath the third bolt. Then, with his hands on his thighs, he pushed up with his strong leg muscles until the third bolt shot up. The outer door to the library flew open and Windbreaker bounded in, whacking at the tip of a tentacle that had wound itself around a hind leg. The tentacle tightened its grip; the centaur spun around and kicked the door shut, severing the tentacle. Then Windbreaker took in a scene more fantastical than any he could have ever imagined. Gathered around the library table were some dozen hard-looking pirates, their eyes closed in most intense concentration. Just beyond the writing table, emerging from a cloud of exploded gunpowder, was the Innkeeper, and he was beyond rage. His eyes were fixed on Blunger and he was reloading a huge pistol with powder and shot.

Windbreaker grabbed Blunger by the belt and the seat of his trousers and in one swing, heaved him, belly down, over his back, just like a sack of flour. Yin tried to leap onto Windbreaker's rump, but fell short. Unable to climb onto Windbreaker, Yin leaped up and grabbed a double handful of the long hairs of the centaur's tail and there he hung, flailing and kicking and oscillating like a pendulum.

The Innkeeper paused in his reloading. One leech remained, dangling from his forearm. The Innkeeper smiled. He had plans for that leech. It had worked hard, tried its best and deserved a new home, a quieter, more gentle, less curdled home. He intended to introduce the worm to Myron Blunger. What Blunger needed to accomplish the task of retrieving the seven-league boots was a strengthening of his blood! Perhaps this most tenacious leech, freshly loaded with Viking blood, would accomplish what the St. Felicia's potion had failed to do.

The Innkeeper raised the pistol with his left hand, squinted, centered the cannon-barrel on Blunger's vitals, brought his right arm across and beneath the barrel to steady his aim. The centaur was trying to escape into Esfandiary. But whose Esfandiary? The Innkeeper concentrated; the scene beyond the door shifted abruptly . . . .

The centaur looked to his left and even as he took in new knowledge, his muscles were bunching. The door to Esfandiary was wide open. Beyond the threshold was greenness, a profound silence, safety for Blunger. Windbreaker couldn't accelerate to a gallop or zig-zag sufficiently to foil the Innkeeper's aim; the floor was too slippery! With maddening slowness, as though trying to gallop through water, Windbreaker made for the open door.

The Innkeeper shifted the reloaded pistol to his right hand; with his left, he nudged the last of Dr. Watson's leeches into the muzzle. Then he sighted on Myron Blunger, and pulled the trigger.

BANG!

There was a loud cry; he'd gotten his target that time! The centaur, Blunger and the imp-gnome vanished behind a screen of black smoke. The Innkeeper fell to his knees. Blood spurted from the corners of his eyes; a magenta curtain ran down his face. Deafened by the explosion of the hand-cannon, blinded by curdled blood and the cloud of burnt powder, he roared a powerful malevolence at the fleeing centaur and his thrice-doomed passenger, and then he laughed. And continued to laugh, for Myron Blunger, seeking escape and salvation, had fled into hell. He was doomed!

His fury abated, the Innkeeper's hold on Esfandiary diminished. Green dissolved into blue . . .

But it was the Innkeeper's Esfandiary that Windbreaker soared into through the doorway, majestic as a stag. Behind him, there was a loud bang; Windbreaker felt Blunger shudder—he'd been hit! Gripping him tightly, the centaur came to ground and tore along a wide trail cut through a green jungle-world. Running low to the earth, he dropped Myron Blunger into a patch of undergrowth where he'd be safe for the moment, then veered across the trail to decoy the Innkeeper, in case he'd been followed. The pain in Windbreaker's tail abruptly ceased; it had been the gnome holding on, and he'd fallen off! The centaur slowed gradually, then turned around.

Visibility was terrible; everything was green, including the air. Yin lay on the ground several dozen yards back, moaning and trying to raise himself. Blunger was further back, nearly lost in a green haze that extended in all directions so that one couldn't see more than fifty yards. Windbreaker started back, gasping after his exertions.

Blunger was sitting up, waving and hollering; his legs were in the undergrowth. Why didn't he get up? Then Windbreaker saw that Blunger was under attack! He was trying to fend off a squat, bowlegged, hairy creature with a long, wide snout and protuberant, upward-curled fangs! It was tugging at Blunger's left foot, grunting and snorting, slowly pulling him into the bushes!

Windbreaker broke into a gallop, flashed back along the trail, keeping his eyes fixed on the patch of dense vegetation into which Myron Blunger was rapidly vanishing!

That final blast wakened the pirates from their creation-trance. As one they rubbed their eyes, then looked to the door to Esfandiary. It was open. They'd succeeded! Long John Silver looked around; Blunger was gone! Too bad; somehow he believed that the landlubber had been fighting their line of creative thought. A keelhawling would be a fine way to inaugurate the voyage!

The Innkeeper had somehow gotten into the library and he was on his knees, laughing wildly, insanely. The Innkeeper wouldn't be joining them at sea, Silver decided. But beyond the open door to Esfandiary was a placid beach, longboats at ready and there, anchored good and proper and with sails furled, the *Hispaniola!* Quickly he organized the order of march to the longboats, putting himself last, with a dirk ready to fly in case the Innkeeper proved troublesome.

Dr. Watson picked his way through the cloud of gunpowder, coughing, his black bag in hand. He was carrying Yang, whom he'd found unconscious in the hallway, over his shoulder. The Innkeeper lay on the floor, roaring with laughter. It was some minutes before Dr. Watson brought Yang about, and some minutes later before the details of what had just transpired were made clear.

"Why did he have to get involved in the affairs of humans?"

Yang wailed. "Why did I let him? What a fool I was! They'll be eaten alive!"

"Eaten alive!" Watson said as he attended to the Innkeeper. "Who'll be eaten alive?"

"Yin," Yang said. "And Windbreaker and Myron Blunger. He shot them into Esfandiary," pointing to the Innkeeper and the now-discarded pistol. "The Innkeeper shot him!" Yang said, shaking from side to side in sorrow for his lost brother.

The Innkeeper attempted to rise, but had not the strength. Dr. Watson, busily dabbing at the curdled blood on his face with a handkerchief, asked, "And what's so humorous?"

"Blunger is gone!" the Innkeeper exclaimed with insane glee. "Gone! I shot a leech into him. Deep, dear doctor! If he were lucky, my shot would have blown him into pieces. Second choice is to go to sleep and bleed quietly to death as the leech's natural anti-coagulant serum does its work. More likely, Blunger'll probably thrash out his last moments hanging from the teeth of a *Thunder Lizard*, with his guts ripped out before his living eyes.

"I don't know where he thought he was escaping to, but it's *my* Esfandiary he's in! *My* Esfandiary . . ." And the Innkeeper shuddered with delight at the thought.

Watson reeled back to Blunger's writing chair, into which he fell. "What are you saying?" he demanded, horrified. "Blunger told me of his experience in Esfandiary. I've been researching it in Freud . . ."

"Forget Blunger!" the Innkeeper roared. "There is no Blunger! Except . . . in my chamberpot, heh, heh."

From an inside jacket pocket Dr. Watson pulled a thick bundle of paper. "He dropped these in the hallway," said the doctor to no one in particular, his voice hushed and trembling. "I picked them up . . ."

Dr. Watson slipped on a pair of eyeglasses and scanned the first pages of *Hope and the Dragon*. The Innkeeper, still chuckling at having triply-dispatched Myron Blunger from the Inn, snatched and read each page as it left Dr. Watson's hands, leaving them on the floor for the gnome Yang to re-order and scan that he might learn for what noble cause his brother had been sacrificed. Then the Innkeeper hoisted himself to a sitting position and with a low growl, tore the sheaf of manuscripts from Dr. Watson's hand. Indeed, the Innkeeper grew quite solemn as he studied the last manuscripts written by Myron Blunger in the Inn at the End of the World.

Yang, lamenting the loss of his brother, had no interest in Blunger's final manuscripts, and joined Dr. Watson who had marched over to the outside door. The doctor lifted him to the peephole in time to see the rear segment of the kraken vanish over the lip of the plateau on which the Inn was situated. Exhausted, bleeding profusely and unable to break down the door through which the half-horse had vanished, the kraken was slowly, painfully inching its way downtrail toward the Deep.

THE WOMAN IN BLACK

*In which Sophie Blunger and her sister Gertrude are brought
into this business, and not a moment too soon.*

Gertrude Weintraub, Sophie Blunger's older sister, lay on her back
and grimly watched the rising sun paint the opposite wall of her
bedroom. Orange. Orange juice. Toasted English muffins with
orange marmalade. Cereal with raisins. Coffee. None of this decaf
nonsense; strong coffee that got the system going; *pischen coffee*. If
not for all the *agita*, she could have been looking forward to breakfast on the terrace with her sister, a good *shmooze*, some sighing
over their problems and watching the earlybirds jog along the
beach. But they'd been up until midnight two nights in a row and
Sophie was still asleep in the living room, on the sofa-bed. And the
Myron problem wasn't solved.

Where was he? Why didn't he phone? And if he was too busy
to phone, why didn't he *answer* the phone? That was Sophie's
version of the Myron problem. Gertrude's version was more philo-
sophical and had to do with a foolish marriage to an impoverished
librarian rather than a butcher or an accountant, both dismissed
by her kid sister when that dreamer Myron Blunger entered her
life. So far Gertrude had managed to keep those thoughts to herself, for the most part.

From the cuckoo clock on the wall opposite the bed came a
tired whirr, some clicks, a *pong*. The door opened and out came
Dickie bird to tell her it was six o'clock, give or take an hour.
Gertrude's right hand felt around on the bed, found a slipper,
flung it at the cuckoo clock. Missed low. Her heart wasn't in it.

Shying slippers at Dickie bird had been Harold's morning thing. Dickie bird bobbed solemnly, peeped once, and retreated. Six o'clock. More likely six-thirty, judging by the rising sun. Only one peep. Dickie bird couldn't count any more. Maybe he was punchy after taking all those slipper-shots. The door to his chalet closed with much creak and clatter of mechanism, and another *pong*. Gertrude found herself blinking rapidly as tears formed in the corners of her eyes. With the kids up and gone and no grandkids on the horizon, Harold had brought home the Swiss cuckoo clock from a business trip to Hong Kong to raise some hell around the place. Poor Harold.

Gertrude turned her head to the left. Spread over the other half of her double bed were an Atlas and an old Texaco road map of the Northeastern States; nowhere was there a reference to Upper Muchness, or a Lower Muchness, though villages of less than a thousand population weren't included. According to Myron's writings, he was at an Inn at the End of the World, somewhere in that unmarked, unbordered whiteness. The Inn at the End of the World.

There were two possibilities. One: Myron had lost his mind. Two: Myron had not lost his mind. In which case one must accept some radical notions: that elves escort the souls of sleeping children through a dream-world called Esfandiary, which is populated by griffins, heffalumps and at least one minotaur; that by writing in the library of this Inn one could transport oneself to the Valley of Upper Muchness; that one fine morning, perhaps *this* morning, Joey Willem would head out to hunt dragons in the Dromedary Mountains, accompanied by Brunnhilde the Valkyrie, who was on vacation from her bed of fire.

Gertrude's instincts pointed to a sudden and complete stripping of her brother-in-law's mental gears.

Dickie bird and Myron. Both clunked out.

All well and good to label Myron mad, but what about the packages? They had arrived at Gertrude's doorstep two mornings in succession, addressed to Sophie Blunger. Sent how? Wrapped in plain brown paper tied with heavy white string . . . wrapping paper with no return address or postage stamps, no postmark, just a yellow-stamped diagram in the upper right corner that looked like a lightning bolt. *A Kee Ess Una Meiseh*. *Broco*. And *The Griffin Problem*. As though that weren't strange enough, the second batch consisted of *The Pizza Vendetta*. *The Dish best served Cold*. *The Battletuba*. *Justice*. No note, no letter.

Gertrude had set aside the wrapping paper and the string for further study; they had some interesting features. The string had been untied and then retied; the original tying had left groove-marks in the wrapping paper that didn't correspond to the string locations when the package had arrived. Either the sender, presumably Myron, had changed his mind about its contents before mailing it, or somewhere between sending and receiving, the package had been opened. Had anything been removed? There was no way to know, short of discovering the means of its mailing. For it had certainly not gone through the U.S. mail, not without stamps.

So who was creeping around the condo development in the night, leaving packages on doorsteps?

Gertrude took up her idea list, which, so far, consisted of three points. One: Sophie was certain the manuscripts were in Myron's handwriting. For better or worse, that was a fact. Two: He hadn't telephoned in four days, nor did he answer the phone. But, he might have turned the ringer down, or the telephone might not be not working at all. Or he might be too absorbed in his craziness to answer it. If it turned out that he was home all this time with the telephone ringer turned down low, while his wife was eating her *kishkes* out from worry, that *shmo* would have the world's first colonoscopy done with a cane, without anesthesia.

Three: it was high time someone entered the apartment. Now she added the idea that had caused her to waken before sunrise— Four: *In doubt, Higher Migher!*

After planting it in the storyline himself, subconsciously or unconsciously or whichever way he turned out his writings, Myron Blunger had interpreted it every which way but the right way. It would take a team of psychiatrists years to deconvolute that clue.

Of course, he would insist it wasn't his fault; he'd done the best he could with the information at hand. Pissing up a tree, yet! What a sight that must have been!

So, One: someone had to get into the apartment. Two: they had to find out how these manuscripts were being delivered. The *Higher Migher* test might shed light on that. The *Higher Migher* test required only a sheet of paper. Gertrude tore one from her idea pad, wrote four words on it, slid to the side of her bed, picked up her cane, braced herself and rose. Snagging the slipper she'd flung at Dickie Bird, she maneuvered it next to its mate with her cane, wiggled her feet into them, dropped a roll of adhesive tape into her pocket and padded out even before visiting the bathroom. There was no time to lose! *Higher Migher.* Hah!

Throwing on her housecoat, she crossed the living room, which was bathed in golden sunlight. There was Sophie, all tangled in a light blanket—she claimed she couldn't sleep without a blanket, even in Florida—the portable telephone on the pillow beside her head in case Myron should phone. Poor Sophie. Trying to ignore the stabs of arthritic pain in her right hip, Gertrude threw on a dress, made her way to the door of her apartment, unlocked it quietly and peered out into the hallway. Good. No package. Not yet. Would there be another delivery? Was Myron written out? Well, there was nothing to lose.

Taping her note to the outside of the door, she closed and locked it, then hobbled to the bathroom to freshen up. Emerging some minutes later, she walked back into the living room where she tapped her sister's shoulder with the rubber tip of her cane. "Rise and shine, Sophie," she said. "*Gai pischen.* Wash up and get dressed!" she said. "Fast! We may be getting company very soon."

Sophie stirred, then unwrapped herself from her blanket and sat up. "Something happened?" she cried anxiously. "Myron!" It was nearly a shriek.

"Not yet," Gertrude replied soothingly. "Wear your walking shoes; there's no telling where we'll end up today. I'm putting up coffee. While we're waiting, I want you to telephone New York; we have to get someone into the apartment."

The apartment. Not *your* apartment. *The* apartment, like in police stories in the papers. Sophie's heart pounded. It took all her will power not to break down. Already slipping into the same wrinkled dress she'd worn the day before, Sophie looked reproachfully at the silent telephone, then made a quick trip to the bathroom. Upon her return, she shook her head and moaned, "So who's going into my place at this hour?"

"Your son Jason?" Gertrude suggested.

Sophie forced a mirthless laugh. "Last night the Sleeping Beauty told me he was at work, meaning I shouldn't disturb him while he's making money. Not to worry; she would drive down to the Bronx first thing in the morning, right from her 'standing appointment'. Myron could be gasping for air on the floor while she gets her hair put up and her nails polished."

"Irving, then!"

"He's in Cleveland, at a conference," Sophie moaned, wringing her hands. "In his college, if you want to be a full professor instead of an associate professor, you have to go to conferences and give talks to other professors. They don't have places for conferences in Manhattan, I've asked him; he has to fly halfway around the world?

"At least his Shirley wouldn't hang up on me. She's working hard to surprise us with wonderful news, if she can just get Alexander toilet-trained. And she had no idea her father-in-law was missing or she have certainly invited him for dinner. She told me she'll go over today by bus, right after Alexander has breakfast and makes potty.

"I'll phone Minsky," she declared after a moment's thought. "She's up already. She'll have to get the key from the super."

"Go ahead," Gertrude said, pouring two orange juices and setting them beside cereal bowls on the kitchen table. Sophie found an address book in her handbag and nervously dialed.

From the kitchen, Gertrude heard Minsky's shrill voice more

clearly than her sister's anguished whispers. "Myron? Your Myron? *Oy, veh*! I thought he'd gone down to Florida with you. Now that you mention, I happened to notice your mailbox is full . . . Modern Maturity, Reader's Digest, the gas and electric . . . you're sure he's not with the boys, Irving or Jacob? Tsk, tsk . . . I'll ask Adele; maybe she saw him. You don't know Adele? Oh. Lovely girl. So young to be a widow. Very friendly, an intellectual, always in the park reading a paperback. I'm sure you'd recognize her. Who would have believed . . . what's that? The super? Sure, immediately I fix myself up a little, he'll let me into the apartment with his passkey and I'll call you right from the apartment. Give me your phone number down there."

Sophie did that, then hung up. There was a clatter from the kitchen, where her sister Gertrude was taking down breakfast dishes. Sophie groaned. She'd come down to Florida to visit her widowed sister with arthritis in the hip! Her sister Gertrude walking with a cane! She'd lost twenty pounds in the year since Harold passed on; she had no appetite, hated to eat alone. Her dresses looked better on their hangers than on her. She'd come down to help Gertrude regain her zest for life, and now Gertrude was taking care of *her*.

Breakfast was on the table. Juice. Bran Flakes with raisins and bananas. Toast with orange marmalade. Strong coffee. They ate silently, nervously alert to the slightest telephone-tinkle that might signal a call from Myron.

What was taking Minsky so long? This was an emergency! Sophie pictured her selecting a dress, changing her mind . . . which shoes went with the blouse . . . ? She regretted having phoned Minsky in the first place. Only God knew what kind of stories she'd be hollering all over the park! And who was this Adele?

Sophie reached for the telephone to call the airlines; by the time Minsky made herself presentable for the super, Sophie could be landing at LaGuardia already.

She pulled her hand back. If she tied up the line, Minsky couldn't get through. Or Myron. Also, maybe Gertrude was right. Maybe the phone was out of order. Maybe they'd forgotten to pay the bill. Suppose she ran home without taking Gertrude out shopping for some clothes that fit and it turned out that Myron had simply turned the ringer down too low? He'd done that once, claiming that the shrillness hurt his ears. And if she berated him for not telephoning, he'd shrug his shoulders and say, "What's to call? I know where you are; you know where I am. Nothing's new."

If Gertrude had been willing to come up to the Bronx for a stay, that would have solved everything; they could have flown up immediately. But Gertrude wouldn't go north; not with winter around the corner. Sophie would have to wait for Minsky to call back.

Gertrude printed *Higher Migher* on a napkin, inverted it, underlined the H and the M, then slid it across the table to her sister.

Sophie shook her head wearily. Exhausted from worrying, she had no time or patience for games.

"Look at it upside down," Gertrude said. "H. M. upside down gives you . . . ?"

The telephone rang. Minsky! Sophie snatched it up, but finding herself unable to speak, passed it to her sister with trembling hands. Sophie Blunger shut her eyes and interlaced her fingers, prepared for the worst. "Minsky?" Gertrude nodded. "This is Gertrude." She adjusted the volume so that Sophie couldn't hear Minsky, in case there was bad news.

"Yes, also a widow," Gertrude said loudly, impatiently.

"Yes, I know, I know . . . it's the worst thing . . . but you're in Sophie's apartment? You found . . . what?" This last shouted loudly enough to echo in the living room. "Where?" she demanded as Sophie fought for breath.

"Oh my God!" Gertrude whispered.

Sophie rose, staggered blindly to the sofabed and dropped onto it, her stout frame shaking.

"No straws, you say?" Gertrude said. "What's his name? Papa Dopoulis? One word? Papadopoulis. The super. Just a minute . . ." Covering the mouthpiece, she whispered, "Your super's name is Papadopoulis?"

Sophie Blunger nodded.

Back to Minsky. "Thank you. Make sure you keep this telephone number, in case something else happens." She hung up and faced her sister squarely.

Sophie, speechless with fright, pushed herself to a sitting position and sat facing Gertrude, her head cupped in her hands.

"The front door wasn't double-locked," Gertrude said crisply. "Just the snap. There's no sign of Myron, no note, no sign of a breakin. In the kitchen wastebasket, a wrapper from Shofar brand kosher bologna, sixteen slices. All gone. Gulden's mustard on the table, open a few days, encrusted. A knife . . ."

Sophie emitted a choked scream.

"For mustard!" Gertrude explained hastily.

Sophie exhaled, moaned.

"And in the living room . . ."

Gertrude caught her breath. "In the living room, a pile of almost-horse droppings. A large pile. Cold. Without the usual pieces of straw, the super noted. Your Papadopoulos says he grew up in Greece, on a farm. With a horse, there's always bits of straw. But centaurs have a different diet! The droppings are from, not a regular horse, but a centaur!

"Papadopoulos. A centaur." Gertrude shrugged her shoulders and recited the rest of the message tonelessly, as though she'd given up. "He's very angry, not about the pile of manure so much, but that you've had a centaur up in your apartment and never told him. Twenty years he lived within a day's walk of the Acropolis and never saw a centaur except on stone carvings and in picture books, as a child!

"Anyway, Minsky says she spoke up for you. She pointed out that she'd been in the apartment many times and had never noticed centaur droppings before, not even horse droppings. But he's still angry and if the centaur ever returns, you're to call him immediately."

Gertrude raised herself and fetched Sophie a glass of cold water. Waiting until her sister had drunk it, Gertrude sat herself down, took her sister's hand in hers and said, "Sophie, dear, let us consider the possibilities. One: Myron may have simply lost his mind, in which case he's probably run off into Van Cortlandt Park to live in the woods like a hobo, taking with him a half-dozen bologna sandwiches and all the paper and pencils he could find in the apartment. He writes, he mails out the stories—don't ask me how they get through without stamps. The manure he left in the living room may have been . . . an accident, a red herring . . . who knows? Straw or no straw, I think we should phone the precinct again and have them check the area around the stables in Van Cortlandt park.

"Two—and this does strain at the imagination—Myron has not slipped over the edge. Everything in his writing is true, he's being held prisoner at The Inn at the End of the World, and is desperately trying to write Joey Willem back to the Inn, under the Innkeeper's orders." She sighed. "In which case . . . in which case . . . well, we should first learn how these stories are being delivered."

The thought resonating within Gertrude's mind was: *But why the horse shit? Unless . . . Myron is clever and resourceful enough to have provided a madness alibi. Alibi? For what? Adele! In case Adele didn't work out! If that bastard is playing house with Adele, may his eyeballs shrivel into raisins and hair grow on the inside of his mouth! Goddamned librarian!*

There was a sound at the front door. Three sharp raps. Gertrude's blood raced. The *Higher Migher* gambit had worked! Did this mean . . . that Myron Blunger's ramblings had a semblance of truth? A shock ran down her spine! She positioned her cane, rose and called, "Coming," then proceeded through the foyer to the door, her heart beating wildly.

"Who is it?" Sophie whispered, hoping against hope that it was Myron, flown down secretly, to surprise her.

"Wilma Hawkins!" Gertrude hissed, waving Sophie back into the living room. "H. M. upside down gives you W. H. In doubt, Wilma Hawkins! And believe me, I have doubts. Stay back; I want to confront her alone. She may be . . . shy." *Or insane, considering*

her upbringing, Gertrude thought to herself. She threw the door
wide open and so startled was she that she lost her breath and
screamed in instead of out.

She faced an apparition, a nightmare, a *dybbuk* from the spirit
world. No larger than Gertrude herself, the creature was covered,
from wide-brimmed hat to high-button boots, in the most utter
blackness. Black was the veil that concealed her face and neck, and
black the dress that hung nearly to the floor. She wore black gloves
and her right hand gripped the knob of a black walking stick. In
the other hand was a brown paper package wrapped in string.
Addressed to Sophie Blunger, it bore no U.S. postal stamps at the
upper right corner, only the same streak of lightning as the earlier
packages.

At the woman's side hung a sack of undulating, tightly woven
metallic thread from whose inside came a constant rustle and crackle
of sound as though a hatful of mice were tumbling about in a
mixture of cellophane and straw. The noise rose and fell in intensity, and was never completely silent.

Gertrude fell back, shocked, unbalanced. She blurted out,
"Who . . . what . . ."

With a sweep of her walking stick, the apparition struck off
the invitation that Gertrude had fastened to the door—*Wilma
Hawkins, please knock!*—and marched directly into the apartment.
"Wilma's gone north. She intends to fall in love with Don Juan,"
said the apparition, "and to give Trenton Interface, who didn't
bother to notice that she'd become a woman, the cold shoulder."
The voice of the woman in black was a pleasant contralto, and
there was in it a power that caused Gertrude to back into the
apartment.

"Don Juan!" the creature snarled from beneath her veil. "Don't
think I didn't warn her! If it weren't for Don Juan and his kind,
this sack would be a good bit lighter! One letter, probably written
while giving his prostate an hour's rest, makes him a suitor!"

Gertrude followed the woman, intending to steer her back

into the hallway but was confounded by the wild flailings of that walking stick.

"Of course, it's Trenton Interface that Wilma's still in love with," the woman said, peering briefly into the small, second bathroom, as though carrying out an inspection. "Wilma, you know, left Upper Muchness because Trenton still thought of her as the little Hawkins girl, with braids. Well, she's no little girl any more; she's a major-general in Lightspeed, with a dashing uniform, sexy black designer boots, a stylish tam, a combat belt loaded with accessories . . . the works. I'd give a lot to see Trenton's face when he sets his eyes on her, but she couldn't wait, couldn't wait! Says its a mess up there, and getting worse, and that's a fact. A terrible, tragic fact."

Encountering Sophie Blunger, the woman in black interrupted herself long enough to thrust the package into her hands, saying, "Mrs. Blunger, Wilma Hawkins asked me to deliver this package to you. Your husband suffers from lack of confidence, my dear. But what can one expect, considering that the most praise he ever received in life was when he finally succeeded in his toilet-training. Since then, it's all been downhill.

"Also, he is inattentive. My Nephew, with Whom I am in frequent contact, advised Myron to give Joey Willem hope. *Hope is the fuel of life*, He said. He did not—repeat, did not advise him to get involved with Dragon Groff."

The stranger-intruder-crazywoman was followed into the living room by a stunned Gertrude, whose plan to meet and question Wilma Hawkins had taken a weird and possibly dangerous turn. *Who was this lunatic? And what was making that noise in her sack?*

Sophie Blunger regarded this otherworld spirit solemnly, then asked, "Where is my husband?"

"I just ran into him in a back passageway at The Inn at the End of the World. By this time, he may have left the Inn, probably forever. If I could just concentrate, I could probably work up a vision."

Gertrude had no doubts about this crazywoman's ability to

work up a vision. She backed up to the unmade sofabed and glanced into the tangle of bedding, looking for the portable telephone. Though slight of frame and not very tall, the woman in black seemed purposeful and was armed with that walking stick. She was well past the boundaries of eccentricity and was probably mad to the core; they might well need help from condo security. Fast. But the telephone was not in sight; it was probably entwined among the pile of sheet and blanket and pillow.

The woman in black had turned to the wallpaper, which she proceeded to study closely, though she did not remove or raise the veil.

"Fantastic! Amazing!" she whispered, tracing the pattern with a gloved fingertip. "Whirls within swirls and the whole thing slipping away within itself," she muttered. "Where did you get this?" she demanded.

Gertrude answered, "Fourteen dollars a roll, from Macy's." *Where was the damned telephone?*

The crazywoman spun about. "You *bought* it for money? If *Bourbaki* knew of this, they'd clear up the fifth lemma in no time! Follow this wallpaper far enough in the right direction and you could get anywhere you have a mind to."

Sophie had the package open. Inside were two stories. "*Hope and the Dragon*," she recited. "Written with Guidance. And *Too Little*. Yes, that's Myron's handwriting!" she cried. "How did you get this?"

"It came down with me, by Lightspeed," replied the woman in black, as matter-of-factly as one might say Parcel Post, or Express Mail.

"Lightspeed?" Sophie asked. "What's Lightspeed?"

The woman took a seat in an armchair near the foyer, placing her noisy sack on the floor and laying her walking stick across her lap. "Lightspeed uses natural wind-tunnels that exist far beneath the Earth's surface," she said in a tired, faraway voice. "They have been known since ancient times, when their surfacings were guarded by priests and oracles. Apparently one surfacing is in the Inn at the End of the World.

"Of the tunnel's origins I can only say that it has, at various times and places, been believed they were created by demons, by the Emperor Suleiman as storeplaces for the newly captured and imprisoned djinns, by giant worms that dwelt beneath mountains when the Earth was young. Wilma Hawkins, of course, has faith only in her father's Theory, which postulates their creation during the second cycle of contraction of the early Earth, when gases blown out from the planet's innards had to travel horizontally beneath the developing crust, or some such nonsense. That is implicit in the fifth lemma, she claims, and I must admit your wallpaper seems to corroborate that. Yet . . . " (and here the woman raised a finger in warning) "I note that she does not travel Lightspeed un-armed.

"In truth, of course, my Nephew created the tunnels, along with all the rest of the universe. The evidence is in the regularity of their interleavings."

"Your nephew?" Gertrude prompted, as she sat at the edge of the sofabed, groping blindly for the telephone. "Who are you, anyway? Who is this nephew?"

"Oh, how stupid of me," said the woman in black. "Who am I? Why, I am God's aunt!"

Gertrude elevated the urgency of finding the telephone and getting condo security up here before God's aunt opened her sack and let loose whatever was making that noise! Probably a snake! She shuddered; whenever the news ran thin, the papers ran ar-ticles on snake cults! This woman, dressed in funereal black . . .

She must not reveal her fear. Crazies were like dogs; they could *sense* fear! Gertrude shook the blanket from the pile, folded it, an acceptable activity for a homemaker. No telephone shook out of it. Gertrude willed herself not to panic. The woman, after all, *had* brought another of those mysterious packages. She might be a little crazy, but she *had* to know something about Myron Blunger, once one got past her interest in wallpaper and the fifth lemon and the Lightspeed tunnels.

Gertrude laid the blanket on the floor and groped desperately under the mattress; no telephone. She couldn't make much of a dash for the door, not with her hip. She signalled to her sister to keep up the conversation, such as it was? *Keep the crazylady talking while I look for the telephone!*

Sophie Blunger did not collapse into howling anguish and despair. Calmly she placed *Hope and the Dragon* and *Too Little* on the coffee table. She had to keep control of herself. Myron was gone, maybe dead, and now God's aunt had dropped in for a visit. There was no point in starting up with Gertrude for opening the door to her. Not now. Later, after the lunatic was gone.

But there were people worse than lunatics! Kidnappers. Murderers. Sophie felt her heart palpitating. She had to fight hysteria, had to think. She and Gertrude were trapped, Gertrude because she couldn't possibly run, and she, because the chair in which God's aunt was sitting was in a direct line with the front door, the only exit from the apartment. She couldn't possibly flee and leave her sister to an indescribable fate. And God's aunt was thin and wiry, probably quite strong. No, they were trapped until Gertrude came up with the telephone.

Unless . . . if she could get enough coffee—strong coffee—into the woman, God's Aunt would have to go to the bathroom. Then Sophie could get Gertrude out into the hallway where they could scream for help.

She caught herself. Help? From Gertrude's neighbors, every one of them a mah-jongg player who only spoke to other mah-jongg players, even in the lobby?

May every tooth in their mouths fall out but one, and that one reserved for toothaches!

The rustling from inside God's aunt sack increased slightly, then diminished to its former level of noise.

She had to keep up the conversation, while she thought desperately. "It's never happened that God's aunt visited us," Sophie offered, facing the veiled intruder but aiming her statements at her sister. "Perhaps you'd like a cup of coffee? Why don't you put up a *big* pot of coffee, Gertrude?" she said. "Strong coffee! Good for *pischen!*" Gertrude nodded knowingly, planted her cane, rose and made her way into the kitchen.

Sophie racked her brains for a simple, non-threatening open-ing question, and came up with, "So if you're God's aunt, what do you do?"

God's aunt pulled that terrible sack onto her lap—how heavy it must be!—reached inside and pulled out a slip of paper. From a pouch at her waist she drew a pair of bifocal eyeglasses, which she slipped beneath the veil. She looked up at Sophie, sighed heavily and said, "I follow the human search for a warrantee on life. One would think that, given the size and quality of your brains, you would have deduced and accepted the truth millenia ago, but you refuse to accept the conditions on which my Nephew granted life, though they've been written out clearly enough, God knows.

"The problem is the curses. Even under the mildest provoca-tions, you resort to maledictions, blasphemies and the most elabo-rate curses; no less than personal violence they are an offense and a rebuke to my Nephew! I try to intercept those wishes before they find their way to my Nephew's ears. Fortunately, I have this magic sack, which collects them."

"The sack is full of . . . curses?" Sophie asked. *What to say? What to ask?* Calmly as though asking whether God's aunt took one lump or two, Sophie said, "That's nice. Then you get an exter-minator? Or do they just stay there?"

It was important to keep up this conversation; who knew what voices were talking inside this crazy woman's head, or what those voices might order her to do at any moment!

"Some stay for centuries," replied the woman in black. "Some are withdrawn. Most get neutralized, sooner or later. It's depress-ing, you know. There's no end to it. No end. There is not one aspect of God's Creation, except rainbows, that hasn't been on the receiving end of a curse at one time or another. Fish are cursed for

being too small, too bony, too salty, too bland, and especially, too
hard to catch. The poor curse the rich, who reply by erecting high
fences topped with broken glass. Recently folk began cursing VCR's,
whatever they may be. Even the unliving cannot escape humankind's
fury! Rocks and stones are cursed by farmers. The weary traveler
stubs his toe and curses his own bones! Curses have been leveled at
every law of science, even the force of gravity, mostly by students
of the second kind taking final examinations. It does not occur to
them that without gravity, there would be no planet! Let them
come up with a better design, I say.

"Somewhere down there," and she tapped the sack with her
walking stick, "is a blessing bestowed by a Hungarian woman who
was being transported off her ancestral property in a wheelbarrow
by the local duke's minions, for non-payment of taxes. Sixteenth
or seventeenth century.

"After she finished cursing the land under the duke's feet, she
invoked syphillus on the duchess, nymphomania on his daughters, the plague on his horses and pustulant sores on his private
parts, all this in a bellow that would have done credit to a sargeant
of the line.

"As it happened, the duchess *did* contract syphillus. History
does not record the state of the duke's privates, but when a plague
broke out at his stables, he promptly wed his three daughters to
the first three single courtiers who walked in the door. The Hungarian woman escaped being burned alive as a witch only because
she struck a deal, blessing the fecundity of the brides in return for
a tax abatement.

"There are those, and I will not name them, who, at the slightest
adverse turn of fortune, cry to heaven against Adam and Eve, the
Pope, Jesus Christ, my Nephew, and me!

"Me, I can take it," she said stoically. "But hurling maledictions at my Nephew! Dangerous, dangerous!" The veil swished
from side to side as she shook her head.

Sophie listened for the sound of coffee dripping; what was
taking Gertrude so long?

"That's why He gave me this job," continued God's aunt. She slapped the sack, from the insides of which a cacaphony of rustling had suddenly erupted. "Here they are. Humankind's gratitude for Creation and Life! A sack full of verbal thunderbolts in every language, from persons of low and high station, from the pious, from the dregs of humanity.

"Oh, what's this?" she said, as Gertrude appeared with a tray of cups steaming with fresh-brewed coffee, some cookies, milk and sugar. She set the tray down on the coffee table, then pulled a hardback chair up to the coffee table and poured a cup of strong brew for their mad guest, and one for herself, which she diluted with sugar and milk.

The woman in black took her coffee under her veil. The black hat bobbed up and down. The cup reappeared, empty. "*Pischencoffee*, eh?" said God's aunt, brightly. "Wonderful! I haven't had a proper flush since I passed through Mexico, six years ago. Maybe now I can concentrate. But I sense that you still don't believe what I have been saying," she said. Sophie Blunger gripped the arms of her chair, preparing to launch herself past this crazy woman with a sack full of curses, out into the hallway and down the fire exit, not stopping until she reached the super's apartment on the ground floor. But how could she leave her sister alone and defenseless? And what about that walking stick with the heavy knob? Maniacs, it is said, have strength out of proportion to their size . . .

God's aunt plunged her hand into the sack and extracted a small piece of paper, which wriggled and twisted until she administered a smack; it then settled down, limp. She fished out another. The black veil turned toward Gertrude and the woman who called herself God's aunt said, "Here are two that just came in. The first: "*If that bastard is playing house with Adele, may his eyeballs shrivel into raisins and hair grow on the inside of his mouth! Another: 'May every tooth in their mouths fall out but one, and that one reserved for toothaches!'*

Sophie sank into her chair, stunned. "I . . . I . . ." she gasped. She looked at her sister, but Gertrude's mouth was hanging open.

God's aunt nodded, thrust the maledictions back down the mouth of the sack and helped herself to another cup of coffee with no sugar, no cream.

After a prolonged silence, the woman in black said, "My Nephew tried to give him help, you know."

"You mean . . . God?" Gertrude whispered. "My brother-in-law, Myron Blunger, spoke to God?" She glanced outside, half-expecting to see from all this blasphemy a storm brewing offshore, but the Sun was even with the top of the picture window and the sky was bright blue, with few clouds.

The black hat bobbed up and down in acknowledgement. "Would you believe that a grown man, an educated man, spoke with my Nephew, the creator and Lord of the universe and failed to ask one significant question? He might have asked about Fundamental Truth, or the nature of good and evil or how humankind has in every generation brought suffering upon itself or, at the very least, the mechanics of Creation."

If that bastard is playing house with Adele, may his eyeballs shrivel into raisins and hair grow on the inside of his mouth! Gertrude was afraid to move, much less talk. Who was this crazy person who could read minds?

Sophie Blunger snapped, "I'll have you know Myron is very intelligent and if he didn't ask those kind of questions, it's because . . . because those questions have no answers! They're trick questions. Also, Myron writes better than he talks; you should see the letters he's written to the landlord about our waterhammer!"

God's aunt rose, her walking stick held out before her. Sophie Blunger took up a sofa-pillow; the crazy woman wasn't used to backtalk; surely she was going to take a swing!

"Now I have to pee," announced God's aunt, firmly. "At my age, it takes a while. While I am gone, read those stories. Upon my return, we will decide upon a course of action. It is all good and well that Wilma Hawkins is on her way north, but one cannot expect even a Major General in Lightspeed to do everything. I . . . I can concentrate. I can . . . see!" she cried out. "Wait for me; do not leave. I sense a vision . . . I see your husband, Mrs. Blunger, leaving the Inn in a great hurry, and suffering from a pain in the rear end."

Gertrude was about to sniff her general agreement with this sentiment, but the woman in black vanished into the lavatory and closed the door behind her. And there were questions to be answered, such as how this intruder had read Gertrude's mind!

So it was that when Gertrude Weintraub spotted the telephone in the opening between the mattress and the back of the sofabed, instead of phoning Condo security, she cradled it, converted the sofabed into a sofa and hurried into her bedroom, leaving Sophie to her husband's manuscripts.

And Sophie Blunger, in silence accompanied only by the steady rustling of fresh curses arriving into the sack and a distant tinkle not unlike that of a small brook rippling through deep forest, read the final two stories written by Myron Blunger at The Inn at the End of the World.

HOPE AND THE DRAGON

by Myron Blunger, with GUIDANCE!

"*Freeeeze!*" screamed Nightwind as it tore down from the Dromedaries. A December wind advanced to Halloween, it lashed at the lifeberry glen below the Saddle, then shrieked down the valley. "*Woooooe!*" moaned the trees stripped of their autumnal crowns. The few birds that remained to face winter had gone to ground, and the furry animals of the woods and fields, shivering, huddled as closely together as possible in their dens.

This was the night, of all the nights of the year, on which the lifeberries ripened. And on this night, the clusters of sweet lifeberries had to be shaken free of their round, burgundy pods and blown down onto the Saddle, there to be swirled by the wind into great piles and mounds, that Dragon Groff might eat therefrom and line his stomachs for the gorging to come.

The sun had dropped behind the Cliff of Night, and a full moon rose over the eastern cliff as though rushing to its perch in anticipation of a grand spectacle. Thousands of stars appeared, twinkling brightly, peering down at the *Kristallfluss*, which never glittered more brilliantly than on Halloween nights. The wind blew faster, colder, more furiously, crushing dry leaves into powder and orchestrating the sighs and moans of the branches throughout the expanse of woods that spread over the northern and western portions of the valley. But it blew in vain this Halloween night. The last great wind of the season of life had found the lifeberry bushes already stripped bare of fruit, their thin branches dry and barren, their protective thorns foiled and purposeless.

Driven from the teaching glade by the howling wind, Elf Miki and Rush squatted side by side in the hollow of a damp, age-rotted treetrunk across the road from the Hawkins house. Elf Miki closed *The Book of the Ways of Man* and exclaimed, "Finished!"

The course was over! Elflet Rush should have been singing and dancing, darting through the air and bursting with relief! Unfortunately, she couldn't do any of those things. Despite the warm corduroi dirndl and double-knit sweater she was wearing, and even though she was triple-wrapped within the folds of a bathtowel with only her blue eyes and the tip of her nose peeking out, she was shivering. What with the wind and the wet ground and the only illumination provided by a ball of phosphorescent moss that Miki recharged by occasional rubbing, the elflet felt miserable. She had suggested holding the final learning session in the common room of The Brambles, a country inn just outside the village of Lower Muchness. She'd heard it was a charming place with scatter rugs and easy chairs and a roaring fire and crackers and cheese and doughnuts and hot tea laced with honey at all hours. Miki had shaken his head, mumbling about exposure and human prejudices, and finally admitting that such things cost money and he had none.

But the course was over! "Am I an elf now?" she asked, her teeth chattering.

"Not yet," Miki said. "You have to take a final exam. Here." He passed her a blue book and a stub of a pencil, suitable for her tiny hand. "Ready?"

"What's an exam?" she asked, turning the pages of the blue book. Why, they were all blank! Oh. That's what the pencil was for! She'd studied writing, of course, but she'd not expected to *do* any of it except to leave mysterious notes in unexpected places, for fun. She'd practiced in secret, composing long sentences with many commas and exclamation marks. But she'd never taken an *exam*! Pulling the towel tightly about her, she added, shrewdly (she hoped), "I hope the exam doesn't go on all night; I'll soon be frozen solid and then I won't be able to take your place and you won't get your promotion!"

Elf Miki, blue-lipped but too proud to admit his shivering, was hunkered down within the folds of a dark green woolen cloak, whose collar came up to his ears. *Won't get your promotion*! Rumor was that a new township was about to open up in California north of Malibu, very near the beach and the Big Surf, which was *the* experience of the universe, according to an elf who'd done it. People would soon be moving in. Babies, infants . . . souls needing guidance and shepherding as they went through the transition, breaking away from the One Soul to their individual identities. The guardianship was still open, unassigned. Big surf. Beach. Sunlight. Warmth. No more cold winters with screaming winds and electricity that interfered with *changings*. No more decaying barriers or frightening adventures that he couldn't cope with and didn't understand!

All he needed was a replacement and a clean slate. He had experience and seniority and, he believed, the favor of the administration, despite his failure to get the boy Joey back to the Inn. Of all the souls in his charge, the boy Joey was the most difficult, the most unsettled, the one that had to be watched extra closely this night! If the boy—and all the other souls within Miki's jurisdiction—were sound of spirit at dawn, promotion and transfer could take place as soon as Rush was officially made Elf. But dawn was dawn and now was now, and Rush *had* to pass this exam!

Miki explained, "An exam works this way: I ask questions and you write the answers in the blue book. Or I give answers and you write the questions. Or I leave a clue and you have to figure out both question and answer! Also, you have to write an essay of a hundred fifty words. And you're not allowed to talk. At all! Ready?" He tore open the examination pack, muttered hurriedly through the instructions on the cover, then opened to Page One and recited, slowly and clearly, "The first question is . . . What are the five W's and their cousin H?"

The elflet pursed her lips in concentration, nibbled momentarily at the end of her pencil, then brightened and whispered to herself as she wrote in her bluebook:

#1. Who, What, When, Where . . . Where . . . ah, Why and . . . and . . . and How.

Glowing with satisfaction, she laid down the pencil, awaiting the next part. This was easy! Soon they'd be finished and could get out of the cold. If only they had money for the Inn in Lower Muchness, with its cozy fire and cups of hot tea laced with honey, and doughnuts. She'd never tasted a doughnut.

Miki glanced at her list and a great relief tinged with pride swelled within his chest; despite her insatiable curiousity and tendency to wander, examine and try things, she'd really learned something! What a stroke of good fortune that they'd been driven from the Teaching Glade to this dank shelter! With no distractions, no flitting away on foolish inspections, the elflet was going to do well! He was about to continue, slowly, deliberately, when he became aware of change, motion, something happening across the road. Miki looked up. A window had suddenly been thrust open and a head poked out into the night!

The elf's heart fluttered wildly. He shook his head in classic denial, a human trait that might, might influence an unfavorable course of events. He watched as Joey Willem slid open his bedroom window . . .

Joey Willem slid open his bedroom window oh so quietly and the Halloween wind shrieked into the room, fluttered through the interview report strewn all over the floor as though demanding, "*Is this the best you can do? Tear it up! Do it over!*"

He would *not* do it over; its heading was perfect, the margins were exactly one inch wide and he'd made a cover page, two pictures in color and a diorama! And it was true! It *was* true! It *was* the best he could do and anyway, who cared? No one believed him, not his friends from school, not Miss Wally the worst teacher in the entire school, not even Aunt Loretta! Mr. Blunger would have

believed him, but he was away again; the attic room that Mr.
Hawkins had given him to live in was empty.

Fibber!—Liar!
Your tongue is all on fire . . .

The taunts of his classmates were more bitter than the wind,
were even worse than being sent up to his bedroom by Uncle
Benison to *consider* his interview report. Wiping the wetness from
his cheeks, he zippered his jacket up halfway, knotted his knapsack firmly shut and placed it on the window ledge. He'd deliberately not closed his door all the way, in case someone happened to
come by and sort of drop in and see what was happening and ask
him what the matter was. But that hadn't happened.

Mr. Blunger would have understood! Mr. Blunger . . . he'd
said it was okay for Joey to call him Myron, but Aunt Loretta said
no, he would be Mr. Blunger until Joey turned twenty-one. But
he was to call her Aunt Loretta, not Mrs. Hawkins, and Uncle
Benison sounded better, less formal, than Mr. Hawkins.

*Less formal! Uncle Benison was nothing more than a . . . than a
dried-up, old . . . numbernose!*

But Mr. Blunger—Myron—was nice, almost like a father,
though Joey didn't exactly know what it would be like to have a
father around. Somehow, he just didn't have one, never had. Mr.
Blunger would probably have made a good father, Joey thought, if
he hadn't spent so much time writing that column for *The Postulate*. But he was away somewhere.

Joey could hear them downstairs in the kitchen. Uncle Benison,
Aunt Loretta and his teacher, Miss Wally. What was she saying?
Joey strained his ears.

"At best, the boy doesn't know the difference between Real
and Pretend! At worst, he's lazy and guilty of plagiarism!"

Aunt Loretta piped up, her slow-thinking mind straining to
address Miss Wally's stacatto barrage of charges. "Lazy? Plagia-

rism! Oh, that couldn't be . . . I'm sure . . . the boy worked so hard on his report . . ."

If his mother were there, she wouldn't have let Miss Wally say those things! She'd have marched the old pruneface right to the door with a broomstick and told her to get out and stay out!

Joey could hear a rhythmic *Rapa-tapa Bang . . . Bang! . . . Rapa-tapa Bang . . . Knock-knock . . .* Uncle Benison was tapping with his fingernails on the table, tapping in time to Miss Wally's list of Joey's shortcomings. If only Mr. Blunger had stayed on! For sure he would have told Miss Wally a thing or two about dragons. Let Wally try to outtalk and bully Myron Blunger! He'd for sure spin Old Walrus's eyes right in their sockets!

Joey put one leg up on the windowsill. A floorboard, relieved of weight, creaked loudly. Uncle Benison called up, "Well? You got yourself straightened out yet, young man?"

Young man! That was bad. Joey hated to be called *young man.* He zippered his jacket right up to his chin and opened the window wide, squinting against the sudden blast. That was it! He *was* straightened out and now he'd prove it! Too bad Miss Ugly Wallface hadn't asked to speak with Mr. Blunger instead of Uncle Benison! Maybe she didn't *know* about Mr. Blunger, that he was a famous advice column writer for Uncle Benison's newspaper.

When Miss Wally had stopped his report right in the middle and sent him back to his seat, even Michael Tooney had smirked. And that, after Joey had secretly shown Michael his new penknife. Miss Wally suggested he was making it up . . . fibbing, as though he didn't even know real from not real! And she'd taken his report, marked it up in red and handed it back to take home for signature. And all the way home on the school bus, the kids had laughed and pointed and sung that stupid rhyme over and over every time he tried to explain . . .

> Fibber!—Liar!
> Your tongue is all on fire!
> Scorch it brown and let it split
> So every dog in town can have a little bit!

Not content with that, the old . . . the old *fartbag* had nothing better to do than to drive all the way up into the valley to *discuss* the report and stay for dinner! And the more she talked, the worse it got, with Joey shaking his head *No, no*! and fighting off tears until Uncle Benison had sent him upstairs to *reconsider*! Well, he *had* reconsidered! Dragon Groff *did* exist and he was going to prove it to *everyone*, including Uncle Benison and Aunt Loretta and all those dummies in his class and especially Miss Wally!

Dragon Groff! Oh, wouldn't it be *great* to see the playground darken and everyone looking up and there was Dragon Groff with his wings big enough to cover the whole school . . . landing right there in the playground, reaching up to the third floor and poking his head in through the window of Room 3A4 and giving old Wally a blast of fire right in her behind! *Then* let her shake her finger at Dragon Groff!

Joey savored the image for a long moment, then determinedly placed both hands behind the knapsack, closed one eye, lined it up and shoved; not too hard. It landed directly at the base of the trellis. Maybe he wasn't so great in basketball, but that shot was perfect! The knapsack was for landing on. It was stuffed with his pillow and two blankets stripped from his bed, and a sweater, to cushion his fall in case the old trellis broke and he went to the ground. And for camping out in case . . . in case finding Dragon Groff took a while. Plus some cookies and a toothbrush and a flashlight and other stuff he might need. Including, for emergency, four dollars and forty cents he'd earned delivering Uncle Benison's weird newspaper to Mr. Broco.

Suppose he fell and busted his leg climbing down; *then* they'd come running, and *then* they'd be sorry they didn't believe him!

Cautiously he thrust his left leg outside and sent it probing for the trellis. But it was more than a yard away; even if he managed to reach it, then what? Stretched between trellis and the window, he'd fall straight down and break his neck.

Both legs had to go out; he'd have to swing his way over. Clutching the windowsill with both hands, he eased himself out and down until he was hanging freely. He peeked down; it seemed a long way to the ground. Cautiously he swung his left leg to the side; it still didn't reach. He tried swinging his legs from side to side, easing himself to the left . . .

The wind was chilling his hands now, trying to break his grip on the windowsill. His arms were tiring; he couldn't climb back up, even if he wanted to! Would the trellis hold? It was old, half rotted, held together mostly by the gnarled, woody remains of a trumpet vine. According to Aunt Loretta, the vine had once attracted hummingbirds, though she hadn't seen one in ten years, and it may have been a cardinal; she wasn't quite sure.

The mischievous wind screeched, *Jump! Fly with me*! but Joey Willem gritted his teeth and swung farther, farther to the side until one sneaker, then both had found toeholds and he had defeated the wind and now he would show them all!

He hurled himself away from the window, reached for the trellis but with a loud *Crack*! the structure fell away and his hands, waving wildly, found only air and he was falling, turning upside down, trying to extract his feet from the latticework! His head slammed into a tangle of vine; instinctively he grabbed it. The old, dry wood crackled loud as a string of firecrackers but held together as the vine tore slowly away from its grip on the wood-frame house and lowered him to the ground. His head hit his knapsack with a thump and he lay there, dazed but unhurt.

After a few moments, he lifted his head and looked around. On the ground to his left was a pattern of yellow rectangles of light from the kitchen window. Over by the road was Miss Wally's old Buick with the crack in the windshield, and beyond it, the blackness of the woods that stretched all the way to the Cliff of Night. Joey looked at Broco Way, the narrow dirt road that ran north, marking the boundary between Mr. Broco's cultivated acres and the great woods. Broco Way ended in a narrow path that led up, up to the Saddle, to the hidden glen of lifeberry bushes and somewhere, somewhere up there . . . to Dragon Groff.

Slowly he got to his feet, expecting, hoping that someone had heard the vine tear away, and maybe would be coming out to see what had happened. But only the wind knew he was there. The wind screamed *Hello*. Joey tightened his collar and hunched his thin shoulders inside his jacket. He was more frightened than he had been in running away from the Inn. He'd had those wonderful boots then, and could outrun anything, even birds! Several times Joey had secretly searched for the boots in the meadow and in the eaves of the adjacent forest, but they were gone, probably forever. He was alone, without magic boots or even a kitchen knife. Jim Hawkins, facing that dreadful Mr. Hands in *Treasure Island*, had had a brace of pistols!

He sniffled, wiped his nose and made a promise. If he didn't find Dragon Groff, he wouldn't come back. He'd keep on going till he reached the Snakeway, where he'd hitch a ride with a trucker and head out west somewhere and hunt for gold and diamonds and things. But he'd never come back to school again, or to the Hawkins's, either, where no one believed him.

Above the wind, he heard an owl hoot. Or was it an owl? Joey peered into the darkness. Was that blackness over there a moonshadow, or a bear? He scurried toward the house, stood by the porch. Of course, he didn't *have* to find Dragon Groff this *particular* night. That big lady, Brunnhilde Valkyrie (wow, what a name that was!) had said something about Halloween night being especially good for dragons. In fact, she expected to be out this night, herself, with *Wildschweinblutmeister*. Joey wasn't sure what she meant by good, and wasn't sure he'd like to meet up with her in the darkness.

He could go the other way, toward the village. That wouldn't be as scary, though the wild woods came right up to the road no matter which way he took. There was going to be a party in the gym sponsored by the PTA. A Halloween party. He could go and have a real great time just to spite Uncle Benison. In fact, he wouldn't even have to walk; there was an old bike that had belonged to Wilma; it lay on its side in the toolshed and Mrs. Hawkins even kept air in its tires, so that when her daughter came home, she could ride it like she used to when she was a little girl. But Joey couldn't go to the school party. The kids would make fun of him again.

Nor could he let Miss Wally brand him for life as a fibber, a liar! With the rest of this school year, and seven more till he graduated high school? He couldn't! With a last, wistful look back at the warm, yellow light spilling out from the kitchen window, Joey Hawkins slipped his arms through the straps of the knapsack, hitched it higher and, bending his head against the wind, started up Broco Way toward the night-enshrouded Dromedaries. And Dragon Groff.

"Who's that?" gulped Elf Miki, spying a figure outlined on the windowsill of Joey's bedroom. Let it not be the boy! This was no night for mischief or trouble! Edging to the lip of the hollow, careful not to disturb his protege, who was concentrating on her examination, he watched anxiously as a package was placed on the windowledge and, after some hesitation, pushed out onto the ground below!

Beside him, Rush peered out from beneath the folds of her towel and, after a moment's thought, wrote in her bluebook,

#2. Who? Joey Hawkins.

Final exam! This was easy as riding a robin! A flush of excitement warmed her momentarily as a dozen thoughts swarmed through her mind. But she said nothing; one did not talk during an exam! Her teacher had said so.

The window was opened all the way and a leg thrust out! Alarmed, Miki gasped, "What does he think he's doing? Not now! Not tonight! Not on Halloween!"

The elflet wrote,

#3. What does he think he's doing? A What question. Ans: Climbing out the window!

Then she smiled. Oh, oh! Miki had tried to trick her up! She wrote:

#4. *Not now* was the answer. The question was . . . when? As
in, *If not now, then when?*

Oho! The final exam was getting trickier! Suppose she didn't
pass! Miki would be so disappointed! Suddenly that answer seemed
too short, too easy. It needed puffing up. Her thoughts drifted to
that roaring fire in the common room and she shivered. Her bottom was getting damp. She added: *Not a fit night for man or beast.*
Her eyes followed Miki's. The boy was hanging outside the window now, his legs stretching along the side of the house toward a
vine on a sort of frame. Well, if one can't fly, life must get awfully
boring at times. So he was being a spider. Rush could understand
that. But on a night not fit for man or beast? Also, he wasn't very
good at it. The elflet watched as he swung over, grasped for the
vine-frame, missed, fell, turned head-for-heels, fell upside-down
slowly as the vine tore away from the frame-thing. There! His head
hit the baggage he'd tossed out earlier and now he lay there on the
cold ground.

Miki dashed out into the night. His cloak, swirling, caught on
a branch and was wrenched away. Heedless, the elf ran toward the
road only to be swept up by a windfury and carried off across the
road, spinning and flailing his arms as he was blown into a copse
of bushes, where he held on with all his strength. Rush jumped to
her feet, gripped the edge of the hollow tree with both hands.
Leaning out into the terrible wind as far as she dared, she cried,
"Come back! Miki, come back!"

She heard something that sounded like "pan" and then Miki
flash-transformed into a royal blue spheroid but that didn't help;
with no tangible hold on the bush, he was carried high in the air
and in no time at all, he'd been blown over the Hawkins house
and was gone.

Clutching her bathtowel about her, Rush ran out, was sent
flying into a low branch and hung on, sobbing, until a lull in the
sudden gale permitted her to drop to the ground and crawl back
toward the hollow trunk, pausing to retrieve Miki's cloak after
many tugs. Throwing it over her back for protection, she made her

way back to the shelter, looking like nothing so much as a large, green bug with a bedraggled carapace. Inside the hollow, she continued to the farthest corner, slipped out of the dirty bathtowel and wrapped herself in Miki's cloak, though it was six sizes too large. And then she remembered that she was taking a final exam, and how did she know this wasn't all part of it? She'd been sworn to silence, and yet she'd called out to Miki! Oh, she'd failed; for sure, she'd failed! But . . . but suppose she hadn't been heard? The exam included essays; Miki had said it would! And one of the famous human essay questions was: Does a tree falling in a forest make a sound if there's no one to hear it? By which they meant, no human to hear it! That was the remarkable thing about humans; they really thought they were the center of the universe! No matter. If Miki didn't hear her, did it count?

That was the essay! And figuring that out was part of the exam! Elflet Rush pushed her hair back out of her eyes, seated herself determinedly cross-legged and started to write. One hundred fifty words, asserting and proving that her blurted cry didn't cound. Exactly one hundred fifty words; she counted twice. Miki didn't reappear. Across the road, the boy shouldered his package and left, vanishing up the dark road toward the Dromedaries. And still the wind howled and Rush felt more and more uneasy. The boy shouldn't be heading up toward the Saddle, not on this night. Why was he, then?

Why? *Why*! One of the W's! The one where she had to figure out both question and answer! So *this* was what Final Exam meant! Oh, it wasn't so easy after all! Rush pressed her forehead, as though to squeeze out a half-remembered passage from something she'd heard. Not something from *The Book of the Ways of Man*. She was sick of that book; nothing made sense! No, not a book. Something she'd heard in Esfandiary! She'd been escorting a group, souls of older children. They'd been through colors and music and were huddled in a circle for storytime and a wizard had appeared— actually an elf in a wizard outfit—with a guitar and he'd sung a few elvish ballads and told them the story of Lazy Turkletoe

Who Wouldn't Think and Wouldn't Grow and how men and women first got started and . . . and of the Valley of Day and Night and the setting of the Barrier and all about Dragon Groff and the lifeberries . . .

Where was the boy Joey heading? Where! Another W! She had to find out where the boy was headed! Before Miki had vanished he'd called out something. What? Where? Why? The W's were attacking her mind! She concentrated on Miki's last cry. Pan. Yes, pan.

"Peter Pan!" she exclaimed, then clamped both hands over her mouth. Why couldn't she remember to keep her mouth shut? Well, words spoken didn't count if they weren't heard! She'd just proved that in a hundred fifty words.

Peter Pan.

What about Peter Pan?

Peter Pan was the answer! The question was: *Who?* Peter had wanted to be Peter Pan; she'd wanted to be Tinker Bell, but had settled for Wendy and had ended up being a heffalump, of all things!

But she'd done it well, hadn't she? And she could be Peter Pan if she had to! Back to Where. Where was Joey headed, on this terrible Halloween night? Not the Saddle! Not tonight!

The elf-wizard's tale came back to her.

After the great crossing-over of the dinosaurs to Esfandiary, dragons were placed that the creatures not return. Dragons, whose powers of mind exceeded all, even Man, whose time was come. That they not consume those with whose safety they were charged, they ate only once a year. On All-Hallows Eve. At midnight. They would start at sundown with lifeberries, greasing their dry throats and swelling their bellies and whetting their appetites! Starting at midnight, they were permitted to gorge on whatever was unprotected by nest or burrow or dwelling!

Where had the boy been headed, and why? She had to find

out to pass the exam! No wandering creature great or small between the peaks of the Dromedaries would be alive at dawn!

There were lights on in the lower windows of the Hawkins house. Lights meant people. She would have to disguise herself as Peter Pan and go into the house and find out where the boy was headed. Without talking. And without revealing her identity, as many humans looked askance at elves and, probably, elflets.

Opening her bluebook, she printed as many potentially useful phrases as she could remember. Then it was time to go. Peter Pan called for green tights and top . . . green slippers and a green, peaked cap with a yellow feather. Rush's dirndl was blue, her sweater, white. All that would have to be concealed. She would have to wear Miki's green cloak. Slipping her bluebook and pencil into a side pocket, she stood up, thrust her arms into the slits and advanced to the entranceway, gathering up the half of the cloak that trailed on the ground like a bride's train. The wind had subsided momentarily. Taking a deep breath, the elflet aimed herself at the front door of the house across the roadway and ran for it, leaping over twigs and stones, stumbling and rising again, hurtling herself forward toward the front walk and the door, which was getting larger, higher as she drew closer. She had never been up close to an adult human; they must be huge!

Shaping her hand into a fist (chapter 5 of The Book), she rapped on the door and stepped out of the way. Nothing happened. No one had heard. She found a stone and, running as fast as she could, banged on the door with all her strength, regretting how, earlier, she'd been foolish enough to think this final exam was easy!

And then . . . footsteps! Loud, clumping footsteps and the door was flung open by a large human with gigantic feet. This would be Benison Hawkins, who figured in some of the boy Joey's dreams. She opened the bluebook to the second page, where she'd printed:

TRICKERTREAT!

WHERE IS THE BOY JOEY GOING?

TOO LITTLE

Nightwind *whooshed* into the open mouth of Benison Hawkins, darted up past his sinuses and explored that marvellous brain which could integrate over 12 dimensions without losing one, which could twist space and time and come out even or slightly ahead. That brain was stymied. The signal coming in from the optic nerve seemed to indicate the presence on Hawkins's doorstep of a charmingly pretty girl enveloped from neck to ground in a hooded, green tent with loose, floppy sleeves. The wind seemed to be toying with her, one moment pressing her against the iron railing, the next moment, lifting her into the air as though to send her up, up over the cliff of Night and out of the valley forever. She was holding onto a vertical railing bar as for dear life.

Hawkins plucked her from the wind and pulled her into the foyer of his house. So, a girl. A girl who barely came up to his knee. A tiny girl who held in her tiny left hand what appeared to be a blue exam booklet.

Ah! Now she was pointing to some words printed on page 2 of the bluebook. Hawkins stooped down and read:

TRICKERTREAT!

WHERE IS THE BOY JOEY GOING?

The mathematician's face fell as his brain deftly came up with an answer consistent with the current state of *realpolitik* in the valley. Somehow, Lucien Broco knew that Joey Willem was in trouble and saw an opportunity to get his hands on the lad! So he'd sent this very small and undoubtedly very clever girl as a spy. This was no hench-child who had braved the dangers of Halloween for a few cookies and some pennies. *Where is the boy Joey going?*

Hawkins supposed that Broco was even now at that ostentatious picture window, peering through binoculars. Well, Lucien Broco would see nothing. Hawkins invited the little one into the house, locking the door against the angry, cheated Halloween wind. Too bad there were no cookies or ice cream on hand, but Loretta always had some kind of goodies about. Lifeberry candy, perhaps; the last of the old stock.

The little one slid gracefully past him into the foyer, then stepped cautiously into the kitchen, where she looked around without uttering a word.

Loretta Hawkins, pleased that someone had come for Halloween treats, wiped her hands on her blue-checkered dishtowel and approached the little one who seemed more a doll than a flesh-and-blood child. Scooping a handful of lifeberry candy from the Halloween dish, she cried, "Oh, Oh, you poor little creature," getting down on hands and knees that her welcome might more completely envelop the little guest. "Trickertreat!" she read, peering through her bifocals at the page in the exam book, which Rush held out before her.

"Oh, treats, treats for my Halloween sweet!" marvelling at this little one's pale skin, blue eyes and fine, golden hair that peeked out from beneath the hood of her much-too-large, hooded cloak. Gushing with love, Loretta filled the cloak pockets with lifeberry candy, trilling "Down the hatch," as she crammed the last into Rush's mouth. "So tiny, so hungry, so cold! Would you rather have pie and milk, or some hot tea? Or some nice, hot soup? Oh, my, your hands," she exclaimed, taking Rush's tiny hands in her own. "Why, they're frozen! Just wait, dear child; I have some delicious heeble soup heating up! I'd offer you some lifeberry pancakes but we're right short this year; the crop didn't come in like usual. In fact, my Joey was up there researching his school report, and he told me there's nary a single berry in the entire glen!"

It took all Rush's self-control to suppress a cry at Loretta's statement. *No lifeberries! They've already been devoured! According to Miki's Book, Lifeberries were Openers, unleashing the dominant functions and organ parts of each species! For humans, the mouth! For elves, the long memories were set spinning, generally affecting balance. And for dragons, they released the appetite glands! Groff's stomachs must be convulsing with hunger!*

She had to intercept the boy! But where was he going? Where?

Shushing his wife, Benison Hawkins said, gruffly, "Forget lifeberries for a minute! Look at the second line there!" and he pointed to the bluebook.

There was no question about it;

WHERE IS THE BOY JOEY GOING?

was a brilliant, succinct condensation of everything they'd been discussing for the past hour! Lucien Broco had sure hit the mark this time! Benison Hawkins overcame his pride, peered out the window and waved, hoping to surprise Broco at the binoculars, but though the lights were on, the library curtains were drawn and Benison could discern no sign of the master of the valley.

Loretta finished her perusal of the little girl. "You must be one of Joey's little friends from school," she declared. Putting her face right up to the elflet's, Loretta asked, sweetly, "Are you in Joey's class, honey?"

Are you in Joey's class? Chapter Eight of *The Book of the Ways of Man* dealt with competition, and Rush remembered that the word *class* meant *prideful status.* Only humans indulged in prideful status. She shook her head and nibbled on a second piece of candy. It was easier to maintain forced silence during a final exam if one's mouth were full.

"Well, that's okay," Loretta said in a motherly tone. "What's your name, dear?"

Rush had expected that question. Turning to page three of her blue book, she pointed to the words she'd printed, following (she hoped) Miki's shouted instruction:

PETER PAN

"Oh, she's Peter Pan!" Loretta cried, clapping her hands. "Imagine that! Well, I'm Loretta Hawkins, and that's my husband Benison and this nice lady is Joey's teacher, Miss Wally." Miss Wally was staring intently at the odd creature who was tinier than any girl she'd ever seen before. And quieter. Was she not being fed properly? Was she mute? Had someone cut out her tongue? What was going on in this house, anyway? Perhaps she'd been hasty in her judgement of the boy Joseph.

Benison chuckled, "Yep, Peter Pan here has put her finger right on the Joey problem. Where's Joey going? she wants to know, and I'd like to know, too! Bad enough the boy's too lazy to go out and do a proper interview, like the assignment said. But to dream one up is ten times worse!"

"He did *not* dream it up," Loretta said, ladling steaming, crackling heeble soup from a tureen into a teacup and forcing teaspoon after teaspoon into the elflet, who was afraid to disobey a rule of etiquette lest she fail the exam, which was *much* more difficult than she'd expected. "While our little guest warms up, why don't you read Joey's interview out loud, Miss Wally?" Perhaps this little girl could help get poor Joseph off the hook, she hoped.

Miss Wally reminded Loretta, "He took his report upstairs. Call him down, Mr. Hawkins; if he admits that he made it up, I'll agree to accept a substitute report. He may interview anyone he likes, but no dragons!"

Benison said, "Well, that's mighty kind of you, Miss Wally," and cupping his hands, he called upstairs, "Time, Joey boy! And bring the report."

There was no response.

"Joey!" Benison shouted. Getting no answer, he stamped to the foot of the stairs and hollered, "Joseph! Get down here *now!*"

Which was followed by his footsteps ascending, an exclamation, a call up to the attic and then a shouted, "He's gone! And the window's wide open! Joey-boy's gone!"

Loretta Hawkins hurried up the stairway only to find him absolutely, definitely missing and gone *out the window!* She stood there peering out into the night, heedless of the wind, until Ms. Wally put both hands on the frame and closed it firmly. Joey's teacher then searched among the scattered papers, looking for a note, an explanation, preferably one that exonerated her from culpability in the boy's decision to run away. She came across a mathematics problem that she didn't recognize having assigned.

'If a man and a half mow a lawn and a half in a day and a half . . .'

It was not Joseph's writing; that left Benison. Upon entering the house, Ms. Wally had noticed the volumes of Benison's Theory on their own bookshelf in the living room. Joseph had frequently boasted of his Uncle Benison's brilliance in mathematics . . . this must be an example.

Taped to the bottom of the page were the outlines of a man and of half a man, the whole figure at the left-hand side, apparently facing a grey-shaded area (one lawn) and the half-man on the right-hand side, apparently facing a smaller area, a half-lawn. Someone, neither Joey nor Benison to judge from the scrawl, had written: 'Starting right after breakfast and allowing an hour for lunch . . .'

Ms. Wally's heart sank; never in a million years would it have occurred to her to solve a problem in such a fashion. Was something defective in her training? The Hawkinses were preoccupied with the open drawers and certain missing items from the bathroom. Miss Wally slid the paper into her handbag, for future study. Or evidence.

On the other hand . . . she sniffed, sniffed again, her brows furrowed in suspicion. "Mrs. Hawkins," she whispered. "Let's go back down to the kitchen. I've been dealing with ten-year-olds for twenty-five years. My guess is he's hiding in the cellar, hoping to outlast anger until it's supplanted by pity. Or smoking a cigarette. We'll give him a half-hour." Well she knew the tricks of ten-year old boys, and the best responses. She'd wait Joseph out until he came out of hiding, tired and hungry and likely crying his little head off. Even if it meant staying the night.

Rush, alias Peter Pan, was where they had left her, perched precariously on the kitchen table's edge. She seemed to be having trouble keeping her balance. Loretta picked her up, hugged her closely and vigorously, then set her down in a less dangerous place, sitting on the floor not too close to the door, with its cold drafts. The big folk took the same seats as before, only now Miss Wally had some pages in her hand. She cleared her throat.

"Two weeks ago," she said, her voice a well-modulated contralto, "I instructed the class in the proper method of interviewing. As a class assignment, each student was to interview an adult neighbor and write a report. This is Joseph's report."

"'Dragon Groff lives in a cramped, narrow cave above the lifeberry glen in the Saddle between the Dromedary Mountains.'

"The first error," she announced triumphantly, "not counting that this so-called interview is made up out of smoke." Cigarette smoke, if her suspicions proved out. "Is the cave in the Saddle, or is the glen in the Saddle? Not clear," she sniffed, then continued.

"'From the front of his cave, Dragon Groff can see the tops of the cliffs and my house and Mr. Broco's on the hill, but not all the way to my school in Lower Muchness. He would like to visit the school. Very much.

"'The cave has no address, but Dragon Groff doesn't get mail so that don't matter. The nearest road to the cave is Route 39, which is the Snakeway, which you get to by Bumbler's Pass. Dragon Groff remembers when they built Route 39. He remembers a lot of things, maybe everything that ever happened in the whole valley.'"

A cave near the Saddle?

Rush's head felt light. The lady Wally was talking . . . talking . . . humans talk, talk . . . don't they ever stop to wonder? What had lady Wally said? Cave? There were dozens of caves in the mountainsides. Which cave? She was dizzy and couldn't concentrate . . .

Miss Wally read, "'Dragon Groff remembers when the valley was filled with lifeberry bushes and pine trees and a stream ran down from the mountain, along the valley floor beneath the dark cliff to a great swamp. He remembers elephants with thick, brown coats of hair and long, curved tuskis.' He means *tusks*, of course," she interjected. "'They were noisy and stupid. Once, when Groff flew overhead, they stampeded and destroyed many lifeberry bushes. That winter, many of them starved, including the little ones. And he remembers the first humans that came to hunt them. They ran around almost naked, with no coats or shoes, even in the deep snow. All that's gone now, says Dragon Groff, and the stream and swamp are dried up.'"

A thrill flashed through the elflet's body as she recalled a tale of the Wizard, about an ancient valley *carpeted from side to side with purple-fruited lifeberry bushes*! And the proper name for those animals was *mammoths*, and Miki had mentioned them once during a history lesson, and he'd even taken her to see a knob of bone protruding from the ground at the south end of the valley, *where the ground was mushy and tiger lilies and cattails grew in clusters*!

Benison Hawkins turned to his wife and challenged her, "You grew up in these parts. You ever hear of elephants or naked folks runnin' around the valley?"

Loretta shook her head. "No elephants, anyway," she whispered, figuring that there was no point in bringing up her brother Herman, who was still a mite peculiar when it came to dressing, particularly in summer. He'd had to repeat grades and hated it. Did this mean that Joey would have to repeat grades?

"No elephants," Benison grumbled.

Loretta leaned over and whispered to the teacher, "Some ten-year olds are still learning the difference between real and pretend. My daughter, Wilma, never cleared it up, even after she . . . became a lady, if you know what I mean. I do wish she'd write more. Go right on; you read beautifully. I'm going upstairs to get some pancakes from the attic, seing as we have company. I'll be right back." Drawing a sweater over her shoulders, she shuffled out of the room.

Miss Wally continued, "'All that seems like yesterday,' says the Dragon Groff, 'and I am older than the hairy elephants. Much older. And I am tired, lonely and very hungry.'"

Rush paled as the words penetrated the fog thickening in her mind. *Much older than the elephants*! Tired, lonely. Hungry!

The candy. Something in the candy. Lifeberries. Miki had warned her about lifeberries. Some species couldn't handle them. Elves? She couldn't remember. All she wanted to do was lie down somewhere and sleep.

She *couldn't* do that! Where was the cave? She should get out of the house, try . . . try to get out of this . . . solid body . . . fly north to the Saddle. But she was dizzy . . . the room was spinning around . . .

Miss Wally raised an index finger and continued. "'When Dragon Groff took sunbaths in the old days, he spread himself out on a flat rock as big as Mr. Broco's mansion-house. In those days, none dared bother him, not even the meat-eaters who thundered up and down the valley, chasing the long-necks who had left the great swamp to lay their eggs or eat ferns. Groff says the swamp protected the long-necks from the meat-eaters. But not always. The End.'"

Rush had to get outside fast. But should she disobey Miki? Break silence? Sound the alarm? Cry out:

DRAGON GROFF IS REAL AND YOU ARE IN DANGER!

She would fail her exam and they wouldn't believe her anyway. Humans didn't believe anything they hadn't seen on television, with commercials. That was on every page of the guidebook.

The elflet rose unsteadily and made her way to the door, waiting until Benison Hawkins opened it. Though her head was awhirl, she lurched down the path to the road against the wind, reoriented herself vaguely north and took one step, was blown back, took another, and another. In no time at all, she was on her hands and knees, crawling beside the roadway.

*   *   *

The cold, windswept world outside Lucien Broco's library was curtained off, the only lighting indirect, unobtrusive. A low fire glowed in the fireplace, its crackle and hiss drowning out the bubbling sound that accompanied each of the valleymaster's breaths. "It's curse enough to feel the rattle in my lungs," he'd snapped at Trenton Interface, "I don't have to listen to it as well!"

From all parts of his body, a web of tubes and electrical leads bound him into a *Max-Relax Life Support System*, a body-fitting waterbed that massaged his muscles and joints with ultrasound while dozens of sensors provided monitoring of his life functions. The tubes and wires were strapped together in neat bundles which snaked off into a large-screen monitor; a parallel cable vanished into an adjacent room where teams of nurses and technicians, supervised by medical specialists from Boston and New York, alternated shifts . . .

" . . . wasting their time and my money, sitting around watching an old man die!" Broco muttered to himself as much as at Trenton, who sat in a hard-backed bridge chair, keeping vigil over his beloved master. Not that there was so much organically wrong with the old man; that was one thing the doctors agreed on. It was his desire to live that was failing. His life force.

Somehow, Trenton had to get Mr. Broco's adrenalin up. Somehow. But the major domo was exhausted, his eyes puffy and half-closed from lack of sleep. He dared not look in the direction of Mr. Broco's recliner; one minute in that and he'd be asleep. Even the floor was starting to look inviting.

Lucien Broco had lost his chance at immortality. The full measure of his despondancy had been made clear when, earlier, he had turned to his major domo and whispered, "See to it . . . that everyone's taken care of . . . properly, Trenton. The henchmen, the kitchen staff, Hawkins. After I'm gone, Hawkins will have a life-pension. It's all arranged. And don't forget what's his name . . . Blunger. The advisor. Do something for him, Trenton. I don't know what, but find something and do it. You will be given power of attorney, of course. And for the medical crew . . . I suppose they did their best . . . double wages, and triple for Sundays and holidays. Isn't tonight Halloween?"

The question pulled Trenton Interface from a shallow doze. "Yes, Mr. Broco," he said quietly. His employer had never displayed interest in holidays, relying on his staff to take care of those things when they turned up on the calendar. Was this the beginning of the end? The doctors had warned him that Mr. Broco's will to live was ebbing dangerously, and he might revert to childhood or worse before the end.

"See that there's candy . . . no, drat candy! . . . money! Money in a dish for the urchins. And double for those in clever costumes! No coins, mind! Washington gave no quarter!"

With an effort, Broco lifted his head from the pillow. "Eh, that was clever, wasn't it, Trenton? Washington gave no quarter! I'm not dead yet, dammit! Give them greenbacks. Ones and fives. Let them learn to respect their presidents!"

His head dropped to the pillow. Trenton's eyes flashed across the dials on the wall monitor, on which was displayed the outputs of the life-support sensors and probes. The readings were all within range, but life was more than a collection of high-tech monitors and gauges.

The game was over. The valleymaster had put all his chips on Hawkins's Theory and the place the boy Joey called Esfandiary, and lost. After sixty years as builder and possessor, maker and unmaker, the Grey Fox (Fortune Magazine) had given up. Now he lay dying, drained of hope and the life-force. No longer interested in his financial matters, in the splendor of the *Kristallfluss* or in the small affairs of the valley, he lay in a cocoon, the curtains drawn. If he were to go this minute, his last words on Earth would have been a pun. Trenton vowed never to reveal that. A tear trickled down his cheek. Lucien Broco was preparing himself to turn off, to die.

The major domo clenched and unclenched his hands. Was this not his fault? Had he not let Mr. Broco down? Why had he admitted those accursed pizzas into the mansionhouse, when he should have sounded the alarm, calling up the hench-army to drive the intruders from the valley? And later, with the entire hench-orchestra at his command, how could he have permitted the pair of griffins to escape? So strong was the love of Trenton for his master that it transcended his own misgivings and doubts regarding this Esfandiary business, which he did not pretend to understand. With a final glance at the cold, impersonal gauges on the life-monitor, Trenton Interface dropped to his knees and clasped his hands in the darkness. If only . . . if only his beloved master could get one more chance at this thing he wanted so much! The challenge alone would restore the life-force in him; Trenton knew it would! Hawkins was a genius. Hawkins *had* to be a genius!

A bell rang. A red light flashed in the darkness! In an instant, Trenton was at the display. But the gauges were steady; the flashing red light was not from the life-support monitor. It was the intruder alarm, one of the infrared beams from the fields, probably responding to the passage of a fox or . . .

"Eh, what's that, man?" Broco called from his cradle.

Trenton thought fast. The lighted box on the panelboard was from sector I-19, a field of honey-clover and beehives just off the roadway and north of the mansionhouse. Any creature larger than a squirrel could have broken the beam; a fox, a deer, a woodchuck. "It appears to be an intruder, sir," he said. "Someone in I-19, stealing honey. Or spying," he added, recalling the effect the intrusion of Augustus Vimstetter had had on his master. He *had* to get Mr. Broco's adrenalin up!

"Let him steal . . . take all the honey he can carry," Broco wheezed. "What's the use, now? As for spying . . . my life will be an open book soon enough, Trenton. Exposes . . . reporters . . . unauthorized biographies . . .

"Tell them nothing, Trenton! Nothing! They'll all want to know how I built forty-two dollars in quarters, a chicken with an eyepatch and a case of out-of-date ketchup into a four billion dollar empire! Well, let them figure it out if they can."

Walking over to the window and parting the curtains, Trenton put the binoculars to his eyes. Darkness had fallen over the valley, and lights were on in the Hawkins house at the foot of the green-sward. As Trenton watched, the upstairs lights flicked off. Then he saw Hawkins pacing in front of the kitchen window. Anxiously; his right hand was waving spastically and he was gumming his teeth. Trenton extrapolated, raised his eyes northward, switching the binoculars to infrared. Ah . . . ah, there it was. A white blob moving slowly across the field. Why so slowly? No matter. It was the boy Joey, and none too soon. Trenton thrust the binoculars into his master's hands, pointing them in the direction of sector I-19.

Broco looked halfheartedly, then pressed the binoculars into his eye sockets to reduce their shaking. "What is it?" he demanded. "The boy? Where is he going?"

"North," Trenton intoned solemnly, not daring cast the slightest doubt on his master's hasty conclusion.

"North!" cried the valleymaster. "The boy Joey has broken with Hawkins! He is returning to Esfandiary. My venturing outfit! Quick. And warm up the halftrack!"

This was it, then! Trenton moved fast, before the medical crew could respond to the dangerous surge in heartrate. A turn of a key locked them into their chamber. Ignoring their pounding and call-ing, Trenton quickly removed the sensors from Broco's frame, helped him into his double-insulated woolen underwear and then, into his steel-grey, puncture-proof venture-suit, guaranteed to keep its wearer safe anywhere, anyhow, short of the vacuum of deep space or external pressure in excess of sixty atmospheres.

Looping Broco's arms around his neck, Trenton Interface half-carried the old man to the book-lined wall and pressed a button. Bookshelves swung to the side. "Just a minute!" Broco snapped, and from behind a rack of encyclopedias, he took a crystal decanter filled with a plum-colored, viscous liquid, which he clutched to his chest as they descended by elevator into the garage. They made their way across the concrete floor, past rows of cars and trucks of every description, until they stopped at a massive, armored halftrack.

Trenton Interface was relieved to find that the valleymaster's muscles had not yet started to atrophy, though they were weak from disuse. Settling Mr. Broco into the passenger seat, he leaped into the driver's seat and started the six-hundred horsepower diesel engine. At the press of a button, the garage door opened and they were headed into the night. "What's that, sir?" Trenton asked, almost jubilant, for it was like the old days. Mr. Broco was humming a tune, and his face radiated its old, wizened smile. And best of all, he'd found something to do! He was joining in, coming back to full life! Yes, Mr. Broco was busily pouring liquid from the decanter into small ampoules, stacking each one into the clip of a high-pressure dart/spray gun. And he'd turned on the long-range infrared scope and put it on automatic. The phosphorescent screen glowed greenish-white, random dots with no pattern, while above them, on the roof of the cab, the detectors rotated slowly, steadily in their hunt pattern, looking for a source on which to fasten.

The flush on Mr. Broco's face was worth all the pills and tonics the doctors had been plying. Trenton determined to prolong the adventure as long as possible.

"What's that?" he repeated.

"Triple-distilled lifeberry serum," Broco chuckled. "The entire crop down to the last berry, concentrated into this one flagon! One drop and you tell everything you know. Ten drops and you spill everything you ever heard. I have . . . here . . . the entire output of the only lifeberry glen in the world. I have cornered the market!

"*Avante!*" he shouted. "I feel like a million dollars! Make that a billion. After taxes!"

The halftrack rumbled down the driveway, turned right and headed north. Lucien Broco's eyes closed and his thin lips trembled with excitement as they had at countless corporate takeovers. Trenton, fighting the weight of his eyes, had all he could do to keep to the road. Neither of them saw the momentary flash of light just above the Saddle of Dromedary Mountain.

The infrared detectors, closing in on a smallish form running erratically across the wide fields to the right, swung up and to the left, searching for the source of that flash, but it had offblinked. Unable to locate the source of the heat-burst, they resumed their search for the boy Joey.

In his prime, Dragon Groff had torched more than one rogue tyrranosaur with his fiery blast.

NORTH BY WAY OF JULIA'S FROCKS AND SOCKS

"Unh! Unh!" *Whoosh*! What in God's name is that old woman doing in the bathroom, Gertrude wondered. She was in the bedroom, where she'd taken the telephone to call the Bronx police out of Sophie's earshot. Ever since the woman in black had disappeared into the bathroom, Gertrude had heard grunting and a steady tinkle of water from behind the door. Was that old woman fooling around with the pipes?

But it was the moaning from the living room that demanded Gertrude's attention. Sophie lay sprawled over the sofa, reading the final pages of *Too Little* for the second time and wailing for her lost husband. A plumber could fix a busted pipe; you can't put the lid on a full-blown depression with a wrench and solder. Anything, even anger, was better than depression. Gertrude covered the mouthpiece with her hand.

"You know what I think?" she snapped. "Your Myron has time to write about an elf running around dressed as Peter Pan. He has time for a ten-year-old boy out hunting dragons instead of attending to his homework. For the wind he has a paragraph. For you . . . nothing. I bet he's landed himself in a psychiatric ward somewhere and this writing business is part of his therapy, along with electroshock." It was major surgery, but Sophie was heading toward a classic depression and Gertrude had no patience with what she regarded as childish self-indulgence.

"Rhauggh! Rhauggh!" *Whoooooom*! An animal cry from the john, followed by a grand roar as of rapids. "Unh! Unh!" *Whoosh*! and now "Rhauggh! Rhauggh!" *Whoom!* The john was doomed, Gertrude thought.

Sophie rose and staggered into the bedroom just as Dickie bird piped once. "Shock treatments on my Myron?" she whispered, wiping her eyes. "I have to go! I have to find my husband before they kill him! Doctors are very forgetful, you know; they could turn the current up and then start arguing about the Yankees and my poor . . . poor Myron . . . lying there . . . sparking . . ."

Sophie Blunger's histrionics were cut off by a thundering from the bathroom, a roar comparable in intensity to that of the great Victoria Waterfall.

Gertrude attended to the telephone, then turned it off and planted herself firmly, a pillar of support for her beloved sister. "That was Captain Gurney, in the Bronx," Gertrude said. "They sent a car down to the stables in Van Cortland Park and carried out a search, but didn't come up with a manure sample that matched in texture and bulk to what turned up in your living room. If Myron doesn't show up within forty-eight hours, they'll list him as missing. There's nothing more they can do. The captain said that this happens all the time, and in nice families, too. It could be a case of amnesia," she added, "or not enough roughage."

From the john came a standard Kohler flush. Gertrude guided Sophie back into the living room and eased her onto the sofa. The woman in black emerged from the bathroom, adjusting her gloves.

"That's much better," she announced with a great sigh. "Sorry if I had to run the water a bit; as I said, at my age, it takes a while to get started."

"My husband . . ." Sophie moaned.

"Your husband," God's aunt said in a somber, almost clinical tone of voice that sent heaves and shudders through Sophie's body. "While I was waiting for my system to function, I had two visions."

Gertrude stared at the black veil. Concealed behind it was a woman who called herself God's aunt, who *shlepped* a sack full of curses, pissed rivers, spoke in complete sentences and had visions. And she was Sophie's only hope. Gertrude focussed on that.

"I saw your Myron departing from the Inn," continued the woman in black, and Gertrude noted that her voice did not waver like Madama Zhoda's did when she was picking horses from a deck of cards at seventy-five cents a race.

"He was sprawled across the back of a centaur, accom-panied by a gnome. The vision, over which I have no control and I beg your pardon, homed in on Myron Blunger's behind, and there I saw a wound made by foreign objects. To wit: a chunk of lead, and a leech, both blasted into his rear by the Innkeeper. That was the first vision."

Sophie Blunger's head nodded as her auditory system tried to force this *mushagas* into the appropriate part of her brain.

"The second vision was definitely from Esfandiary," God's aunt continued, "and is fuzzy, which means it hasn't happened yet. But not too fuzzy; it's coming right up. A small, boar-like carnivore has Myron by the foot and is dragging him to its lair deep in a primeval forest, where its mate waits along with their raucous, snoutish and very hungry offspring."

"Can't you do something?" Sophie Blunger cried, throwing herself at the feet of the woman in black. A gloved hand was laid lightly on her shoulder, and she raised herself, sobbing. "If I could, I would," God's aunt said gently. "But I am not omnipresent, and I am here, in Florida. I don't even know into which Esfandiary your husband has been sent, though I suspect the worst."

"I have to get there," Sophie Blunger said, slowly and firmly, though her hands were trembling. "I want to leave now. I must help him."

Gertrude shook her head at this sign of madness. "Get where?" she said. "You can't . . . you can't . . . . " She looked at the veiled woman in black, for confirmation.

"She is correct," said the woman in black. "You cannot get to Esfandiary by any means. But you could get to Lower Muchness, if you were determined to. It is possible that, if Myron Blunger survives present and future dangers, he could end up in Upper Muchness." *If he is not already distributed among the bellies of the Boar-Snout family*, she thought.

"To Muchness, then," Sophie declared, unflinchingly. "Is there a train?"

God's aunt leaned forward. "Better. You will take the *Lightspeed*. Pack warm clothing in a shopping bag. Wear walking shoes. Carry thirty-six dollars and fifty cents plus bus fare and a flashlight.

"Take the bus to Ocean Avenue. Enter Julia's Frocks and Socks, on the corner of Market. Go to the rear, to the discounted rack. Without trying it on, buy the yellow sun-dress, the one with exactly fourteen buttons and half-sleeves, size twelve, marked down to $36.50; take it into the last dressing room. Shut the door firmly, change into that dress, but do not fasten the final button until you have picked up your shopping bag and have it securely on your arm. Then close your eyes and, as you fasten the last button, step into the mirror firmly and with confidence and say *"Lower Muchness."*

"You may feel dizzy for a moment. If the system's working right, you will slip away through the mirror, as Alice did once upon a time, then a great wind will support you.

"You will be carried north by *Lightspeed*, to the edge between reality and what-might-be. You will be flung into a haystack just outside of the village of Lower Muchness. Behind you will be a hill of black rock that extends underground until, in the valley of Upper Muchness, it surfaces and becomes the Cliff of Night.

"The cave is the Cave of the Winds; it is part of the *Lightspeed* system. Take care not to fall backward into the cave; without an announced destination, you would circle the Earth endlessly, miles underground. If I recall correctly, a sign points toward the path that leads to the road to Upper Muchness. If you hurry, you may catch up with Wilma Hawkins; she is dressed in the uniform of a *Lightspeed* General. Explain the circumstances; she will try to get you into Upper Muchness, perhaps by means of the school bus if other means fail."

"And suppose the mirror trick doesn't work?" Gertrude asked, even as her sister hurried into the kitchen to select a sturdy shopping bag from the collection crammed between the refrigerator and the wall.

God's aunt's hat and veil oscillated from side to side. "Then you will break your nose against the mirror," she answered impatiently.

"You have to believe! Now, the path will lead you to a road that is both uneven and odd," God's aunt said. "For some folk, it is an ordinary road, with more than the usual bumps and dips. Joey Willem's teacher, Ms. Wally, is one of those, otherwise she wouldn't have reached the Hawkins house.

"For others, it seems that no matter how carefully one puts one foot in front of the other, he ends up exactly where he started, or vice versa, with no recollection of having turned around."

"I'd better go, too," Gertrude said.

The hat and veil bobbed slightly; presumably God's aunt was nodding. "Yes," she said. "Go. Your sister is overwrought and will need support. Remember to take a flashlight and heavy sweaters. I must leave now."

Was Myron Blunger still alive? God's aunt was more determined than ever to persuade her Nephew to bring about Blunger's repatriation to the Bronx, to the arms of his loved ones. She took the elevator down and walked into the bright, midmorning sunshine. She needed to sit quietly and organize her thoughts.

"Wotan!" she muttered as she made her slow way down the street toward a small shopping mall. What chance did Myron Blunger have after crossing the false god Wotan? For at the moment of truth, when her system opened fully, God's aunt had received a third vision.

She had seen a great hall dimly illuminated by black candles and Wotan stretching his arms out to the creatures of the night, trolls and ogres, goblins and were-creatures. Behind him were figures that God's aunt could not identify, and behind them, frost giants.

However, her Nephew *was* omniscient and all-powerful, and that could be an advantage if she could but get Him involved in Blunger's problem.

Omniscient. All-seeing. She pondered the word and its implications. Being omniscient could be a disadvantage at times, such as when trying to concentrate on a difficult golf shot, she reasoned. God's aunt reached deep into her sack, into the largest compartment, the one reserved for golf, and retrieved a handful of choice maledictions. A powerful curse on putting. A five-iron malediction that invariably sent balls into the rough. A sand-trap blessing . . .

Reluctantly, she returned them to the sack. There was another way, if she could just find a bookstore.

It was getting hot, and the sack of curses seemed to gain weight at each step. God's aunt wondered if it wouldn't increase her efficiency if she used a shopping cart. Like the one at curbside. Why, it wasn't being used and was empty except for a few crumpled fliers.

She heaved the sack into the cart, sighed, indulged in a full body-stretch, then proceeded to march along the street, keeping one eye out for displays of winter coats while she pondered the Blunger problem.

She did not notice the blue and white, four-door sedan that had started to move, keeping half a block behind her. In it were two burly men with wraparound sunglasses. One was speaking into a microphone.

And there was a book shop, and on the sidewalk, a rack of discounted paperbacks and, what she most needed, a bench, presumably meant for brousers. A gentleman wearing a white linen suit and rather old-fashioned brown and white wing-tip shoes sat primly at one end. A wide-brimmed Panama hat and dark glasses hid his face. One hand rested on a walking stick of plain, unpolished, natural wood. He might be watching the passersby, or half-dozing behind those dark glasses, or just reflecting on times past . . .

Laying her staff on the bench to separate her from the gentleman, in case he should think her forward, God's aunt took a seat and began picking through the titles, looking for a book on etiquette. A nice, thick, pretentious book . . .

Her eye happened to fall upon one of the titles in the rack. *Gloria's End*. That could be about etiquette . . .

She took the book, opened it to a page at random and read a paragraph . . .

From the slow roll of the cabin cruiser in the swells, Gloria knew that they were well out from the harbor, maybe fifty miles out. Stars. No moon. She lay in the stern, dazed, cold, her wrists bound behind her with cruel rope. One ankle was lashed to a heavy anchor. Her eyes were puffy from the beating and her mouth was encrusted with dry blood. She shivered.

She was cold because she was naked. They'd stripper her, looking for another knife, but she didn't have another. Had her two or three thrusts killed Slade? She hoped so. More likely he was in the cabin, bandaged up, counting the heroin blocks, trying to figure out how many she'd taken. Three. She'd taken three and hidden them well; Slade would have to take the boat apart to find them. Evidence. In a pre-arranged location. In case she weren't around when the police searched the boat. In case the job went sour. In case she wasn't around at all.

Naked. No more secrets. The undercover agent was uncovered. Now the one called Pig was crawling toward her to indulge himself . . .

Shocked, God's aunt thrust the disgusting book back into the rack. She took another, titled *Doing Wright*, opened it near the center . . . .

"Please to put down your head," said the one they called Doctor Wright, pressing the tip of the machete against Detective Stoker's naked sternum. Doctor Wright's voice was soft, reasonable. The blade of the machete pressed against Stoker's skin and warm blood was already running down his waist into the blanket.

This was what they'd done to Hector, furrowing his spine, over and over, a little deeper each time with this same machete, until he'd talked. But Hector didn't have the key, did he? So they made him a quadraplegic . . . for nothing. Stoker had the key. And Stoker was lashed face-down to the iron corners of the kind of bed that comes with a twelve-dollar a day flop.

Detective is one tough job, man.

"Now, you want to give me the key, Mr. Detective, or you want to be a basket case, like your partner?"
Horrified, God's aunt scanned book after book.

. . . Knives . . . bullets . . . rape . . . incest . . . "Four million cash, or I'll pull your lungs out through your nose!"

"The weapon was her flaming red hair; it drove my client mad, your honor!

. . . bodies everywhere, alive, dead, copulating, squirming . . .

Every one of these dreadful books was filled with violence and inhumanity of the worst sort! The curses she'd been collecting were simply the scrapings of a malevolance she'd never imagined! And the art on the covers!

And then she found, on the lowest shelf,

Of the stuff of stars I made them, and of Myself, for I am life. It was written by a Miss Lowery.

An odd title for a book, but there it was, right on the cover, and opening it, God's aunt found that it was a book on etiquette! The book had an index, and under Birthdays there were five headings. Aunts' birthdays . . . yes, yes . . . there it was, exactly what she'd expected to find!

But that title—why did it ring a bell?

"You have any I.D., lady?"

The woman in black looked up; two men in uniforms with badges and wooden clubs and guns in holsters towered above her; in the street was a car—a police car—with rotating lights.

"What's in the bag, honey?" asked the second officer, eyeing the sack suspiciously.

"Possession of more than a gram of marijuana is a felony," the first officer recited. "Also, that shopping cart is the property of Enright's Supermarket. You have some identification?"

The second officer was speaking into a machine. "Perp dressed as old woman in black with veil . . . Petit larceny/Shopping cart, vagrancy. Possible Mary Jane. Carrying a large sack and a long stick or club . . . we'll bring her in for prints and a strip-search."

Instinctively the woman in black returned the book to the shelf and reached for her protective staff, but the second officer already had it, plus her sack, which he was holding gingerly by the neck. "What'cha got in here?" he repeated.

"You don't have . . . have to answer that!" It was the gentleman. His hat still covered his face, but his diction was slurred. One had no difficulty imagining bloodshot, rheumy eyes behind those dark glasses and a breakfast drunk from a silver flask. "I am a lawyer. Yes, a lawyer, by God!" He chuckled and, pointing a forefinger at the cops, declared, "You need a search warrant."

"Sure, Jack," said the second cop. He was about to open the sack, but the first officer held his arm and nodded, his hand dropping onto the handle of his billyclub.

"We go by the book, eh?" said the first officer. "We'll get a warrant. And so the lady ain't without representation, Jack, we'll take you along for a breath analysis. Vagrancy, spitting on the sidewalk. Unless you'd rather clear out now, peacefully.

"Now, please lift your veil, ma'am," he asked, with rule-book politeness.

God's aunt shook her head violently; lifting her veil in public would cause a great deal of trouble!

"Your name and address?" asked the officer. The second cop was hefting the sack. Not heavy enough for the hard stuff. Marijuana? Had they nailed a middleman, a street distributor? "I am God's aunt. I will leave." She rose, somewhat unsteadily without the staff she'd gotten used to.

"Not with this, honey," said the second officer, putting the sack and staff into the trunk of the patrol car. He then called into his portable police radio, "She says she is God's aunt . . . that's right . . . G. O. D. . . . God's aunt," followed by, "Possible Mary Jane, pending search of sack. Need a warrant."

"First name, please?" asked the first officer, less patiently than before.

The gentleman reached over and put his bony hand around God's aunt's wrist. "Say nothing without . . . counsel," he ordered. "I am counsel.

"And do not . . . do not try to lift her veil," the sidewalk lawyer said in an imperious voice to the first officer, just as he was about to do that. "You can not touch . . . touch her any way; sexual harrassment! Civil code S439. I am her counsel!" he said, proudly. "You touch one thread of her clothing or her person, I will have you fired! And I mean *fired*! I am her attorney at law!"

The attorney at law was escorted into the rear seat of the patrol car without difficulty and without handcuffs. Had God's aunt had her staff in hand, she might have escaped the indignity of being likewise transported to the stationhouse, booked for theft of a shopping cart, vagrancy and possible possession of drugs. She would not have been held in an unpleasant cage while a search warrant was obtained. At one-thirty in the afternoon, the supermarket manager, satisfied to retrieve his shopping cart, decided not to press charges.

The search warrant arrived at three in the afternoon, and several more hours were spent in making photocopies of the material in the sack, over which a magistrate's clerk pored for several hours, trying to match known forms of mental illness with the behavior of a pervert who chose to drag around with her a sack full of the most heinous and graphic curses he'd ever laid eyes on! In the end, the magistrate threw the whole thing out except for the vagrancy charge, on which the woman (if it was a woman; she refused to lift her veil and the court matron, a devout Catholic, refused to search her against her will) was finally freed at eight thirty at night, on her own recognizance, with her lawyer at her side.

The *starstuff* phrase had run through her mind during her entire incarceration. She had heard that phrase a long time ago, in a profound setting. Who had said it? Where? Why? Why did it obsess her now, with all she had on her mind?

Side by side they walked down a wide avenue lined with palm trees. Store windows were lit, but there were few shoppers. And in the middle of a block empty of pedestrians her attorney whispered,

"*Of the stuff of stars I made them . . .*"

She whirled about and thrust her staff into her attorney's chest. "You!" she shouted.

He laughed and tilted His hat up just enough to reveal His countenance, then lowered it..

"*. . . and of Myself, for I am life.*" He whispered without a trace of a slur.

"You . . ."

"Yes," chuckled God. "I snap-edited the title of that book on etiquette, just to see if you'd notice it."

"It's not nice to fool aunty," she grumbled. "I thought You were playing golf." She surruptitiously kicked the sack to make it rustle more loudly and remind the Lord God of her difficult assignment.

"It's not nice to consider sending three golf curses heavenward!" her Nephew snapped. Nearby windows rattled inexplicably and for a mile around, resting birds took to wing. "I have an important game tomorrow. How am I to concentrate on My putting?

"But perhaps it's for the best," He sighed. "You saw the books in that rack. Violence. Lust. Degradation of the human body and spirit on every page! Wotan the false god did not stroll out of hades unbidden; he felt a summons. Had the boy Joey Willem not taken the seven-league boots, Wotan would today be striding the Earth, preparing his reign.

"But he wants to rule Earth who cannot even guide his own daughter. Hear this, auntie. For five hundred years, by the will of her own father, Brunnhilde lay on a cold, marble slab, dreaming. Of what would a healthy girl dream ..."

God's aunt nearly blurted out, "A new winter coat," but kept her mouth shut.

" ... but a hero to come for her?" God continued. "And Brunnhilde is a large, healthy, fun-loving girl! In five hundred years of dreaming, her expectations have magnified beyond all reasonable bounds. Yes, whether she finds her hero or not, Wotan will have his hands full." God laughed, a belly-laugh such as accompanies the ending of a great responsi-bility.

"I put a part of Me into every human born; apparently it is Wotan they want. Well, let them have a taste of him. But enough of that; how do you like my disguise?"

God's aunt tapped his walking stick.

"From the tree of life."

"But why the drunkenness?"

"Myron Blunger," was the solemn reply. "In the darkness of the back corridor of the Inn, frightened and disheartened, he wondered if I had ever put Myself into serious trouble, and what effect that might have on My attitude toward humans.

"I accepted the challenge. I have done just that, disguised as a defrocked, somewhat inebriated attorney.

"So I have wandered over the land, talking with plain folk about business and taxes, joining a congregation of fancy-dressed people at prayer, sitting in on a course on ethics. I have been threatened for money I did not possess, ignored when begging for food, wounded in a drug-related crossfire, offered perversions of body and spirit ..."

God raised His right hand and thundered, "*I destroyed Sodom and Gomorroh with fire for lesser evils than I have experienced in this place!*"

His aunt, terrified that He might destroy Everything, took His hand and slowly, gently lowered it. Though not permanently damaged in body—and she had little doubt that He had rewarded the miscreants with prompt and thorough Judgement—her Nephew was hurt more deeply than a human could ever understand. Rejected, denied by those he loved most dearly, and facing replacement by an *ersatz* god. Not for the first time. Oh, He could destroy Wotan with the wave of a finger, but what would that prove? Another pretender would come along.

"Too much ego?" God's aunt asked, as another woman might suggest, "Too much salt?" in discussing a recipe.

"Ego is in the genes," her Nephew replied. "It was necessary, that mankind compete successfully. But they were supposed to learn humility. Life has gotten out of balance. I designed mankind with free will, but invariably he has hooked to the left."

"Blunger . . ."

"I will not intervene on behalf of Blunger!" the Lord declared.

"Then I declare today my birthday!" God's aunt retorted. "In that book on etiquette, I found that an aunt—and especially a maiden aunt—is entitled to a birthday, complete with luncheon at a nice restaurant and presents. I have never had a birthday. So . . . today is my birthday."

The Lord God nodded reluctantly, suspecting a trap. "You are entitled to a birthday," He admitted. "What present would you like, auntie?"

Beneath her veil, God's aunt smiled. "I would like You to do something for Myron Blunger. I am not asking for a miracle! I saw him in that back corridor at the Inn; he was humping along pitifully, carrying a hot tureen of *cholent*. I couldn't be certain, but I think his soul had slipped out. He certainly wasn't all there! We must return him to his habitat, to the Bronx." She stopped walking; they were beside a department store and in the display windows were some very becoming winter coats.

God said, "Myron Blunger, descendant of Morris the Decent, is the most religious person I have encountered in this era. His religion, of course, is food, and he prays three times a day, and sometimes four, which is more than I can say for most folk.

"Perhaps I have devoted myself too much to golf and not enough to the doings of my children. Like his namesake, Myron Blunger did open My eyes to the dangers and temptations under which they dwell. And Myron Blunger brought forth laughter, in which I did take pleasure.

"I will not intervene, but I will test Myron, and if he passes, I will do him a kindness."

"What test?" God's aunt asked, uneasily.

"I will put Myron Blunger to the same test that the 'other' Moses passed easily."

"What test was that?" asked the woman in black. Had she created a great jeopardy for the poor, beset Bronxite?

"It is not difficult."

"You will frighten him."

"He will not know who I am."

"How many questions will you ask?" The woman in black was thinking of Rush's examination in *Hope and the Dragon*, which seemed endless. From the little she knew of Blunger, he could never pass such a test.

"One."

One question, to decide whether or not Mrs. Blunger becomes a widow. Yet, if it were an essay question, and the Lord gave part credit . . . "And how will he answer?"

"By one word. So we will again learn how Myron Blunger, descendant of Morris the Decent, compares with the 'other' Moses."

One word. So much for part credit, thought God's aunt.

She raised her staff to point at a nice, black coat with a velvet collar and a silk lining, but her Nephew declared, "These coats aren't for you, Auntie. This night will see an end, a finale to the Blunger affair. Tomorrow morning, after making My rounds, I shall play eighteen holes against Lucifer. No tricks, of course. Mind that you keep those curses locked tightly! Then I will meet you in front of Lord and Taylor in Manhattan.

"Take this." He put into his aunt's hand a key on a ring. An ignition key. And then He was gone.

For a long moment, the woman in black stood at the window, examining the styles and wondering what Lord and Taylor might be showing.

But her Nephew had said the word *finale*. The affair was coming to a conclusion! And she'd been given the key to the yellow schoolbus that served the Muchnesses. Why?

She had to get north! With no money for carfare, God's aunt started walking toward Julia's Frocks and Socks, reaching that shop just as the owner was putting out the lights. Demanding the use of the facilities in a no-nonsense voice, she headed toward the back dressing room, bypassed the formality of purchasing a dress—God's aunt had travelled gratis via *Lightspeed* for centuries. It was one of her perks.

As she stepped into the mirror and felt the wind take hold, she regretted having mentioned Blunger's name. After all he'd been through, what kind of test would her Nephew subject him to? And what if he didn't pass?

CONVERGENCE

I am cold.

There are no lifeberries. While I slept, the bushes were scavanged. My belly is shrunken; my throat dry as old bones. I am beyond hunger. Night and the wind rule the valley.

The youth comes this way.

*   *   *

Joey Willem dropped to the ground and lay curled up, shivering from cold, night-damp and fear. Maybe he should have stayed on the road, but hiking across the open field was less scary than having the woods just a few yards to his side. Also, there was thunder over the Cliff of Night. At least, it sounded like thunder, though Joey saw no lightning.

This was probably a short-cut if he just kept the moon to his right. This must be the darkest night of the year, he thought. The wind seemed to be dying down. Still, he was shivering. Why were there dry leaves in a field? Were the woods that close?

OOO . . . eee . . .

He jumped to his feet. It came from behind and to the left. It had to be the wind, starting up again. By sheer determination, the boy fought off another round of the shivers. But they'd come again, Joey knew. And again. Up on the Saddle, the wind must be fierce! The jacket wasn't enough; he needed his sweater, also. Gritting his teeth, he removed his jacket as fast as he could and grabbed from his knapsack the woolen turtleneck Aunt Loretta had knitted special for him, pulling it over his head. One sleeve on, the other . . . where was it? Everywhere he thrust his fisted hand it encountered material and where was the headhole? Frustration and fear escaped his mouth in the form of a muffled cry.

Suddenly leaves were rustling behind him and to the left. He stood still, trapped within the heavy-knit sweater. Trembling but afraid to give in to panic, he forced himself to probe for the sleeve opening. He found it! He yanked the sweater down, felt his head pop through the tight neck-opening and rammed his arms into the jacket sleeves.

CRASH!

Now it was close by! Silence, then a gutteral throat-noise and a loud rustle of leaves . . . something large was following him! Joey snatched up his knapsack and jacket and ran blindly. A little mewing sound rose as high as his throat but only got out in pieces with each labored exhalation. His legs pumped and his arms beat the air; the knapsack swung this way and that and Joey didn't dare look back at whatever was chasing him.

Everyone knew that animals could smell fear. He could hear his heart beating, pumping . . .

The thing behind him could hear it, too, and to that thing he was food! Food! He hadn't asked Groff what dragons ate! That wasn't one of Miss Wally's interview questions, was it? It should have been.

Cold was streaming through the knitting-holes in the sweater; without breaking stride, he managed to shove his hands into the jacket sleeves.

OOO—eee!

He dashed to the right, to the left and then something had him by the ankle and he went down hard and now there was grunting and the crackle of dry leaves. Instinctively he tucked himself into a tight ball, his arms protecting his closed eyes. He whimpered, bit his lips. Whatever had him hadn't started to chew or

bite; it was just holding him! It. Did dragons play with their vic-
tims before eating them? Yanking the flashlight from his knapsack, he flashed it just for an instant, his heart stopped from pure
terror.

"Joey!"

Something very large towered over him. It was Brunnhilde
Valkyrie! "It's you!" he cried, joyously.

"Why, it's the boy Joey out dragon-hunting!" Brunnhilde said,
stooping down. "But why are you lying down; you will not find a
dragon in the grass. You must call. *OOO—eee*!"

"Something's got m . . . me by the ankle," the boy sobbed,
tears streaming freely now that he'd been found. It took all his
courage to turn on the flashlight and shine it on his trapped ankle.

"It is wires," said the Valkyrie. "Just [*choost*] a fence got you."
She pulled the wires apart, freeing Joey's leg. "That is better?"

"I . . . I guess so," Joey admitted, steeling himself for a scold-
ing as he stood up and put his weight on the ankle. After a long
minute, he said, "I ran away, you know. I have to find Dragon
Groff. Everyone thinks I'm a liar, that there is no such thing as a
dragon."

"And what will you do when you find him?" asked the giantess as she strode ahead, her eyes scanning the area between the
mountains.

"I . . . I'll talk with him again. I'll ask him to fly down the
valley and over to the village. Just once! During recess! He spoke to
me, once. He really did," Joey said as he hurried along beside the
Valkyrie, three steps to one of hers.

"I went up to pick lifeberries for Aunt Loretta, but there were
almost none left, just small ones. While I was picking them, he
spoke to me from where I couldn't see him. He asked me to leave
them for him. He said they were his. I was so . . ."

"Frightened? Of course you were," said the Valkyrie, placing
her hand on the boy's shoulder as they rejoined the road and continued north. From time to time, she thumped the butt of
Wildschweinblutmeister into the dirt.

"He didn't exactly *tell* me that he was a *dragon*, you know," Joey admitted. "He *showed* me that, with pictures."

"Uh, huh," grunted Brunnhilde. "What does Dragon Groff look like? Is he very large?"

Joey shuddered. "Bigger than . . . an elephant!"

"And how large is an elephant?" Brunnhilde asked.

"You've never seen an elephant?" Joey asked, surprised. Back in the Bronx he'd been to the zoo, once. It pleased him that he knew something that this enormous and fearless woman didn't.

"No," she said. "But I have seen a dragon. Fafnir. But I did not kill that one."

"Well," Joey said, "Dragon Groff's teeth are as long as . . . as my arm. And he spits fire but not at me. We're . . . friends." The Valkyrie found Joey's little hand, and enveloped and warmed it.

They continued in silence until Brunnhilde said, "You would not like to see Dragon Groff harmed, then. It is your friend."

Joey nodded.

"So," she said, but kept her thoughts to herself. "We will see."

The road started to rise; they had reached the lower foothills of the Dromedary Mountains. The cutoff to Bumbler's Pass was behind them and from that point, Broco Way diminished to a narrow dirt lane that zig-zagged through dense woods.

The ascent steepened and now, to their right and below, the open fields of the Broco landhold shone cold and white. To their left and up the mountainside, the woods was so dense, the blackness so absolute it hurt the eyes to try to penetrate it, even with the flashlight held out front. The road ahead was a kinetic patchwork of silver and black, not unlike a roadside warning of danger ahead. The way back was equally forbidding.

As they started up the Glen Trail, the entire sky flashed violet. Joey gripped Brunnhilde's hand tightly.

The halftrack prowled in its *Whisper-glide* mode, in which horsepower was traded for silence by an arrangement of heavy-duty mufflers. The road ahead was scanned, not by headlights, but by high-resolution radar. No external light, no sound revealed the progress of the vehicle. So smoothly did it ride that when Broco demanded that Trenton Interface follow the boy off the road and across the open field, the major domo could only rationalize his refusal by claiming that dirt or damp would damage delicate electronic instruments mounted in the underchassis. It pained him to lie to Mr. Broco; of course, the halftrack could, if necessary, wade through quicksand. Had Mr. Broco insisted that they chance it, the major domo would have disobeyed, asserting with convincing reluctance that the valleymaster's medical balance was so delicate that even his venturing outfit would not spare his internal organs possibly fatal accelerations or collisions. The truth, which Trenton could not speak at all cost, was that by keeping to the road, Trenton hoped to prolong the chase and his beloved master's last shot at life.

It was important that Mr. Broco participate in the venture, thus his position as gunner-navigator, his responsibility to track the boy by infrared and keep a record of the relative coordinates, preparatory to a surprise interception. Broco's adrenalin surged when, increasing the beamwidth, he discovered a second white blob on his monitor screen coming up from the lower left. This second blob was more intense than the first, indicating a larger source of heat energy. The second, larger blob was advancing on the first, which had stopped moving. They merged, then continued together, angling back toward the road. Good old Trenton, anticipating that they should stick to the road! Genius!

It was time for the capture! Nab them both at once! Broco scanned the command panel before him, thrilling at the awesome power that was his to unleash at the mere touch of a button.

Laser-guided armor-piercing rockets. Fore and aft Scatterblast for crowd dispersal. Computer-controlled Sequential Grenade launchers! Smoke dispersal cannisters . . .

Broco guided his forefinger over the array, found *Intercom* to Driver, stabbed it, pulled the overhead mike to his lips.

"Gunner to driver, gunner to driver," he intoned, thrilling at the very sound of the word *gunner.* "Projected interception coordinates two—zero—niner, one—three—three. ETA twenty three niner, repeat; ETA twenty three niner. Over."

Trenton Interface brushed away a tear that had started down the cheek out of his master's field of view. Trenton Interface's lachrymal glands had so seldom been called upon to deliver that the sudden appearance of a tear nearly caused him to veer off the road. What a tragic end to a builder of industry, a creator in his own right, a commander of thousands.

Laser-guided armor-piercing rockets! Fore and aft Scatterblast for crowd dispersal!

All nonsense. A dummy panel of buttons that pressed, would produce nothing more destructive than impressive sound effects, some flashes of light and appropriate roars as imaginary rockets blasted off, as an audio tape simulated the chatter and growl of motorized, small-calibre machine guns swivelling around to wreak destruction. The halftrack had been designed by Lucien Broco in his freewheeling heyday, when his secret and unfriendly takeover of an international chemical cartel had triggered the first sign of paranoia. Trenton had quietly ordered the armament modifications, that the valleymaster might play soldier without doing harm to himself or others. The vehicle had never been used until this night, certainly the last night of Lucien Broco's life. The childish delight on Broco's face tore at Trenton's heart.

Mr. Broco expected, "Received, over and out," but something odd and unexpected had suddenly taken Trenton's attention. He put the vehicle on automatic, in which mode it slowed to a cautious five miles per hour, computer-coupled side-scanning radars taking over the steering. The screen before him revealed the same two blobs that Broco was calling to his attention. Plus another blob, so faint that it was barely distinguishable from background noise, beside the road some hundred yards ahead. Something there was alive, but motionless. Trenton's hand on the steering wheel returned control of the halftrack to him. His eyes alternately darted from the screen to the windshield until the heat-radiating object was mere yards away.

If it was a fox or racoon, it must be nearly dead. Braking to a halt, Trenton opened his door, dropped to the ground and crossed the road. Very quickly he spied a pile of leaves and beneath it, the source of the faint heat radiation: a tiny figure on the ground, asleep, hurt or near death from exposure. He dropped to his knees, picked it up . . . it was a child! An impossibly small girl child buried within a cloak, half frozen, unconscious! Her arm moved! She was alive! Bundling her within the cloak and holding her to his chest, he carried her into the halftrack, placed her in front of the heater vent and turned it on high.

"What's that you've got?" Broco asked, peeling back the hood of the cloak to uncover a beautiful chalk-white face framed by a tangled mass of yellow hair.

"I'm not sure. Very small." It was too mature of form to be a child, too slight of build to be human, but Trenton kept his thoughts to himself.

She stirred; the cloak fell away. Though near death from exposure, the little one was gripping a blue book in both hands. Unhitching his safety harness, Lucien Broco bent over the still form and breathed warm air onto her little hands. Then he opened an ampoule of lifeberry serum and put it to her lips.

Gradually Rush stirred more and more until, though her eyes were still closed, her lips parted and words long suppressed began tumbling out . . .

"Tell Miki . . . Joey's gone . . . Dragon Groff . . . . " and more and more until Broco and his major domo had pieced together a plausible account of why the boy had run off and where he was headed. Ecstatic, Broco refastened his harness.

"North to the Saddle, man!" Broco demanded. "But quietly, quietly . . . we don't want to startle Dragon Groff, do we? Uunngh!"

"What was that?" Trenton snapped, instantly alert for the dreaded stroke or heart attack.

"Nothing," Broco said. "Just . . . an odd sensation, as though a brush had whisked across my mind. Move out! Get going!"

But Lucien Broco's eyes stared blindly at a point in space beyond his monitor screen and his dry lips were working as though endeavoring to frame words that would not come out. Something—a secret pain? an old guilt?—had brought terror to the old man.

Trenton wondered whether he should head back to the house for medical treatment, but if the quest ended here, Broco would surely fail. And the girl-child was coming around quickly now; she was looking around the interior of the halftrack with huge eyes, though she said nothing. Trenton Interface had no choice but to throw the transmission into Drive and continue the venture, though he was careful to lag behind the two white blobs, who had crossed the field together and were now climbing up the Glen Trail, according to the image on his monitor.

As he drove, Lucien Broco turned on the short-wave radio and snapped instructions to Henchman Gribbs, second in command to Trenton Interface. The orchestra was to be assembled at once and marched along the rim of the Cliff of Day, entering the Saddle from the eastern side. Pipes, muffled drums, trumpets, the battletuba . . . Lucien Broco's ascension through the portal into heaven was to be accompanied by appropriate music.

*   *   *

This valley was created with cliffs and mountains to mark Day and Night, Good and Evil, Passage and Denial, Hope and Despair, Life and Death.

He made for me a hidden place in the mountains wherein I

might dwell and He charged me to rule over the valley, and I have faithfully done so.

Now the fruit of life has been taken, leaving not even a merciful tithe, and he who ordered this thing that he might live forever, comes this way.

I, Dragon Groff, keeper of the barrier, have swept his mind and found an abundance of greed and human arrogance. I await him.

I await all of them.

Even Myron Blunger.

ESFANDIARY

"NO—MORE—CHOPPED—LIVER—HELP!

"NO—MORE—CHOPPED—LIVER—HELP!" shouted Myron Blunger.

With his right leg he kicked and swung and pushed at the tusked, long-snouted creature whose jaws were clamped firmly on his left foot! It was slowly, inexorably pulling him into a dark thicket of malodorous, cabbage-like vegetation and leafless, black thorn-bushes.

"Help!" he screamed. The creature snorted, braced itself and tugged him another half-yard. Now only Myron Blunger's head and shoulders were outside the perimeter of the beast's little patch of territory. Blunger whacked repeatedly at the creature's snout with the heel of his left shoe, which the pig-thing had ripped off his foot and discarded with a grunt. As his left hand wielded the shoe, his right hand clawed the ground in search of a strong root or a bush; *something* to anchor him! His face slid into the shadow of a bush. He smashed and whacked and wished he held a good old rock in his hand instead of a shoe. And then his right hand did slide across a palm-sized rock. He tore it from the ground, raised it above his head. Roaring "NO MORE CHOPPED LIVER!" Myron Blunger brought it down upon the pig-head.

He was in Esfandiary, where belief is a power!

It stopped tugging for a moment, but didn't release him. Myron Blunger delivered another slam with the rock, followed by a counterwhack with the heel of the shoe, right over the thing's little red pig-eyes! It squealed but pulled all the harder and now

Blunger was deep in the thicket. The pain in his foot was unbearable.

The fate of most creatures is to be eaten alive.

Myron Blunger had read that somewhere, but he'd never *understood* it! There was so much he'd never really understood!

Blunger struck again, whacking this way, that way, every which way, looking for a sensitive spot on the beast's head, which was now filthy with mud, spittle and his own darkening blood! At one time, Myron Blunger would have passed out at the sight of it, but a double threshold had been crossed.

God Himself had recognized him! And given him a *benefit*!

And in shooting him in the *tuchus*, the Innkeeper had gone too far!

Blunger's ears picked up the thunder of the centaur's hooves pounding, pounding, but far away, too far away to do any good. It was up to him!

And then the air was split, rent by the *charge*! as sounded by the horn of Roland in that alien place. Again it sounded, and this time the creature released Blunger's foot and, sniffing and grunting, lifted its head. Blunger saw its curled tusks and rows of sharp teeth, saw its pig-eyes taking in the approaching enemy. Blunger's foot, gnawed and bloody, was immovable. Determinedly he lifted his right arm, sighted and flung the rock at the animal, catching it directly between its little red pig-eyes!

Grunting, it pulled back a few inches, glared at its prey and in those precious seconds, Windbreaker closed to within fifty yards . . . forty and the beat of his hooves drummed on the trail and now he was nearly upon them, the sword *Excalibur* whirling and flashing. The pig-thing squealed its anger, turned and bounded into the underbrush.

In the distance, something trumpeted its reply to Windbreaker's horn-blast. Something large. Very large.

The centaur bent at the waist, located Blunger in the half-light of the thicket, hauled him out and into his arms. Windbreaker immediately spun around and sped to the prostrate gnome.

Windbreaker laid Blunger on the ground beside Yin, who was sitting up, unharmed, though dazed and unfocussed. "What happened?" asked the gnome, weakly. Then, "Where is this?" as he pulled himself to his feet.

"Esfandiary, I guess," Windbreaker said, and he knelt and examined Blunger's leg and ankle, probing gently. Blunger's foot was bleeding, the flesh torn in numerous places. His ankle was bruised, swollen, possibly sprained, too tender to walk upon. Removing Blunger's trousers, he saw that the poor fellow's backside had been drilled by a bullet and was bleeding profusely. At the opening of the wound, a leech was gorging on a brand of blood it apparently couldn't get enough of. Windbreaker flicked the loathsome thing away; it landed on a tree trunk and remained there. Windbreaker proceeded to remove Blunger's undershirt and methodically tear it into strips, with which he cleansed the wound as best he could.

"A fine job I made of it!" the centaur grunted. "Your leg . . . is it broken?"

Myron Blunger gritted his teeth and exclaimed, "Broken? By a *woods-pig*? Hah!" Followed by, "I don't know. Maybe. Probably. It doesn't matter," he said stoically.

"I heard you call . . . something about chopped liver," Yin said. He had recovered sufficiently to do some scholarship; his notebook was out and he held a pencil stub. "What is the meaning of chopped liver?"

Blunger winced at the pain. "No more . . . chopped . . . liver," he said. "Chopped liver means someone who always gets pushed around. My whole life, I'm chopped liver. Never made chief librarian or even adult reference, always signing over my pay to a landlord, no money for this, no money for that . . . no money to send the boys to summer camp . . .

"A failure, a failure, a failure! Sophie knows it. She wouldn't say a word, of course. No matter what, *not a word*! Oy, the woman's a saint!

"Made a few dollars on a book—the TV series gets cancelled! No paperback.

"And then . . . kidnapped. And why? For a pair of boots! But no more! I am going to give Joey Willem hope! God told me to! The boy needs me! Me! Myron Blunger! I am going to Upper Muchness to give my boy *hope!*"

With that, Myron Blunger looked about for the first time and shut up. He was at the edge of a trail about twenty feet wide. A trail through a jungle of unusual trees. Unusual because their green trunks glimmered with a million colors. Unusual because they were draped with a dense tangle of heavily flowered vines. The air was also unusual; it was tinted green. He took a quick look at his skin; it seemed tinted green, also! He sniffed cautiously, then inhaled deeply and felt light-headed, almost dizzy. The air was sweet, aromatic.

"This isn't a golf course," he said.

Windbreaker shook his head. "Must be a different part of Esfandiary. Well, let's go. Can you ride proper?" he asked Blunger, who still lay on the ground.

"Ride?" Blunger echoed, blankly. "Ride?" Automatically, Myron Blunger looked around as though expecting to see a taxi or, better, a subway. "Ride what?" he asked, weakly.

"Me!" the centaur snapped. "And fast; something answered when I blew the horn. Something big. Get on; we have to get out of here. Mount from the left side," he said, lowering himself to enable the partly crippled Blunger to climb up. With much help from the centaur and the gnome, Blunger struggled to his undamaged foot, hopped alongside Windbreaker, and amid much huffing, gurgling and yelping was lifted, hoisted, draped over the centaur's back in the flour-sack position. Windbreaker then lifted Yin to his shoulders.

Before moving out, the centaur happened to glance at the treetrunk to which the leech had stuck. Half the bloated thing was wiggling frantically; the other half, apparently embedded in the treetrunk, was being ingested. A closer examination of the treetrunk revealed a smooth, green, resinous sheath in which innumerable thousands of insect wings were stuck fast, embedded in pairs. Where the bodies had once been, there were only faint dimples in the sticky, resinous sheaths. Wind-breaker decided not to mention this phenomenon for fear of starting a panic.

Yin was no happier. Shuddering to find himself so far above the ground, the gnome clamped his hands to both sides of the centaur's head. About to close his eyes from fear, he noticed a length of vine less flowered than the other foliage, banded yellow and green, with a flat, orange head, two ruby eyes and a black, flicking tongue. Part of it was coiled about a section of vine with whose flowers its coloring blended perfectly; the front part was lowering itself directly at him. He screamed. The centaur side-stepped, nearly losing Blunger but avoiding the snake as it writhed furiously, then withdrew amid a rustling of vines.

Windbreaker slashed at the overhead foliage with *Excalibur* to prove to the terrified gnome (and himself) that the snake had departed, then looked about carefully, studying his options. The canopy of intertwined, heavily flowered vines and hidden dangers continued upward as far as he could see. What sunlight reached the ground was so diffused that there were no strong shadows.

Windbreaker shied toward the center of the trail and tried to think. He could go uptrail—the direction from which he'd come, or downtrail. Staring at the ground, he became aware of a series of large circular depressions at both sides of the trail. They were more than two feet across and at least four inches deep in firm soil. Footprints, though such was their symmetry that the centaur couldn't determine their direction. Windbreaker didn't wish to burden Blunger with uncertainty. *No . . . More . . . Chopped . . . Liver!* Blunger had picked a fine time to renounce what apparently was his religion.

Windbreaker trotted some distance in the direction from which he'd come, but found no sign of the door to the Inn. Some hundreds of yards further, the trail sloped downward and the centaur found himself sinking more deeply into softer soil. Finally he halted, looking ahead at a dark, fetid marsh, into which the circular tracks disappeared. Though he heard no roar or hiss, the very silence of the place was oppressive; the centaur would go no further. Also, he was fetlock-deep in mud and sinking.

That left down-trail, and no direction for retreat, should that become necessary. He turned and hurriedly retraced his steps. The path was straight as far as he could see, though visibility was only a hundred yards or so before details were lost in the green haze. He proceeded at a slow, cautious trot.

Myron Blunger's belly was taking a pounding. "NO—MORE—CHOPPED—LIVER!" he muttered. "I will not ride draped like a sack of herring! I will ride like a *mensch*!"

Calling a brief halt, Blunger slid his body parallel with the centaur's, carefully eased his wounded leg over the ridge of Windbreaker's back and pulled himself erect. As the centaur broke into a trot, Blunger leaned forward and grabbed Windbreaker's waist in a desperate bear-hug. Windbreaker's attempt to concentrate on his footing was made more difficult by Blunger, who was generating a large amount of noise, even for a neophyte to riding. Each step elicited a short cry of pain.

Unfortunately, Myron Blunger had corroborated his own hypothesis regarding testicle placement and horsemanship, as explained to the charming Adele in the park, half a lifetime ago. The clutching of the centaur's waist required that he ride with a pronounced forward tilt, and such was the location of his most sensitive parts that, pressed between centaur and rider, they were taking great punishment. The tenderness of his posterior made it impossible to ride erect, like the English princes and dukes who played polo for a living.

Blunger's agony finally forced the centaur to take action. He called to his passenger, "Press your knees into my sides—more firmly! Don't worry, it doesn't hurt! The literature is full of horses from which even a Blunger from the Bronx cannot, repeat cannot physically fall off," he declared. "Shadowfax, for one. And Pegasus, probably.

"Trust me . . . and don't be so rigid; bounce a little.

"There you go . . ."

As the centaur instructed Blunger in the art of posting, Yin considered the air. It was warm, moist and alive; what made it pale green were tiny motes, gnats, winged spores . . . whatever . . . they darted and zipped silently, ceaselessly in all directions. Listening, he became aware of harsh screeches, long, wavering hoots, piercing whistles, chuffing grunts from the underbrush . . . and then a prolonged, challenging roar that set his hairs on end. Whatever had made that noise was too close. Even if it were a hundred miles away, it was too close.

Something wet and sticky dropped on Windbreaker's shoulder; startled, the centaur looked up and saw a branch-stump with a splintered end, leaking sap. And another, further along. Orange sap. Fresh sap. This trail had been smashed through the jungle . . . and not long ago. By an unimaginably huge, ponderous creature. Had it meandered through the jungle, munching vegetation? Or had it been in flight? The centaur saw no stripped branches, no ends of vines a-dangling, no indications of a placid luncheon stroll. The thing was beyond imagination in size, and it had been driven.

Studying the trail more closely, Windbreaker noticed another set of tracks. Three-toed, with a heel spur; not so large or deep as the first set, but large enough and deep enough . . . they ran down the center of the trail, and had deep depressions at the front end. Claws. Large claws. From their size and spacing, the creature that had left them was much larger than a centaur. Centaurs are built for brief charges on open plains and meadows, not for slogging through swamps or racing along forest trails. Against whatever had left those tracks, Windbreaker had no chance.

Listening intently, the centaur moved ahead slowly, cautiously. He was weary, burdened with over two hundred pounds of deadweight. He was in alien territory and Blunger was leaving a trail of blood. The centaur's right hand gripped the handle of *Excalibur*, but would King Arthur's sword obey him? In his left hand was the horn of Roland, which was reputed to possess mystic powers when blown by a hero. But Windbreaker was not yet a hero, was he?

And despite Windbreaker's assurances, Blunger was likely to fall off at the slightest chance of pace or direction.

They proceeded slowly, Windbreaker carefully avoiding the depressions left by the hunter and its prey. The trail began to twist and double back, as a hunted creature might do to throw off its pursuer. After completing a doubling-back, he saw another of the boar-like things by the trail snuffling at a dark pool, from which vapor was rising. Blood.

The blood of whatever had made this trail was still hot.

Windbreaker's head swivelled warily from side to side. And then he heard it. A roar and a prolonged, mammoth bellow that ended in a horrible bubbling gurgle. Windbreaker stopped abruptly. The sound came from directly ahead, but the centaur was almost sure he'd heard another, answering sound. From behind. He turned, but saw nothing on the trail. Forward, then, slowly, with *Excalibur* in hand.

Meanwhile, another problem had occurred to Yin. It was of a delicate nature and, bending down from his shoulder perch, he spoke to Windbreaker in a low voice. "About this curse . . ." he started.

"What about it?" Windbreaker snapped. Picking his way along a treacherous, unfamiliar path in an unknown direction while looking out for predators was quite enough without being distracted by items of a personal nature.

"It occurs to me," Yin said in a conversational tone with hardly an overtone of strain, "that if you should be put to a truly heroic test . . . not that you haven't done most excellently . . ."

"Thank you," Windbreaker said, drily. "Were you not on my shoulders, I would kick you into next week."

"Again, sorry, but . . . suppose you met the accepted standards for heroism and the curse were lifted. If you revert to human form . . . on the spot . . . here and now . . . we'd all find ourselves . . . in a difficult situation, if you catch my drift. Including yourself. Up the creek without a canoe, so to speak. Does your curse revert immediately? Or . . . is there a waiting period? Perhaps a committee that has to pass on it?"

The centaur rounded a curve and studied the path ahead before replying, "I don't know." In fact, the thought had never occurred to him.

"You don't know," the gnome mused in what he believed a scholarly tone. "Now . . . now I really understand the significance of time. Suppose . . . something . . . large and dangerous suddenly appeared . . . and you fought it with utmost bravery and skill until sunset . . . and won, that might get you converted to human form on the spot."

"We'd have to . . . Oy! . . . to walk the rest of the way!" Blunger exclaimed, sensing that an important conversation was taking place, and dispensing with his posting in order to listen in.

"I suppose so," Windbreaker said. *Walk the rest of the way!* The gnome's sentence produced a very profound alarm in the centaur, which he decided to keep to himself. How the devil did bipeds walk, anyway? More importantly, how did they manage running? How did they balance themselves? In truth, he didn't remember much of his earliest days, as a child walking and running over the family estate in Greece. He'd have to learn all over again. Here. On the job, in dinosaur-infested Esfandiary. It was a no-win situation!

"And speaking of the way, do we know where we're headed?" Blunger asked.

Thank you, Windbreaker thought.

"We're . . . following the trail," Yin said as positively as possible, sensing a trace of panic in Blunger's voice and feeling a sudden tension in the centaur.

Windbreaker added, rather uncertainly, "It's bound to bring us somewhere."

"Oh." Blunger said, and as he bounced up and down on Windbreaker's back, he said, "There was a time . . . oy! . . . when I would have given up. Oy! I would have said, What's the point? Everything and everyone is against me! Oy! If I lean forward I crush my balls. Oy! Posting is like hitting my busted ass . . . oy! . . . with a hammer! If I lean back . . . oy! . . . I'm going to fall off and break my neck.

"The Innkeeper turned against me. Joey Willem doesn't obey . . . Ah! . . . If God wanted me to lose twenty pounds, why did He invent *cholent*? And what about . . . Elflet Rush and Dragon Groff? And Lucien Broco . . . oy! and the Hawkinses and Joey Willem and Trenton Interface? Oy! With no writing going on, they're stuck!"

"I don't think so," Yin said quietly.

"Oh? So who . . . how . . . " He fell mute.

"Exactly. They've been charting their own course for some time now."

At that moment, it became apparent to all three travellers that they were being followed.

There are two schools of thought on the method used by *Tyrranosaurus Rex* to capture prey. According to one theory, the King of Dinosaurs simply waited, hidden in high foliage beside a path, perhaps near a water hole, and let the prey come within lunging distance. On the other hand, *Tyrranosaurus Rex* is generally portrayed with extremely muscular hind legs, such as sprinters develop. The possibility that both theories are correct, that tyrranosaurs, male and female together, acted in pairs, one driving the prey forward, one lurking by the trail ahead, does not seem to have occurred to researchers.

Windbreaker had just stepped cautiously around a bend in the trail and taken a dozen steps when he heard, from the rear and above, a roar designed to paralyze. To look back would be to surrender; he broke into a full gallop, simultaneously watching the trail lest he step into a hole and break his leg, constantly adjusting his direction so as to keep Blunger's center of gravity roughly above his back and blowing furiously on the horn of Roland. After some two hundred yards, he glanced back without breaking stride and saw, some hundred yards away, the ultimate predator. Its jaws were agape and its dagger-like teeth were capable of scissoring him right through the middle with one snap and it was smiling a reptilian smile as it bounded confidently along. The creature's scaly brown head was mounted upon a short, muscular neck and the monster was coming at a steady pace. Its smallish but lethal-looking foreclaws were pressed into its plated body. It was apparently content to keep him in sight, as it was not making any effort to catch up with him.

Passing the horn up to Yin, the centaur used his free hand to hold Blunger in place; the fool was slipping and sliding this way and that and whooping and howling! If he fell off now, he'd be very lucky to break his neck quickly and cleanly, considering the alternative! Oh, to have Pegasus's wings! Windbreaker wished as he virtually flew along the path, mouth open wide. There was no sidepath, no choice but to try to outrun the monster. Windbreaker ran as never before and still there was a steady *thumpa, thumpa* from behind and then another deafening bellow, as if the thing were taunting him, challenging him to run faster, faster!

And then the trail widened into an arena, a wide clearing of fallen, blood-soaked trees and crushed undergrowth smashed out of the jungle by a creature so enormous that Blunger swung his head one hundred eighty degrees in taking in its full expanse from its grey, boulder-like head to its tail, which vanished into the jungle. It lay on its side, its head jerking and rolling on the ground and its body heaving and pulsing spasmodically as its poor, dumb heart pumped rivers of crimson blood into the dirt through countless gaping wounds. Past groaning, it was barely able to hiss its final, shallow breaths, though its tail was still lashing from side to side. It would not do to get in the way of that appendage. Windbreaker pulled to a halt and backed up to the edge of the clearing. As he'd feared, from behind the bulk of the dying mountain rose another head, a large, scaly, brown head grinning with white dagger-teeth dripping blood and chunks of flesh. Another tyrannosaur! The unfortunate, vegetarian Seismosaurus, after having been chased through the jungle until too weary to take another step, had been pulled down and was being consumed alive!

In a flash, Windbreaker realized the strategy of the carnivores!

Unable to maintain a sprinter's pace for long, they had only to locate one of the behemoths outside the safety of its swamp, cut off its retreat and drive it through the jungle, creating a hunting channel for future prey. No sooner had Windbreaker figured that out than the first beast appeared at the only opening to the clearing and he heard the heavy clump, clump of its mate rounding the carcass, preparing to close in from the opposite side. The jungle was impenetrable. Windbreaker wheeled about to face the original monster, which had started to advance into the clearing. Its forepaws were still folded, its jaws open wide, its head tilted slightly as it stepped forward.

Grabbing Yin from his shoulder, he pressed the gnome to his chest with one hand, while with the other he held *Excalibur* straight out before him. "Get your head down and hold on tight, Blunger!" he said between clenched teeth. "We're going to find out what's in me, if anything!" And with that, he sucked his lungs full of the foul air and charged directly at the monster blocking the trail. It reared up, its foreclaws extended and slashing, and from its throat came a volcanic roar. Windbreaker galloped directly at it, then, as it started to lower its head to bring its dagger-teeth into play, the centaur bent head and chest nearly horizontal and skittered directly between the monster's legs, slashing at the base of its tail as he passed through. The monster bellowed and its mighty tail lifted high in the air, then whipped down to crush this pesky nuisance. But Windbreaker had already swung to the left and the three thousand pound whip of bone and muscle smashed into the earth several feet to his right. At that instant, the centaur gathered his remaining strength and leaped, soaring high into the air, just clearing the tail as it lashed sideways. Landing beyond it, he leaped ahead. Behind him, the dinosaur turned and roared its rage.

Windbreaker dashed along the trail several hundred yards, then slowed to a canter, then a trot, then halted altogether and splayed his legs outward in a rest position, utterly exhausted.

"Thanks God," someone said.

Windbreaker, Yin and Myron Blunger turned and stared at an

apparition in the center of the trail. It was Tom, Blunger's soul! "There's no time to spare!" Tom cried. "I've been searching for you! Come; we have to get out of this Esfandiary! We have to get to Upper Muchness!"

"How?" chorused the three.

"First, you and I have to rejoin!" Tom said. "Think positive thoughts!" And with a loud *Pop* and a whirl of color, Blunger's soul vanished. At the same instant, Blunger felt an electric shock course through his body.

"Wow!" he cried. And then he knew! He closed his eyes, concentrated on the Lord's golf course. A gentle hill was behind him, and in the distance, a water trap. He recalled the smell of the grass, the blue of the sky, a breeze from the left. He concentrated."

Somewhere, not distant enough, he could hear a dinosaur bellow.

This was the Innkeeper's Esfandiary; he had to overcome that, he had to *be* in his own Esfandiary. His jaws clenched, he concentrated. The ground shook. Sweat poured down his face.

He concentrated.

Then he opened his eyes, and there was the Lord's golf course before him! He was by the water trap, which was the size of a small lake. Myron Blunger gratefully swung/fell to the ground with a grunt and lay prostrate, but entire, body and soul together.

Blowing the horn of Roland in lieu of anesthesia, Myron Blunger lay steady as Yin and Windbreaker set about removing the foreign material from Blunger's backside, using the tip of *Excalibur* as a scalpel. The wound was flushed with water from God's water trap, which *had* to be pure, and soon, they bound up Blunger's backside to let healing commence. It was some time, however, before Blunger felt able to mount Windbreaker, and the only position he could tolerate was the 'flour sack', which elicited a constant stream of 'oofs' as the trio headed toward the downed barrier, the crossing of which would bring them to the Saddle at the head of the valley of Upper Muchness, shortly before midnight.

Windbreaker focussed on the terrain, Yin took advantage of the respite to wonder how this experience might be written up from a scholarly viewpoint, for publication.

Myron Blunger, adjusting for his flour-sack perspective, concentrated on the appearance of the Saddle between the Dromedaries. With the barrier down, there was no reason why, with his new confidence, he could not get them there in one mighty burst of belief.

He did, and just in time.

DRAGON GROFF

Needles of glaring moonlight reflected from bits of quartz embedded in the granite of the Saddle. Blacknesses that might be cave openings, or shadows, or something else entirely. And a violet glare that originated somewhere north of the Saddle. All of these made Joey Willem's eyes ache as he peered cautiously from behind an old treestump at the edge of the lifeberry glen, searching for a glimpse of Dragon Groff.

Dragon Groff was up here, somewhere. Probably in a cavern cut deep into the heart of the mountain, a vast chamber with cold, damp walls. Brunnhilde Valkyrie had told him that the dragon Fingal dwelt in a cave fifty feet high! Joey shivered.

Groff's cavern was most likely at the western edge of the Saddle, where a nearly vertical wall of rock marked the rise of the mountain. The wall was streaked with obsidion, studded with deep shadows, any of which could mark the entrance to Groff's cavern. Joey's heart pounded as he visualized Dragon Groff emerging from his cavern onto the granite of the Saddle. First his head would emerge. Then his long neck and then his enormous bulk—much larger than an elephant's—and finally his whip tail. His wings would span . . . .

But where was he? From some of the openings, Joey was certain he saw sporadic flashes. Moon-dazzle? Or dragon fire? There was no use asking Brunnhilde; she was again reading that dumb letter.

Indeed, the Valkyrie had other things on her mind. Slipping a much-creased letter from her bosom, she held it up to the moonlight.

"Listen to this, Joey," she whispered. Her eyes glistened as she read:

> "'*Dearest Brunnhilde,*'
> "That is special, *nicht war*, Joey? '*Dearest!*'. . .

"Then he says:

> "*Thank Wotan I waited for you! I have just now learned of your five hundred year ordeal on the bed of stone, surrounded by fire, and your recent search for a held, a hero worthy of your passion for life! Know that your story has struck a resonance within my heart.*"

"Hmmm," to herself, then,

> " . . . *going each night to my bed alone, cursing my collection of rusting armor, my unscratched shield, my untried broadsword.*
>
> " . . . hearing of your beauty and character and immense physical strength, I have faith in you as in the sunrise, that we are kindred spirits, darling Brunnhilde. Our destinies are intertwined. Writing this is difficult, for my eager fingers caress the instrument that should be you, my dearest.
>
> . . . you are preparing to bid adieu to those glorious but confining breastplates, and welcome your held. It is time Wildschweinblutmeister was retired to a closet.
>
> Give my regards to your father, Wotan the god.
>
> your truly intended,
>
> Don Juan'

"Don Juan!" she exclaimed, folding the letter carefully along the creases and lovingly pressing it inside her breastplate. "Don. Donald. Frau Donald Juan! Oh, you are too young to understand such things."

To herself she thought, sadly, *And this is why I must take Dragon Groff, even if it makes the boy sad. Mein held is coming! Shall I greet him with a rabbit pelt for a dowry? Well, the boy must get over it in time, and the story of the taking of Dragon Groff will come in handy when he sets out to woo maidens.*

Joey Willem had no interest in a woman's letter carried next to the heart. He was listening fearfully for the voice of Dragon Groff. It had been one thing to talk with a friendly, shy dragon when the sun was high and he needed an interview for a school report; it was quite another to be up here on the Saddle on Halloween night with a gusting wind and hypnotic flashes of light. Were it not for the giantess, he would have turned back long ago. But he could not shame himself before her, nor have her think him a liar. Dragon Groff *did* exist!

"Hello?" Joey called tentatively.

"Hello!" boomed Brunnhilde, stepping out onto the plateau and hollering from between cupped hands, her spear nestled in the crook of her left arm. The sooner this was done and over, the better.

Joey shivered.

"Well, what do I see here?" Brunnhilde said, looking down at her feet. Joey Willem scrambled to her side. The giantess was studying parallel furrows in the rock of the plateau. Perhaps a foot deep. Easily a foot apart. At least ten feet long. Four of them. And off to the side, four more. In that pale moonlight, Joey saw that Brunnhilde's countenance, cheerful up until then, had grown serious.

"This I have seen never, not even by Fafnir," she said in a subdued voice, almost a whisper. "This is where your Dragon Groff digs his talons into the rock, while stretching in the sun like a cat. He is not so small, this one."

Joey took out his flashlight and flicked the beam on. It wavered as his hand shook. Even Brunnhilde's spear would not be much protection against something that can gouge solid rock, he knew.

The patches of black appeared to shift, creating illusions of movement in the shadows. Was that due to clouds moving? Or was that something slithering quietly down that dark fold in the mountainside? Was that shadow widening, as a cave opened right before his eyes?

"Groff?" he called out, in a thin, wavering voice.

Dragon Groff woke from a dream-reverie and sniffed the air. Warm-bloodeds were nearby. The memory of hunger surged from his shrunken stomachs, but he had no lifeberries, no saliva, no fire.

Again came a noise to tantalize him. "Groff!"

Weak, yellow light flashed across the opening of his den, but did not penetrate deeply enough to reveal him.

"They're still here!" shouted Joey, shining the pale flashlight beam on a cluster of half-shrivelled lifeberry fruits some dozen yards from the wall of rock.

"So," grunted Brunnhilde, gripping her spear tightly, keeping an eye out in all directions, wary of the tricks of dragons. "And what are these?"

"Lifeberries. When Groff called to me, I was in the lifeberry glen, picking whatever leftovers I could find. He asked for them, asked me to leave them behind. But . . ."

"But not to bring them to him," Brunnhilde said, her voice edged with doubt. "Nor did he come out for them. Why not?"

"Groff!" Joey shouted, tearfully. "Are you here? Answer me! It's me! Joey! Please, please!" Joey flashed his beam this way and that, high and low, wherever he saw a shadow that might be the cave-dwelling of Dragon Groff.

"Don't feed the dragon!" came a shrill screech from down the Glen Trail. Startled, Joey whirled about to see a lean elfin figure less than half as tall as himself, clad in a green cloak. The elflet—for Rush it was—stumbled onto the plateau, followed by two shadows, one supporting the other. The first carried a powerful electric torch in one hands, and over his shoulder was slung a double-barreled gun of odd design, compared with what the boy had seen in pictures in the library of the Inn.

The elvish one's green slippers were tattered from sharp rocks and thorns and she picked her way gingerly, painfully across the Saddle toward Joey. Halfway across, the creature paused, took a deep breath and recited a string of enticements from appendix I of the guidebook, applicable to males aged 8 to 12: "Ice cream . . . television . . . pizza and seven-layer-cake . . . time to go home."

Joey's beam revealed a lean, pale face that was scratched, smudged and tear-stained.

"Who are you?" Joey asked.

"Peter Pan. No, Rush Sore-Foot," sobbed the creature. "Elflet Rush. Oh, I am ruined, ruined. I talked. I have failed the examination." Then, with an effort, "Get away from the Saddle! Stay away from Groff!"

"Yes, leave Dragon Groff to us, eh, Trenton?" It was Mr. Broco, Joey realized! He was completely enclosed in an odd-looking hard-plastic suit, and a clear dome covered his head. Haltingly, he maneuvered his right hand until it found a miniature console built into the suit. He pressed a button; tripod legs shot out and down from his seat. A built-in chair. Mr. Interface helped him fall back gently until the tripod legs supported his weight. Mr. Interface played the electric torch over the terrain, then shined it directly into Joey's face, effectively blinding him.

"Now what's this about a dragon, Joey boy?" Broco asked in a syrupy voice.

There was no point in trying to run away, not from Trenton Interface. Joey Willem closed his mouth and clenched his teeth, determined not to speak.

"Dragon Groff!" Lucien Broco barked, his voice amplified by electronics built into his suit. Recovering his temper, he said, as sweetly as he could, "Trenton and I were out for a Halloween drive, looking for little ghosts and elves and witches to give candy to. And we happened to meet up with Mistress Rush, lying by the roadside, freezing to death. Well, the antidote for freezing, as everyone knows, is lifeberry serum, which I happened to have with me. We gave Mistress Rush a good dosing, and in turn, she told us all about Dragon Groff and your little excursion. She couldn't really help herself, could she?" he laughed.

"She said quite a bit, Joey," Trenton added. "The effect of lifeberry extract . . . on certain persons . . . is to stimulate speech."

Lucien Broco leaned forward toward Joey Willem. "Now, whoever she is, this Rush did spend some time in the Hawkins house just now, and that fool may have stuffed her head so full of his Theory that she doesn't know up from down. But I know you, Joey. We're friends. Joey, do you believe that there's a dragon in the neighborhood? An old dragon?"

Joey, feeling obligated to say something, opened his mouth just enough; Trenton swung the weapon around and squeezed a trigger; a jet of purple fluid shot into Joey's mouth. It was sweet wine and ether and purple fire from the inside of the sun, all together. Joey tried to spit it out, but most of it seemed to slip right down his throat. He gulped. Wheels of fire spun and burst in his head and he no longer controlled his sayings or doings. He nodded.

Brunnhilde, afire with thoughts of her *held*, had watched and listened to all this nonsense dispassionately. But by the second oscillation of Joey's head, she had torn the spray-weapon from Trenton's grasp and had hefted her spear menacingly. Trenton Interface, wisely, did not try to retrieve the spray-weapon.

"He's here. Somewhere," Joey said, miserably listening as the words spilled out of his mouth. He had no illusions as to Dragon Groff's fate if Mr. Broco had his way.

"Ah," Broco said, smiling. "And where is it . . . is he?"

"And what do you want of the dragon?" the Valkyrie asked, drily.

"The most precious thing. Time," Broco wheezed. "This dragon, if it exists at all, must be old. Very old. I am prepared to renounce all the hours of my life spent in the acquisition of wealth.

I want those hours back. I . . . need . . . more time!" Broco gasped this last, then fell back into his suit-chair, exhausted.

"*Yo, ho, ho* . . ."

Broco opened his eyes; the men's chorus of his orchestra! The schedule called for a triumphal oratorio to accompany his translation into heaven, or Esfandiary or whatever they called it. So they were tuning up.

"*Yo-ho-ho, and a bottle of rum!*"

Bottle of rum? Or was that *drums*? His hearing was slipping. What about the drums? Why didn't he hear drums? And where was the battle-tuba? Broco turned his head; he saw no ensemble assembled at the eastern side of the Saddle.

"*Fifteen men on the dead man's chest* . . ."

Over the north ridge and onto the Saddle came a ragged line of swarthy, hard-eyed men armed with cutlasses. Their leader was a one-legged, grizzled fellow with a green parrot on his shoulder and a pistol thrust into his trouser-belt.

Trenton Interface, weaponless, moved close to his employer. On Mr. Broco's chest-console was a red button that would summon the half-track, which they'd parked below the lifeberry glen that they might approach the Saddle in silence. But the halftrack would only come to them if that button were pressed! And the valleymaster seemed unaware of the band of thugs who were gathering around him.

Long John Silver recognized Joey Willem, and clapped his arm on the boy's shoulder, grinning.

"Long John Silver!" gasped the boy, recalling the pirate's treatment of Jim Hawkins in *Treasure Island*. If only he had those boots . . . but then he remembered that they didn't work in the valley. What would happen to him now? Mr. Broco was angry with him. Mr. Interface had no weapon and Brunnhilde was re-reading her stupid letter. If only Mr. Blunger were here, Joey wished. He'd know what to do!

Long John Silver had no difficulty figuring which of this party was the wealthy Lucien Broco. But apparently his arrival had interrupted something important; Long John decided to wait and see what developed. In the meanwhile, he would size up this very large and confident woman with the formidable spear. As Trenton Interface turned to confront the buccaneer, the powerful beam of the electric torch happened to flash into a deep crevice between two enormous slabs of fallen, interlocked granite and was reflected from the depths by a pair of green, vertically-slitted eyes no farther apart than those of . . .

"A lizard!" Broco gasped, who happened to be looking in the right direction. "There's our Dragon Groff! A damned, two-bit lizard!"

Nictating membranes closed over Groff's eyes; he blinked and tried to shrink farther into the crevice, but couldn't.

"Groff?" Joey cried, running to the crevice and trying to squeeze inside. Failing—it was too narrow—he turned and buried his face in Brunnhilde's mail skirt. "No! No! It's not him! Groff is huge and fierce, with fangs and claws!"

Lucien Broco, enraged, snatched the gun from Brunnhilde's hand and, pulling a second trigger, fired round after round of ampoule-loaded darts directly into the crevice. "Dragon Groff!" he screeched, switching triggers and sending a stream of purple fluid directly at the creature. "It's a fraud! A trick!"

Trenton Interface strode toward his master, bent as though to whisper in his ear, surruptitiously pressing the red button on Broco's console. Twice. Emergency! Interface stepped back.

From below the Saddle came a roar as the half-track came alive, located its master by means of the continuous short-wave tracking signal emitted from Broco's venture-suit. The onboard computer radar-scanned the terrain and calculated the fastest route that would bring it to Broco's side. Up the glen trail roared the machine, smashing and crunching bushes and scrub. It careened over the lip of the Saddle and slammed to the ground, its roof-mounted electric torches illuminating the plateau as the machine charged toward Lucien Broco. The pirates scattered as the halftrack closed in; it came to a halt, its doors flung open. Trenton Interface, in a single motion, took Broco in his arms, determined to get him into the safety of the halftrack at any cost to himself.

But Lucien Broco had no further interest in safety. He struggled and kicked and his fingers kept the trigger depressed; lifeberry concentrate continued to arc at the diminutive creature hiding in its little cave. "A real, live dragon, eh?" he snarled. "Not enough hide on him to make a wallet! Go ahead, Joey boy, talk to the great, big monster. Ask him about the dinosaurs and the mammoths and the old days in the valley!" Lucien Broco's tirade dissolved in a fit of coughing as the last of the lifeberry concentrate vanished down Dragon Groff's throat, which was now wide open. The vallymaster dropped the now-useless gun to the ground, turned to his major domo and snapped, "Get him out!"

Trenton Interface strapped Broco into the navigator's seat, took the wheel and gunned the motor. Joey sprang back; even Brunnhilde stepped aside as the halftrack ground up to the crevice and halted. Trenton Interface jumped down and analyzed the situation quickly.

"What are you going to do?" Joey cried, afraid for the creature inside that had pretended to be a dragon.

"Get it out," Trenton replied, his mechanical instincts taking over as he considered the forces that would be required to move the great slabs of rock that had evidently fallen together, imprisoning the creature. "Get it out and take it back with us." Mr. Broco wanted the lizard; whether for pet or profit wasn't Trenton's affair. Mr. Broco was disappointed. And Mr. Broco didn't take disappointment well.

The freeing-up would tax the power of the electric winch to the fullest, Interface judged; huge rocks had slid sideways and needed to be pulled apart. From the tool-chest he took a three-quarter inch steel cable and fastened it to the half-track's electric winch; the other end of the cable he snaked and fastened around what he judged to be the critical point in the cleft of rock, and climbed into the machine's cab. Gunning the engine, Interface activated the winch. The cable lost its slack, then began to tighten.

Some yards away, Long John Silver watched, learned and smiled. There were new things in the world, and folk who knew how to run them. This servant of Broco, for instance; he could come in right handy. Him and his machine. He might or might not want to go piratin', but he'd like as not shape up if he saw a flintlock at the head of his master. Ay, before this night ended, Mr. Lucien Broco would have himself a new partner.

The cable tightened. The breeze strummed it higher and higher in pitch as the tension increased. Long John Silver, by means of signs, winks and head-nods, deployed his men to where he would want them when the action broke.

Brunnhilde looked on sadly, oblivious to these foolish little men and their doings. She would have no dragon head as a dowry, after all. What would her *held* think? Rather than appear stupid, perhaps it were best if she terminated her vacation and returned to the Inn, to her marble slab and the ring of fire.

But the rope of steel was a marvel; never had the Valkyrie imagined such a wonderful thing! It sang higher and higher as the machine pulled on it. This was music she loved. Steel and wind and rocks about to crash! Oh, yes; the crevice could open slightly, freeing the poor little creature, or the rocks could slip and crunch together, crushing Groff flat and perhaps starting a landslide! *Gotterdammerung!* They might all be buried! So what else did she have to look forward to? Another five hundred years of exasperating, tantalizing, unfulfilled dreams? Death would be better than rejection by her *held* for lack of a dowry.

She laughed! With all this clamor of force—the singing cable, the groan of stressed rock—there *must* be a ring somewhere! She hummed along—*The Ride of the Valkyrie!*—she sang aloud— "*Yo ho ... Yo ho ...*" until she heard thunder in the mountains!

Boom!

Boom. Boom!

Not thunder, drums! She looked around, and there they were! Those musicians, the same travelling band that had entertained her with their parade the night she'd first eaten pizza, were filing onto the other side of the Saddle, with great drums and pipes and the battletuba!

She opened her mouth, held her spear that would never attain the title *Drachblutmeister* and sang The Ride!

Her sisters, the Valkyrie, would hear, and come on their flying stallions! How she longed to ride with them again!

There was a loud *crack* from the rock joint.

By the light of the electric torch, Joey Willem saw that the trapped creature was retreating; it would never get freed unless it pushed forward, unless it tried! He thrust his head into the crevice and found that the opening had increased slightly; now he could squeeze inside!

He did, wriggling, pressing, tearing the skin from his knees and elbows, ignoring the groan of rock, the dank stench and the darkness. He called to the creature, "Come on, Groff. It's okay, Groff. It's me, Joey. We're gonna get you out of here."

Joey Willem did what had to be done; bravely, he reached past the creature's open jaws and grabbed its scaly forelegs, one in each hand. Praying that it wouldn't turn on him, he pulled. Two of the pirates grabbed his ankles and tugged so hard he thought his feet would tear off!

Again a loud *crack* from the rock joint; now there was a bit more room. The creature was trying; its claws were digging into the solid rock, seeking purchase. From its open throat issued hoarse grunts alternating with piteous bleats. From outside there came a terrible screeching sound as the halftrack's treads slipped on the glassy obsidian. The cable slackened. One rock slipped and pressed into Joey's back. He closed his eyes but didn't lose his grip on the creature's forelegs. Rock splinters fell and the narrow gap filled with dust, and Joey Willem pulled harder.

Again the sound of a diesel motor being gunned and again

the rock groaned as the cable tightened and slowly, slowly the fissure widened. There was an ominous muffled *crunch*. "Now!" Joey screamed, and yanked the forelegs of the creature as hard as he could. It slid forward! He yanked again, and with a sudden jerk, boy and creature were out of the fissure and sprawled on the plateau of the Saddle.

Trenton Interface descended from the half-track, released the cable from the winch and jumped back as the rock that had held Dragon Groff captive crashed into the crevice. It is only common sense that one does not walk away from a system under stress; one never knows what will trigger relief of that stress.

The major domo then proceeded to examine the creature. From the tip of its narrow, green-scaled snout to the end of its tail, the thing measured no longer than a mid-sized alligator, which it resembled except that its legs did not bow outward and its jaw structure was narrower. Yet its scaly hide seemed loose, as though it had once been larger. Much larger. Its skull indicated a brain cavity disproportionately large for a creature so small. It opened its jaws, closed them on one of the half-rotten lifeberries that Joey had left on the Saddle and gulped it down, pit and all. Trenton saw that some of its teeth were missing and there were white blotches on its gums.

And its tail was horribly mangled. Clearly it had been caught in a rock-slide and pinned inside its den. There had been no rock-slide in the Saddle in Trenton's memory, which meant that Dragon Groff had been trapped in that crevice for over twenty years, probably subsisting on small animals that had ventured inside. And bugs, when there were no animals. And much of the time, nothing at all.

"Get that thing in the half-track," Broco snapped. "We'll find a use for Joey Hawkins's Dragon Groff! Maybe I'll make it into a wallet."

Joey Willem's side ached from where the rock had pressed into it. There was drying blood on his fingers; he wiped them on his pants. His eyes were watering from the rock-dust and dis-appointment.

Dragon Groff. What a joke! The *boom, boom* of the bass drum echoed from the cliffs as the band settled in and the battletuba struck up the triumphal march to which the valleymaster would ascend to heaven without the discomfort of dying. So angry and dejected was Lucien Broco that he didn't bother to dismiss them. Nor did he object when a one-legged pirate slipped quietly into the driver's seat, closed the door and bent his head toward the valleymaster's with a knowing wink.

And then there were drums from a different quarter. Loud drums. Battle drums. *BOOM! BOOM!* A horn sounded and a sheet of lightning lit the sky. Brunnhilde looked up and saw the outline of a man atop the Cliff of Night.

The Innkeeper? Was her vacation finished already? How nice that he had come for her, with drum music.

Another flash of lightning, and now her face paled.

Yes, atop the Cliff of Night was the one who had wakened her from slumber and sent her on vacation. But it was not the Inn-keeper! No! Even at that distance she saw that his left eye was covered by a dark patch.

It was her father! Wotan! On his head was a horned Viking helmet. Girded in bearskin and linked armor and a great-cloak that draped to the ground, he stood with his legs planted apart and regarded her coldly. In his hand was the trumpet Yvgr, which Loki had stolen from Darkalfheim.

And there, beside Wotan, were the rest of the Aesirgods: Loki and Balder and Hod and Tyr and Vidar . . . all of them, with their swords and their spears! Thor, with his hammer, and Bragi and Ull . . .

Again lightning flashed and Brunnhilde saw that behind the Aesirgods and pressing forward were long-armed trolls carrying axes and nail-studded maces, pale goblins, huge ogres bearing lengths of rope and behind them, white-whiskered frost giants clad in bearskins. They had been raised from their biers in the subcellar of the Inn by her father, though Brunnhilde knew nothing of that icy tomb.

A length of rope fell over the lip of the cliff and, uncoiling, dropped to the floor of the valley. Another rope, and another. As quickly as they were made fast at the top, the ropes were flung down and now the first goblin was sent over and down, rapelling against the cliff until in an eyeblink, he was below the treetops and as each rope was tested, more creatures descended, trolls and then ogres. And now Wotan's gaze took in the entire valley and the land beyond the Cliff of Day.

The emotional strain on the ten-year-old was too much to be borne; tears streaked down his cheeks as he stared helplessly at the monsters that would soon be making their way across the valley floor to the base of the Saddle. Up through the lifeberry glen they would swarm, with their sharp swords and knives . . .

And then the sky flashed brilliantly and Joey Willem found himself looking *right into Esfandiary*! Esfandiary and Upper Muchness were connected!

And there was Windbreaker—tall and broad-shouldered in his armor, with bows and arrows in a quiver and lances and a gleaming sword in hand! Atop his shoulders he carried the gnome Yin! And astride the centaur, with his left hand was wrapped around Windbreaker's waist and his right hand pressing his backside for good luck, was Mr. Blunger! The centaur's hooves clacked on the granite as Windbreaker approached.

The boy's heart lifted; Mr. Blunger would know what to do! Mr. Blunger was an advisor's advisor!

All eyes turned to the centaur and the gnome and Myron Blunger, who had arrived just in time!

Love welled up within Brunnhilde's bosom as she stared at Windbreaker with calf-eyes.

Mein held! she whispered, scarcely breathing, prolonging the glorious moment of revelation as long as possible.

His countenance was stern, but there was kindness in those flashing eyes! He was breathing deeply, as though he had just completed a danger-filled *helden*-journey, and Brunnhilde wished she could wipe his brow, draw him a hot bath, prepare a *helden*-banquet with her own hands! And those muscles! From the waist up, he was magnificent! As for the rest, that could be worked out, also; one can't expect everything. But would he notice her? Would he . . .

Here was her held and yet she had no dowry! To slay a pipsqueak dragon would make her look foolish, stupid! But she could display kindness, show off her womanly potential, fatten the poor, starved creature up a bit . . .

Spotting the little pile of overripe lifeberries, she knelt, scooped them up in one hand and with the other, forced open the dragon's jaws. In went the lifeberries; she tipped Groff's lower jaw up, leaving the debilitated dragon no choice but to gulp them down. It did, blinking.

Dragon Groff rose, shook himself, breathed deeply and opened his jaws wide.

Windbreaker looked upon the woman with the winged helmet and his hearts thumped wildly. Until that moment, getting reverted to human form had been an abstract desire; now it was an organic need. He *had* to perform a heroic act *this night*, or never!

Joey Willem happened to be closest to the dragon, and it was he who noticed the section of Groff's back unfold, revealing expanses of dark, membraneous skin stretched between thin bones. Wings. He opened his mouth to shout warning, but froze.

With Captain Silver aboard the half-track, Mr. Hands was in charge. It was he who spotted the talons of Dragon Groff scratching into the granite and motioned the men back.

None moved.

They couldn't. Nor could Yin, Windbreaker or Trenton Interface.

Dragons are telepathic, and do not rely on craft or subtle persuasion to achieve their desires.

Myron Blunger was not affected, perhaps because of the three molecules of St. Felicia's potion in his brain. Brunnhilde, also unaffected by the dragonspell, approached her *held* as in a trance. She raised herself on her tiptoes and permitted her lips to brush against his, ever so lightly. Her heart pounded.

And immediately the fearful silence on the Saddle was broken by two sounds. *Crack*! *Clang*! A metal hemisphere was rolling and ringing on the granite. *Crack*! *Clang*! Another.

So, on the threshold of battle, with the very air crackling with tension, Brunnhilde the Valkyrie was relieved of her breastplates.

HERO TIME

"Gertrude! Look at the sky! It's gone all violet!" Sophie Blunger cried. But her sister's eyes were fixed on the uneven ground illuminated by the beam of her flashlight. Grimly she led the way across an endless tangle of snake-and rat-infested poison ivy that covered pitfalls at the bottom of which wildcats and snapping turtles awaited their prey. And those were but a sample of the dangers Gertrude assured Sophie lurked underfoot and overhead and in every direction and this wouldn't have happened if she'd taken Gertrude's advice and married the accountant!

Their discharge from the Cave of the Winds had been unceremonious. Sophie had burst out of the Cave of the Winds first, landing in a haystack placed exactly to catch neophyte users of the *Lightspeed* system. Gertrude arrived moments later, shrieking and whooping as the final wind-blast sent her full-tilt into that prickly, damp catchall.

"Ten plagues on that woman and her sack of curses!" Gertrude moaned as she collected herself. God's aunt had said there'd be a sign indicating the path that pointed toward the road that led to Muchness. But there had been three paths and only one weatherbeaten wooden sign, which was inscribed, so far as Gertrude could make out:

Follow your nose.

After brief discussion, they had decided to follow Gertrude's nose and it had led them along a path which had led through a clearing to another path which soon dwindled to nothing, and trying to retrace their steps, they'd gotten thoroughly lost. There was no sign of Myron Blunger or a road or any kind of Muchness, Lower, Upper or Lesser, which would have at least placed them in England.

How could they have been so stupid as to listen to the rantings of someone who called herself God's aunt? Okay, she'd done a trick, guessing Gertrude's malediction in case her brother-in-law were playing house with that Adele! Big deal; Gertrude had seen dozens of card tricks as clever as that.

Wherever they were, it was a lot colder than Florida. Fortunately, they had both packed shopping bags full of sweaters, as God's aunt had suggested. Gertrude was wearing an extra cardigan buttoned to the very top and a shapeless, brown pullover. Sophie had added a warm Irish double-knit sweater and on top, a hand-beaded cocktail sweater which was dressier, for when they should find Myron.

Since losing their way in this God-forsaken wilderness, Gertrude had flavored every step with maledictions, half on her brother-in-law, half on the woman in black.

Follow your nose! As she made her way in no sure direction at all, Gertrude imagined her curses weighing a pound each, so that, finding their way into her precious sack, their weight would cause the demented woman who called herself God's aunt to double over so extremely that her head would pass between her legs and bury itself in her rear end and all of her follow her nose until she tightened and wound herself down to the size of a pumpkin and was swept by *Lightspeed* to Bombay, India, where a monsoon awaited for the express purpose of blowing her along an open sewer to the ocean.

The creation of such blessings sustained Gertrude in her attempt to be the big, brave sister; forced silence would have led to weeping and a total breakdown of the natural order.

"*Lightspeed!*" Gertrude snapped. "It's a wonder we weren't killed! Such a wind! I'm half-deaf from the howling! I was bounced around like a cork in a storm and I swear someone pinched me on my bottom! You'd think they could light up the place!"

She caught her breath, then announced in a dreadful monotone, "Oh, God; it is violet! The sky is violet! Why didn't you tell me? Where on God's earth are we, where the sky is violet?" She paused to catch her breath and regard this omen of terror to come.

"I don't know," Sophie said, miserably. She only knew that her husband Myron was up here somewhere and she had to find him. Though she ached from collisions with the walls during the passage north in total and frightening darkness, she didn't *think* anything was broken; the tunnel was apparently lined with a rubbery material. Anyway, she could walk and there was no point in *Lightspeed* adventure; Gertrude, as always, would complain enough for both.

After much stumbling about in the dark, it was Gertrude who spotted a pair of beautiful, yellow, close-set school-bus headlights bouncing and slewing in a trajectory that would soon intersect their meander. She waved her flashlight and in short order, a yellow school bus bounced and ground to the requisite squeaky halt just inches from a major tree. The front door unfolded with much clatter and Gertrude stepped up, followed immediately by Sophie, who did not want to be alone in that place for an instant.

Gertrude reached the top step and flew forward, intending to remove that black hat and veil from the head of the driver with her left hand and then to whack, bang and thump the craziness out of her.

And then the woman's staff was between them and Gertrude Weintraub stopped short and, in a halting voice, apologized profusely for inconveniencing the driver, who must have encountered difficulty finding her way over the broken land. She then tucked her flashlight into her shopping bag and backed into a seat, explaining that after leaving the Cave of the Winds, she had lost her way in the darkness because she wouldn't listen to her sister, who had wanted to take a different, and probably correct, path.

Sophie Blunger, hearing this, gripped a metal railing, bent

down and stared into her sister's eyes, which didn't *seem* dilated or fuzzed over. Nevertheless, Sophie took a seat facing Gertrude, just in case. Neither noticed the presence, several seats back, of a person decked out in the uniform of a general in *Lightspeed*.

God's aunt wrestled with a lever until she managed to close the door. "Whew!" she said. "Somehow, He makes it look easy. Now how do you turn around? I've watched Him do this once or twice . . . let's see . . ." She stepped on pedals and fiddled with the gear-thing, pushing it this way and that way until the bus lurched backward, backfired and stalled. God's aunt twisted the key and restarted the engine.

"Your Nephew—God—drives this school bus?" Sophie asked. In fact, it was in rather good condition for a school bus. There was no graffiti on the seats, and their spacing was comfortably sized for adults.

"First thing every morning," replied God's aunt, turning the steering wheel as far as it would go to the right and stepping on the accelerator. "Then eighteen holes and back by three o'clock sharp to take the children home. He considers it His most important job, these days." The bus lurched forward, gears grinding and brakes squealing as the driver stepped on whichever pedal wanted stepping-on at that point in time without regard to its effect on the bus's state of motion.

"Mrs. Blunger."

In the aisle stood a young woman dressed in white military-cut jodhpurs and a scarlet tunic trimmed with gold braid. A number of leather pouches were clipped onto a wide, black belt that circled a waist that was respectably, but not absurdly trim. Her jet-black hair, which cascaded to her shoulders, framed a pert, intelligent face. Above her left breast was a golden lightning-bolt-shaped device on which was inscribed

General Wilma Hawkins.

Dangling from it by two chain-links was a horizontal strip of brass inscribed *Project Blunger*. She was carrying what appeared to be a slim attache case, from the inside of which came a steady hum.

Project Blunger.

"I am Wilma Hawkins. General Wilma Hawkins, of Lightspeed."

Sophie Blunger felt the hairs on the back of her neck rise, in anticipation of danger.

Project Blunger!

"I am Sophie Blunger," she said, coldly, glancing uncertainly around the rear of the bus to see if Myron might be back there, dozing. But he wasn't; the bus had no other passengers.

So who was this brazen tartlet who dressed from comic books and dared sport Project Blunger in writing? Wasn't it enough that Sophie was already worrying about Adele, back in the Bronx? Was Myron, *her* Myron, running around the countryside making himself a project for single ladies?

Wilma Hawkins sat herself across the aisle from Sophie Blunger, laid the attache case on her lap and popped it open. What Sophie had taken for an attache case was a laptop computer. Apparently the machine was already running; words and numbers were scrolling down the top of the luminescent panel and vanishing at the bottom faster than one could read. Wilma Hawkins's fingers flew over the keyboard. The screen split into two sections; while scrolling continued on the lower section, a steady message appeared on top:

LIGHTSPEED OPERATIONS
PROJECT BLUNGER
TEST SEARCH

1. EXODUS XXX11 9,10
searching: DEUTERONOMY XVI

In rapid succession another I was added to XVI, and then another, and then two I's were replaced by a V and then the I vanished altogether, only to reappear at the end . . .

Wilma Hawkins kept one eye on the screen as she asked, "Your husband's name?"

"Myron. Do you know . . . ?"

"Children?" interrupted the *Lightspeed* officer.

"Irving and Jacob," Sophie answered, perking up somewhat. "Not just Irving; Irving, Ph.D.; he's a physics professor and very bright, except for picking a wife, who is an intellectual with a child, Alexander, from a mistake. Her first marriage, I mean, not the child, who is gorgeous except for his nose, which he got from his biological father.

"Jacob . . . what can I say?" she beamed. "He owns a big pharmacy—you know, hardware, home furnishings, children's clothes, auto parts—and has twin boys and a beautiful house in Westchester. His wife shops."

Wilma frowned as though she'd just received bad news, then nodded toward Gertrude and asked, "Who is she?"

Gertrude had sat in uncharacteristic silence, apparently transfixed by the encounter with God's aunt's staff. "Who is she?" broke the spell.

"Gertrude Weintraub," snapped Sophie's sister. "Of DelRay Beach, Florida. It's about time the government caught up with that . . . that nutcase impersonator!" She pointed toward the driver, under whose guidance the bus was again careening and zigzagging, lurching and bucking so unpredictably that the sisters gripped whatever seemed bolted to the floor, holding on for dear life. "She claims to be God's aunt," Gertrude said. "You'd better tie her up good when you arrest her."

"First of all, I am not with any government," Wilma Hawkins said quietly. "*Lightspeed* is an organization established by the Treaty of Germelshausen at the end of a long-forgotten European war in which the use of wind-tunnels to transport militia and arms was declared forbidden for all time. Unfortunately, the town of Germelshausen vanished before budget arrangements could be made; *Lightspeed*, dedicated to the maintainance and peaceful use of the Earth's natural system of connected wind-tunnels, operates solely on found money.

"Secondly, she *is* God's aunt, so you'd best watch your words."

Sophie Blunger gripped Wilma's wrist. "Where is . . . my husband?" she demanded between bounces.

"Ask the driver," Wilma said, her attention given over to the computer screen. The top section now read:

LIGHTSPEED OPERATIONS
PROJECT BLUNGER

1. EXODUS XXX11 9,10 search completed.

On the bottom section, there appeared two sentences:

> 9. And the Lord said unto Moses: 'I have seen this people, and, behold, it is a stiffnecked people.' 10. Now therefore leave Me alone, that My wrath may wax hot against them, and that I may consume them; and I will make of thee a great nation.

"That's it," Wilma called out to God's aunt, who was pumping the accelerator vigorously as the bus struggled up an incline toward a narrow dirt road. "Exodus XXXII, 9 and 10. The test is . . . *make a great nation of thee!*"

God's aunt guided the bus onto the unlit road, then stamped hard on the brake pedal while throwing the gear-thing into reverse. As she had already learned by trial and error, this was a sure way to stop the engine and, eventually, the bus itself. Turning around, she raised her veil just the slightest amount, as though it had muffled Wilma Hawkins's statement.

"Exodus XXXII, 9 and 10?" she asked, her voice trembling.

"Yes!" Wilma said, firmly. "The computer searched the entire Old Testament."

"Oh," said God's aunt. "Mrs. Blunger, how well does your husband do on tests?"

Sophie Blunger answered the question. "Pretty good, God willing. On his last visit his urine was clear and his blood perfect except for the cholsterol. If he would just cut down on eggs and red meat, Dr. Greenberg says . . ."

"Examinations, Mrs. Blunger. Mental examinations, with answers."

"Oh. Not so good in the orals; he gets excited and talks too much. He does better in essays. Nice, wide margins, four sentences to a paragraph. He writes in Palmer, you know. And he has a master's degree in library science from City College! *Where is he?*" she screeched.

God's aunt's hat and veil bobbed once. "Please, Mrs. Blunger. As I came north by *Lightspeed*, I had a vision.

"I saw your husband in Upper Muchness, alive and sound except for a small injury to his behind, which he was massaging as best he could. He was among friends, a scholar named Yin from the tribe of gnomes and a well-armed and heroic centaur named Windbreaker.

"Unfortunately, he was also in the company of the infamous pirate and murderer Long John Silver and his gang of merciless brigands. And Lucien Broco, a scheming multibillionaire who would sell his grandmother to the devil for another day of life. And Dragon Groff, who is fast recovering from years of accidental imprisonment and near-starvation. Too fast, if you ask me.

"And I thought I saw the Aesirgods, Wotan and Loki and Thor and that gang, plus a host of trolls and demons, swarming down the face of the Cliff of Night as though they intended to lay waste to the valley of Upper Muchness."

Sophie Blunger's mind, avoiding the undigestible, sensibly rejected all but the first item. Shaking her head from side to side, she asked, "The injury to his behind . . . it's not serious? Has he seen a doctor?"

"Not yet," God's aunt said. The hat and veil bobbed upward

and slightly to the right, as though the wearer were studying Sophie Blunger in the rear-view mirror. "It's the result of impact by a leech and a bullet. Fortunately, in that order. Had the bullet opened a path for the leech, it would have dug itself in proper and his right *gluteus maximus* would be paralyzed from loss of blood.

"But the leech splattered on contact; only a bit the size of a threepenny nail got into the wound created by the bullet. Of course, this is all from a fleeting vision. I'm not omniscient. Now, about the test."

Ashamed to ask the size of a threepenny nail, Sophie fixed on the only phrase that made sense. "What test?"

"The Lord God, Creator of the Universe, my Nephew, is going to test Myron Blunger, your husband.

"We'd better get going. Now, how did I get this thing started . . . ?"

God's aunt turned the ignition key, stamped hard on all the pedals and honked the horn in all combinations until suddenly the engine coughed, then roared into life. She forced the gear-thing into second and stepped on the accelerator. With a lurch and a thump, the bus headed out along the narrow road, with God's aunt hunched over the steering wheel. They were headed directly north, toward Upper Muchness, where the sky had turned violet. "A test with one question, my Nephew told me," she called back to Mrs. Blunger.

"What's the question?" asked the practical Gertrude.

"It's the same test He gave to the other Moses," said God's aunt. Gertrude nudged her sister.

General Wilma Hawkins said, "As soon as God's aunt caught up with me and informed me of this development, I programmed the computer to take the Old Testament apart line by line, look-ing for questions asked specifically of Moses. Apparently her Nephew mostly *commanded, spoke with* and *argued* with Moses. The few questions we've found tend to be rhetorical; it's hard to imagine a test coming out of them. But there seems to be one candidate. It's not a question, it's a temptation; that's what worries me."

"Tell me, Sophie," asked the driver, "suppose my Nephew, God Almighty came before you and told you that He was disgusted with all the evildoing. Suppose He said He was going to cleanse, say, the Bronx, and start over. He asks you to get out, to go up to Westchester so He can level the Bronx as He did Sodom and Gemorrah. Suppose he offered to repopulate the Bronx starting with your children and their children and so on. We think that's the test. What would you say?"

Sophie Blunger leaned over to whisper with her sister; Wilma stayed her with a hand. "No talking."

Minutes passed. The bus ground its way up a hill in second gear. Sophie's face contorted as she tried to steal a sign from Gertrude. Wilma stuck her thumbs into Gertrude's armpits and, amid much squawking and shrieking, lifted and frog-marched Sophie's sister to another seat.

As the bus reached the top of the hill, Sophie blurted out, "No!"

God's aunt jammed on the brakes *without* pushing on the clutch, which was the secret to stopping. Indeed, the bus came to a halt with a terrible clatter and shaking of its engine. Carefully setting the emergency brake, God's aunt turned around. "But that's wonderful!" she exclaimed. "You gave the right answer, just like the other Moses did. That's part A. Now explain it! That's part B, and it's as important as part A. *Why* `No?"

"First of all," Sophie said, stalling for time while she thought furiously, "why the Bronx? Why is everyone always picking on the Bronx?"

"Okay. There we're guessing. Maybe He'll decide to level Queens, also," God's aunt conceded, impatiently. "And Brooklyn. We don't know what He'll offer."

"What about Manhattan?" Gertrude called out. Ten years earlier, her purse had been lifted on forty-eighth street and Sixth Avenue, in broad daylight.

"Not Manhattan," God's aunt added. "Never Manhattan."

"And why not?" Gertrude interjected as dormant outrage surfaced.

"Music. Sacred music. Gospel music. Choirs. Masses. The best-paid operatic cantors. All in Manhattan. Do you ever hear the Verdi Requium being sung in the Bronx? Always in Manhattan. That offsets an awful lot of stock market shenanigans.

"So let's assume He asks you to leave so He can utterly destroy the Bronx and Brooklyn and Queens. You answered, 'No.' Now, why shouldn't He?"

"Okay," Sophie said, nervous from the responsibility of this exchange, afraid that she might omit something by mistake and do a terrible damage. This had started with her poor, missing husband. Now, all of a sudden, more than half of New York was at stake, waiting on her answer. She felt persperation dripping down her neck.

"Why shouldn't He?" Sophie said, selecting her words with care. "Well, there's no subway to Westchester so my son Jacob would have to drive down before the fire and brimstone started, and pick Myron and me up in his new Lincoln. That is, if Tiffany hasn't taken the car to go shopping. You think I'm going to ask my son to drive down to the Bronx just when God's about to . . . to take care of the . . . evildoers?" She was breathing heavily. "What's an evildoer?" she continued. "You know, a pharmacy a cash business; sometimes one of his clerks sells some hosiery or a roadmap for two dollars and the accountant might forget to record the sale for taxes. A mistake on a two dollar sale isn't evil."

God's aunt sighed and kept her eyes to the road. The other Moses had put forth high, noble, *God*-protecting reasons, without regard to tax problems or his children's place in history.

Would Myron do as well? Assuming he got the first part right, could he, would he come up with reasons why three boroughs of a major city far larger than Sodom and Gomorrah together shouldn't be levelled, solely that Irving Blunger, Ph.D. and his brother Jacob and their wives and offspring might inherit?

Because of a backfire, Wilma hadn't exactly heard God's aunt correctly. The built-in dictionary in her laptop had failed to come up with a definition or description of *Eraser-gods*, and the *Lightspeed* general was loath to bother God's aunt while she was concentrating on getting the bus safely to the bottom of a steep hill, which was, mercifully, quite straight. Downhill turns frightened her.

Sophie leaned over the railing separating her from the driver. "He wouldn't really *destroy* the people, would He?" Sophie Blunger asked anxiously. "He could send frogs, maybe. A warning. He did that once, you know. In Egypt."

"Mrs. Blunger," God's aunt said, "you made a good start on the test. You got part A. If your husband does as well, I'll put in a good word for him. We hope he'll pass. We must try to help him through part A.

"We're about to enter Upper Muchness; hold on tight."

The bus negotiated hairpin turns and squeezed through narrow passages where bushes and saplings had overgrown the road, all this in second gear with the engine whining and growling. And then the road ahead was straight and the sky from horizon to horizon was violet.

General Wilma Hawkins stowed the laptop in the overhead rack and scanned the countryside. "Well, this is it," she announced, softly. "This is where I grew up." She sniffled once, blew into a handkerchief emblazoned with the *Lightspeed* logo. "We're on Broco Way. After we pass the mansionhouse on your right, you'll see my house.

"And there are the Dromedary mountains and between them, the Saddle," she said, pointing to the horizon directly ahead.

God's aunt pressed both feet on the brake pedal hard and swerved to the left. The bus tipped, nearly going over onto its side and came to a stomach-wrenching halt not five feet from a white horse lying by the side of the road. A white horse with enormous white wings that stretched across the width of Broco Way to the opposite hedge.

"Out! Out! I can't take it any more!" Gertrude screamed, while

Sophie dropped across the double seat, gasping and trying to press her heart back into rhythm with both hands after the near-accident. *A winged horse, yet!* Wilma Hawkins ran to the back, tugged the emergency lever and jumped out the rear door.

God's aunt, tired of fighting the front door lever, followed, taking her staff but leaving her sack behind. Sophie Blunger exited next, worked her way unsteadily down the narrow steps; she needed air. Gertrude emerged last and kept a respectable distance from God's aunt and that black staff. It was Gertrude who smelled something burning and spotted tendrils of smoke pouring out from under the hood, from all four wheels, the rear of the vehicle and both rear-view mirrors. The bus was *kaput*. Just as well, she thought.

"Pegasus," God's aunt declared, stooping down beside the animal. Its flanks heaved. Putting her ear to its chest, God's aunt could hear the great heart pumping. The creature was soaked with cold sweat. It was exhausted. A saddle was in place; someone had ridden the creature to its limit of endurance and cruelly abandoned it.

Wilma dashed back into the bus and returned with her officer's hat and a sealed container of pure water, kept behind the driver's seat in case of radiator overheating. Kneeling by the creature's head, she poured water into the hat and held it at Pegasus's muzzle. It drank greedily and whinneyed for more. God's aunt pulled a small silver flask from her pocket and spilled a few drops of a colorless liquid into the next hatful of water.

The hat was refilled many times, God's aunt adding a few drops of her elexir, until the container was empty of water and the creature's vital signs had improved. For a short time, it rested. Then it struggled to its feet, shook itself thoroughly and spread its mighty wings. It stamped its left foreleg, tossing its head as if to say, *Let's go!*

"Holy water?" Wilma asked, pointing to the now-empty flask.

God's aunt shook her head, glanced about and whispered, "Oozo. Greek fire. I keep some about, to fight off rheumatism."

Gertrude whispered to her sister, "Remember that gasoline

company with the flying horse symbol? Mobil-gas? There was a station just off Tremont Avenue."

Sophie remembered. "That flying horse was red," she whispered.

Gertrude said, "So?"

"So when I tell Myron I saw a white flying horse, he'll tell me that flying horses are red."

"The poor thing was exhausted," God's aunt said, wiping its head with a damp handkerchief. "Who would walk away, leaving an animal in such distress?"

"I think I know," answered Wilma Hawkins quietly as she regarded the animal stretched the muscle cramps from its wings. "A short while ago, I received an amorous letter signed by one Don Juan, whom I've never heard of nor met. I assumed it was from a wooing service—a form letter—and threw it away."

"An amorous form letter?" Gertrude said.

"A wooing service?" Sophie gasped.

"A wooing service. Why not?" Wilma shrugged. "I guess there are lots of men who read the personals and want to make a good impression on a girl but they're too shy or don't speak well on the phone. So they hire a wooing service—they're listed in the Yellow Pages—to send out letters. The service does some research and comes up with a guaranteed personal love letter. Handwritten is ten dollars extra. And for another ten dollars, they write it on the flyleaf of a book, which is supposed to be more spontaneous and sincere and romantic than on twenty pound bond paper. I had my staff look into it."

She sighed and gazed north. "I left the valley at seventeen, fresh out of high school and in love with Trenton Interface. Why should he notice a skinny girl with dull brown hair and scrapes on her knees and elbows from chasing chickens and gathering heebles and lifeberries? Trenton was the most handsome, loyal, intelligent, talented man in the world, and I went out into the world to make myself worthy of him.

"I put myself through college and worked two jobs until I

enlisted in *Lightspeed* and I admit, I did get lonesome. One of the things I learned was that the world's greatest problem is the loneliness of single women." She sighed.

"So here I am, returned to the valley a general in *Lightspeed.* I . . . sort of wonder what Trenton will think when he sees me . . . in this uniform and all." From one of her belt pouches General Wilma Hawkins took a pair of zoom binoculars, focussed them and looked intently at the Saddle. Alarm appeared on her face. She swung the binoculars to the right, then to the left. Descending the Cliff of Night by ropes were dozens upon dozens of figures. Scampering down ropes like monkeys were imps of the type that infested certain sections of the *Lightspeed* system, pinching and frightening transients. Long-armed, naked, hairy creatures with axes and swords clamped between their teeth were climbing down and vanishing into the trees. And there were other shapes, black as the Cliff itself, but with eyes that glowed red.

Dropping the binoculars, Wilma shouted, "Hurry! Hurry!" She dashed into the bus and turned the ignition key again and again. The engine coughed, but didn't catch. Red lights appeared on the dashboard and gauges oscillated wildly. A trace of smoldering bakelite was discernible and black smoke issued from the glove compartment. Clearly the engine was gone. Wilma scrambled to the ground, ran to Pegasus and was about to leap on when Sophie Blunger grabbed her arm.

"No!" she screamed, pointing toward the Saddle. "My Myron is there! I know it. I have to go to him!"

Wilma hesitated, reluctant to thrust the anguished woman away but determined to join Trenton Interface, who was surely among the little group she'd spotted on the Saddle. Gertrude, who had retrieved the binoculars and sized up the situation, gripped Wilma's other arm and settled the issue with one rational plea. "Our only hope is for your Nephew to intervene, and for Him to do that, Blunger must pass that test. If a strange woman general flies up to him on a winged horse and hollers, 'The answer to part A is No!', he won't know what the hell you're talking about.

He's trained to obey Sophie, no matter what. She has to get up there, and the horse can't carry two!"

So it was that Sophie Blunger's left foot was slipped into a stirrup, her bottom pushed into a saddle and reins placed in her hands by Wilma, who knew a thing or two about riding horses. God's aunt whispered something into Pegasus's ear and the flying horse, its energies restored sufficiently for a short run, cantered, galloped faster and faster along Broco Way until it left the road and flew north toward the impending battle.

Its neighs blended with a series of terrified whoops from its rider and soon they were dark specks against a violet sky.

Wilma set out alternately jogging and fastwalking, determined to reach the Plateau in time to stand side by side with Trenton against the devil's horde.

Gertrude refused to leave the valley without her sister. Unable to keep pace with the *Lightspeed* general, she declared her intention to walk to the Broco mansionhouse, demand sanctuary and rest there until Sophie returned. God's aunt offered her the staff, but Gertrude declined; she didn't trust it and would take her chances with her flashlight and a hatpin she kept in her purse.

God's aunt watched Gertrude until she was out of sight, then took her sack from the bus, intending to trudge back to the Cave of the Winds and resume her endless journey. She had not gotten a hundred yards, however, before she heard an odd noise in the dark of the woods that bordered the road. It was a stentorian sigh, a groan as of a planet in pain. She raised her staff and, peering into the darkness, was nearly blinded by the radiance of her Nephew.

He was seated on a fallen log with his head between His knees, gasping for breath. The Lord God was attired in white shorts, a short-sleeved jersey on which was inscribed the name of a jogging club, and running shoes. His chest was heaving.

"Are You okay?" she cried, rushing to His side.

"No," God said. "I am greatly discouraged. Having vowed nonintervention in the affairs of Myron Blunger, descendent of Morris the Decent, I could not drive the bus into the valley of Upper Muchness. I prepared Myself to run behind, that I might see to your welfare and continue to observe the everyday dangers to which mankind is daily put.

"You are the worst driver conceivable, auntie," said the Lord God, and there was wonder in His voice. "You barrelled along in near-darkness, heedless of trees or pitfalls covered by poison ivy, You crushed snakes and rats, nearly hit two deer and frightened a wildcat. And if snapping turtles weren't lake-dwellers, you would have taken a toll there, also. I am astonished at the insight of Gertrude Weintraub, who has dwelt in high-rise apartments her entire life.

"Had I not run along behind the bus, momentarily and locally bending the laws of gravity, energy and momentum conservation as necessary to keep you on the road, the very Earth would have swallowed up bus, passengers and driver. As it was, I saved your lives a hundred times over. What discourages Me, however, is that when I took a brief instant to explore the mind of a driving evaluator in the borough of Manhattan, I found that following such a performance you would, in fact, have been granted a license forthwith, the only fault being that you failed to sound your horn at frequent intervals! I now understand why Myron Blunger, descendent of Morris the Decent, is partial to the subway."

Then God rose, straightened Himself and in an eyeblink, He was attired in yellow and white plaid knickers, a pale blue blouse with a pair of tablets inscribed above His chest on the left side, spiked shoes and a white cap. A set of clubs in a golf-bag hovered at His side, the bag vibrating as though it were anxious to start the round.

"Wait," His aunt said. "What about Your promise to test Myron Blunger?"

But she was talking to empty space. He was gone, no doubt to practice His golf before tomorrow's game.

God's aunt hoisted her sack of curses and trudged another

hundred yards south. Then she threw the sack down, thought of Sophie Blunger who, though terrified, was bravely riding a flying horse to be with her husband. And Wilma Hawkins, weaponless and without a budget, hurrying north as fast as she could, to be at Trenton Interface's side when battle commenced. God's aunt tugged her burden higher on her shoulders, turned around and proceeded to walk as fast as her legs would take her toward the place—wherever that might be—where golfers practiced their driving and putting. Her Nephew had promised Blunger a test. Maybe, if he did well, God would give him a break and send him home, where he belonged.

Also, it is not polite to walk out on one's aunt, even if one was the Lord God.

Not on her birthday.

IN WHICH DON JUAN LOSES HIS HEAD

"Have you any final words before I take your head off and leave it for the worms and maggots?" The midnight air was still and the Commandant's bass voice resounded throughout the lifeberry glen.

"Si," Don Juan gasped. His heart was racing and he was surprised at the steadiness of his voice, with death but a swordthrust away. "Two things. One: as a *hidalgo* I ask you to . . . bury my head in the soil, lest a maiden taking the air come upon it . . . and weep. Two: With respect to my seducing your daughter and killing you in a duel; it was not my fault. I have a doctor's note!"

Halfway up the glen trail, the don had fallen to the ground, exhausted from being chased the length of Broco Way and up the steep path without respite. The tip of the Commandant's sword was pressed against his larynx and it was all he could do to breathe. *Have you any final words?* Life and death were ironic jokes, the don mused. Had God wanted him to be a scholar, he would have been provided with a powerful brain. Had God wanted him to labor in the fields, he would have had broad shoulders. But God had designed him to succor the lonely, the overlooked, the unappreciated women of town and countryside. Which he had done, faithfully, in all weathers and seasons. All his life he had simply obeyed nature, only to be done in by nature. The nature of a horse.

Pegasus had barely made it to ground before collapsing. But even in that final glide, the horse had steered toward its kind, toward the white stallion it remembered from the race in the paddock. A horse is a herd animal, and despite its uniqueness in having wings, Pegasus was, at heart, a horse. No sooner had the don extricated himself from the collapsed animal than he had felt the Commandant's sword at his back.

Don Juan had rolled to the side and leaped to his feet—a gymnastic trick that had saved his life more than once—starting for the woods only to be slapped back by the flat of the Commandant's sword. Whirling, he darted south on the road, only to hear hoofbeats and find the white stallion blocking his way. So he ran north, and the Commandant's steed trotted behind like a sheep-herding collie, ensuring that he stick to the road. Tricks and dodges were rewarded with the flat of the Commandant's sword on his back and shoulders; his blouse was near shreds and he was bleeding. He knew better than to draw against his nemesis; his blade, of the finest Toledo steel, would snap against the devil's sword wielded by the one he'd slain in the flesh.

So it was over at last and the don lay on the ground, too fatigued to take another step. It was ironic, he thought with a bitter smile, that at the end, his loins ached as never before and he was rewarded with one final look upward toward the Dromedaries, a pair of *grand tetons* outlined against a beautiful lavender sky.

The Commandant was not interested in the don's so-called proofs, but the other request had struck a nerve. The Commandant was, if anything, excessively alert to the sensitivities of women, and the digging of a shallow hole for the seducer's head seemed reasonable, except that he had no shovel. Would it be consistent with the niceties of revenge to require the don to dig his own head-pit with his bare hands?

Yes. And as the Commandant explained his codicil to the don's request, his marble eyes glowed at the appropriateness of this end to the vendetta!

But just as his captive commenced digging, there came, from the direction of the road below, a new sound. Commandant d'Ulloa called a halt as a man came into sight pulling a heavily loaded child's wagon by a length of rope. The wagon was loaded with thick books, and smelled as though it had recently been used for the transport of rancid fruitcake, though that seemed unlikely.

Two women were in back, one pushing the wagon while the other retched into the shrubbery. As the Commandant watched, they switched roles.

Women were so delicate. The Commandant would not permit Don Juan to continue his digging within earshot of women; if the villainous seducer and murderer made a scene, they would succumb to the vapors or such. Holding his sword rock-steady, he waited for the party to pass by.

They did not.

"Who's there?" whispered Loretta Hawkins, peering through the shrubbery at the white horse and its master, who were half a rope-length from the path.

"Commandant d'Ulloa," came the reply in a bass voice.

"There's someone on the ground," Miss Wally said, wiping her mouth with a handkershief and taking a cautious step toward the frozen tableau. "Oh!" she cried, seeing the sword-tip pressed to the throat of the downed one.

"Remove that sword immediately!" she snapped in her best schoolteacher voice. "Take it away before I confiscate it!"

And because he was a gentleman, Commandant d'Ulloa did back the sword away from the don's larynx, though only by several inches.

"Who are you, young man?" Ms. Wally asked, and her voice found a lower, more mellow register than was its custom. She was rewarded with a brief and relatively accurate account of the events that had led to this denouement. Throughout the telling the name Don Juan resounded within her fluttering heart and elsewhere like a volcanic fire. Indeed, though a great battlehorn sounded in the distance, she dismissed it as of no matter, for Don Juan lay at her feet and his eyes, dark, liquid eyes with unusually long lashes, were on hers.

Don Juan . . .

. . . whose life was about to be snipped because of an alleged seduction—and who knew which party had instigated it?—and a duel of honor carried too far.

Don Juan . . .

. . . whose continued existence depended entirely on the belief of others. Oh, could Ms. Wally believe when she put her mind to it!

Bravely, she crowded the Commandant so that he was forced, out of *noblesse*, to withdraw the sword until it no longer touched the don at all. "You say you have proof?" Ms. Wally asked of the don.

Don Juan withdrew both Dr. Watson's medical finding and Portia's case-at-law from an inner pocket and handed them over. The moonlight was sufficient for reading, and Ms. Wally an experienced enough teacher to decipher Watson's scribblings, which she read aloud. Finally she nodded, returned the slips of paper to the don, and turned to the Commandant.

"You have pursued this poor . . . this gentleman for more than three centuries, I understand."

"Correct," replied the Commandant, with a bow.

"I'm not a lawyer," Ms. Wally said, "but I know harrassment when I see it. I'd advise you to desist, before the lawyers get you into court."

"Who will summon them?" the Commandant sneered. "His voiceless mouth that will roll in the dust as soon as you have gone on your way?" Though annoyed, the Commandant remained considerate of the gentle sex; he did not divulge the purpose of the bowl-shaped depression in the ground that the don had already excavated. Nor did Ms. Wally note the dirt beneath the don's fingernails, though they would never have passed morning inspection.

"The don's heirs will summon the lawyers, if for no other reason than to fight over the estate!" Ms. Wally snapped, stepping protectively over the recumbant form of the don. "As he *is* a don and a *hidalgo*, there will be an estate. And as a direct result of his lifelong fight to alleviate his internal pressures, there are bound to be heirs. Many heirs, perhaps numbering in the hundreds—and their descendents—and not one of them with papers to prove exclusive rights to the don's fortune. You will know what it is to be hounded! A battalion of marshalls will serve papers on you to bear witness at a thousand court hearings; an army of lawyers will question you, gently at first, then viciously as Hollywood takes notice and motion picture rights take precedence over *habeus corpus* and the like. And remember; this is all multiplied by dozens of likely heirs."

"I fear no earthly court!" the commandant shouted. "Do you not see the violet sky? All is connected; heaven and earth and hell are one; the past is the present, and there is no future!"

Somewhere in the west, in the direction of the Cliff of Night, drums rumbled, a bass horn trumpeted low, and was joined by another.

"So much the worse for you," Ms. Wally said, taking the don's hand and helping him to his feet. "If indeed the past is summonable, you will be hounded not merely by one, but by fifteen generations of heirs and their attorneys."

"Fifteen generations of lawyers?" the Commandant said reflectively, fingering the edge of his sword.

"At least," said Ms. Wally. "To compensate for their eighty-hour workweeks and poor public image, they breed like flies. As for the senor, I . . . I offer myself as . . . as a guardian and role model. In short, I claim this man as my own. You've had your revenge. Enough! The poor man has been reduced to a shadow of his former self."

"Not quite, madam," whispered the don as he regarded his savior with grateful eyes.

The Commandant looked upon this interfering, dominating woman and a shadow of a smile formed on his alabaster countenance.

"So be it!" the Commandant said. "Don Juan de Tenirio, this woman has put claim to you. Woo her, then! Say some sweet thing on the instant or I shall surely put my sword through your organ of lies!" And the point of his sword again pressed on the don's adam's apple.

Lying helpless on the ground, Don Juan turned to Ms. Wally and said in a beautifully-cadenced baritone, "Do you know why the breasts of women, once formed, remain shapely even after weaning their babies? In the entire animal kingdom, this happens only in the human species."

"Really?" she whispered back, kneeling and shyly putting her hand in his. "And why is that?"

"You see, God, in His wisdom, tried to make it easier for a man to determine friend from possible foe at a distance. Permit me to say that, though you were on the horizon and a fog between us, I would know you for a friend."

Ms. Wally, who had never thought her bosom particularly attractive, blushed. The Commandant smiled coldly, took a jewelled ring from his own finger and handed it to Don Juan.

"This Ms. Wally has claimed you as her own. Do you accept? Do you swear to be faithful to this woman, forsaking all others for all eternity?"

The don nodded, blinking away tears of gratitude and joy at this unexpected deliverance.

"Then rise, and by the power invested me as a Commandant at the court of his glorious majesty, King Juan Carlos, I pronounce you man and wife." The Commandant passed his sword over the couple, then sheathed it.

"You may put the ring on the bride's finger. But know, Don Juan, that I command you to dig a hole beside your door with your two bare hands, large enough for you-know-what. Should you fail your marital pledge in the slightest regard, the hole will be filled."

"Whooppee!" sang Ms. Wally, planting a full, passionate kiss on her husband's lips. Then she helped him to his feet and turned to the Commandant. "Now, lend us your horse to pull this wagon to the plateau; we're exhausted. In return, the don will agree not to press any charges. A *quid pro quo*. An exchange . . ."

"I know what *quid pro quo* means!" laughed the Commandant. He motioned his steed to follow and supervised the attachment of the wagon rope to the pommel of its saddle.

"What is this we are transporting?" the Commandant asked politely.

"My Theory," said Benison Hawkins, his first words since the encounter. "The sky has turned violet, an event predicted quite nicely in the sixth volume. It has occurred to me that it is time my Theory was pushed to the limit. Fortunately, we had this wagon lying about . . .

"By the way, I am Benison Hawkins. The one back there propping the wagon is my wife, Loretta, who is also keeping an eye out for our missing quasi-adopted son, Joey Willem. Say, it was right nice of you to marry Ms. Wally off like that, no fussing with dresses or flowers or invites. That's the way it should be. She's Joey's teacher, you know."

The Commandant's smile broadened. The doctor's note claimed that the don's problems stemmed from an excess of prostate pressure and balls the size of Valencia oranges. Though the Commandant was ignorant of the sciences, he knew that the cure for a push was a pull. And from her shortened stride, the Commandant suspected that Mrs. Don Juan's thighs were already pulsating furiously. The don would not last til year's end, and would die of a collapsed prostate, in agony.

They moved rapidly up the glen path, in single file, the Commandant leading his horse, Mrs. Don Juan behind her husband. He slipped back and bent his head to hers. The Commandant did not hear her reply, but he smiled ever more broadly as the entourage approached the lip of the plateau between the mountains known as the Dromedaries. Yes, his petty revenge, a quick beheading, was hardly punishment for this despoiler of maidens, compared with being coupled, even temporarily, with a member of the most demanding species of female. A teacher.

By the time they'd reached the edge of the Saddle, the teacher and Don Juan were walking hand in hand and kissing fervently. But Benison Hawkins had come to a halt and was pointing at something at the far end of the Saddle.

Saliva from the jaws of Dragon Groff dripped onto the granite, forming small pools. The creature, his throat lined with lifeberry juice, now towered over the warm-bloodeds, but his stomachs were empty of meat and his concentration wavered. More warmbloodeds had stepped onto the plateau, plus one that appeared warmblooded to the eye, but emitted no body-heat, nor did the horse.

They hesitated. With a telepathed command, Dragon Groff bade them approach. They did.

"Oh! Oh, my God!" Mrs. Don Juan screamed at the sight, and, fainting away, would have dropped had Don Juan not swept her up and cradled her in his arms.

"My. My, oh my oh my . . . . " Loretta Hawkins babbled.

"A dragon!" Benison Hawkins cried rapturously. "An otherworld dragon! You see that, you *Bourbaki* idiots?" he shouted gleefully into the sky. "My Theory . . . is RIGHT!"

Then the dragon-spell took them, and they advanced across the plateau under its command. The Commandant, not affected by the mental pressure, mounted his stallion, turned back and vanished down the glen path.

"Ooooh . . . Ooooh . . ." The cry came from above. Brunnhilde's blood surged with excitement as she spotted the flying white horse soaring high over the Saddle. Her sisters were coming! Protected from the dragonspell by her metal helmet, she answered the call.

"Yo ho! Yo ho!"

"Ooooh . . . Ooooh . . ." came the reply as the horse dipped low and passed over the group.

Myron Blunger blanched. There was a flying horse overhead. A white horse with wings. Not red as advertised; white. And on that flying white horse with wings was his wife, Sophie! But Sophie was supposed to be in Florida! How could she be here? And when did she learn to ride a horse, much less a flying horse! She was always so busy. He waved.

Each time the flying horse streaked overhead, Sophie leaned over and shouted: "Ooooh. Ooooh." But that made no sense at all to her husband.

A great burden was lifted from Sophie Blunger's heart to see her husband below, standing on his two feet, holding his behind and waving. She wanted nothing but to descend and embrace him—carefully, mindful of his wound—but she had no idea how to steer the flying horse down. Nor was Pegasus desirous of landing on a patch of rock occupied by a formidable creature of uncertain disposition.

So for the moment, the best Sophie could hope for was a series of overflights. And so swift was Pegasus that Sophie had no time to shout the entire instruction: *The answer to the question is No*, therefore she focussed on the essence of it. *No!* But consonents don't propogate through air nearly as well as vowels, and fifty feet from the ground, the N's were dead.

"Ooooh . . . Ooooh . . ."

Due to her excellent physical condition and *Lightspeed* training, General Wilma Hawkins arrived at the Saddle only somewhat short of breath, having jogged the length of Broco Way and climbed the Glen Path in record time. At the sight of Dragon Groff, she stopped, then looked about quickly, efficiently, as she'd been trained by *Lightspeed*. Her weight was on the balls of her feet, and she was prepared to sidestep, matador-like, should the monster lunge. Why was everyone frozen? The *Lightspeed* training program is thorough, but does not include *dragonspell*.

There was her beloved Trenton, standing protectively beside a halftrack. The Broco halftrack! Growing up in the valley, Wilma had heard of this military vehicle, loaded with laser-guided rockets, frag-morters and other armaments! Its powerful diesel engine rumbled as though awaiting a command to rev up and clear the valley of the murderous scum! And it was her Trenton who had thought to bring it along! Oh, he was so clever, so resourceful and Wilma Hawkins loved him and yearned for his touch.

Where was Lucien Broco? Why were they all motionless?

A boy knelt by the dragon's left foreleg, staring up at the creature's wings, which were partly unfolded. Who was he? Had her parents had another child in her absence and not even sent her an announcement?

No time to worry about that. There was an assortment of ill-attired knaves bearing cutlasses and daggers, but all were motionless.

All except a tall warrier-lady and a portly fellow whose right hand disappeared into his trousers; they were the only ones who weren't transfixed. Having apparently sung herself out of *Yo, ho's*, the warrier-lady had taken a position beside a centaur and was looking apprehensively toward the Cliff of Night and hefting a wicked-looking spear. The centaur was young, handsome and well-built, and his white upper part and midnight black horse part matched the color motif of the moonlit Saddle.

There was also a gnome, but he was just sitting cross-legged on the ground, engrossed in what appeared to be a notebook. General Wilma Hawkins dismissed him as irrelevant. The portly fellow had to be Myron Blunger, the focus of Project Blunger. He was standing crookedly, as though favoring his left foot. Not quite transfixed, he was waving to something or someone overhead with his left hand; Wilma didn't dare look up for fear of the Northern Lights, which at that latitude were magnificent enough to transfix anyone.

Beside Myron Blunger were her parents—her mother seemed stouter and her father's hair was definitely thinner—and a gentleman attired in medieval garb—doublet and trunk hose—though his blouse seemed the worse for wear, with dark stains that could well be dried blood. The gentleman was holding a woman in his arms. As General Hawkins assimilated this data, the woman stirred and was gently stood upright, the gentleman's motions slow, dream-like. Why, it was Ms. Wally, her former teacher! And she finally had a beau! And what a beau! He intertwined his arm with hers in precisely the manner in which Wilma had long dreamed Trenton Interface's arm would one day encircle her own.

But first things first; the minions of the false god Wotan were even now swarming over the valley. War impended. An assessment of force was the first order of business. The centaur and the giantess were armed.

Ms. Wally's natural weapon was the standard-issue eighteen-inch ruler and she was not above clapping board erasers against the ears of a troublemaker. She'd best be put to shelter in the half-track. Anyway, she had swooned again. Her beau carried a sword. Blunger appeared weaponless, but General Hawkins had read the dispatches. This overstuffed, seemingly inept fellow was tough. His right hand, vanished into his trousers, likely gripped the butt of an Uzi or perhaps a string of grenades, and his awkward stance was probably the first position for a karate sequence.

Her father, she saw, had his Theory. No help there.

At the other side of the Saddle was a mixed bag of musicians— General Hawkins recognized Lucien Broco's travelling orchestra. Mostly drums, horns and homemade bamboo flutes, which were churning out a dirge of some sort. Not a proper weapon among the lot.

The musicians' families, off to one side, made a large support group, clapping and dancing. Would they clap when Dragon Groff opened those jaws and set the very rocks smoking with fire? Would they dance when the hordes of the false god Wotan clambered onto the Saddle and laid swords to their throats? No, as soon as their shift was over and they could punch their timeclocks they would start screaming and stampeding, fleeing the Saddle in all directions. Wilma Hawkins had heard the contract terms Mr. Lucien Broco had forced upon the Henchpersons' Union in return for their trumpets and drums.

As for the dragon, its eyes were half-closed and its long tail lay, untwitching, on the granite floor of the Saddle. The creature seemed exhausted, or dormant.

A plan was required. How to shape this rabble into an effective force? And why were they so . . . phlegmatic?

It came to her in a flash. *They were under a spell!* All of them, save the tall warrior lady and Blunger, though he seemed partly transfixed. The warrior lady remained in control of her actions because of her winged, *metal* helmet! In one fluid motion, Wilma Hawkins snapped open one of her belt-pouches and pulled out a standard-issue metal-mesh hairnet with four bronze stars. In an instant it was down over her forehead, secure at the nape of her neck and tucked under her ears. If whatever was affecting these folk was electromagnetic in origin, she would be shielded.

Had Dragon Groff not been too weary to include this new-comer in his holding spell, her action would have come too late. It didn't matter. There was one here, a Ms. Wally, who did not be-lieve in dragons. Groff would provide her with something she *could* believe in. He woke her from her daze, lifted his head, now nearly as large as that of a tyrranosaur, high in the air and consummated his existence, driving into the minds of all assembled a page from his history, a page that would not soon be forgotten.

The meat-eater, twenty feet high and nearly fifty from tooth to tail, thudded awkwardly along the muddy shore of a swamp-edged lake on its powerful hind legs. The reptilian grin of Tyrannosaurus Rex bared six-inch, dagger-sharp teeth to its prey, a crested corythosaurus that had just started to lay a clutch of cannonball-sized eggs to hatch in the sun's heat. She heard the clump-suck, clump-suck of the taloned feet pulling heavily through the thick mud, saw the meateater coming across the flat; instinct took over. A thrust of her powerful tail brought her upright. Lumbering heavily on elephantine hind legs but forced to securely plant each stumpy foot before she could trust it with her ponderous weight, she lurched across the mud-flats toward the water's edge. Her massive body and tail careened from side to side in her desperate flight.

But while she had been concentrating on dropping her eggs, the tyrannosaur had moved to cut off her line of flight. She was doomed.

Suddenly the sky over the western cliff blazed, lit by a column of fire—red and yellow. The tyrannosaur did not slow down; the event in the sky was not a competitor for its prey. Steadily it advanced, its jaws distending wide for the kill. It taloned feet sunk more deeply into the watery mud.

Clump-suck. Clump-suck.

A hundred yards away, at the swamp's edge, mud-coated antecedants of alligators woke from their mid-day torpor and swung their heads to watch the chase. The huge carcass would belong to the great beast through the remainder of the day; by night, they would engorge themselves, especially if the tyrannosaur killed her near the water.

Dropping her eggs, the crested corythosaurus lumbered across the flat, ignoring the column of fire in the sky. Deeper and deeper she sank as she wallowed through the swamp. Then the ground heaved violently and the earth shook and mud and land parted with a terrible roar; a gaping fissure suddenly extended from the forest across the mud flats and the swamp. In the lake, the water parted and cascaded into that crack in the earth. Swampwater rushed into it, carrying the alligators into the earth's depths. The tyrannosaur screamed, but could not halt its momentum; falling into the fissure, it bellowed with rage and terror until its head smashed into a wall of rock and its neck was broken and it started to die the death of reptiles; slow and decentralized. Its jaws snapped reflexively as the herbivore thudded single-mindedly toward the safety of her home, the doomed lake whose surface suddenly boiled, alive with terror.

Then came the aftershock and the dying tyrannosaur screamed at the pain transmitted through the earth to its body. Far to the south, a twenty-trillion ton mountain from space had streaked down from the sky and smashed into the planet Earth.

The impact had relieved accumulated ground-stresses for thousands of miles around the impact site. The air-borne shock wave that followed tore up century-old trees and blew gasping, screaming creatures of all sizes over a landscape suddenly afire. The tyrannosaur, not accepting its death or that of the world, convulsed its way deeper into the crevasse. Hours later, after the equally doomed alligators had blindly torn away much of its living flesh, it succumbed in all its parts.

A great darkness descended. Fire came and ate the forest and that marked an end and a beginning.

Such was the reminiscence of Dragon Groff, and it was understood by all. A tiny "Oh!" escaped the lips of Ms. Wally, who now noticed her pupil, Joey. She nodded her apologies, positioned herself in the arms of her husband and re-swooned slowly, graciously, deliciously surrendering herself to long-repressed dreams in which neither interviews nor dragons played a part.

Between swoops of the flying horse, Myron Blunger became aware of Joey Willem, huddled beside a creature that seemed remarkably sedentary for one so large and scaly. He wanted to scurry to Joey Willem's side and deliver a sentence or two, something positive and life-affirming, but found himself capable of only limited motion. [Myron Blunger had no way of knowing that the shampoo he'd used faithfully for decades contained chelated iron, which partially shielded his cerebrum from the dragonspell.] He could follow the swoops of the flying horse, and he could wave to his wife.

"Oooooh!" sang Sophie as she flew away toward the cliff of Day.

Windbreaker struggled against the mind-clamp that held him nearly motionless. He had watched as the lizard grew, expanding into a monster that equalled in size the tyrannosaur he had escaped earlier. It was urgent that the centaur break the hold on his physical self. There was no use attempting to hurl one of his lances at the dragon, or attempt to give *Excalibur* a swing; by spell or curse or black magic, the power had been sucked from his arms. But he still had breath! And the horn of Roland was in its pouch, dangling from his pommel on the left side. And the horn of Roland had power . . .

He closed his eyes, concentrated on his left hand—imagined it grasping the pouch, opening it, taking the horn . . .

Imagining wasn't enough. He *commanded* his arm to lower, to move slightly back, to place his hand in position . . .

His arm jerked, vibrated as wills contended . . . now he could feel the soft pouch and the horn within. He had it. By force of will he made his fingers clamp it, take it out, raise it. It was as though he were lifting hundreds of pounds; his right arm hung, useless, as the muscles of his left arm trembled, threatened to spasm. And then the horn was at his lips. He gathered a double-lungful of breath, and blew!

And it was as though a clamp was loosened. Loosened, but not removed. The head of Dragon Groff swung around and the heavy-lidded eyes focussed on the centaur. The dragon's mouth opened. Again Windbreaker blew the horn of Roland. The beast spread its wings, putting a quarter of the Saddle into deep shadow. For the third time, Windbreaker blew on the horn of Roland. The dragon recoiled. Windbreaker found that he could move freely; the dragonspell was broken.

A spear sailed over the edge of the Saddle, thudded into Windbreaker's leather body-armor and fell to the ground. Another arced high and bounced harmlessly from the hard scales of Dragon Groff's back. Blunger bundled the boy to his belly and scurried away to a defendible position behind a boulder.

Suddenly, long-armed, hairy creatures were swarming over the edge of the Saddle, throwing spears and swinging axes. The pirates, after flinging some daggers and cutlasses with little effect, retreated to the ridge, turned and vanished down the trail that led to the sea beyond, where the *Hispaniola* was anchored. Handing his bride to Trenton Interface, Don Juan drew his sword and joined Brunnhilde and the centaur as they dashed to the edge of the Saddle, taking advantage of the high ground as they made a stand against some dozen trolls, slashing and thrusting furiously, returning hastily-flung spears with effect until the invaders fled. But the centaur's keen eyes detected a swarming at the base of the glen. This was just an exploratory sortie; the valley must be flooded with the things.

Windbreaker would have followed the retreat, but was held back by Don Juan, who suspected a trap. Brunnhilde's attention was held by the dark figure of Wotan, atop the Cliff of Night. There was more mischief coming.

General Wilma Hawkins didn't know what to do next.

Long John Silver did. Shielded from the dragonspell by the steel body of the hatchback, he and Broco, after rapid and efficient exchange of thought, had come to an understanding. Slipping out the rear of the half-track, Silver helped his new partner down onto the ground.

Placing his loudspeaker against his major domo's ear, Lucien Broco spoke in bursts.

"Good man, Trenton," Broco said affectionately. "Won't be going . . . back with you, though. Joinin' up . . . with Long John. A new life! A new start! We're goin' to . . . convert the *Hispaniola* to a cruise ship. Operate down in the Leewards. Pirate theme. Charge five thousand a week times thirty passengers; make a fortune!"

"Glory Line Cruises! Capstan chanties!" Silver chimed in. "Tops'ls bellyin' in a following wind! Him what shaves gets keel-hauled! Every man passenger a Captain Blood, every woman a beauty. Searching for treasure on a private island!"

"That's what folks want today," Broco cried, gleefully. "Action, an escape from drab, silly cocktail parties and such!"

"Aye," Silver said. "Good grub, of course!"

"Air conditioning," Broco joined in. "Carpeted plank. We're

going to call that package The Search for Cap'n Kidd's Buried Treasure!

"And for two thousand a week more, the Weight-loss Adventure package! All the above minus the good grub. Instead, the passengers participate in the capture of a treasure-laden Spanish galleon, swinging aboard on knotted ropes, cutlass in mouth and a bloody kerchief around their heads! Make the captives walk the plank! Fondle the women; strip 'm of their jewels. Sharks, blood, rum swizzles. All mock. Except the rum swizzles and the fondling and maybe the stripping. But safe as a church pew. Eh? Actors and actresses'll aboard the merchant vessel will get a chance to break into show-biz! All participants bonded, all events insured! We'll make a fortune, Silver and me.

"Of course, I won't be on board; I'll be ashore in my mansionhouse, a landlubber. I'm going to . . . be a stereotype, Trenton. Fleet owner. Heh, heh. Rich, greedy, gnarled old bastard stereotype. It's me, Trenton. I love it already!"

Life eternal as a stereotype wasn't so bad, the pirate had explained as they exchanged dreams and visions in the halftrack.

It wasn't the treasure or the stacks of money that gladdened the heart and made for dinnertime conversation, they had agreed. It was the scheming, the double-crossing and finagling that went into getting it! Oh, would it be grand!

With that and a handshake, they were partners.

Lucien Broco, safely on the ground, tore off his venture suit and took a deep breath. "Now don't worry," he assured the dismayed Trenton. "You're taken care of for life! You and the boy. And the henchmen. Look after Joey boy. And the landhold; see that the greensward gets mowed!" Tears glistened on the major domo's cheeks.

"Thanks, Trenton. Thanks for everything. Give . . . give yourself a raise! Give . . . everybody a . . . a threefold raise!" He took Long John Silver's arm and they started off toward the ridge and the long downhill march to where the *Hispaniola* lay at anchor.

Dragon Groff was flapping his wings slowly, letting their tough membranes turn leathery, suitable for flight. A shower of arrows; another sortie. One caught Dragon Groff in the unscaled flesh of his throat. He roared and turned slowly. He opened his jaws and spat a stream of dragonfire onto a half-dozen trolls that had crawled onto the Saddle. A dozen others flung lances without taking aim, turned and fled down the slope.

But when Dragon Groff tried to send a fireball as a parting gift, only a few drops of warm spittle came from his fire-glands. The lifeberries had lined his system, but had not filled his bellies. He was weak from hunger. Trolls had always given him gas, but he was starving and there lay six of them, seared if not cooked to perfection.

Groff crept to the edge of the Saddle, lowered his head and for some time the loudest sounds on the Saddle were of bones cracking and meat being gulped.

After greeting her parents, who were very surprised to see her at all and especially in such a 'getup', as her mother put it, General Hawkins tapped Trenton Interface on the shoulder. Time to deploy the halftrack! Trenton was staring at the form of the valleymaster, Lucien Broco, silhouetted at the top of the ridge at the far side of the Saddle. Lucien Broco, the valleymaster, was gone, forever.

It was some few minutes before Trenton Interface, tears streaming down his face and his voice choked, turned his attention to the woman in military dress. But it didn't take long to explain that the weapons systems were all dummies. Then Trenton asked to be left alone for a while.

General Hawkins considered deputizing Myron Blunger, but he had crept out from behind a boulder and was alternately motioning the flying horse down, and waving it off. He explained that his wife was aboard.

Well, why didn't she come down to him?

Whispering, lest he distract the very large and hungry dragon from his dinner, Myron Blunger explained. On the one hand, he one moment signalled anxiously for her to come down before she fell off the horse; the next moment, realizing the selfishness and stupidity of asking her to share his danger, he waved her off.

The dilemma would resolve itself, and very shortly. Pegasus was tiring; the swoops were getting lower.

And now the gnome, whom General Hawkins had already dismissed as inconsequential, was tugging at her sleeve.

"I've finished my research and I have an important suggestion!" he said, waving his notebook.

"Speak quickly," General Hawkins snapped. "I'm very busy," though, in truth, she was very desperate and out of ideas.

"We must close the loop!" Yin shouted.

"Close the loop," Wilma Hawkins replied, with remarkable civility under the circumstances. "You did say, 'Loop', did you not?"

"You don't understand!" Yin cried. "Loops must be closed. When we ... er, spirited him from the Bronx, Blunger had been dreaming of the king of France. In Esfandiary, he even tried to contact the king of France, but the king didn't reply. For a while, I assumed he was too busy reviewing his army. *But now I know the truth of it*!"

"Army? What army?" General Hawkins snapped, stooping to look this small one eye to eye. "What army?"

"'The king of France/ and twenty thousand men/ marched up the hill/ and ne'er marched down again.' An English children's folk-song, recalling the battle of Agincourt. The French lost the battle; their children sing 'Frere Jacques'. The English won. A million English children sing that song every day. They even got Shakespeare to make a play about it. *Shakespeare*! If it weren't for the belief of English children, the king of France wouldn't be in Esfandiary or anywhere."

"But we must hurry; I've figured out why the king didn't respond to Blunger! I know how to save Earth from Wotan and his gang of dreadful minions!"

LA VACHE ESPAGNOL

"Blunger, pay attention!" Wilma Hawkins slapped Myron Blunger's unwounded rump with the official *Lightspeed* French-English/English-French dictionary she'd retrieved from one of her belt-pouches, but he continued limping in tight circles, shouting encouragement toward his wife at each swoop of Pegasus and making contradictory motions with the hand that wasn't massaging his wounded buttock. The flying horse, its ozoo-derived energies spent, was spiralling down toward the Saddle, its wings barely pushing air.

Through the open door of the half-track, Loretta Hawkins clapped at the performance of her daughter. "You hear that, Blunger?" she cried. "Pay attention!" Laughing merrily at her daughter's dramatic return, she rached back into the half-track and tugged the former Ms. Wally, now Mrs. Don Juan, to the door so she could see better. The Don had ordered his bride to take refuge in the armored vehicle, for safety, and just in case an opportunity arose to consummate their marriage.

Trenton Interface, still distraught at Mr. Broco's departure, was doing his best to entertain the teacher by playing the soundtracks of mock rockets and machine-gun fire on the public-address system. The soundtracks sounded most realistic when the diesels were rumbling; the backfires were like mock explosions. So even though the half-track was nearly out of fuel, Trenton permitted the diesels to idle for the sake of atmosphere, despite the objections of Mrs. Hawkins. After all, how could Loretta give the new bride a crash course in sex and home-making with all that racket? It was no wonder she'd lost her train of thought and was sitting at the open door, swinging her legs and cheering her daughter.

So far as Don Juan was concerned, if the opportunity for conjugal relations arose—and he had little doubt that it would arise; his internal pressures were building up to a new high—the mathematician's wife could leave or remain as she chose, but the door would have to be closed. It would be challenging enough to bring his bride to the threshold of ecstasy amid the din of gunfire and rockets; one could hardly be expected to establish a natural rhythm once battle started in earnest! Arrows and flashing spears, the clickety-clack of swordplay. And there was the chill wind to reckon with . . . yes, the door would have to be closed.

But God, that Valkyrie was awesome!

"Over there, beyond the violet, is Esfandiary," General Hawkins shouted to Myron Blunger, "and somewhere in Esfandiary is the king of France, whom you offended by singing that English song of triumph."

"Poop on the king of France," Blunger cried, wringing his free hand. "Look how low he's coming in! They're going to crash into the dragon!" Indeed, Dragon Groff was stretched out comfortably, his eyes shut in a light doze, his talons nestled in the grooves that he had worn into the granite during countless millenia of minding the barrier. Tendrils of dark green smoke curled upward from his nostrils and were carried away by the breeze. Dragon Groff would not take well to being awakened from his postprandial nap.

"We *need* the king of France!" General Hawkins screeched. She was getting dizzy from looking up words in the dictionary while running beside him. "Under his command are twenty thousand mounted knights and foot-men armed with pikes and battle-axes. Dragon Groff is . . . *hors de* . . . *hors de bon appetit*! Only they can save us from Wotan's minions! Now call out to the king of France and start your apology!"

"I apologize!" Blunger shouted.

"In French, damn it!" She put her finger on the first of the apology forms Yin had written down after much research. "Repeat after me: Je vous present . . ."

"Je vous present . . ."

" . . . mes excuses pour avoir . . ."

" . . . mes excuses pour avoir . . ."

" . . . chante cette chanson chauvine!"

" . . . chante cette chanson chauvine!"

"Aidez-nous, s'il vous plait!"

"Aidez-nous, s'il vous plait!"

"Your accent is terrible!" Mrs. Don Juan screeched from the half-track. "You must talk more through your nose." But Blunger's attention was on the descent of Pegasus, who was coming down too fast. Blunger lifted his free arm, signalling, *Up*! *Up*!

"Not loud enough!" General Hawkins screamed into his ear. "French has to be shouted."

"Aidez-nous!" Blunger roared. "S'il vous plait."

"Better," Mrs. Don Juan called. "But you mispronounced *nous*—it is not a gallows noose. B-minus!

"And you forgot the apology and the 's'il vous plait' was weak," General Hawkins said. "Try it again. And loud!"

"Je vous present . . . mes excuses pour avoir . . . chante cette chanson chauvine! Aidez-nous! S'il vous plait!"

"B-plus," Mrs. Don Juan said grudgingly, but the king of France did not appear at the threshold of Esfandiary, nor his army.

Blunger stopped massaging his wound and watched Pegasus's final approach. No way he was going to clear the dragon.

"Part two!" General Hawkins said. "Je vous present . . ."

"Je vous present . . ."

" . . . mes excuses pour mon accent provincal. Etc."

" . . . mes excuses pour mon accent provincal. Aidez-nous, s'il vous plait!"

But no army appeared.

Brunnhilde and Windbreaker were patrolling the edge of the Saddle, keeping watch against another sortie. Don Juan would have helped out, but his attention was now consumed in wonder at what material that was which clung so nicely to the general's tight little ass.

The flying horse swooped low, lifted its legs, cleared the dragon's back by mere inches and made a four-point landing, snorting and panting. Myron Blunger caught his wife as she was about to fall from the right side of Pegasus. "From the left side, darling," he said, taking her foot from the stirrup and prying her hands from the pommel. "Windbreaker taught me that, with horses, one always tries to fall from the left side."

"Thank God you're alive!" Sophie took advantage of their embrace to whisper: "The answer to the question is No."

Blunger blinked. Tears formed at the corners of his eyes. He whispered back, "That's nice! While I'm dying a thousand times over against my will and you're taking a nice Florida vacation, with flying horse lessons, you *shlepp* all the way up here to the end of the world to tell me No? It's not like I . . . ask every Monday and Thursday . . . like some husbands . . ."

God's aunt finally tracked her Nephew down in a copse of birch trees below the Cliff of Day. Resplendent in robes of majesty, the Lord God was seated upon His throne which He had called to Him and in His arms, he cradled two small figures who were sound asleep. His bag of golf clubs bobbed gently at a distance.

"What about the test?" she demanded, wearily easing herself down onto her sack. She was grumpy because it was very late and her shoes were wet from dew and her feet hurt and the wind was blowing through her ratty old coat and she felt her Nephew wasn't doing His share.

"You said You were going to test Myron Blunger and if he passed, You would do him a kindness. I was hoping that You might offer to help him get back to the Bronx. He doesn't really belong here, You know. And his wife Sophie is . . ."

God put His forefinger to His mouth. "Do I not know where Sophie Blunger is, and why?" He whispered, with a cautionary nod at the sleeping figures cradled in His arms. "As for the test, I would have administered it hours ago, if a certain woman in black who covets a new winter coat had not disclosed the exact wording of that test to the aforementioned Mrs. Blunger, who went to great lengths to pass the answer to her husband.

"I offered the original Moses the honor of siring a great lineage; as you know, he declined and his sons did not succeed him. As a result of that overwagging tongue of yours, I have decided to abide by the results of a different test, a far more difficult one.

"Myron Blunger is being tested right now."

"You . . . changed the test?" God's aunt gasped. She wondered who these little ones were, upon whom the Lord God had extended the warmth of His hands. "More difficult? What . . . kind of test?" Her heart sank as she realized that, in trying to do good, she had probably doomed Myron Blunger and his wife to a terrible fate.

"He has to recite."

"Blunger has a tongue," God's aunt said, relieved.

"In French."

"Oh, no."

"To twenty-thousand French knights and foot-soldiers, each of whom believes that his dialect is what is spoken in Paris."

"Oh, my God, no!" gasped the woman in black, whose business caused her to spend much time in France. "And Blunger's grade . . ."

" . . . will be decided by the king of France!" God threw His head back and laughed softly.

"And . . . the result?"

"We will soon know. And the answer to your other, unasked, question is that these are Elf Miki and Rush, who passed her examination with honors. They are both exhausted. Now hush, auntie, that I may observe the events taking place to the north . . ."

"The answer to what question is No?" Brunnhilde demanded. At Pegasus's landing, she had rushed over, eager to greet one of her sisters, and was annoyed to find an imposter.

"God is going to personally test my husband," Sophie Blunger explained, with just a touch of smugness. "We have the question, and the answer."

"What kind of test?" Blunger asked, anxiously.

"It's a Moses test," Sophie said calmly. "Every Moses takes it sooner or later. Just remember," she said to her husband, "the answer is No. Better yet, No, thank You."

Myron Blunger shrugged his shoulders. "No is no. So?"

Having lost track of the line of argument, Brunnhilde turned her attention to the dozing dragon. Now that it was large enough for its head to serve as a fine dowry, it had fallen asleep. One could not slay a sleeping dragon. Somehow she had to make an impression on this magnificent Windbreaker, at the very sight of whom her skin trembled. Marching to the lip of the Saddle, she peered over the edge. Down below, at the base of the slope, she spotted moving shadows under the canopy of trees. So they were forming into groups. Hundreds of them. Perhaps thousands. A full-scale attack was imminent. The iron wagon was issuing battle-noises and farting quite nicely, but showed no spears or arrows; it might well be impotent. She hefted *Wildschweinblutmeister* and resumed her patrol.

"We're not finished, Blunger!" General Wilma Hawkins said, pulling Myron from his wife's tearful embrace. "Now you must apologize for not being French! And then, Long live the king! Repeat after me: Je vous present . . ."

"Je vous present . . ."

" . . . mes excuses pour ne pas etre Francais. Vive le roi!"

" . . . mes excuses pour ne pas etre Francais. Vive le roi!"

This was delivered with fervor and spirit, now that Myron Blunger's Sophie was safely down on solid ground.

Safely?

"What's th . . . that?" Sophie screeched. She was looking at Windbreaker.

"A centaur," Myron muttered, rather put down at the 'Answer is No' business. After that, if Sophie expected him to *explain*

Windbreaker, she had another think coming! Then he paled as he realized that his wife, who could spot a pinhead-sized ketchup stain against a red shirt, had been so involved in calling "Ooooh" to her husband that she had not noticed the enormous dragon over which she had just flown and that now lay directly behind her. She probably thought it was a hill! It was vital that she not turn around. Not until he'd had a chance to prepare her. He groaned and pointed to the region of his wound.

Solitiously, tenderly, his wife probed his rump until she hit the jackpot.

"Oy!" he shouted.

"Hold still!" she demanded as she tugged at his belt.

"Not here!" Myron Blunger hissed, pointing to the lady general. "Over there, behind the tank-thing!" He maneuvered Sophie to where the bulk of the half-track hid the existence of Dragon Groff from Sophie Blunger.

There she undid his trousers, refrained from commenting that they badly needed a cleaning and pressing, and slid them and his shorts down enough to reveal an ugly, black gash in her husband's rump-flesh. It didn't *look* like the kind of wound one would get from an aggressive young widow, but Gertrude's veiled warnings about one Adele were still echoing in Sophie's mind.

And who was this young creature in uniform who'd been dancing around with her Myron while his wife was frightened out of her mind and half-seasick from flying? Sophie posed the question to her husband, while examining the separated flesh to inspect for pus and infection.

"Arrgh!" Myron Blunger screamed in pain.

"That's my daughter, General Wilma Hawkins!" exclaimed Loretta Hawkins, dropping down from the doorway of the halftrack and squinting at Myron's wound, which appeared even more sickly than one might expect, because of the violet light.

"Kneel down and turn to the right so I can get a good look," Sophie demanded. Myron Blunger did so.

"Come here, Mrs. Juan," Loretta called. Trenton Interface

helped Mrs. Don Juan descend and then there were three heads bobbing and exchanging diagnoses over Myron Blunger's rump-wound. "It could be a bite-mark," Mrs. Don Juan said in response to Sophie Blunger's whispered question. "I have a second-grader, Elizabeth, who bites when she doesn't get her way."

"It looks infected," Loretta Hawkins said. "I wonder if my daughter, the general, has some salve in one of her pouches."

Instantly, a tube of ointment was pressed into Loretta Hawkins's hand. Instantly, because General Wilma Hawkins was on her hands and knees, nose to nose with Myron Blunger. "Encore," General Hawkins said, pointing to the set of apologies.

Between applications of the ointment, which burned fiercely, Myron Blunger produced a second round of apologies, shouted northward with fervor and passion.

And then a figure emerged from the violet haze. It was a young man wearing the blue and white dress uniform of the king's guard. Unarmed, he carried a pole on which were a white flag and above it, the standard of the king of France. He marched stiffly across the width of the Saddle, saluted General Hawkins, helped her to her feet, stooped and handed Myron Blunger a sheet of carefully folded parchment sealed with wax. Blunger motioned to his wife to pull up his drawers and trousers.

"Not yet!" she hissed in his ear; "I'm working the ointment into the wound." Opening the message, Blunger read aloud:

Vous parle le Francais comme une vache Espagnol. The signature was an ornate symphony of flourishes authenticated by a strip of tri-colored ribbon affixed by an elaborate wax seal.

Mortified at having been forced to receive such a splendid and ornate missive on hands and knees, with his *derriere* exposed, Myron Blunger pushed his wife's hand away from the wound, pulled up his drawers and trousers and hoisted himself to his feet. Fastening his belt, he bowed deeply, grimacing at the pain.

The emmisary turned to the center of the violet aura and sang in a clear tenor:

"Allons, enfents de la patrie . . .

La jour de gloire . . . est arrivee . . ."

"Blunger passed the test!" God announced, and He grinned. Elf Miki stirred, but did not awake.

"Thanks God!" whispered His aunt, bowing to her Nephew. "Shh!"

"They're coming!" Blunger announced, and indeed, with a blast of trumpets and a ruffle of drums, there appeared out of the violet haze a line of sturdy, grim-faced pikemen, followed by another and another . . . armored knights on horse, pennant-bearers, a row of buglers, more knights and more, a platoon of high-kicking camp-followers wearing red garters, blue blouses and red skirts but no stockings at all, six kitchen-wagons drawn by oxen and finally the king's guard and the king himself on a white charger . . . .

And just in time! Trolls and ogres, demons and goblins by the hundreds, having silently crept up through the lifeberry glen, now poured onto the Saddle behind a fusillade of lances and arrows! Trenton Interface lifted Mrs. Don Juan and thrust her inside the halftrack; likewise he hoisted Loretta Hawkins and the one who'd arrived by flying horse. Then he pulled the door shut and activated the smoke dischargers. Instantly the vehicle was enveloped in a black miasma.

Don Juan distinguished himself, saving the weaponless gnome Yin from a troll's saber with a series of lightning thrusts and parries that terminated in the skewering of the foul thing. Windbreaker and Brunnhilde carried Myron Blunger, who could not run on his swollen ankle, to safety inside a kitchen-wagon guarded by an elite corps of gourmet knights. They then worked their way to the center of the fray, Excalibur flashing to the right while to the left, Brunnhilde used *Wildschweinblutmeister* as a scythe, decimating the invaders in wide swathes.

Wilma Hawkins rushed to her father's side, weaponless but determined to die if necessary to save him and his Theory. Observing this on the infra-red detector, Trenton Interface slid down the emergency escape hatch, secured it behind him and, keeping low, dashed to the general's side, scooping up discarded lances as he ran. Wilma Hawkins had returned and she was weaponless and beautiful and brave! Together they stood guard over Benison Hawkins, who squatted beside the express wagon, doggedly watching his Theory. And as his daughter and Trenton Interface and a handful of pikemen beat off assault after assault, and trumpets sounded and horses screamed and blood ran freely over the granite of the Saddle, Benison Hawkins saw the first volume of his Theory rise slowly into the air. He held his breath. Before his bulging eyes, the second and third volumes likewise levitated and soon all twelve volumes were floating up and back, away from the battleground. Up they soared in formation and so furious was the battle that only Benison Hawkins saw his Theory gain ascendency. Without shame, the mathematician wept as his Theory soared higher and higher and then vanished into the nexus of the violet beams, into Esfandiary.

Still more of Wotan's minions poured over the lip of the Saddle, but now the king of France had deployed his army and defined his strategy; this group of invaders faced an unbroken wall of sharp pikes held fast by three layers of sturdy soldiers. Their efforts at breaching the barrier repulsed, the assault ground to a halt. A trumpet was blown; the wall of pikes receded by the count: "*Un . . . deux . . . trois . . .*"

And into the space just opened charged the king's knights. Trumpets sounded the *Marseillese*! Waves of mounted and armored knights swept across the line of battle, their horses' hooves sparking on the granite, their swords flashing in the brilliant moonlight. In wild disarray, the invaders were driven back. Again and again the knights charged across the width of the Saddle, singing to the accompiment of the orchestra. Flights of arrows and hurled lances threatened to break the line of pikemen; yet the regulars held. Windbreaker longed to join them, but his place was beside this beauteous woman-warrior who made his heart pound and his frame shudder.

The din roused Dragon Groff, who woke disoriented. He struggled to his feet. He had been dreaming of the olden days, when lifeberries abounded from cliff to cliff and he had been the overlord of the valley. There were no meateaters in view, only a miriad of two-leggers. Who were these who swarmed over his place where he once lay in the warm sunlight? He swung his head to the left and to the right and saw the rage of battle on this place that had been his eyrie.

Spreading his wings, he thrust down against the night air and stepped toward the edge of the Saddle. Again he beat his wings. And again. But there was no lift, nor did his powerful hind legs provide the upward thrust that would send him aloft.

He had lost his strength, his fire, his purpose. His days were ended.

Skirting the carnage, he made his uncertain way to the edge of the Saddle and projected his thoughts and then he knew that evil swarmed over the valley that was his to guard. The horse-men fought bravely, but for every hundred of the evil ones whose carcasses befouled the lifeberry glen, a thousand more were making their way up the hillside.

And then a fireball flew out of the night and exploded directly at his forelegs, lacerating his underparts with white-hot splinters. Dragon Groff reared up, bellowed his rage and pain, tried to spit fire, but shot forth only a thin stream of phlegm. Another fireball crashed into the melee, and the din of screams and cries reached a crescendo.

Another fireball arced high and exploded above the fray, showering fiery, crystalline needles onto pikemen, trolls, goblins and knights alike. Groff saw that the fireballs were coming from the top of the Cliff of Night! This sacrilege, in the valley he was sworn to oversee and protect! He bunched his shoulder-muscles and thrust down with all his might and felt uplift! Again, and again! He crouched, then simultaneously pushed off and thrust downward with his wings.

And Dragon Groff was airborne. In his prime, he would have

needed but a half-dozen wing-thrusts to achieve altitude. Now it was all he could do to keep above the treetops as he aimed himself toward the Cliff of Night. A well-thrown spear pierced his right wing; he lost altitude and very nearly crashed.

"*Come on, Groff!*" entered his mind. It was the boy, Joey; he had made his way to the top of the ridge that ran along the rear of the Saddle, and was shouting as he ran parallel to the dragon. This Groff read in his mind.

"*Get 'em, Groff!*"

And the boy, using the butt end of a spear as a pry-bar, released a heavy rock from its resting place to roll down and across the Saddle and into a band of invaders. "*Get 'em, Groff!*" Dragon Groff fought his way up against gravity and arrows until he came level with the top of the cliff. But he had no fire, no strength. Nor could he bend the will of these who stood in a row atop the cliff, coldly regarding the battle. They would descend, when there was no longer opposition.

Dragon Groff had only his massive bulk as a weapon, and strength only for one pass. As he began that final glide along the edge of the Cliff of Night, he saw that a weapon had been hurled directly at him. If he veered to the left, he might glide safely to the ground, leaving behind this final battle for which he had no strength or hope. Or he could slip to the right and down to the valley floor and possibly survive.

For what purpose?

The hammer of Thor caught him full in the chest and cracked his breastbone. His next breath was as of raw fire and the one after was his last. But a great cry arose from the top of the Cliff of Night as Dragon Groff, though near death, soared along the cliff-edge, spilling the army of Aesir-gods and frost giants from the cliff-edge into space and finally coming to rest with his head atop their leader.

So stunned was Wotan that his spirit slipped from the body that it had usurped and was one with the foul vapor that rose from the battle site. Awakening to find the muzzle of a dragon resting on his chest, Blondevik Ungdworker lay still until he had regained his full strength and senses. Much later, when he had resumed his duties as Innkeeper, he had the art department portray that scene in a series of murals, with which he decorated the dining-hall.

Along the length and breadth of the valley of Upper Muchness, and over the expanse of the Saddle, the tide of battle turned. Leaderless, the host of the false god Wotan—even the demons—abandoned their weapons and ran, shrieking, down the lifeberry glen and into the woods, seeking escape. And at the stroke of midnight, when their shift was technically up and they could have fled, Lucien Broco's hench-orchestra played over and over their rendition of the Marseillaise.

"The battle is over!" God's aunt said, happily.

"Not quite, auntie," said the Lord God. "There are thousands of trolls and goblins and the like crashing about the valley. Who will attend to their departure? The king of France will not."

"Dragon Groff . . . I could not see . . ."

"Even now the soul of Dragon Groff ascends into heaven."

"You . . ."

"Nay," God said quietly.

"Then who?" God's aunt demanded, and in her righteous anger, she marched to the bag of golf clubs and held it tightly behind her back. "Thou shalt not hit one more ball until this matter is solved entirely!" she said, and, tearing off her veil, she looked her Nephew directly in the eyes.

For a long moment, He said nothing. Then he chuckled, snapped His fingers and the bag of clubs was again at a distance, bobbing gently. "You win, auntie," He said. "If you had been paying attention to all that has happened, you would know the answer."

"I don't," she admitted.

"The closing of loops. The final blow will be dealt by . . . yourself!"

"Me?"

"The sack. You have been collecting curses for millenia. Why do you not put them to use? Open the sack; let the breeze sweep your blessings across the valley that they may affix themselves as needed."

God's aunt laid her sack on the ground, opened the neck and jumped back. Bits of paper and parchment flew out and were carried by the breeze over the trees and out of sight, in a westerly direction. Curses flew by the dozens, by the hundreds, by the thousands. The Lord God closed His eyes as a great clamor of noise and wailing pealed across the valley of Upper Muchness.

"It is done," said God to His aunt. "A use has finally been found for your collection of `Go to hells!'.

"Not completely," she replied. "According to that book on etiquette, a maiden aunt is entitled to more than a winter coat for her birthday. There is the matter of the Blungers, and her sister Gertrude. They must be returned to the Bronx. Windbreaker has earned his reward. It would be nice to give the boy Joey a proper family. And there's the matter of Hawkins's Theory. I'm not asking for a *Deus ex machina*, just a few birthday presents. Besides the coat."

The Lord God smiled and His countenance shone. "You figured it out, didn't you, auntie?"

"Figured what out?"

"That I am a forgiving God, gracious and generous, especially to those who summon the courage to speak boldly with Me. Very well.

"Hawkins's Theory has been recognized. He is in a state of grace. I pity his friends and neighbors; were I to intervene, I would grant them deafness, as a boon.

"Joey Willem saved the life of Dragon Groff; he is Lucien Broco's sole heir. He will sojourn with the Hawkinses, and I will guide him Myself to use his fortune for good, and not for evil. I will guide him; I will not direct him. So long as he follows the path of righteousness, My countenance will shine upon him and he shall know peace all the days of his life.

"As for the centaur, I will visit him in his sleep and grant his wish. Brunnhilde deserves better than a half-man."

"That leaves only the Blungers," God's aunt said. "And Gertrude."

"Myron Blunger shall be rewarded," God said. "I have not forgotten that he has given me mirth, which I never received from the other Moses. For him I have done what I have not done even for the other Moses. I have created a *machina ex Deus*."

God's aunt looked around but saw only meadow.

"It is over there, at the foot of the Cliff of Day," God said. Then her eyes were opened and God's aunt saw two green electric lights and a stairway descending into the cliffside.

"Within the cliff is a subway," God said with a grin. "One car, complete with motorman and strange writing in colors on the sides. The Blungers and sister Gertrude will be guided there, following a late, celebratory snack at the mansionhouse. The subway will bring them to the Pelham Parkway station, where they can find a bus."

"That's double fare," God's aunt said. "Please send the subway to Pelham Bay Park; they can take the number 6, change at One Twenty-Fifth Street for the number 4 and go uptown . . ."

"Woodlawn, then," God snapped. "I will send it down through Van Cortlandt Park to the Woodlawn station; they can change to the number 4. And they will remember sufficient for their welfare but will find it impossible to discuss their adventures except with each other, and that will suffice."

"Thank you, my Lord and Nephew," God's aunt said. "Now I'd better get back to work . . ."

"Not yet, auntie," said God. "One loop remains to be closed."

The Lord God extended His finger and a ray of light illuminated a nearby scrub pine. His aunt approached it, and there, side by side, a pair of boots lay on the ground.

"Thank You," she exclaimed, which is the proper response to a

Printed in the United States
2933